PRAISE FOR THE DO-IT-YOURSELF MYSTERIES

Flipped Out

"Bentley's well-developed characters are what makes this cozy so endearing, entertaining, and enthralling."

—*Blogcritics*

"The reader will be drawn in like a moth to the flame. This is probably the best book in the series to date."

—*Debbie's Book Bag*

Mortar and Murder

"With plot twists that curve and loop . . . this story offers handy renovation tips, historical data, and a colorful painting of the Maine landscape." —Examiner.com

"Mystery author Jennie Bentley has nailed together another great mystery with *Mortar and Murder*." —*Fresh Fiction*

Plaster and Poison

"A delightful small-town Maine sleuth . . . Solid and entertaining." —*Midwest Book Review*

"[A] thrilling story that keeps the readers guessing and turning pages." —*Fresh Fiction*

continued . . .

"A believable and beguiling mystery. Each novel in the series delights, and the third installment only raises the stakes." —Examiner.com

"A pull-no-punches mystery." —*The Mystery Gazette*

"This is one solidly built mystery . . . Attractive characters and a beautiful setting round out this wonderful read." —*RT Book Reviews*

Spackled and Spooked

"Smooth, clever, and witty. This series is a winner!" —*Once Upon a Romance*

"Bound to be another winner for this talented author. Home-renovation buffs will appreciate the wealth of detail." —Examiner.com

"I hope the series continues." —*Gumshoe Reviews*

Fatal Fixer-Upper

"An ingeniously plotted murder mystery with several prime suspects and a nail-biting conclusion." —*The Tennessean*

"A great whodunit . . . Fans will enjoy this fine cozy." —*Midwest Book Review*

"Smartly blends investigative drama, sexual tension, and romantic comedy elements, and marks the start of what looks like an outstanding series of Avery Baker cases." —*The Nashville City Paper*

"Polished writing and well-paced story. I was hooked . . . from page one."
—*Cozy Library*

"There's a new contender in the do-it-yourself home-renovation mystery field . . . An enjoyable beginning to a series."
—*Bangor Daily News*

"A strong debut mystery . . . Do-it-yourselfers will find much to enjoy in the first of this new series."
—*The Mystery Reader*

"A cozy whodunit with many elements familiar to fans of Agatha Christie or *Murder, She Wrote*."
—*Nashville Scene*

"A fun and sassy journey that teaches readers about home renovation as they follow the twists and turns of a great mystery."
—Examiner.com

"The mystery is unusually strong. Home-renovation and design tips are skillfully worked into the story, the characters are developed and sympathetic, and the setting is charming. The climax leads to a bang-up ending . . . A first-rate mystery and a frightening surprise ending."
—*RT Book Review*

Berkley Prime Crime titles by Jennie Bentley

FATAL FIXER-UPPER
SPACKLED AND SPOOKED
PLASTER AND POISON
MORTAR AND MURDER
FLIPPED OUT
WALL-TO-WALL DEAD

WALL-TO-WALL DEAD

JENNIE BENTLEY

BERKLEY PRIME CRIME, NEW YORK

THE BERKLEY PUBLISHING GROUP
Published by the Penguin Group
Penguin Group (USA) Inc.
375 Hudson Street, New York, New York 10014, USA
Penguin Group (Canada), 90 Eglinton Avenue East, Suite 700, Toronto, Ontario M4P 2Y3, Canada (a division of Pearson Penguin Canada Inc.) • Penguin Books Ltd., 80 Strand, London WC2R 0RL, England • Penguin Group Ireland, 25 St. Stephen's Green, Dublin 2, Ireland (a division of Penguin Books Ltd.) • Penguin Group (Australia), 250 Camberwell Road, Camberwell, Victoria 3124, Australia (a division of Pearson Australia Group Pty. Ltd.) • Penguin Books India Pvt. Ltd., 11 Community Centre, Panchsheel Park, New Delhi—110 017, India • Penguin Group (NZ), 67 Apollo Drive, Rosedale, Auckland 0632, New Zealand (a division of Pearson New Zealand Ltd.) • Penguin Books (South Africa) (Pty.) Ltd., 24 Sturdee Avenue, Rosebank, Johannesburg 2196, South Africa

Penguin Books Ltd., Registered Offices: 80 Strand, London WC2R 0RL, England

WALL-TO-WALL DEAD

A Berkley Prime Crime Book / published by arrangement with the author

PUBLISHING HISTORY
Berkley Prime Crime mass-market edition / September 2012

Cover illustration by Jennifer Taylor / Paperdog Studio.
Cover design by Rita Frangie.
Interior text design by Laura K. Corless.

For information, address: The Berkley Publishing Group,
a division of Penguin Group (USA) Inc.,
375 Hudson Street, New York, New York 10014.

ISBN: 978-0-425-25556-8

BERKLEY® PRIME CRIME
Berkley Prime Crime Books are published by The Berkley Publishing Group,
a division of Penguin Group (USA) Inc.,
375 Hudson Street, New York, New York 10014.
BERKLEY® PRIME CRIME and the PRIME CRIME logo are trademarks of
Penguin Group (USA) Inc.

PRINTED IN THE UNITED STATES OF AMERICA

10 9 8 7 6 5 4 3 2 1

—Prologue—

Derek pulled the boat up to the rickety pier in the cove just below the house on Rowanberry Island. Looking at the old center chimney Colonial, I was reminded, forcibly, of how it had looked the first day we'd come out here to start work on it, some four or five months ago now: run-down, decrepit, and listing to one side, with broken windows, a weather-beaten plank exterior, and a hole in the roof big enough to land a helicopter through.

Now it looked like a different house. Straight and sturdy, gleaming with white paint and a brilliant red door under a fan-shaped window.

"It's gorgeous."

Derek glanced at it over his shoulder, in the process of tying up the boat. "Yup."

"We did a good job."

"Yes," Derek said, "we did. C'mon, Tink."

He extended a hand and hauled me up onto the pier, with special care for my bandaged hands.

It was just a few days since I'd narrowly escaped immolation when my garden shed went up in flames. I'd been locked inside it at the time, and had to fight my way out, to the detriment of my manicure. My hands were blistered and sore, the skin extra sensitive, and I was currently using salves and strategically placed bandages to get through the days. Derek was gentle as he lifted me from the boat, one arm snaking around my waist to take most of my weight as he pulled me up to stand behind him. "I'll get the basket."

He jumped back into the small craft and then crawled back onto the pier a few seconds later, picnic basket in hand.

It was late July, the weather was beautiful, and we were both alive and—as the saying goes—young and in love. The television crew we'd been saddled with for the past week had left town just a few hours ago, headed for their next assignment, and it had seemed a good idea to take the rest of the day off to relax and regenerate. We'd spent the past week working practically around the clock to renovate a little house in the historic part of Waterfield, the Village, for a television show called *Flipped Out*, and while that had been stressful enough in and of itself, things had gone from bad to worse when the owner of the house had turned up dead, followed by a whole lot of other complications, including that burning garden shed. I was exhausted, both physically and mentally, and when Derek suggested we take a trip out to Rowanberry Island and spend the day there while the weather was still warm enough to enjoy the water, I'd jumped at the chance. We'd packed a lunch, borrowed a boat from a friend, and here we were.

"I like it here," I said, gazing around at the pine and birch forest framing the house, and the blue sky, dotted with fluffy white clouds, bleeding into the equally blue water.

Derek glanced around, too. "Nice place. Although after what happened to you back in April . . ."

During a particularly nasty spring fog, I'd been stuck on this island with a killer. The ferries had stopped running, and I'd been responsible for the lives of a handful of other people as well as my own. I'd made it out alive—just like I did from the burning shed—but if there'd been a fog creeping in right at this moment, I think I might have been less happy about being here.

"It turned out all right," I said, turning back to him. "Just like this time."

"Sure," Derek said, but he didn't sound like he meant it. "Where do you want to sit? On the porch, as usual?"

During the months we'd spent out here working, we'd often eaten lunch on the porch. If the weather was bad, we'd stayed inside the house, but we rarely brought a blanket to spread on the grass. The porch was easier.

"That's fine."

"C'mon." He hefted the picnic basket in one hand and put the other against my back as he guided me across the meadow toward the house.

Once we reached the porch, he put the basket down and dug into his pocket. "Since we're here, we should probably make sure everything's all right inside."

I nodded as I watched him pull his keychain out of his pocket and sort through the keys before he found the one that fit the lock. "Any reason to think it won't be?"

He glanced at me as he twisted the key. "None at all. But people have been coming and going for a few weeks, looking at the place. Melissa told me we've had a handful of showings since she put the place on the market."

Melissa James was our Realtor—who also happened to be Derek's ex-wife. I wasn't thrilled about having to work with her—indeed, I'd spent the past year doing my best not to have to work with her—but after our regular Realtor got married and left Maine for Miami, we didn't have much choice.

"At least they've made sure to keep the door locked," I remarked as Derek struggled with the key.

He nodded, and finally got the door unlocked and the key extracted. "Sticky lock. I'll have to bring some oil next time I come out here." He pocketed the key and pushed the door open. It swung smoothly, without the squeal of hinges it had on our first day here.

"Looks the same," I said, glancing around at the tight run-around staircase and the edge of the old-fashioned sailcloth rug—painted by yours truly—I could see through the door into the living room on the right.

Derek nodded. "Let's walk through, just in case."

"Sure." I went in one direction, he went in the other. When we ended up in the kitchen at the back of the house, I said, "Nothing wrong that I could see."

Derek shook his head. "Let's go eat."

Sure. We headed back out onto the porch, where Derek unpacked the picnic basket.

He'd packed it as well, without help from me—or to be more accurate, he had thrown himself on the mercy of Kate McGillicutty-Rasmussen, our friend who ran the Waterfield Inn B&B, and begged for help. Kate's hand in the basket was obvious. For one thing, I'm pretty sure it would never have occurred to Derek to bring genuine cloth napkins or real crystal glasses. Or a tiny bud vase, into which he shoved a couple of stems of tiny blue flowers that grew along the side of the house.

"What's the occasion?" I wanted to know.

He glanced up from the basket, a flash of blue eyes the same color as the flowers—and the sky. "Do we need an occasion?"

"I guess not. It's just . . ." I trailed off when the bottle of champagne appeared. "Derek?"

"Fine. I'm celebrating the fact that the TV crew has left and we survived the week." He pulled out two wrapped sandwiches and put one on my plate and one on his. Lobster rolls, from the deli in downtown Waterfield. In Derek's opinion, the best lobster rolls in Maine.

"Lobster rolls and champagne?" I said.

He grinned. "Why not? And whoopie pies for dessert." He brandished them. "Do I know how to plan a date, or not?"

Definitely. I watched as he popped the champagne cork and filled my glass and then his own. "Cheers."

I raised my glass. "Cheers. To a better week than the last one." I'd had my fill of dead bodies and complications for a while; I was ready for life to settle back down.

"I'll drink to that," Derek said, and did.

We ate in silence for a few minutes. Derek likes food—he has one of those metabolisms that's always cranking, so he's pretty much always hungry—and the fresh sea air and trip across the waves had given me an appetite, too. And to tell the truth, I was preoccupied, mulling things over in my mind. Something was going on; I could feel it. I just didn't know what. But something was up. He was restless. Maybe even nervous. Or worried. Eating too fast, even for Derek.

"Ready for dessert?"

He polished off his lobster roll while I still had almost half of mine left, and then he handed me my whoopie pie and started unwrapping his own. I followed suit, since I figured I probably couldn't finish the rest of the lobster roll as well as the whoopie pie anyway, and I certainly wasn't about to turn down dessert.

The whoopie pie is the official state treat of Maine, not to be confused with the official state dessert, which is blueberry pie. It consists of two rounds of chocolate cake—or in some cases pumpkin or spice cake—with frosting between them, and commonly, it's the size of an average hamburger. That said, the biggest whoopie pie ever created was made in South Portland in 2011, and weighed in at 1,062 pounds. But I digress.

I love whoopie pies, and Kate had made these, which made them even better. I had unwrapped the treat and was about to sink my teeth into it when something about it caught my eye.

"Something wrong?" Derek said innocently.

I ignored him. I had stopped with my mouth still open, the pie an inch from my lips, and now I squinted down my nose at the top of the chocolate cake, where something sparkled. Whoopie pie isn't supposed to sparkle, FYI.

I moved my hands back a few inches and waited for my eyesight to adjust, heart beating faster. My mouth, however, stayed open, but for a different reason now.

Derek had stopped eating, and was watching me. I glanced at him, and back to the whoopie pie in my hands again.

"Derek?" My voice shook.

"Yes," Derek said, and he sounded like he was farther away than just on the other side of the tablecloth.

"Is that . . ."

My heart was beating so hard it was difficult to get the words out.

"It isn't a cherry," Derek said.

No, it wasn't. Wrong color.

Very carefully, I lowered the whoopie pie to the porch floor and stared at it, much the same way I might stare at a spider, or something else I was worried might jump up and bite me.

"Derek? What . . . is that?"

"Pick it up and see," Derek said.

I reached out, with a hand that shook. And pulled out a ring.

"Derek?"

"I thought I'd lost you," Derek said. "You went home alone and you almost died. I don't want you to go home alone anymore. I don't want anything to happen to you because I'm not there. I want to marry you, so your home will be my home and no one can come into it and hurt you again."

I blinked.

"I called your mother," Derek added. "She approves."

Of course she did. My mother likes Derek. And besides, I was thirty-two. It wasn't like I needed my mother's approval to marry.

"I love you, Avery." He looked at me across the tablecloth, those blue eyes beautifully sincere.

"Derek," I sniffed. Somehow it was the only thing I could manage to say.

"Is that a yes?"

Of course it was a yes. I just couldn't get the word out. So I nodded, and threw myself across the tablecloth so champagne and small blue flowers went flying. He caught me and pulled me in for a kiss.

"I love you, Avery."

"I love you, too," I sniffled, and let him rescue the ring from my grasp and slide it, whoopie pie crumbs and all, onto my finger. Where it fit perfectly and looked—as the saying goes—like it was where it belonged to be.

—1—

"This is a waste of time," my fiancé grumbled. I glanced over at him as I slotted my spring green VW Beetle into a parking space outside the condominium building where Josh Rasmussen lived, and cut the engine. It was a few days later, and truth be told, I didn't need the Beetle; I could have floated here on the invisible pretty pink clouds that still surrounded me from Derek's proposal.

"We don't know that. And even if it is, you owe it to Josh to be nice about it. He's trying to help."

"Yeah, yeah," Derek said and opened his car door. "I'll be nice. But I want it on record that I'm against this."

I swung my legs out, too, and addressed him across the roof of the car. "Listen, you got your way when we bought the house on Rowanberry Island. We spent all spring and most of the summer renovating it, not to mention all the money in our account, and we're still waiting for it to sell. I'm not saying it wasn't fun, and a once-in-a-lifetime opportunity, but if we have to lower our standards for a while, and renovate a two-bedroom condo in a 1970s building—a condo that has none of the architectural elements that make your heart go pitter-patter—you'll just have to suck it up and deal with the situation. If you want to get married in October, we need the money. Weddings aren't cheap."

The date we had picked was only six weeks away, but Derek didn't want to wait, and neither did I. My mom had raised her eyebrows at the timeline, but it was an afternoon wedding, so I didn't need a proper gown. We had booked the church and the minister, and had settled on the adjoining reception hall for the celebration, and everything was proceeding apace.

"I don't want to get married in October," Derek said. He waited until I was close enough so he could snag my wrist, and then he pulled me even closer so he could look deeply into my eyes. "I want to get married right now. Or at least pretend we are."

I squirmed, as those cornflower blue eyes had their usual effect on my insides. "There's a little old lady watching us."

Derek straightened up. "Where?"

"First-floor apartment on the right. White lace curtains."

"Oh yeah," Derek said as the lace curtains fluttered. He smiled down at me, dimples and all. "Wanna give her a thrill?"

"You're awful." But I let him kiss me, and as usual, my stomach swooped.

"Break it up, you two!" a voice yelled, and when I turned my head, I saw Josh Rasmussen, along with his best friend and brand-new girlfriend, Shannon McGillicutty, hanging out of the window of Josh's third-floor apartment. They were grinning. I grinned back and lifted a hand.

"We'll be right up."

Josh nodded. "I'll buzz you in. Mr. Antonini's apartment is on the second floor. Meet you there."

They withdrew from the open window and closed it behind them. I looked up at Derek. "Remember, be nice."

"I'll be nice. And then afterwards, you can be nice to

me." He gyrated his eyebrows exaggeratedly. I burst into laughter, and he grinned back. "C'mon, Tink. Let's get this over with. Then we can take the honeymoon early."

I smiled. "By all means."

He flung an arm around my shoulders, and I snuggled into his side as we walked toward the front door.

. . .

My name is Avery Marie Baker. I met Derek Ellis some sixteen months ago, when I inherited my aunt Inga's old Victorian house in the tiny hamlet of Waterfield, Maine. He was the renovator I hired to help me fix the place up, since my ninety-eight-year-old cousin a few times removed—the "aunt" was a courtesy title—hadn't been in a position to maintain or update the house. My plan was to sell it, pocket the money, and go back to my perfectly blissful existence in Manhattan, with my textile design career, my rent-controlled apartment, and my boss-cum-boyfriend, Philippe. But over the course of the summer I fell in love not only with Maine but with Derek, and I ended up staying. We've been together, personally and professionally, ever since.

Josh, whom we were here to meet, is the son of the Waterfield chief of police, Wayne Rasmussen. Wayne married my best friend, Kate McGillicutty, last New Year's Eve. Kate is Shannon's mother. That makes Josh and Shannon sort of stepsiblings, which is a little weird when you consider that Josh has been in love with Shannon since she and Kate moved to Waterfield when Shannon was thirteen. The infatuation came long before the sibling relationship, though—in fact, I think it was Josh who introduced Kate and Wayne. And the romance is brand-new. It took Shannon quite a while to warm to the idea—she was afraid she'd lose her best friend if things didn't work out—and it took them both plunging off the cliffs and into the Atlantic Ocean recently to make her realize how quickly it could all go away. (Sort of the same thing that made Derek finally pop the question, I guess.) It had been horribly scary and we'd all been very worried, but they'd both been mostly OK, and the person responsible got caught, eventually. They've been working things out for the past week or so, and when they came to unlock the front door for us, we could see that things seemed to be going well. Josh had a trace of lipstick at the corner of his mouth, while Shannon's long mane of black cherry hair was tangled, as if someone had had his hands in it quite recently.

Derek grinned. "Having fun, kids?"

Josh blushed and adjusted his glasses. Shannon grinned back. "Yes, in fact."

I elbowed Derek's ribs. "Leave them alone. They're over twenty, they can do what they want."

"Of course they can," Derek said. "And I'm thirty-five, so I can give them a hard time."

I shook my head, exasperated.

"Knock it off," Josh said, "or I won't show you the apartment. If you're going to keep doing this to me, maybe I won't want you working downstairs from me."

I shot Derek a look that said, *Don't you dare tell him to go ahead because you don't want to see the apartment anyway!* And he put his hands up in the classic pose of surrender. "I'll be good."

"I'll believe that when I see it," Shannon said, and smiled at me.

I smiled back. "So tell us about Mr. Antonini and the apartment. What's going on?"

"Mr. Antonini," Josh said as he fit the key into the door of the condo on the second floor, right above the little old lady with the lace curtains, "bought this condo when the building was new. He lived here for years with his wife and a couple of kids. The kids grew up and moved out, and eventually Mr. Antonini retired. He and his wife became snowbirds."

A snowbird, for the uninitiated, is a Mainer—or someone from another of the cold Northern states—who migrates south in the winter. Many snowbirds are retirees, who keep two residences: one in the northern U.S. for the summer, one in Florida, Alabama, or the islands, for the winter.

"They're in their seventies now, and they're tired of the traveling. So they've decided to sell the condo and just spend all their time in Florida."

"And that's where we come in," Derek said.

Josh nodded, struggling with the door. It seemed to be going around. "They've owned the place for more than thirty years. It's paid for. It didn't cost much when it was new—not compared to what real estate costs these days. And it needs a bit of updating, since they haven't done much to it in the time they've owned it."

"So we can get it cheap." Derek glanced at me.

"Not to say cheap," Josh said, finally pushing the door open and pocketing the key. "Condos in this building, all fixed up, go for over two hundred thousand these days. You'll probably have to pay a hundred for it. But you'll be able to make a bit off the deal."

"It depends on how much updating it needs," I warned him as Derek led the way into the dark hall, peering left and right. "If it'll be prohibitively expensive to renovate, he won't want to do it."

I already had my hands full convincing him that redoing a small, bland flat could be interesting. We'd been spoiled so far, between Aunt Inga's Victorian, Kate McGillicutty's carriage house from World War One, and the 1783 center chimney Colonial on Rowanberry Island.

Josh nodded. "I told Mr. Antonini that. He understands. He'd prefer to get this taken care of quickly, with minimal fuss—and from Florida—so he'd like to avoid listing the house with a Realtor and going through all the time and effort it would take to market it, but if it doesn't work out, it doesn't work out. Have a look around."

I did, following Derek inside.

Like Josh's place—like all the apartments in the building—it was a two-bedroom, one-bath flat. The front door took us into a dark and narrow hallway with parquet floors and papered walls. To the left was a kitchen; I could see vinyl and avocado green appliances through the doorway. To the right was a bedroom. Next to the front door was the door to the only bath, and roughly opposite was the doorway to the combination living room/dining room. It had a little balcony off the back, just big enough for a minuscule table and two plastic chairs, overlooking grass and pine trees. Off the other end of the room, where the dining table stood, was another door—this one to the second bedroom.

"Split bedrooms," I said.

Derek nodded. "Hard to find in apartments from the seventies. They liked to group things together back then."

"It's a good thing, right?"

"Oh yeah. People like split bedrooms. Put the kids down on the other side of the house and turn in with no worries that they'll wake up from the mattress squeaking and the bed banging against the wall."

So the split bedrooms were a plus.

"This is a good-sized room." I turned in a slow circle, taking in the living room/dining room combination. "Airy. Lots of light."

"That wall of windows out to the balcony is great," Derek agreed. "Though I'm not sure I'd call it a good size, Avery."

"That's because you haven't seen the apartment I grew up in in New York City," I said. "It was only about half the size of this. Three of us lived there. And we still managed to fit in two bedrooms, a bath, a living room, and a kitchen. Some people have much less."

"Up here people are used to enough room to stretch their legs," Derek answered. "But it isn't too bad. Let's look at the rest." He headed out into the hallway to look at the kitchen and the bath, where most of our efforts—and funds—would be spent.

Everything was neat and clean, but dated. The wallpaper in the kitchen was mustard yellow and green tartan plaid. The vinyl floor was made to look like brick—in perfect condition, but sinfully ugly. The appliances were green, the counter yellow. The bathroom floor was also vinyl, and the tub had a molded plastic shower wall. An oak vanity cabinet with a single basin completed the 1970s look.

"What kind of people live in this building?" Derek asked over his shoulder.

"All kinds," Josh answered from the hallway. "There are eight apartments, two on each floor. The Antoninis lived here: two parents with two kids, until the kids moved out and only the parents were left. The other second-floor apartment belongs to two guys named Gregg and Mariano. Gregg works at the hospital. I think he's a resident. Your dad probably knows him."

Derek's father is Benjamin Ellis, Waterfield's GP. The plan was for Derek to take over the practice, until my boyfriend decided he liked working on houses more than he liked working on people. He quit doctoring to start Waterfield R&R some six years ago.

"Mariano commutes to Portland to work," Josh added. "I think he's in the hotel business. Below them is William Maurits. Single guy in his fifties, likes Eastern religion and abstract art. Insurance adjuster. He commutes to Portland, too."

"Below us on this side is Hilda Shaw," Shannon contributed, peering at us around Josh's shoulder. He's as tall as his father, close to six and a half feet, and although Shannon is half a foot taller than me, she looks almost dainty next to Josh. I was happy to see that the bandage she'd had on her forehead since the accident had been replaced with a much smaller Band-Aid.

"The lady with the lace curtains?" Derek asked.

Josh nodded. "She's lived here as long as the Antoninis. She's an older lady, lives on Social Security or disability or something. No job. Spends most of her time sitting at the window watching people come and go."

"If you decide to buy the place," Shannon added, "be prepared that she'll tie you down and not let you up again until she's turned your brain inside out. She knows everything there is to know about everyone who lives here, right down to what's in their refrigerator and what they wanted to be when they were eight. Everyone has to pass by her door to go in or out, so she knows everyone's business. There are no secrets in this place. Miss Shaw knows them all."

Josh looked uncomfortable for a split second before he pushed through it. "One of the third-floor apartments is mine, or rather, Dad's. The other third-floor apartment is a rental, and a couple of girls from Barnham College live there. Candy and Jamie. You'd recognize Candy; she works at Guido's Pizzeria."

"The blond waitress with the ponytail?" I said. "She's a little annoying. Whenever we go there to eat, she always fawns on Derek and ignores me. Makes it hard to order."

"She's a bit of an airhead," Shannon confirmed. "But Jamie is nice. Can't imagine how the two of them ended up being roommates; they have nothing in common."

"Local girls?"

Shannon shook her head. "Just Candy. Jamie is an out-of-stater." She pronounced it "out-of-statah," like any self-respecting Mainer.

"Flatlander?" I suggested, since that's what the native Mainers call people not from the mountainous New England states.

"Mississippi. As far south as you can get. And I guess it's pretty flat down there. Cotton country, isn't it? Then Josh is across the hall from them, and on the top floor . . ."

"A woman named Amelia Easton is on my side," Josh said.

My ears pricked up. "Her name sounds familiar."

"She started working at Barnham College last year. Took over Professor Wentworth's job, remember?"

"Of course." Martin Wentworth had taught history at Barnham two years ago, during Josh and Shannon's first year there, and had been replaced by Professor Easton the following autumn.

"What about the last apartment?" Derek wanted to know. "Who lives there?"

"That'd be the Mellons," Shannon said.

"Like the fruit?"

She spelled it.

"Mellon. Right. And what do they do?"

"The husband works for your friend Peter Cortino," Josh said.

Peter is a Boston transplant who married Derek's high school sweetheart, Jill. They run Cortino's Auto Shop, so the guy on the top floor must be a car mechanic of some sort.

"The wife stays home with a little boy," Josh added. "He's two. His name is Benjamin, and hers is Robin. Her husband's Bruce."

"Bruce and Robin?" Derek's lips twitched.

"Yeah. Why?"

"No reason." But he grinned.

"What?" I asked.

"I'll tell you later. So the building has four single people, a family, and two pairs of roommates?"

"Gregg and Mariano aren't so much roommates as a couple," Shannon said. "They'd probably get married if they could, but they'd have to move to Massachusetts to do it."

I nodded, since I knew what Derek was thinking. If we were to take on the project, who was our targeted buyer? "The best thing to do would probably be to renovate for single or double occupancy. Two bedrooms, one that could be used as an office if the buyer is single. Most families probably wouldn't choose to live in a place this small these days."

Josh shook his head. "Robin and Benjamin moved in with Bruce almost a year ago, and they've been talking about finding a place with a yard ever since. I don't know why they don't."

"Money?" Shannon suggested.

Josh shrugged. "None of my business, I guess. And

they're quiet enough. I'm sure Benjamin would like a yard to play in, though. I had one growing up—we didn't move here until after my mom died—and it just isn't the same."

"Convenient for your dad," I said, since the new police headquarters was on this same side of town, a few miles down the road. "And I'm sure it would have been hard to stay in the house after your mother was gone."

"Sure. Anyway, that's it. Everyone who lives here. So what do you think?" He looked around.

"I like it," I said. The fairly compact space reminded me of being back in Manhattan—not that I wanted to be; I loved Maine and Aunt Inga's old Victorian house, but the reminder was sort of nice—and I thought it might be fun to make such a little space functional and exciting. A totally different scope from the big Colonial we'd put so much time and effort into. Between then and now we'd spent a couple of weeks slapping lipstick and polish on a compact 1930s cottage in Waterfield Village, but it had been a rush job, work-for-hire, with the TV crew dogging our footsteps, and it hadn't scratched the itch much at all. But I could sink my teeth into this, and put to good use some of the tricks I'd picked up in thirty years of living in Manhattan, for how to make something small seem more spacious and how to make something a little dull and dingy seem fresh and new. "It'd be fun. And it wouldn't take long to do. A month maybe."

Not like the house on the island, which took forever to renovate and would take just as long to sell. People who can afford half-a-million-dollar Colonials on the coast of Maine don't come along often enough.

I added persuasively, "It's a good location, and if we price it right, we could probably sell it quickly."

"Would we need approval from the condo association to do the work?" Derek asked.

Josh shook his head. "Not for what you're planning to do. If you want to enclose the porch, or do something else that would affect the way the building looks from the outside, you would, but as long as you're just renovating the interior, you can do whatever you want."

Derek looked around. "Did Mr. Antonini give you any idea what sort of price he might be willing to settle for?"

"I didn't ask," Josh said. "I didn't think it was any of my business. I don't think he wants to give it away, but on the other hand, he's ready to sell. I have his number. He said if you were interested and you wanted to talk, to give him a call." He dug in the pocket of his jeans and pulled out a slightly crumpled business card.

"Thanks." Derek put it in his own jeans pocket. We stood in silence for a moment.

"So?" Shannon said. "Are you going to do it?"

I looked at Derek. He looked at me.

"I expect we are," he said.

I smiled.

. . .

"Did you meet Miss Shaw?" Kate asked an hour or two later.

I was back home, at Aunt Inga's house, and Kate had come over to help me with the invitations for the wedding. I was making my own paper, with pulp and water and small blue flowers—the same kind Derek had stuffed into the bud vase before he proposed. Because making paper takes a lot of time, Kate had volunteered to help, to make it go faster. I'd said yes, since I had something I wanted to ask her. But first I'd mentioned the trip out to Wayne's old condo building to look at a possible renovation project.

I shook my head. "She was watching us from the window, but we didn't meet her."

"You will," Kate said ominously, up to her elbows in pulp.

We were set up in the backyard, near the remains of the garden shed—Derek hadn't had time to build a new one yet—and we were busy pulping old newspapers, both because it was quicker and easier and because I didn't feel like cutting down any trees. Jemmy and Inky, the two Maine coon cats I had inherited from Aunt Inga along with the house, were watching from a safe distance, while Mischa, the small Russian Blue kitten I had rescued from Rowanberry Island this spring, kept trying to play with the pulp.

"That's what Shannon said, too." While Kate was filling wooden frames with pulp, I was aiming my hair dryer at the ones that were already filled, in an attempt to make the paper dry faster.

"Oh, was she there?"

"With Josh. Looks like they're working things out?" I aimed the dryer at Mischa, and sent him scurrying away from the pulp.

"They seem to be," Kate said with a shrug. "She doesn't talk to me about it."

Shannon was an adult; it probably wasn't so surprising that she didn't discuss the progress of her love affair with her mother. Especially when her mother's new husband was Shannon's boyfriend's father.

"Is Miss Shaw giving her a hard time?"

"No more than she's giving anyone else," Kate said. "Or so I assume. She was all over me when Wayne was still living there. She's one of those people who has to know every little detail about everyone else's life, probably because she doesn't have one of her own."

"A life?"

Kate nodded. "She just sits inside her apartment all the time. Never leaves. I'm not sure whether it's agoraphobia or just that she's allergic to everything on God's green earth, but she lives vicariously through other people. If you end up renovating the place, just be prepared that at some point she'll dig up every bit of information on you that she can. Who you are, where you live, why you moved here, what happened to your aunt . . ."

"Let her. I don't have anything to hide."

"In that case," Kate said, "you have nothing to worry about. How's it going?" She nodded at the still moist note cards.

"It's getting there. I wanted to ask you something."

"Shoot," Kate said.

"I appreciate your help with the invitations. Can I ask you one more favor?"

"You want me to do the food for the reception?"

I lowered the hair dryer to stare at her. Mischa took the opportunity to reinstate his investigation of the pulp. "God, no. I'd never ask you to do that."

"I'd be happy to," Kate said.

"I appreciate it, but that wasn't what I was going to ask."

"What, then?" She shooed Mischa away gently.

"I thought you might want to be my maid of honor. Or matron of honor, I guess, since you're married yourself."

She blinked at me for a moment before she said, "Isn't there someone else you'd rather have? A friend from New York? College roommate?"

I shook my head. "There isn't anyone left in New York I'm that close to. I sent a couple of invitations to people down there, but I don't want any of them to be my matron of honor. My mom and Noel are coming from California, but I can't make my mother my matron of honor, either, no matter how well I get along with her."

"No," Kate agreed, "that probably wouldn't look right."

"I'd like you to do it. If you don't mind."

"I don't mind. Of course not. I'd be honored. If you're sure . . ."

"I'm positive," I said. "Please."

Kate nodded. We worked in silence for a few minutes, both of us probably a bit more overwhelmed by emotion than we ought to be.

"So are you going to renovate the condo?" Kate asked finally. I accepted the change of subject without quibbling.

"I think so. Derek went to look at our finances and to talk to his dad. He likes to run these things by Dr. Ben."

Kate nodded. "It's nice that he has such a good relationship with his family."

It certainly was. Especially since my own family, which

consisted of my mother and her new husband, was clear across the country on the California coast.

"Let me know what you decide," Kate said. "I'll be happy to help out with the work, if you want."

"We never say no to extra hands. You know that. We'll see what Mr. Antonini says."

Kate nodded, and we went back to our pulp and our hair dryer.

—2—

"Still like it?" Derek asked two weeks later, standing in the hallway looking around. We'd closed on the place about an hour before, and had headed over to inspect our new purchase.

I glanced up at him. He's over six feet, I'm five two. "Don't you?"

He shrugged. "I didn't like it much to begin with. But I figure I owe you one. I had to talk you into getting excited about the midcentury ranch on Becklea Drive, and I had to talk you into believing we could handle Kate's carriage house, and I had to twist your arm to get you to agree to give the Colonial a try . . . I figure it's your turn to choose, yeah?"

"I guess it is. But I'd be happier if you were happy, too."

"I'm not unhappy," Derek said, looking around. "I'd just like it more if it had some fun features I could play with."

"I know. You like crown molding and arches and wide plank floors and tall ceilings. This has none of that. But it has a lot of other benefits. We can get in and out quickly and probably sell it pretty fast, too. And I bet if we try, we can figure out ways to make it look more interesting."

"It's not the same thing," Derek said, but he sounded a little more positive. "What did you have in mind?"

"I'm not entirely sure. But it's such a blank slate that we could do almost anything to it. We could start by taking out the plain hollow-core doors and putting in solid wood doors with panels instead."

"That'd help to make things look more solid. What else?"

"Depends. What would you say to putting in a pocket door to the bathroom? It would save space in the hallway. It's a little cramped the way it is."

"That's a good idea," Derek said. "Except instead of a pocket door, why don't we make it a sliding door with a rail? It could rest here"—he put his hand against the wall between the two doors, the one to the hallway and the one next to it, to the bathroom—"when it's open."

"With the rail actually visible?" I squinted up, trying to picture it.

"Remember when we first met last summer?" Derek said. "You were enamored with the industrial look? Exposed ductwork, concrete kitchen counters, all that jazz?"

I nodded.

"Remember how I wouldn't let you do any of it because we were renovating your aunt's Victorian cottage and it just wouldn't look right?"

I remembered it vividly.

"Here," Derek said and threw out a hand to indicate the space we were standing in, "it would look great."

"Really?"

"Sure. The ceilings are a little low for exposed ductwork, and besides, the ductwork is routed through the walls anyway, but we can give this place an industrial look if you want. It's from the 1970s. Things were pretty streamlined back then."

Huh. I looked around with new appreciation, visions of

steel beams and corrugated metal dancing in my head. "How do we go about it?"

"I'm glad you asked," Derek said. "New tile in the bathroom. Something sleek and modern. And a new vanity cabinet. Maybe a floating one."

"Floating?"

"Without feet. Mounted to the wall."

Oooh. I nodded.

"Sliding door on the bathroom to maximize space in the hallway. New kitchen cabinets . . ."

"What kind of cabinets did you have in mind for here?"

Derek hesitated. "We could go to the lumber depot and buy new oak cabinets and stain or paint them."

"With picture frame doors?" I could feel my nose wrinkling. "They're so old-fashioned. How about we get the kind with smooth doors, if they have them, and then we give them a few coats of paint and a few coats of high-gloss polyurethane and make them look like they're lacquered? I saw that once, in a DIY magazine. It looked great. Like high-end IKEA cabinets, but better quality."

"What color did you have in mind?" His voice was resigned, even as his eyes registered interest.

"Turquoise?" I suggested, since that had been the color of the cabinets in the magazine article. "Concrete counter, like you suggested. Maybe a backsplash of those little clear glass tiles—or glossy subway tiles with just a band of glass tiles; it'd be cheaper—and we could even put those industrial floor tiles down, you know, the sort of hard plastic ones?"

"With the speckles? Sure. It would fit the style of the place." He looked around. "Maybe this won't be so bad, after all."

"That's the spirit. How about we go grab some dinner and celebrate? And plan what we'll do tomorrow?"

"What did you have in mind? The Waymouth Tavern?"

"Guido's Pizzeria," I said, and watched his eyebrows rise. "It's on the way home, and you can tell Candy that you'll be working downstairs from her for a month. I'm sure she'll be thrilled."

"You can't be jealous of Candy," Derek said, leading me out and stopping to lock the door behind us.

"Of course not." The only person I'm ever jealous of, and that only on rare occasions, is Derek's ex-wife. And I'm even getting over that, since Derek has told me repeatedly that there's nothing in the world that would induce him to go back to her. "They have good pizza."

"Fine with me," Derek said with a shrug, "I'm always up for pizza." He headed down the stairs. I followed, only to bump into him when we got to the first floor. When I peered around him, I saw that he was facing Miss Hilda Shaw's door, and that the door was open and Miss Shaw herself was standing there waiting for us.

This was the first time I'd seen her, other than as a pair of disembodied eyes peering out from between the folds of the lace curtains moved apart by an equally disembodied hand. Up close and in the flesh, I saw that she was younger than I'd expected. I'd envisioned some small and wrinkled Miss Marple lookalike, frail and white-haired. What I got was a sturdy women in her late fifties or early sixties, with frizzy ginger hair shot through with gray, wearing a flowery, faded housedress and fuzzy slippers. Her arms were pudgy, her ankles thick, and her cheeks doughy. When she spoke, it was in a raspy voice that hinted at what was either a pack-a-day habit or laryngitis.

"Hello," she said. "I'm Hilda Shaw."

There was an expectant pause. The compulsion to answer was irresistible—and was obeyed.

"I'm Derek Ellis," my fiancé answered. "This is Avery."

He reached behind him and pulled me forward. Misery loves company and all that. I wiggled my fingers. "Hi."

"A pleasure to meet you both," Miss Shaw rasped. "I saw you here two weeks ago, too." She fixed Derek with an unblinking stare out of dark eyes.

"We were looking at the Antoninis' condo," Derek said. "Have they decided to rent it out?"

I shook my head. "They've decided to stay in Florida full time. We just bought the place."

"Oh." A shadow crossed Miss Shaw's broad face. Then it cleared and she looked back at us. "Are you moving in?"

"We'll be renovating the place," Derek said at the same time as I answered, "We've already got somewhere to live."

"Where do you live?" Hilda Shaw wanted to know.

I hesitated, but couldn't think of a reason not to tell her. Waterfield is a small town; half of us already know where the other half lives. And besides, Shannon and Kate had both said Miss Shaw never left the building; the chances that she'd suddenly show up at the door wanting to be let in were slim.

"I inherited a house from my aunt last summer. It's on Bayberry Lane in the Village. Derek lives on Main Street in downtown." Because Waterfield is such a small place, especially the historic district and the downtown commercial area, we're only four or five blocks apart. The condo complex was on the west side of town, a few miles from the historic district, near the new police station and about halfway between town and Barnham College.

"So is this a place for you to share?" Miss Shaw wanted to know.

Derek shook his head. "We're just renovating it and putting it back on the market. And we may be making a bit of noise over the next few weeks. Sorry."

"So you're not married?" She looked from one to the other of us.

"Not yet," Derek said.

"Engaged?"

He glanced at me and grinned. "Yes."

"For how long?"

"A few weeks." I gave her a bright smile as I took a step toward the stairs. "It was nice to meet you, Miss Shaw."

"You, too," Hilda Shaw said. "So you'll be starting your renovations soon?"

"Tomorrow." Derek looked trapped, like a deer in the headlights, too polite to cut and run.

My mother did her best to instill politeness into me, but I am, after all, a New Yorker. We tend to be direct. "I'm sorry, Miss Shaw," I said, grabbing Derek's arm. "We really have to go. We have a lot to do before tomorrow morning."

"Of course." Hilda Shaw sounded conciliatory, but the look in her eyes was avid, as if she really wanted us to stay longer so she could finish turning our brains inside out and shaking them to see if anything of value was left.

"We'll be back in the morning," Derek said, unable to help himself. I resisted the temptation to roll my eyes. "We'll see you then."

Miss Shaw nodded and withdrew into her apartment. By the time we got downstairs and were getting into the Beetle, she was back behind the lace curtains again. I could see them flutter.

"You were much too nice to her," I chastised Derek after the car doors were closed and I was plugging the key in the ignition. "Now she'll never leave us alone."

"She's a lonely old lady," Derek answered. "I feel sorry for her."

"She treated us like we were suspects in a crime."

"It wasn't that bad," Derek said, buckling his seat belt. When we're working, we pretty consistently use Derek's truck for everything—it's a Ford F-150 with plenty of room in the back for all our supplies and tools, quite unlike the Beetle—and when we're not working, I enjoy driving my zippy little car. It was a gift from my mother and her husband last Christmas, since I hadn't had a car when I first arrived in Waterfield. In New York City, there's not much point in owning one. Having to drive to get anywhere was a new experience for me, but I'd found I was enjoying it.

"Yes, it was." The engine caught, and I put the car in reverse and backed out of the parking space, narrowly avoiding a collision with a Jeep coming in the opposite direction. It slid into a parking space a few slots down. After a moment, the door opened and a young man got out. He was in his early or mid-twenties and olive-skinned, with black hair and a strong nose, dressed in black pants and a white shirt. He headed for the front door at a good clip, without even looking our way. The lace curtains went into a frenzy of flutters.

"Who do you suppose that is?" I said. "Bruce, Gregg, Mariano, or William Maurits?"

"It isn't Maurits. He's quite a bit older. And I think I've met Gregg once. My money's on Mariano."

"Or Bruce maybe?"

"It could be Bruce. Do you want me to stop him and ask?"

He was being sarcastic. I chose to ignore it.

"Of course not. He looks like he's in a hurry. I don't want to interrupt him. I'm just curious. These are our new neighbors, after all."

"You're as bad as Miss Shaw," Derek said. "Nosy old spinster."

I shot him an offended look as I concentrated on turning the Beetle out of the parking lot and onto the Augusta Road in the direction of Guido's. "Am not."

"Are, too. Or you will be if you don't look out. You already live alone with three cats."

"I'm getting married!" I said.

My boyfriend grinned. "Yes, you are. And your future husband is just giving you a hard time. You won't ever turn into Hilda Shaw. You have too many friends and too many interests to end up sitting behind your kitchen curtains petting Mischa and watching the neighbors."

Jemmy and Inky loved my aunt, but they merely tolerated me. They wouldn't let me pet them, so if I were to sit behind the kitchen curtains petting a cat, it'd definitely be Mischa. I wouldn't be watching the neighbors, however; the kitchen faces the back of the house, and all I can see from there is the backyard, with what's left of the garden shed, and the trees.

"Thank you," I said. "I think."

"My pleasure," Derek answered and stretched his legs out.

Five minutes later we pulled into the parking lot outside Guido's Pizzeria.

It was barely five o'clock, but already the place was hopping. The parking lot was more than half-full—a few trucks, plus a whole army of small economy cars with out-of-state license plates—and although I've seen the inside more tightly packed than it was right now, there was someone at almost every table. We made our way through the crowd, ducking and weaving, until we got to a small table for two near the swinging door to the kitchen. Candy, in her customary tight jeans and cropped pink top, was wending her way between the patrons, ponytail bopping and bubble gum snapping.

"Hi!" she said when she got around to noticing us—or rather, Derek. "What can I get you to drink?"

Derek ordered a beer for himself, and since he had Candy's attention and I didn't, he added a Diet Coke for me.

She popped a pink bubble. "Be right back."

"See?" I told Derek when she'd sauntered off, tail swinging, "It's like I'm not even here."

He grinned. "Don't worry about it, Tink. *I* know you're here. Who cares what Candy thinks?"

He reached across the table and took my hand, looking deeply into my eyes. I leaned forward, irresistibly drawn, while tucking a strand of yellow hair behind my ear. That's the reason he calls me Tinkerbell: lots of kinky, Mello Yello hair I often pile on top of my head when I work, like Peter Pan's little fairy friend. That, and the fact that when he came up with the nickname, last summer when we first met, I was pouting a lot, because I wasn't getting my way. Oh yes, and he thinks I'm cute, or "cunning," as they say in Maine. For Halloween last year, we dressed up as Peter Pan and Tinkerbell. Derek looks quite fetching in tights.

"Who do you want to be for Halloween this year?" I asked dreamily. Those blue, blue eyes never fail to have an effect on me.

Derek straightened and let go of my hand. "Don't you

have enough to worry about without making Halloween costumes? We're getting married in October, aren't we?"

I sat back myself. Obviously the hand-holding was over. "We could combine the two. How would you feel about getting married in costume?"

"Not good," Derek said.

"People do it, you know. Themed weddings. And it would be fun. We could be Peter Pan and Tinkerbell again. Or you could be Robin Hood and I could be Maid Marian. You already have the green tights and the tunic from last year, and the hat with the jaunty feather. All you'd need is a bow and arrows."

"And then for Halloween I suppose you're gonna repurpose the bow and arrow and turn me into Cupid? With little angel wings and a diaper? No thanks."

"But I really wanted to be Maid Marian," I said, pouting.

"You can still be Maid Marian," Derek said. "I'll be Friar Tuck."

"You look nothing like Friar Tuck." Tuck—at least the stereotypical Tuck—is short and fat and bald. Derek is tall and lean and still has all his hair. It's dirty blond bordering on light brown, with streaks through the front and crown in the summer from time spent in the sun, and it's almost always just a touch too long. I'm rather fond of it, and I'd hate to have to shave a bald spot to make him look the part. It would grow back in, I know, but still . . . not something I'd want to remember from the happiest day of my life. Just imagine the wedding photos.

"Fine," Derek said. "I'll be the Sheriff of Nottingham."

"Maid Marian can't marry the Sheriff of Nottingham. And besides, he wore tights, too. They all wore tights back then. Friar Tuck probably had tights under the cassock."

Derek huffed. "I'm not getting married in tights. In fact, I'm not getting married in costume at all. No themed wedding. A monkey suit is as far as I'll go."

"Tuxedo?"

"If you insist," Derek said. "Now can we *please* talk about something else?"

"I suppose. What?"

"The condo. Talk to me about the condo."

Fine. "We start by tearing out, the way we usually do. Get rid of everything we don't plan to keep. The old kitchen cabinets and sink, the avocado green appliances, the vanity cabinet and commode."

"Not the commode," Derek said. "It's the only bathroom in the apartment, and I'd hate to have to knock on Miss Shaw's door to ask her if I can use the facility. She'd probably watch me through the keyhole."

I shuddered. "Lord, yes. No, let's make sure we won't have to do that. That should take us most of the first day, don't you think?"

At that point, just as Derek was nodding agreement, Candy came back with our drinks and derailed the conversation for the moment. She pulled her order pad out of her back pocket. "What'll you have?"

Derek ordered a pizza with everything except pineapple and anchovies, and Candy turned away. She was just about to slip through the door to the kitchen when a man grabbed her arm and held her back. He looked to be a few years older than Derek, late thirties, and was good-looking, in a slick sort of way. Dark-haired and olive-skinned, he reminded me of the late and mostly unlamented Tony "the Tiger" Micelli, former reporter for Channel Eight News.

Candy smiled when she saw the man, but whatever words he muttered in her ear made the happiness slip right off her face. When he walked away a few seconds later, without a backward glance, she stood watching him, for once chewing on her bottom lip instead of her bubble gum.

"Uh-oh," I said. "Who is he?" Derek grew up in Waterfield; if anyone knew, he would.

"Who?" He glanced over his shoulder. I indicated the man, now on his way into the hallway in the back, where the bathrooms were. Derek shook his head. "No idea. He's not from around here. Or if he is, he's new."

Over the past five or six years—since Melissa dumped Derek and started selling real estate, extolling Waterfield's virtues as a sleeper community for Portland and Augusta—our little town's population has practically doubled. There have been new subdivisions cropping up like toadstools all over the place, many of them built by my now out-of-business cousins, the Stenham twins. This guy must be one of the newcomers.

"He's too old for her," I said.

"It's none of your business," Derek answered. And since he was right, I left it at that.

—3—

"I can't imagine living under this kind of scrutiny every day of my life," Derek muttered under his breath the next morning as we stood in the parking lot under the watchful eye of Miss Hilda Shaw, unloading tools from the back of the truck. "No wonder the Antoninis left."

I grinned. "Guilty conscience?"

He shook his head. "No. But I don't have to have done something wrong not to want someone watching my every move."

Too true. We had only been here twice, and Miss Shaw was already getting on both of our nerves. Didn't she have something better to do than sit behind her curtains watching everyone else? Couldn't she go read a book or something? Or watch a soap opera?

"Maybe she'll get used to us," I said optimistically. "Maybe she's just interested in us because we're new."

"She's not."

It wasn't Derek who said it. I looked up to meet the gray eyes of a short and slender man in a charcoal gray suit, who had stopped beside the sedan in the next parking space. He stuck out a hand. “I’m William Maurits, 1B.”

“Avery Baker,” I said, shaking the hand, “2A.”

Derek reached past me to shake Maurits’s hand as well. “Derek Ellis. We’ve met before. What’s that you said?”

“It’s not because you’re new,” William said, and switched the briefcase back into his right hand now that the handshaking was over. He lifted his chin, perhaps in an effort to appear taller, since he wasn’t much bigger than me. “I’ve been here for ten years, and she still watches my every move.” He shot something akin to a glare at the lace curtains. “Nosy old biddy. Always has to have her beak in everyone’s business.”

“Maybe she doesn’t have much of a life of her own,” I suggested.

William glanced at me. “She doesn’t. Never married, never had children.” He chuckled. “Not that I have room to talk. I never married or had children, either. Married to the job, I suppose.”

“So maybe she’s lonely.”

William shrugged. “Possibly. All I know is, she spends all her time sitting at that window. I’ve never seen her come outside the building. She even has groceries delivered.”

“Is she ill? Or disabled?” Some sort of mental illness maybe? Agoraphobia, like Kate had suggested. That’s what it’s called when people are afraid to go outside, right?

“No idea,” William said. “All I know is, she’s a nuisance.” He nodded politely before disarming his car alarm and getting in.

“Cheerful fellow,” Derek remarked when William had pulled out of the parking space and was waiting to join traffic on the Augusta Road. “You got what you need?”

He ran an experienced eye over the tools I had assembled.

“I think so. If you’ll take the big toolbox, I’ll take this little one. And if we need anything else, the truck will be right downstairs; it’s not like it’s a long walk to get something.”

"I don't want to parade in front of Miss Shaw any more than I have to," Derek said, and hoisted the big toolbox. "C'mon, Avery. Let's get this show on the road."

"Let's." I grabbed the small toolbox and followed him toward the front door, twiddling my fingers to Miss Shaw on the way.

Just as we reached the front door, it opened from the inside, and Candy tumbled out, followed by another young woman. She was shorter by an inch or two and, unlike Candy, seemed determined to make as little of herself as possible. Like Candy, she had a blond ponytail—baby-fine hair scraped straight back—but it looked less jaunty, just sort of hung there. Candy was polished to a high sheen, with iridescent blue eye shadow, a thick layer of mascara, and pink lip gloss, while her friend looked like Plain Jane, with not a stitch of makeup on her face. I had wondered whether Candy's faded jeans and cropped top were a uniform of sorts, clothes she wore to Guido's to maximize her earnings, but it must be her usual mode of dress, because she was wearing the same tight jeans and the same short and tight sort of top now, when I assumed she was on her way to school. Both girls had bags over their shoulders, and Jamie was jingling a set of car keys in her hand. Unlike Candy, she was dressed in leggings and an oversized and baggy sweater that hung almost to her knees and hid any hint of a figure. The color was a dark navy blue bordering on black that overwhelmed her pale complexion and delicate features.

"I always told you it was stupid—" she said, with a soft Southern drawl to her voice, and stopped abruptly when she saw us. "Sorry."

"Good morning." Derek flashed his patented Derek-grin, the one that never fails to give me a little swoop to my stomach. Candy blinked. After a second, she seemed to recognize him.

"Oh. It's you. Hi."

"Hi," Derek said, just as a clatter from inside the building announced the arrival of someone else. After a moment, a pair of long legs in jeans appeared on the stairs, and a second later, the rest of Josh Rasmussen became visible.

"Oh," he said when he saw us. "It's you."

Derek arched a brow. "Didn't you expect us?"

"Yeah. Sure. It's just . . ." He shook his head. "I gotta go, or I'll be late for school. I'll see you later."

He pushed past us and headed for his car, a small, brand-new, dark blue Honda parked in the lot. It had replaced the dark blue Honda he used to drive, after that one had ended up in the Atlantic Ocean a month or so ago, and had been declared a total loss by the insurance company.

"Probably can't wait to see Shannon," I said to Derek. He nodded.

"We'd better go, too," Jamie told Candy. "Don't want to be late. Excuse us, please."

They disappeared into the parking lot and went in different directions. Candy headed for a small white hybrid, while Jamie got into a nondescript compact, pale blue. A few seconds later, all three cars were lined up at the exit, waiting to merge with traffic on the Augusta Road.

"Want to take bets on which of the neighbors we'll see next?" I asked Derek.

He shook his head. "I'd rather just get inside before we see any of them. We'll never get any work done this way."

Since he had a point, I scurried through the door and up the stairs after him, with only a sideways glance at Miss Shaw's door on my way past.

We spent the next several hours causing major destruction. It's quite cathartic, actually. I enjoyed ripping out all the worn and torn ugliness, and imagining all the pretty and shiny we would be installing it its place. Derek went to work with pliers and wrenches, taking the plumbing to the kitchen and bathroom sinks apart preparatory to tearing out the sinks themselves, while I armed myself with—of all things—a shovel, and went to work ripping up the vinyl floor in the kitchen. That took us through to lunch, when we broke out the sandwiches and drinks I'd packed and made ourselves comfortable on the small balcony.

The front door was actually on what I'd consider to be the back of the building, where the parking lot also was. On the front—or other—side, there were balconies overlooking a wide expanse of grass and a line of trees. We were into September, and among the fir trees were a few oaks and birches that had just started to turn yellow, bright against the blue autumn sky. Some of the leaves had given up the ghost and were drifting lazily toward the green grass.

I took a deep breath, filling my lungs with the crisp, clean air. "Pretty."

"It's a good place to live," Derek agreed.

I glanced at him. "Did you ever want to live anywhere else? You were a doctor; you could have gotten a job anywhere."

He shook his head. "I always planned to come back here, to take over Dad's practice."

"What about Melissa? You were married when you graduated. Did she want to live somewhere else?"

"If she did, she never said anything about it," Derek said. "She's still here, yeah?"

She was. And I'd wondered about that. She'd come to Maine with Derek, and after their divorce, she'd stayed on with my cousin Ray Stenham. But he was out of the picture now, too—and would continue to be for a while longer, I hoped—and since then, Melissa's most recent beau had met with an untimely death. It wouldn't have been surprising if she'd decided to leave Waterfield to start fresh somewhere else. After all, there wasn't really anything left for her here.

Except her career, I suppose. She's Waterfield's most premier real estate agent, which means she's doing quite well financially, and from what Derek had said, she'd always been concerned with position and social standing and with being "somebody." That's why she'd made sure to marry a doctor, he'd said—for the money and the prestige. If living in Waterfield gave her both, then that might be reason enough for her to stay. I could understand, even if I sort of wished she'd pack up and get out of what was now *my* town.

"What about you?" He glanced at me. "Is this your way of telling me you're sick of being here and you want to go somewhere else?"

"Oh, no." I shook my head. "I'm perfectly happy."

"Good to know. Why did you ask?" He stretched out his legs and leaned back on the plastic chair. It groaned in protest.

"Just curious. I never used to consider living anywhere but Manhattan. I was born there. I went to college there. I lived there my whole life. When I first came here, I didn't think I'd survive the summer."

Derek grinned. "What changed your mind?"

I smiled back. "You did. I figured you'd never agree to move to Manhattan with me."

And at that point I'd noticed all that Waterfield had to offer. There was clean air and a slow pace and friendly people—not that New Yorkers aren't friendly; they're just busier as a rule, and don't have as much time to sit and talk—and there was Aunt Inga's house, and the cats—who wouldn't be happy in a New York apartment, especially one where I wasn't allowed to have pets—and Derek, and everyone else I'd gotten to know, and did I mention the clean air and the slow pace and—oh, yes—the ocean? We New Yorkers like being close to the ocean.

Downstairs, we heard the sound of a door opening, and a second later, a tiny figure burst out onto the green grass. A little boy, maybe two years old, in striped overalls and a red shirt. He had a shock of jet-black hair, and was squealing with laughter as his short legs pumped. A few steps behind came a woman with long, blond hair, whose voice floated up to us. "I'm gonna get you! I'm gonna get you!"

They tore across the grass, laughing and yelling, until the little boy tripped and fell and rolled. His mother fell right along with him, and she grabbed him and tickled him until he was breathless with laughter and was hiccupping for her to stop.

"Must be Robin and Benjamin," I said.

Derek nodded, his eyes still on the pair down on the grass.

"Have you ever wanted children?"

He glanced over at me. "It never really seemed a possibility before."

"You and Melissa never got to that point?"

He shook his head. "I told you. We were pretty young when we got married, and circumstances were never conducive to kids. At first I was in school, then there was residency, and by the time we got to Waterfield, I wished I'd never married her."

I nodded.

"What about you?" he asked after a moment. "Do you want children?"

"I'm not getting any younger."

Derek smiled. "That's not really an answer, is it?"

I smiled back. "I guess not. Sure, I think I'd like a child. Before it's too late." A little copy of Derek running around in striped overalls, squealing with laughter.

"One thing at a time, OK? Let's get married first."

"Let's," I said.

. . .

By the end of the day, we'd accomplished what we'd set out to do, and had cleared the sinks out of both the kitchen and the bath, along with the vinyl flooring and the kitchen counter. Tomorrow we'd start ripping down the kitchen cabinets. After that, a trip to the lumber depot was in order, to see what was available to replace the cabinets we'd torn out, so I could start designing the kitchen.

It's one of my favorite aspects of the job. I didn't go into interior design after Parsons—I've always liked fabrics and sewing too much for that—but I'd taken my share of design classes while I was there, and the fact that I got to put some of that knowledge to use now was wonderful. Derek's heart is more in restoration anyway; whenever there's something old and salvageable, he wants to keep it, and he finds great pleasure in tinkering with it until it's good as new.

"Space is at a premium in this one," I said as we locked the door behind us and headed down the stairs to the parking lot. "Wherever we can make something seem bigger, we should. And wherever we can tuck things away out of sight, that's good, too. Open and airy feels bigger than cluttered."

"Like?" He glanced at me over his shoulder as we descended the stairs. Miss Shaw was not lying in wait for us this time, and we made it past the first-floor landing without incident.

"A friend of mine in New York had an old fireplace in her apartment that didn't work anymore. So she put her TV in there and had a frame built for it, so it was actually built into the fireplace. And someone else had an apartment with a really great closet—one of those with double doors, you know?—but not enough room for an office. So she bought an extra armoire for her clothes and turned the closet into an office. She bought a long counter and installed it inside the closet, along with a lot of shelves above, and then she could push the chair inside and close the doors whenever people came to visit."

"Genius," Derek said.

"It was, actually. You've never lived anywhere like that, but—"

"Actually, I have." He pushed open the door to the parking lot and held it for me. "In medical school. The apartment I shared with a buddy was no bigger than this one."

"Then you know what I'm talking about. My mom and I had this table in the kitchen in the apartment in New York—after my dad died and it was just her and me, you know—and it hung on the wall under the window. It was this little half-circle with hinges, fastened to a sort of base, and the half-circle part could flip down when we didn't use it." I illustrated using my hands.

"Genius," Derek said again.

I elbowed him. "You're being facetious. I don't like it."

"Sure you do." He grabbed me around the waist and swung me around so my back was against the truck and he was in front of me. "You like me. Admit it."

I wound my arms around his neck. "Fine. I like you."

Just as he bent to give me a kiss, I turned my head. "Not here. Miss Shaw is watching."

"Damn Miss Shaw," Derek said and kissed me anyway.

—4—

By the time we reached the condo building the next morning, Josh's Honda was gone from the parking lot, along with Candy's hybrid, Jamie's compact, William Maurits's sedan, and Mariano's Jeep. Indeed, the only car still there was an older model Ford Taurus station wagon, gold colored, parked over in the corner. I spied a child seat in the back, so I guessed it must belong to Robin and Benjamin. Everyone else, it seemed, had gone to work or school. Even Miss Shaw's curtains hung quietly for once.

We spent the first part of the day taking down the kitchen cabinets. It's a two-person job, since someone has to hold the cabinet while the other person unscrews the screws holding it to the wall. If not, the cabinet will fall and hit someone on the head. Derek held while I unscrewed, and I won't deny that I enjoyed watching the play of muscles in his arms under the short sleeves of the T-shirt as he wrestled with the cabinets. I may even have taken a little longer than I should to unscrew a few of the upper ones, just because I was distracted by the view.

Once the cabinets were down and stacked in the bed of

the truck, along with yesterday's bathroom cabinet and sink, we left for a while, to drop the spoils off at the local reuse center, where someone else might have use of them, and to grab a couple of Derek's favorite lobster rolls.

We were sitting there, on orange plastic benches facing one another across an orange plastic table, when the door to the street opened and Jill Cortino maneuvered herself inside.

Peter Cortino's wife and Derek's high school sweetheart is a plump, slightly frumpy, somewhat plain woman in her mid-thirties, with blond hair and blue eyes. Between Derek, who's gorgeous, and Peter, who looks like a Roman statue, she's managed to snag two of the best-looking men Waterfield has to offer. The reason for that is personality. She's one of the nicest, most genuine people I've ever met, and it's frankly a little surprising to me that Derek, after dating Jill, would even look twice at Melissa, who's downright stunning but nowhere near as nice.

Anyway, Peter and Jill have been married for seven years, and have three kids plus one on the way. Peter Junior is six, Paul is five, and Pamela is two and a half. And Jill is about to burst. When she stopped beside our table and we invited her to sit, she put a hand against her back and puffed like a beached whale. "I won't fit."

She was right, she wouldn't. There wasn't enough room between the orange bench and the edge of the orange table for a nine-months-pregnant stomach.

"You're enormous," Derek said, getting to his feet to pull a plastic chair over from another table and carefully lowering her into it. "Are you sure there's only one baby in there?"

Jill swatted him. "Yes, there's only one. And no woman likes to hear that she's enormous."

"You're beautiful." He kissed her cheek, and Jill gave him a crooked smile.

"You're too charming for your own good, Ellis. Always have been." She winked at me. "How are you doing, Avery? Getting everything ready for the wedding?"

I told her I was fine, and yes, things were coming together.

"The invitation was beautiful," Jill said, making herself comfortable on the hard chair. "Where did you find it? I'd love to have some of that paper for birth announcements or shower gift thank-yous or something."

I told her I'd made the invitations myself. "When we're both recovered"—Jill from labor and sleepless nights, and I from getting married—"we can get together sometime and I'll show you how."

"I'd like that," Jill said. "Maybe I can make the invitations to Poppy's christening."

"Is that the name you've chosen? Poppy?"

Last time I'd asked, they hadn't been able to decide between Penelope, Piper, and Portia. My joking suggestion of Petunia hadn't even made the first cut, and Poppy hadn't been in the running, as far as I could recall. But it was another P-name, so I guess I shouldn't be surprised.

"I wanted to call her Lucia," Jill confessed. "Or Anne Marie. Or Cindy. Something that didn't start with a P. I think we have enough P's by now, don't you?"

She waited for my noncommittal murmur before she continued, "But Peter said that since we'd started, and all the others have P-names, this one should, too."

"Poppy is a pretty name."

"It's better than Pippa," Jill said darkly, by which I guessed that Pippa might have been the front-runner in Peter's mind.

"Are you ready?"

Jill turned to Derek, who had asked the question. "We've been through it three times already. By now it's just another trip to the hospital."

Just another trip to the hospital, like just another trip to the grocery store—except instead of cereal and milk, you came home with a baby. "You'll let us know if there's anything we can do, right?"

"Sure," Jill said, "but my parents are taking the kids,

and my mom will be around after the baby comes. And Peter's mom will come up from Boston to spend a couple of weeks, too. We're all set."

"You'll let us know when it happens, though, won't you? Derek's right, you do look like you're about to pop."

"Any day now," Jill confirmed. "My due date is in just over a week, but sometimes they come early."

"Did the others?"

She shook her head. "Paul was a day late. Petey was two days late. Pamela was right on time. With that in mind, it sounds like Poppy might be early."

She put her hands against the table and levered herself up to her feet, wincing, as the cashier waved to let her know her take-out order was ready to go. It took her a second to find her center of gravity once she was upright. "I'll make sure Peter calls you when it's time. It won't be too much longer, I think. Or so I hope anyway."

She waddled over to the cashier and then out the door with her lobster rolls. On her way back to the auto shop with lunch for her husband, I assumed.

"She looks great," Derek said.

"For being the size of a small house, you mean?"

He grinned. "For being pregnant. Pregnancy agrees with her. Makes her glow."

Good thing, too, as many times as she'd been through it. Counting back in my head, I calculated that Jill had been expecting babies for thirty-six out of the past seventy-two months. Wow.

"You ready to get outta here and back to work?"

I nodded. "We're going to the lumber depot, right? To look at kitchen cabinets?"

"Fine with me," Derek said. "On our way back to the truck, let's go by way of the hardware store and pick up some paint samples."

I nodded.

And regretted it as soon as we turned from the little side street where Derek's favorite deli is located, onto Main Street.

Waterfield's main drag is a turn-of-the-last-century construction: three blocks full of two- and three-story red brick Victorian commercial buildings starting at the harbor and going inland. There are businesses, shops, and restaurants on the first floors of the buildings, and offices, storage, and sometimes living space up above. The hardware store was about halfway down the street, in a two-story building. The second floor is a loft: Derek's loft, to be precise. And directly across the street from it is another loft, one that belongs to Derek's ex-wife. She'd bought it after she sold the McMansion she and Ray Stenham had shared, some seven or eight months ago now. Ostensibly, the reason was to be closer to work—the offices of Waterfield Realty are also on Main Street—but I'd always suspected she did it at least partly because she knew it would annoy me. Or maybe that's just my paranoia rearing its ugly head.

Anyway, when we turned the corner onto Main Street, there she was, on her way up the sidewalk in our direction, looking like the proverbial million bucks.

The first time I met Melissa James, she knocked on the door of Aunt Inga's house to introduce herself and to tell me she could sell the house for me. Aunt Inga had been dead for only a few days, and Melissa didn't know me from Adam—or Eve. At that point, I had no idea she used to be married to Derek—I hadn't even met Derek yet—and I also didn't know she was involved with my distant cousin Ray Stenham, whom I'd always known to be a nasty bit of work. Even without any of that knowledge, she managed to rub me wrong in amazingly short order. It was the way she looked, the way she spoke, the way she looked at me: down the length of her perfect nose, as if I were a grubby teenager with pigtails while she was the lady of the manor.

She's taller than me by about five inches. We're both blond, but while my hair is the aforementioned kinky Mello Yello, Melissa's is like a sleek cap of spun moonlight. We both have blue eyes, but mine are the chlorinated blue of faded denim while hers are a fabulous Elizabeth Taylor indigo.

I could go on, but I won't. And the reason I won't is that although Melissa used to make me feel insecure, she doesn't anymore. Now that I've heard Derek tell me, repeatedly, that she made him miserable and I've made him happy again, and that before he met me, he never considered getting remarried, I can look at her and feel pity for someone stupid enough to throw away the best thing that ever happened to her. In fact, I can even be grateful to her, since her loss—so to speak—is my gain. Derek is the best thing that's ever happened to me, too.

I smiled at her. "Hi, Melissa."

She stopped. "Hi, Avery. Derek." There was a purr to her voice when she said his name that was missing when she said mine. My smile turned into a grin.

"You look lovely, as always."

She did. Today's outfit consisted of a pair of slacks in Melissa's trademark cream—her Mercedes is that color, too—along with a sapphire blue silk blouse that set off those stunning eyes. She'd paired it with sapphire earrings and—I couldn't help noticing—the lima-bean-sized diamond engagement ring Tony Micelli had given her. I'd have thought she'd stop wearing that now that Tony had died.

"Thank you." She preened. Those fabulous eyes looked me over, from head to toe and back—Tinkerbell hair, plain cotton T-shirt, faded jeans, sneakers; all of it dirty from the day's labors—and it came as no surprise when she chose not to return the compliment. I guess I should be grateful she didn't tell me how she really felt. "So what are you two up to?"

"New project," Derek said, putting his arm around my shoulders.

Melissa pouted. It didn't make *her* look like Tinkerbell. "You bought another house? Without my help?"

"The owner wanted to avoid involving real estate agents," I said. "He thinks you're untrustworthy money-grubbing bottom-feeders."

Melissa sniffed. "I'll have you know we have a strict code of ethics we have to go by—"

"Avery's just joking," Derek said, squeezing my shoulders in warning. "A friend came to us and said his neighbor wanted to sell his condo, quickly and easily. He'd moved to Florida and just wanted it off his hands in a hurry."

"Where is it?"

Derek explained the location of the condo building, and Melissa nodded. "That's a good spot. And there's very rarely any turnover there. When will it be ready?"

Derek glanced at me. I shrugged. "Four weeks," he said.

"Wonderful." Melissa showed all her teeth in a bright smile. She seems to have more than the usual number, brilliantly white. "Would you mind if I stopped by sometime, just to check how you're getting along and perhaps to give you some input on what buyers are looking for these days?"

I opened my mouth to tell her to stay away, but Derek got in before me. "Of course, Melissa. We'll be there most days. Come by whenever you have time."

I closed my mouth again.

"Lovely." Melissa turned to me. "Avery, dear . . . I got that sweet little invitation of yours in the mail yesterday."

Note the condescension. I certainly did, but I didn't let it bother me. "Good. I'm glad."

She lowered her voice. "Are you sure you meant to send it to me? You do remember that Derek and I used to be married, right?"

I giggled. "Yes, of course I remember." That's partly why I'd invited her. So she could sit there and watch him marry someone else. And know he'd never be hers again. "We're all friends, aren't we?"

"Don't feel you have to come, Melissa," Derek said. "We realize it might be awkward. But Avery wanted to invite you just in case. She didn't want you to feel left out."

He smiled at me, a smile that gave me more credit than I deserved. Of course, I didn't tell him that. Instead, I just smiled back before I turned to Melissa. "Don't feel obligated, Melissa. But we'd love it if you wanted to share the occasion with us."

"Thanks," Melissa said, and I was pleased to hear that for a second or two she wasn't quite able to hide her grumpiness. Then she pasted on another big smile. "I should get going. Busy, busy. I'll give you a call and arrange a time to come by and see the place, Derek."

"Sure," Derek said. Melissa continued up the sidewalk toward her office, her posterior swaying seductively. I turned to my fiancé.

"Why did you tell her she could come by and give us advice?"

"Is that a problem?"

"Now she'll think we'll use her to sell the place."

"We have to have someone list and market the property," Derek said, his voice reasonable as he guided me toward the hardware store. "It might as well be her. She's already trying to sell the house on Rowanberry Island for us."

"Trying" being the operative word. She wasn't succeeding. And part of me wanted to use that as an excuse to fire her. But as I mentioned, buyers for half-a-million-dollar Colonial houses on tiny islands out to sea don't grow on trees, so chances were no other real estate agent would have been able to do any better. Much as I wanted to, I couldn't really hold it against Melissa that she hadn't.

. . .

We got back to the condo complex just after two o'clock, with our paint samples and measurements for the kitchen cabinets. The parking lot was just as deserted as it had been earlier. More so, in fact, since the Taurus station wagon was also gone now. Our truck was the only vehicle in the lot after we'd pulled in and parked. And Miss Shaw's lace curtains still hung unmoving in the kitchen window.

"You know, that's freaking me out a little," I confided to Derek as we moved toward the front door. "Every time we've been here, she's been sitting at that window, watching us. I thought it'd be a relief when she wasn't, but instead it's weirdly strange."

"She's probably just gone out," Derek answered. "We haven't been here but a few times, Avery. You can't really judge by that. Just because she hasn't left her condo in those couple of days doesn't mean she never does."

"I guess not." Even though Kate and Shannon had both said she never left. It simply couldn't be accurate. Sometimes, surely she had to leave? "She could be at the doctor's. Or the hairdresser's. Or shopping." Her hair and wardrobe could both use some attention, frankly.

"She could have hopped a bus to the Penobscot High Stakes Bingo with fifty other seniors," Derek said. "Or maybe she has a secret life we know nothing about, and she's in Monte Carlo, sipping champagne on a hotel terrace overlooking the Mediterranean."

I laughed, which was probably the purpose of the suggestion, since no one in their right mind would seriously consider Hilda Shaw a candidate for a jaunt to Monte Carlo. The gambling trip to the Native American casino was somewhat more likely. Most likely of all was that she had a daughter, or maybe an octogenarian mother or a niece, somewhere in Waterfield, and they were spending the day together.

"You're right," I said. "I'm being silly. We should enjoy it while it lasts. She'll probably be home by the time we leave tonight. And when we get here tomorrow morning, I'll be complaining that she's watching us through the curtains again."

"That's the spirit," Derek said, and let me precede him up the stairs.

We spent the next few hours on our various tasks. I'd brought my laptop, and while Derek stayed busy scraping paint and capping pipes, I settled on the porch with my feet up on the railing and the computer in my lap. There are several programs available for interior design, and I'd downloaded one last winter when we were working on Kate's carriage house. Now I plugged the dimensions of the kitchen into the program, added its various electrical outlets and water pipes—when you renovate, it's so much easier, not to mention cheaper, to leave those things where they are and work around them—and then I started adding virtual cabinets and drawer bases.

It took the rest of the afternoon to come up with a working design, one where I felt I had made the absolute most of every square inch of the kitchen. It wasn't big, just eight feet to a side: more like a galley, really, once I'd measured for cabinets along each wall. There was no room for an island, or even a peninsula, but I did manage to squeeze in the minimum of necessities: a lazy Susan, a couple of drawer bases, a fridge and stove, apartment-sized dishwasher, mounted microwave . . . there was even room for a small, built-in wine rack between two cabinet bases where nothing else would fit.

"Wine rack?" Derek said, looking over my shoulder. "We're buying a wine rack?"

I shook my head.

"Let me guess. I'm making a wine rack?"

"Not at all. I'm making it."

He arched his brows. "You know how to make a wine rack?"

"Sure. It's easy. I did it once in New York, for a friend. You buy a bunch of mailing tubes—"

"A bunch of what?"

"Mailing tubes. You know, the cardboard tubes you mail posters and blueprints in? Like paper towel rolls, only a lot bigger?" Big enough to accommodate a bottle of wine, in fact.

"OK," Derek said slowly, as if trying to picture it.

"You build a frame—or I do. Then you cut the mailing tubes to the length of a bottle of wine, glue them together inside the frame, and voila, wine rack." I smiled.

"Only you, Avery," Derek said and dropped a kiss on the top of my head.

"You don't like it?"

"I'm sure it'll look great. Your ideas always turn out

great." He straightened and lifted both arms above his head, stretching. The bottom of the T-shirt separated from the low-hanging top of the jeans, baring a stripe of tanned skin, lightly dusted with fair hair. "You about ready to call it a day? All this talk of wine is making me hungry."

Me, too. "Italian?"

"Whatever," Derek said, which coincided rather nicely with my own feelings. We gathered our things, the ones we didn't plan to leave in the condo overnight, and locked the door behind us. Only to stop a floor below, when we got to Miss Shaw's door. A woman I'd never met stood in front of it, knocking. When she heard our steps on the stairs, she turned around, and then—I guess upon realizing she didn't know us—her face registered disappointment.

"Oh."

"Something wrong?" Derek asked.

"I'm not sure," the woman answered. She was short and thin, just an inch or maybe two taller than me, with light brown hair and eyes the color of whiskey, dressed in a navy blue business suit and black patent leather heels. "It's not like Miss Shaw not to be sitting at the window."

"I thought the same thing." I introduced myself and Derek, and found out that this was our upstairs neighbor, Barnham professor Amelia Easton. "We just bought the Antoninis' condo and started renovating it. Miss Shaw has been sitting at the window every time we've been in and out so far. Except for today. We thought maybe she'd gone out."

Professor Easton shook her head. "She never goes out. I've lived here over a year, and I've never seen her leave the building."

"She wasn't at the window when we got here this morning. We left for lunch, and when we came back, we still didn't see her. Do you think something's wrong?"

"It isn't like her," Amelia said.

"I don't suppose you have a key? Or know of anyone else in the building who does?"

"I'm afraid not," Amelia said.

"If she never goes outside the door," Derek contributed, "there's not much need to hide a key. There's no chance she'll lock herself out."

"We could go upstairs and get a screwdriver and take the lock off the door."

"We could," Derek agreed. "But that's a little drastic, don't you think?"

"That depends. If the place is empty, it won't take long to put it back on. But what if something's happened to her? What if she's fallen and can't get up? What if she's broken her hip? Or she's flat on her back in bed with measles? She'll die if no one takes care of her!"

"Not from the measles," Derek said, but he sighed. "You've knocked, right?"

This was addressed to Amelia Easton, who nodded. "For at least five minutes. There's no answer."

"Does she have a phone?"

"I'll get the number," I said, pulling out my cell phone. It was a quick minute before I had Hilda Shaw's number and was dialing it. We could hear the ringing start behind the locked door, but there was no answer. Eventually I gave up and disconnected. "I guess she doesn't have an answering machine."

"She doesn't need one," Derek said, "if she never leaves the apartment."

"Well," I shot back, "if she never leaves the apartment, then she's in there right now. And if she's not answering the phone or coming to the door, then that sounds to me like something's wrong."

Derek sighed. "I'll go get the screwdriver." He headed up the stairs.

I turned to Amelia. "He can be a little slow to get behind things sometimes, but he's good with power tools."

She smiled politely, so maybe it wasn't as funny as I thought.

Derek *is* good with power tools, though, so by the time he got back—with the battery-driven screwdriver—it was quick work to take the lock off the door. Derek put the lock and screwdriver aside before pushing the door open and peering into the dark hallway. "Miss Shaw? Hello?"

I added my voice to his. "It's Derek and Avery from upstairs. Are you OK?"

There was no answer.

"Smells bad in here," I muttered as a combination of odors assaulted my nostrils. The sour stench of bodily functions, along with a hint of something sickly sweet, all of it overlaid by the fresh scent of a Glade Plug-In. Tropical Breeze.

Derek nodded, his mouth tight. "Stay out here, Avery. You, too, Professor Easton."

"Are you sure?" I asked. "I'll be happy to come inside with you." For moral support, or whatever. And yes, saying that I'd be happy to do it might have been overstating the case just a little, but if he wanted me to, I'd go inside with him.

He shook his head. "Better not. If I'm right, the fewer people who traipse through here, the better."

I swallowed. "She doesn't have the measles, does she?"

His eyes were gentle. "I don't think so. But until I make sure, just stay out here. And keep anyone else from going inside."

I nodded. "Should I call Wayne?"

"Better wait until we know for sure."

He gave me a quick smile before squaring his shoulders and plunging into the dark hallway, leaving Amelia and myself cooling our heels on the landing.

—5—

"What does he think happened?" Amelia asked.

I turned to her. "I'm sorry. But I think Miss Shaw might be dead."

Amelia blinked. "How would he know that?"

"He doesn't. But she's not answering the door or the phone, and there's a certain smell . . ."

And frankly, once you've smelled the odor of death, it never leaves you. I'd once spent the best part of a night and a day locked in a tunnel underneath an old house on the cliffs outside Waterfield with my ex-boyfriend Philippe and a rotting corpse, and I didn't think I'd ever be able to get the smell out of my nose. It lingered for weeks, and even now, more than a year later, it took very little to bring me back there. I shivered.

"What?" Amelia said.

"Nothing. Just remembering something I wish I didn't."

"Oh," Amelia said, biting her lip. She looked nervous.

"Don't worry. Even if she turns out to be dead, it won't be a big deal. Wayne is nice. The chief of police. He's Josh Rasmussen's dad."

Amelia nodded. "I met him once or twice when I first moved in. He left shortly after that."

That's right. Wayne had lived here until Derek and I finished renovating Kate's carriage house, and she and Wayne got married New Year's Eve. Amelia would have met him last fall.

"Looks like some kind of food poisoning," Derek said when he came back outside. "Something she ingested didn't agree with her. Her body tried to rid itself of it, but it didn't seem to have worked."

That explained the sour smell.

"I'll call Wayne," I said.

Derek nodded. "The medical examiner's office will want to do an autopsy."

"For food poisoning?" Amelia exclaimed, and then looked like she wished she hadn't.

Derek turned to her. "Unattended, unnatural death. An autopsy is pretty standard."

"She had allergies," Amelia said as I dialed Wayne's cell number. "Severe allergies. That's why she never went outside. She was allergic to bees, and pollen, and things in the air . . ."

She sounded a little bit desperate to get us to believe her. It's not an uncommon reaction when someone has died. There's this need to convince everyone, including oneself, that it was an accident, it was natural, nothing is wrong.

"Avery?" Wayne's voice said in my ear. He sounded just a little worried, I thought. "Is everything all right?"

"I'm sorry," I said. "We're at the apartment, and there's been an accident—"

His voice went from worried to tight. "Is Josh OK?"

Oh God. "Of course. I'm sorry. This has nothing to do with Josh. I should have said so right off. I haven't seen Josh all day, but the last time I saw him, this morning, he was just fine."

"Oh," Wayne said. I could hear him draw a breath. "Good. Thank you."

"No problem." I should have realized he might expect

the worst, when he knew Derek and I were working here in Josh's building. "We do need your help with something else, though."

The worry was gone from his voice, and now he sounded merely resigned. "What is it this time?"

"One of the neighbors has died," I said. "Miss Hilda Shaw. She lives . . . lived on the first floor."

"I remember Miss Shaw," Wayne said. "How do you know she's dead?"

I explained about the lace curtains, and how Miss Shaw was always sitting there watching people come and go.

"Yes?" Wayne said.

"When she wasn't there this morning, we thought maybe she'd gone out. To the doctor, or something. I mean, she'd have to leave sometime, right? To go shopping at least?"

"Shaw's Supermarket delivers," Amelia muttered.

I glanced at her, but talked to Wayne. "But when we went to lunch, she still wasn't there, and then she wasn't there by the time we got back from lunch, and when it was time to leave, Professor Easton, who lives on the fourth floor, had come home from work and tried to get hold of her, and Miss Shaw wasn't answering her phone and her door."

"Uh-huh," Wayne said. "What did you do, Avery?"

I took a breath. He probably wouldn't be happy about this next little bit, and I was preparing myself. To make it easier, I got it all out in a rush. "Derek went upstairs and got a screwdriver and then we took the lock off the door."

There was a slight pause. "I see," Wayne said.

"It's not a problem to put it back on again."

"I'm not worried about the lock. Did you go inside?"

I said I hadn't.

"Did Derek?"

I said he had.

"Put him on," Wayne ordered.

I did, and stood there listening to the singularly unhelpful half of the conversation that came out of Derek's mouth.

It went something like this: "Uh-huh. . . . Uh-huh. . . . Yes, I know. . . . That's right. . . . Uh-huh. . . . Yes. . . . Yes. . . . Probably not. . . . No idea. . . . Of course. . . . We'll be here."

He gave the phone back to me. "He's on his way."

I stuck it in my pocket. "What did he say?"

"Nothing," Derek said, which seemed a rather blatant disregard of the truth. Wayne had said a lot. But it was possible he'd said nothing I needed to know right now. Or nothing Derek thought Amelia Easton needed to know.

He turned to her. "You don't have to stand here. It smells bad, I know."

Amelia nodded, biting her lip, but she seemed reluctant to leave. "I'd be happy to wait with you if you want."

Derek shook his head. "That's not necessary. You didn't go inside, and I'm sure you'd be happier upstairs. If Wayne wants to talk to you, he knows where to find you."

"OK," Amelia said, but she was dragging her feet reluctantly up the stairs, and just before she disappeared, she looked back at us over her shoulder, still gnawing on her bottom lip.

We kept silent until we'd heard the door on the top floor close behind her. Then I turned to Derek.

"What did Wayne say?"

"Nothing," Derek said, looking surprised. "I told you."

"I thought maybe you said that because Amelia was standing here."

He shook his head. "What was there to say, Avery? He called the ME's office and he's on his way. With Brandon."

Brandon Thomas is Wayne's youngest and most gung-ho deputy. He'd like to spend all of his time fiddling with forensic evidence and crime scene investigations, but Waterfield has a minuscule police department, and everyone has to do their share of patrolling and directing traffic. Whenever he gets the chance to gather hairs and fibers and spread fingerprint dust, he's like a kid in a candy store, though.

"He said to stay out," Derek added, "and make sure no

one else went in, and not to do anything to disturb the scene. You know the drill."

I did. "And that's it?"

"That's it. He's on his way. We wait."

"Fine." I put my back to the wall and slid down until my butt was on the cold concrete of the floor. Derek followed suit, and there we sat, side by side, until I broke the silence again.

"I knew something was wrong."

Derek turned to look at me, and I clarified, "This morning. When she wasn't at the kitchen window. She was always there. Every morning when we got here, and every night when we left."

"It's only been a few days, Avery."

"I know that. But if I'd made you open the door this morning, maybe . . ."

Derek shook his head. "It wouldn't have made a difference. She was dead before we got here today."

I sniffed, and then wished I hadn't, as the smell permeated my nostrils. Better to breathe through my mouth for a while. "How do you know?"

"Do you really want me to explain rigor mortis and all the other things that happen to a body after death?"

Not really, no. "So she died last night?"

"The medical examiner will be able to make that determination better than I can," Derek said. "I was just a general practitioner, and not for very long, and I dealt mostly with patients who were still alive. We lost one every once in a while, especially when I rotated in and out of the ER, but I've never had to do much on the forensic side. But if I had to guess, I'd say she probably died around nine o'clock last night."

I swallowed. At nine o'clock, we'd been at Aunt Inga's house, curled up on the sofa enjoying each other's company.

Derek reached out and took my hand. "Don't blame yourself, Avery. It has nothing to do with us."

"I know that." I turned my hand around and curled my

fingers through his. "I guess I feel bad because I didn't really like her."

Derek nodded. "It's worse when it's someone you don't like. When someone you like dies, you're sad and you mourn. But when it's someone you don't like, you feel guilty."

He had that right. Not that I'd had a whole lot of experience with people dying. My dad when I was thirteen, but I'd been too young to really reflect on the deeper issues of what had happened, I think. My dad was gone, and I missed him, but I don't know that I thought much beyond the immediate grief. Aunt Inga died last year, but I hadn't really known her, and besides, I'd been in New York when it happened. And although there's been a fair few deaths here in Waterfield since that time, I hadn't known many of the victims well, either.

There was a sound downstairs—the front door unlocking, I realized—then footsteps in the hall below and up the stairs.

"That was fast," Derek remarked.

"Maybe it's someone else."

The footsteps didn't sound like Wayne. They were quicker, lighter. A moment later, the top of a sandy blond head appeared on the stairs, followed by a narrow face with a prominent nose, and a male body dressed in pale green surgical scrubs with the words "Waterfield Hospital" stamped on the chest. I didn't need Derek's greeting to know I was looking at Gregg Brewer, the resident from the second floor.

Gregg blinked for a second, as if unsure, and then his face cleared. "Derek, right? Dr. Ellis's son?"

Derek nodded. "This is Avery, my fiancée."

I managed a smile. "Nice to meet you."

"Likewise." Gregg nodded politely. "What's going on?"

"She wasn't at the window this morning."

"I noticed."

"She wasn't at the window this afternoon, either. Amelia Easton, from the fourth floor, thought something was wrong. So we took the lock off to see."

Gregg looked around. "Where's Professor Easton?"

"I sent her upstairs," Derek said.

"And no offense, but what are you doing here?"

"We bought the Antoninis' condo a couple days ago. We're renovating it."

"Ah." Gregg's face cleared again. "Mariano mentioned that someone was working on it. Guess he didn't realize I'd know you." He shot another glance at Miss Shaw's door. "So what's going on?"

"She's dead," Derek said.

Gregg blinked pale eyelashes. "Dead?"

"Last night. Looks like something she ate."

Gregg didn't speak for a second. "Have you seen Mariano?" he asked.

It was my turn to blink, this time at the abrupt change of subject. "Sorry. No."

"Do you need any help?"

Derek shook his head. "She's way past the point where a doctor can help her. The police are on their way."

"Police?"

"Unattended death," Derek said. "Standard procedure. We're just waiting until they get here and can secure the place."

"Right." Gregg glanced up the stairs in the direction of his own condo. "If you've got it covered, guess I'll just go upstairs."

"They'll come find you if they need you."

Gregg nodded. "See you later, then."

He continued up the stairs, two steps at a time. By the time he reached the next landing, he was whistling. It took me a second to place the song, and then it hit me: *Ding-Dong! The Witch is dead . . .*

Derek glanced at me, but didn't speak. I shrugged. Upstairs, we heard the key jingle and then the door open. The whistling stopped and Gregg's voice called out, "Mariano? You here, babe? Did you hear the news?"

The closing of the door cut off the rest of the statement, if there was more, and we couldn't hear Mariano's answer.

"*He's* not feeling guilty," Derek said.

I shook my head.

"He was upstairs last night, *and* he's a doctor. If he doesn't feel guilty, you shouldn't, either."

I nodded. "I think maybe I should go downstairs and wait for Wayne. It takes a key to get inside."

"He used to live here," Derek answered, "and his son still does. In an apartment I'm sure Wayne still owns. He'll have a key."

"I could use some fresh air."

"That's a different story," Derek said. "Go ahead. I'll just sit here and make sure no one goes inside."

"I'll be back in a few minutes." I got to my feet. "It's the smell. It reminds me of that night in the tunnel under Cliff House. I'm feeling claustrophobic."

The hallway felt too narrow, as if the walls were closing in. And although maybe we couldn't really smell the odor through the door that Derek had pulled mostly shut, it was there in my nose.

"You don't have to come back. I'll do this." He dug in his pocket. "Take the truck."

"I don't want to abandon you here—" I began.

"Don't worry about it," Derek said. "I'll get a ride home with Wayne. Or Brandon. Or Shannon. She'll probably be by at some point to see Josh."

"Maybe I'll go visit Kate. If Wayne won't be home for dinner, she might like some company." Not for dinner, though. The thought of food wasn't appealing at the moment. But the thought of company was.

"I'll call you," Derek said. "If I can't work it out any other way, you'll just have to come back for me."

No problem. I just needed to get away for a while. I took the keys and headed down the stairs to the parking lot.

I was on my way out of the lot when Wayne's police car came down the Augusta Road and turned in. He lingered for a second next to me, and we both rolled down our windows. "Leaving?" he said by way of greeting.

I nodded. "The smell is bothering me."

Wayne wrinkled his nose. "Is it bad?"

"No, actually. But ever since that night I spent under Cliff House, it's bothered me more. You don't need me for anything, do you?"

"Know where to find you if I do," Wayne grunted.

"I was thinking of heading over to the B and B to see Kate. Is she busy?"

"No more than usual. Tell her I'm sorry I won't be home for dinner." He put the police car back into gear and rolled into the parking lot. I turned the truck onto the Augusta Road in the direction of Waterfield Village.

. . .

The Waterfield Inn started life in the late 1890s as the home of the fabulously wealthy Ritter family, and is a gorgeous three-story Queen Anne construction in the heart of Waterfield's historic district. It's painted yellow with white trim, and has towers and turrets and porches and bay windows: every architectural excess imaginable, the very hallmark of the Queen Anne style.

By the time Kate got her hands on it, it had been turned into three apartments with three skuzzy little kitchens and three marginal bathrooms. She and Derek spent the better part of a year restoring the place to its former glory, and then last winter, Derek and I spent a few months turning the old carriage house on the back of the property into a love nest for Kate and Wayne. The chief of police, it turned out, didn't want to live in the main house, where the guests might come across him wandering down the hall to the bathroom in his boxer shorts in the middle of the night.

Kate was in the carriage house when I got there. It was the middle of the week, so business was slow, and at dinnertime she doesn't usually have much to do anyway, since a bed and breakfast is only licensed to serve breakfast and cold, boxed lunches. Most of the work happens early in the day: cooking and serving breakfast, cleaning up, changing sheets and towels . . . By the time the end of the day rolls around, there isn't a whole lot left to do except hang out and be available for questions. And with a mostly empty house, Kate had gone home—across the grass to the carriage house—and started cooking dinner for herself and the husband she expected to arrive soon.

She wasn't thrilled when I told her he would be a while yet.

"Another one? You found another body?"

"I couldn't help it. When we didn't see Miss Shaw, we got worried. It just wasn't like her not to sit at the window and watch everyone."

"She was a nosy old bat," Kate said, "God bless her soul." She turned down the heat simmering under the homemade spaghetti sauce.

I nodded, grateful that the bubbling sauce—redolent of garlic, sundried tomatoes, and oregano—was helping to remove the sickly sweet stench in my nose. "One of the guys on the second floor was whistling 'Ding-Dong! The Witch Is Dead' when he went to tell his partner the news."

"Most people don't like a busybody," Kate said. "I doubt she'll be missed, poor thing. You want some dinner?"

"I could eat," I said, surprised that I meant it. The delicious smell of the simmering sauce must have chased any lingering nausea out of my system. "But what about Wayne?"

"What about him?" Kate turned to pull flatware and glasses out of the kitchen cabinet. "If he can't make it home for dinner, he can't complain if someone else eats it instead."

She took one look at my face and started laughing. "I'm joking, Avery. There's plenty of sauce for all of us, and when he gets home, it's a matter of ten minutes to toss a handful of noodles in a pot. Don't worry about it; you're not taking food out of my husband's mouth."

"Oh. OK." I started breathing again. "In that case . . . sure, I'd love some dinner."

"Make yourself comfortable." She filled the plates with droopy strands of angel hair pasta before ladling chunky sweet-smelling sauce over top. My stomach rumbled.

"Smells good."

"Hopefully it'll taste good, too." She put a plate in front of me. "Dig in."

I dug.

Kate is a half-dozen years older than me, and a year or two older than Derek. They went out once or twice when she first moved to town and he'd just gotten dumped by Melissa, but things didn't work out, for which I can only be grateful. She and I became friends as soon as I drove into Waterfield.

She's taller than me—most people are—with a head full of bouncy copper-colored curls, framing a friendly face with freckles and warm hazel eyes. And although she's not pretty in the conventional sense, the vivid coloring and Jane Russell figure make her a knockout. It's no wonder at all that Derek liked her. She's extremely likable. And it was obvious that marriage to Wayne agreed with her, because she was practically glowing with happiness.

"You look good," I said.

She glanced at me across the table. "I feel good."

"The house working out for you?" I glanced around at it. It was too small for a designated dining room, so we were sitting in the eat-in portion of the kitchen, at a small round café table for two, looking out at the yard behind the bed and breakfast. The kitchen cabinets were white, the counter marble, and the floors dark-stained wood. I'd done my best to make the whole carriage house look like a Parisian apartment, because Paris was where Kate and Wayne spent their honeymoon, and I wanted them to remember it every time they looked around.

"The house is great," Kate said. "Why?"

"No reason. I'm just thinking about the condo." Another fairly compact space I needed to spruce up.

She tilted her head. "You had a small apartment in New York, didn't you? What did you do there?"

I thought back. It had been a rental, like most apartments in New York. Two bedrooms, like the condo, but on a much smaller scale. No dining room, nor any eating area in the living room. Just a small space for a small table and two chairs in the kitchen.

"We couldn't do much to the space itself. We didn't own it, even if we lived in it my whole life. Until my mom married Noel and moved to California three years ago."

"And then you lived there alone?"

I nodded. "Until Aunt Inga died and I came here. A friend of a friend sublet it, and then ended up taking over the lease when I stayed in Waterfield. We made sure the furniture was small—both Mom and I are little people; small scale furniture was fine for both of us—and we used a lot of mirrors to open the space up visually. And Mom liked landscapes, since she thought they made up for not having a lot of windows."

"Bringing the outside in?" Kate suggested.

"That, plus visually extending the space. Pictures of landscapes give the perception of depth. And there's not a lot of green space in New York, so the landscapes made up for some of the concrete, too."

Kate nodded. "So what do you plan to do about the condo? You won't be decorating it, after all. No pictures, no mirrors, no furniture."

"Not sure," I admitted. She was right about that; furnishings and decorations have a lot to do with making a place look bigger or smaller, and without them, I'd have to come up with other ways to do the job. "Play with paint colors, maybe. Horizontal lines make a room look bigger. We talked about going with the warehouse look for some architectural interest; Derek thinks the space is too bland and boring—"

"Why am I not surprised?" Kate grinned. "I suppose vertical lines makes the space look smaller?"

"Taller, anyway," I said. "Smaller . . . that depends on the width of the stripes. Wide stripes make the wall look longer than skinny stripes. It's all about tricking the eye." I thought for a second. "It's possible I could talk John Nickerson into letting me borrow some furniture from his store to decorate the place. He lent me a few things I used to stage the house on Becklea Drive."

John Nickerson owns an antique store on Main Street, down the street from Derek's loft, and the house on Becklea

Drive was a midcentury ranch we'd renovated last fall. The previous owner had worked for John some years before, so he'd felt a certain proprietary interest in the place, and since his store specializes in midcentury furnishings and art, all of his merchandise looked great in the house. The sleek midcentury lines would probably look equally good in the condo.

"Can't hurt to ask," Kate said, and got up to put her plate in the extra narrow dishwasher we'd squeezed into the pint-sized kitchen. I'd fitted one into the design plans for the condo's kitchen as well. "Do you have to run, or can you stay and visit?"

"I can stay for a while." I brought my plate and utensils over to the counter.

"Not going crazy with the wedding prep yet?"

"The church is booked, the minister is hired, and the hall is rented, but that was no big deal. There was never a question about it. Derek and I both want Barry Norton to marry us, and we'll have the reception in the church hall. It was just a question of picking the date. I finally got the invitations out."

"I got mine in the mail." Kate nodded, pointing to the front of the stainless steel refrigerator where the invitation hung, fastened with a magnet in the shape of the Eiffel Tower. "How's everything else going?"

"The only two things left to decide on now are the food and the clothes."

"I'll do the food."

"You can't do the food. You're the matron of honor."

"Shannon will help," Kate said. "And if I ask Cora and Beatrice, I'm sure they'll help as well. And Jill, if she's up and about again after the baby. And your mom will be in town by then, too. Between us we'll get it done."

"You don't have to cater my wedding. I can hire a caterer."

"I want to," Kate said. "Except the wedding cake. I don't do cakes."

"I'll get one of the bakeries to do the cake." Wonder if

there was such a thing as a whoopie pie wedding cake to be had? If it existed anywhere, it would exist here in Maine.

"Let's turn on the TV," Kate said, "and watch the Cooking Channel. Start making a list of what you want."

"Works for me." I snagged a pen and notepad off the counter and settled into the sofa in the living room while Kate reached for the television remote.

—6—

Wayne came home after another hour, with Derek in tow.

"Saw the truck," my boyfriend said when I raised an inquiring brow. "I was gonna walk home"—everything in downtown Waterfield is just a few minutes from everything else—"but then I realized you were still here."

"Hungry?" Kate asked. "There's plenty of sauce left. I'll make more spaghetti."

"I could eat," Derek said, while Wayne nodded.

"I'll go take a shower while the pasta cooks."

"If you want to wash up," Kate said to Derek as she got up from the sofa to start boiling water for more angel hair pasta, "you know where the bathroom is."

He nodded, and disappeared in the direction of the first-floor half bath, while Wayne headed upstairs to the master bath and shower.

"How did it go?" I asked a few minutes later, when Derek came back out to the living room with water stains on his T-shirt and wet strands of hair around his face.

He blew out a breath as he sat down next to me on the

sofa and put an arm along the back of it, and behind my shoulders. "About as could be expected. She's still dead."

"I didn't think she wouldn't be. Any idea what happened?"

He shook his head. "Not until the medical examiner has had a go. But if I'm guessing, and if Amelia Easton is right and Miss Shaw had food allergies, I'm gonna say she died of anaphylactic shock, from eating something she was allergic to."

"Don't people with food allergies usually keep medicines around that they can take in an emergency? You know, the same way someone with asthma keeps an inhaler?"

"It's called an EpiPen," Derek said, "and yes, they do. Usually."

"Did you find one?"

"I didn't look," Derek said. "I waited for Wayne and Brandon to get there, then I showed them the body and told them what happened. They looked around while I reinstalled the lock on the front door. The van from the medical examiner's office came and took the body away, and then Wayne and I left and came here."

"Brandon's putting in a couple of hours on the scene before calling it a night," Wayne said, coming down the stairs toweling his hair dry. It's dark and curly like his son's, shot through with gray now that he's in his late forties. He had changed out of uniform into a T-shirt and jeans, and his feet were bare. He dropped a kiss on Kate's cheek on his way to leave the towel in the laundry room. When he came back out, he added, "I don't think we'll have any problems with this one. Just a simple, unattended death. But the boy enjoys doing his CSI thing, and he may as well get the practice in. If I don't keep him happy, I'm afraid he'll leave me."

He took a seat in one of the armchairs.

"Is he talking about leaving?"

Brandon Thomas is a native Waterfielder, whose mother, Phoebe, suffers from multiple sclerosis; I'd be very surprised if Brandon moved away and left her.

Wayne shrugged. "He's dating that girl from the state police now. And Augusta isn't that far away."

Augusta is the capital of Maine, situated about forty-five minutes north of Waterfield. It's where the Maine state police headquarters are located, and where Daphne, the girl Brandon was dating, worked. She's a canine handler, who had brought her partner Hans, a German shepherd cadaver dog, down to Waterfield last fall when Derek and I had found a skeleton buried underneath the house on Becklea Drive. Daphne and Brandon had hit it off, we'd seen her—and occasionally Hans—several times since then, and now I guess they'd made it official.

"Has he mentioned leaving?" Kate asked, a tiny wrinkle between her brows.

Wayne shook his head. "He hasn't mentioned anything. I just know he'd rather be doing forensics and crime scene stuff all the time, and if the state police can offer him that, it'd be stupid to turn it down. I'm sure they'd be happy to have him."

Anyone with sense would be happy to have Brandon, who's a personable fellow, a hard worker, and a joy to be around. However, I could quite understand why Wayne was worried.

"You've had plenty of dead bodies here in Waterfield in the time I've been around. He's been keeping busy."

"He seemed happy when we left him," Derek added. "Like a pig in slop. The way he snapped on those latex gloves reminded me of me, the first time I did an annual exam." He winked at me.

I hid a grin, as the comparison was irresistibly funny. "I don't think he's going anywhere, Wayne. He chose to stay in Waterfield and join the police rather than go away to law school, just so he could be close to his mother if she needed him—I don't think he'll leave now."

"Maybe not," Wayne said. The words lacked conviction, but he looked a little happier, and when Kate announced that the food was served, he and Derek toddled over to the café-table-for-two in the eating alcove and got down to it. Kate and I went back to watching TV until they were done.

"Getting ideas for the wedding?" Derek asked as he sat himself back down next to me on the sofa with a replete sigh.

I nodded, patting his thigh as it came to rest next to mine. "Kate has volunteered to do the food."

He shot her a look. "You don't have to do that."

"I know I don't have to," Kate said. "I want to. Everything except the cake. I don't do wedding cakes."

Derek shrugged. "Far be it from me to try to talk you out of it. I've eaten your food. You'll probably give us a break on the price, too, won't you?"

"We'll work something out," Kate said serenely and snuggled into Wayne's arm.

"There's no reason we won't be able to go back to work tomorrow, is there, Wayne?" I wanted to know. "Miss Shaw's death has nothing to do with us, right?"

"Not unless there's something you're not telling me," Wayne said.

"Like what? If she died of anaphylactic shock, that's nobody's fault. Is it? It's an accident, right?"

I glanced at Derek, who nodded.

"I'm sure Brandon will finish up in her apartment by lunchtime tomorrow," Wayne said, "but you're welcome to go into your own apartment anytime you want. The investigation is limited to hers."

"Will you be talking to the neighbors?"

He arched his brows. "Any reason I should?"

None I could think of, really. As Kate said, Miss Shaw probably wouldn't be missed. Nobody had liked her much. But that's no crime, and it wasn't like she'd been murdered.

"If the medical examiner determines that cause of death was anaphylactic shock," Wayne said, "and it seems to be leaning that way"—he glanced at Derek, who nodded—"then I don't see any reason why I have to conduct interviews. She ate something that didn't agree with her, and she died. It happens."

It did. Nice and easy. About time we discovered a dead body that didn't turn out to be murdered. I leaned back against Derek's shoulder with a sigh of my own and focused my attention on the television screen and the plans for the wedding that were bouncing around in my brain.

. . .

When we got to the condo building the next morning, Brandon was already there. The black-and-white patrol car was parked in the lot, and Miss Shaw's kitchen window was open, with the lace curtains blowing in the breeze. When we got up the stairs, we saw that the apartment door stood open as well, with a piece of yellow crime scene tape strung from one side of the door to the other.

"Airing out," Derek said.

The stench was a whole lot less noticeable today. I raised my voice. "Brandon? You here?"

"Bedroom," Brandon's voice came floating back.

"Can we come in?"

"May as well," Brandon said, "everyone else has been through the place." He sounded grumpy.

I arched my brows at Derek and ducked under the tape.

Miss Shaw's apartment was laid out exactly like the one above, with the same rooms in the same places, and the same hollow-core doors and plain but serviceable vinyl and parquet floors. Any similarity ended there. The Antoninis' place had been empty when we took it over: broom-clean condition, in real estate terms. Hilda Shaw's home was a mess. Lots of mismatched, overstuffed furniture, with doilies hiding the threadbare arms of the sofa and chairs.

There was stuff everywhere: Hollywood gossip rags in piles on every flat surface, a line of pill bottles along the top of the toilet tank, boxes of cereal decorating the kitchen counter. And books. Stacks upon stacks of books. Mysteries and thrillers, many of them true crime. For some reason they were stacked all over the floor in front of the bookcase rather than on the shelves.

Brandon was in the back bedroom, and he wasn't alone. Josh was holding up the doorjamb, and his lanky height made Brandon look shorter than I knew him to be. As we walked in, Josh said, "I swear to God," in the tone of voice of someone who'd said the same words a few times already, "I locked the door last night. Nobody could have gotten in."

"Someone did," Brandon answered, "or do you think I left it looking like this?"

He indicated the drawers in the oak dresser, open with fabric tumbling out—the plain but serviceable white cotton underpants of an older woman with no significant other in her life—and the open doors to the closet, where sack-like housedresses were hanging on hangers where they hadn't tumbled to the floor.

A strapping young man who played football in high school, Brandon is twenty-three or -four, a few years older than Josh, and as fair as Josh is dark. He has blond hair that he keeps in a regulation buzz cut, with bright blue eyes, and an equally bright smile. He and I had gotten to know each other quite well the first few weeks after I moved to Waterfield last summer, since someone was trying to force me out of Aunt Inga's house, and that same someone kept breaking in and leaving me little souvenirs, like all of Aunt Inga's china smashed on the kitchen floor, and a step in the basement stairs sawed through, so I fell and twisted my ankle. I kept Brandon quite busy for weeks, dusting Aunt Inga's house for fingerprints and looking for hairs and fibers.

"What's going on?" I asked, peering past Josh's side, while Derek leaned to look over my head. His front was warm against my back, and he slipped an arm around my waist to pull me a little closer.

"Someone was here after Josh locked up last night," Brandon said. "I don't work like this. I don't tear things out of drawers without putting them back. If something falls on the floor, I pick it up. I would have put the books back on the bookshelf, not left them lying all over the floor."

"What's here that anyone could possibly want?"

"I don't know," Brandon said, "but I'm going to find out." He went back to riffling the contents of the bedside drawer.

"If it was here," Derek muttered in my ear, "don't you think whoever was here last night would have taken it?"

I shrugged. Maybe, maybe not. There was a lot of junk here. It would depend on what it was the unknown somebody had been looking for, and whether he or she would have had time to find it in the mess that was Miss Shaw's apartment. "Have you found anything interesting?"

"Nothing that anyone else would be interested in," Brandon grunted.

"Any word on cause of death?" This was Derek's contribution.

Brandon shook his head without looking up from the drawer. I could see his fingers sifting through packets of folded tissues, cough drops, and other odds and ends. "Too early. The ME hasn't started the autopsy yet."

"There's going to be an autopsy?" Josh asked. He sounded almost concerned. I glanced up at him, but he didn't meet my eyes.

"Gotta be." Brandon nodded, straightening. "Unattended, unnatural death. The ME will probably call it an accident—anaphylactic shock, the victim ingested something she shouldn't have—but we have to know."

"There's no reason to suspect foul play, is there?"

"Not as far as the death goes," Brandon said. "She clearly had health problems. All the stuff in the kitchen is gluten-free. There's nothing with strawberries, nuts, or shellfish anywhere. And she took a ton of medicines."

"EpiPen?" Derek said.

Brandon glanced at him. "Is that a medicine?"

"Emergency injection for anaphylaxis."

"Syringe?" Brandon shook his head. "Haven't found anything like that."

"Keep looking. If she had severe allergies, she should have had an EpiPen." Derek pulled me backward out of the doorway. "We're going upstairs. Let us know if you need anything."

"Will do," Brandon said. Josh followed us out and headed downstairs to the parking lot with a murmured good-bye. He still looked worried.

—7—

"What's up with Josh?" I asked Derek when we were inside our own apartment with the door closed so neither he nor Brandon had any hope of hearing us.

"What makes you think something's up?"

"He looked worried. Frazzled. Tired."

"Can you blame him?" Derek asked, digging wrenches and pliers out of the toolbox in the hallway. "If he forgot to lock the door last night and someone was inside Miss Shaw's apartment . . ."

"He said he didn't."

Derek straightened, tools in hand. "Well, what was he gonna say?"

"If he forgot, I hope he'd admit it."

Derek didn't answer, and I added, "He doesn't seem like the type who'd forget something like that. He's the son of the chief of police; if anyone knows how important it is to keep a crime scene secure, it would be Josh."

"It isn't a crime scene," Derek said.

Point taken. "Strange that he'd be the one locking up in

the first place. Wonder why Brandon didn't. It isn't like him to leave it to someone else."

"Maybe he got called away abruptly," Derek said. "Girlfriend emergency."

"Maybe."

He disappeared into the bathroom, where he went to work on the plumbing. I busied myself taking down the wallpaper in the kitchen. It's a surprisingly time-consuming chore, but a mindless one that leaves plenty of time for thinking.

The situation downstairs bothered me. I didn't doubt Josh's word that he'd locked the door last night. But I also didn't doubt Brandon when he said that someone had been in the apartment overnight. He really wouldn't have taken all the books off the shelves and left them on the floor. For one thing, he'd have had no reason to—all he was doing was making sure there was no evidence of foul play, that Miss Shaw's death had indeed been what it appeared to be: an accident. And second, if for some reason he did move the books, he'd have put them back. He certainly wouldn't have taken them down, left them on the floor, and then lied about it.

So who else had been there last night? And why? What had they been looking for? Jewelry or money? Something they could hock? Or something else?

"What kinds of allergies can kill someone?" I called through the wall to Derek.

"Any kind," floated back to me.

"Cats and dogs? Ragweed and pollen? Mold spores?"

"If someone's allergic enough." He appeared in the door. "Usually, when someone dies from anaphylaxis, it's food related. Either that, or a sting. Some people are deathly allergic to bees. If they get stung just once, they can die within thirty minutes."

"Did you see any bee stings on Miss Shaw?"

"I didn't examine her," Derek said, folding his arms across his chest. I admired, distantly, the excellent musculature in his biceps and chest. "It wasn't my place to do, and besides, she had a rash. I wouldn't have been able to see anything like that."

"Rash?"

"Hives," Derek said. "Someone with that kind of severe allergy will break out in hives if they are exposed to the allergen."

"What are the other symptoms of anaphylaxis?"

His eyes went vague, as if he were picturing the pages of a textbook. "There's itching and rash followed by rapid pulse and possibly a sense of impending doom. Then comes swelling of the throat and tongue, which brings on difficulty in breathing and swallowing, and finally there's loss of consciousness followed by sudden cardiovascular collapse."

"Wow." So the whole system shuts down essentially.

Derek smiled, his eyes back in focus again. "Out of all the people who present with an allergic reaction every year, only about one percent get to the point of dying from it. The rest get helped before it goes that far."

"Why didn't Hilda Shaw get helped?"

"I don't know," Derek said. "Maybe she ran out of epinephrine?"

"Does that make sense to you? That someone so allergic wouldn't make sure she had what she needed in case of an allergic attack?"

"Maybe she'd run out and she just hadn't had a chance to call the pharmacy for a refill. Or if she got her medicines by mail, the way a lot of older people do, she might have ordered one, but it didn't arrive yet."

"Maybe." It was a big chance to take, though. So perhaps the EpiPen had somehow developed legs and walked off . . . "Was there anything at all that you saw yesterday that made you think maybe it wasn't an accident?"

"Nothing," Derek said firmly. "She died of anaphylactic shock. I'd stake my medical license on it."

I smiled. "The one you don't have anymore?"

He grinned back. "A minor detail." And then the grin disappeared and his voice changed. "Don't worry about Miss Shaw, Avery. There's nothing we can do. Nothing we could have done when it happened. Let Wayne and Brandon worry about it."

I nodded and went back to scraping wallpaper. Although I didn't stop thinking.

. . .

A couple hours later, when I left to pick up lunch, Miss Shaw's apartment was locked up tight and the crime scene tape gone, but there was a notice on the bulletin board downstairs in the hallway, outside the laundry room, that a meeting had been called for seven o'clock that night in the building's community room. All residents were expected to attend. The note carried Wayne's name on the bottom, but in Brandon's handwriting; I guess Wayne must have called and told Brandon to put it up before he left.

As soon as I was outside and in the truck, I called Derek to let him know. "There's a meeting tonight in the community room. I didn't even know this place had one."

"It's in the basement, behind the storage rooms," Derek said. "Are we expected to attend?"

I pulled the truck out of the parking lot and onto the Augusta Road. "I assume we are. Now that we own a condo in the building."

To be honest, I don't much enjoy driving Derek's Ford F-150. It's too big and bulky, and it feels heavy and hard to maneuver. I like my Beetle: small and zippy and good for taking corners and slipping through traffic. And a bonus: It has no bad memories attached. I once drove Derek's truck off the road into a ditch after someone had messed with the brake cables, and every time I crest a hill and head down the other side in the truck, I remember that runaway feeling.

"You'll have to go alone," Derek said.

"I will? Why?"

"Don't you remember? It's Ryan's bachelor party tonight. And the wedding tomorrow."

Of course.

Ryan is an old friend of Derek's from high school. He lives in Portland now, forty-five minutes away, and he was getting married that weekend. I'd forgotten all about it in the excitement over the condo and Hilda Shaw's death.

"You're spending the night in Portland, right?"

As far as I knew, Derek and his high school buddies were going out drinking, the way men do at stag parties, and rather than missing out on the fun because he had to drive home afterward, Derek had booked a room in the reception hotel. He'd have to be back in Portland tomorrow afternoon anyway, unless he wanted to miss seeing his buddy fitted with the ball and chain, so he figured he may as well just sleep in, and I'd meet up with him before the ceremony. That way I'd have somewhere to change into my fancy dress, too, and I wouldn't have to wear it on the ride from Portland, or make my toilette in one of the hotel restrooms. And we could spend the night after the reception in the hotel, instead of driving home—in separate cars—in the darkness of night.

OK, then. Change of plans. "I'll just go to the meeting by myself," I said.

"You don't have to go. You already know everything that's going on, and I'm sure Wayne wouldn't care if you came with me to Portland instead."

"What am I going to do while you and your friends carouse? Sit in the hotel room and watch HGTV?" I shook my head. "No thanks. I'll stay here and go to the meeting and take care of the cats and drive up tomorrow morning."

Ryan's fiancée and her bridesmaids were having their own shindig tonight, but I hadn't been invited, since I didn't technically know Carla. Staying in Waterfield and listening to Wayne discuss Hilda Shaw's death and Brandon's mishap with the neighbors sounded more interesting. And then there were the cats. Mischa gets mopey when I leave. After months of living under the porch on Rowanberry Island, you'd think he'd be used to being alone, but ever since I brought him to the mainland with me, and into Aunt Inga's house, he's been more like a limpet than a cat. The other two have made independence and self-sufficiency a religion, but Mischa is happiest when I'm right at home and he's right where he belongs, in my lap. And although Derek might be right, that I did know everything that was going on already, it was possible Wayne had dug up some little tidbit of information I hadn't heard. And I was damned if I would miss out on it. Not to sit in a hotel room in Portland watching HGTV.

"Do what you want," Derek said. "I need to get back to work. We have to knock off early today as it is."

"I'll be back in thirty minutes. Roast beef OK for lunch?"

Derek allowed as how it was, and we hung up. I headed into town and down Main Street to one of the cafés, where I ordered two roast beef sandwiches on rye to go. It was while I sat there waiting for the food to be made and handed over that the door opened and John Nickerson walked in.

He's a small, skinny man with an Elvis haircut and a limp left over from Vietnam, usually dressed in a vintage 1960s suit with skinny pants or a vintage 1970s ditto with bell-bottoms and appliqués of flowers and peace symbols. Sometimes he even sports rhinestones. He's totally enamored with midcentury chic—1950s, '60s, and '70s—which is pretty much all he sells in his store. Finn Juhl–inspired sofas, teak tables and TV stands, shag rugs, and wall hangings with giraffes and zebras. He also has an outstanding selection of pictures of big-eyed children with puppies and kittens.

When he saw me, his thin face broke into a grin. "Afternoon, Avery."

"Hi, John," I replied. "How's it going?"

"Good, good. You?"

I said I couldn't complain.

"Derek not around?" He looked over his shoulder.

I shook my head. "He's working. I'm picking up lunch to go."

"New project?"

I nodded, and told him all about it. Including the fact

that one of the neighbors had just kicked the bucket last night. John nodded sagely. "That's no surprise."

"What isn't?"

"That Hilda Shaw is dead."

"And why is that?" Other than the fact that she was getting on in age and we're all going to die sometime.

"I knew her," John said.

OK. But that wasn't a reason for her to be dead, either. Or was it?

"We're the same age. Went to school together. I've wanted to kill her myself on occasion."

Ah. "I guess I didn't make myself clear. She wasn't murdered."

John tilted his head. "Really? That's surprising."

I know murder isn't a laughing matter, but I couldn't help the surprised giggle that escaped my lips. "What makes you say that?"

"In school she was voted 'most likely to die mysteriously.' "

"You're kidding?"

John admitted that he was. "But she was the kind of girl who liked to know things about people. And once she figured out something juicy, she liked to hold it over their heads."

"Blackmail?"

"More or less. There was this girl that I liked, back when I was thirteen or so. Her name was Susie Lawrence. She had no idea who I was, and I preferred it that way. So, of course, when Hilda found out, she threatened to tell Susie, unless I gave her the dessert out of my lunch box every day."

"I thought she was allergic to gluten."

"I wouldn't know about that," John said. "I do know that she was allergic to nuts. One day, my mom put pecan sandies in my lunch instead of chocolate chip cookies, and that took care of the problem."

"She realized they were bad for her?"

He shook his head. "She ate them. And then she had to

go to the hospital with some sort of allergic reaction, and that was the end of it. Her mom knew she hadn't packed anything with nuts, so Hilda had to have gotten the cookies somewhere else. Mrs. Shaw got the whole story out of Hilda, and she made Hilda apologize to me. I got to eat my dessert in peace after that."

"What about Susie Lawrence?"

"Oh, Hilda told her," John said with a shrug. "But it's going on fifty years ago. I'm over it."

"Was Susie nice about it at least?"

"She couldn't care less," John said. "That's why I didn't want her to know. It's no fun having a crush on someone who doesn't know you're alive."

"She knew you were alive after that, though."

He shrugged. "You sure Hilda wasn't murdered?"

"Not entirely sure," I admitted. "The medical examiner hasn't done the autopsy yet. But Derek said it looked like anaphylactic shock. The ME will probably concur."

"If Derek says it's anaphylaxis, I'm sure it is."

"Although there was one sort of weird thing. Or if not weird, at least interesting."

He tilted his head, birdlike. "What's that?"

"Well, everyone seems to agree she had allergies. Amelia Easton, the neighbor, said she did. There were a ton of medications in the apartment, and some very specialized foods. Gluten free, no nuts, no seafood, that kind of thing. And now you're telling me she had allergies when she was a child."

"Uh-huh," John nodded.

"Well, it seems like she should have had an EpiPen. You know, emergency injection of epinephrine. But she didn't."

"Really?"

"Brandon didn't find one. And he spent a lot of hours, both last night and this morning, going through the place. Derek thought that maybe she'd run out and just hadn't been able to get a refill yet, but it's interesting."

"Very," John agreed, as the cashier nodded to me, white

plastic bag with wrapped sandwiches in her hand. I got to my feet.

"I should get back. It isn't fair to let Derek do all the work. Even if I'm sort of in the way at this stage of the game." I don't update electrical plugs or change out plumbing; those sorts of things are Derek's domain. My contribution comes either before, in the design, or a little later, with painting and adding finishing touches. Once he got done with the major mechanicals, which wouldn't take more than a couple of days in a small apartment like that one, I could start throwing myself into the project as well, but until then I was mostly relegated to making lunch runs and appreciative noises.

"I'll see you around," John said. And added, "I almost forgot. Got your invitation in the mail the other day. He finally got around to popping the question, huh?"

I smiled. "I've only been in town a little over a year. It isn't like we've been dragging our heels."

"Seems longer," John said.

I nodded. It seemed longer to me, too. In some ways, it felt like I'd always been in Waterfield. "You'll be able to come, right? To the wedding?"

"Wouldn't miss it," John said before he turned his attention to the cashier, who was waiting patiently for him to tell her what his to-go order would be. I took myself and my sandwiches out the door and down the street to the truck.

. . .

At five we knocked off work for the day. Derek drove me home and dropped me off before going to his loft to shower, change, and drive to Portland with his nice suit in a garment bag for tomorrow. I took a bubble bath, washing all the grime and dust from the renovations off in Aunt Inga's clawfoot tub, and made myself some dinner. I petted Mischa a lot, making him purr hysterically, and I made sure the other two cats were fed and watered and had what they needed before I got in the Beetle and headed back to the condo building.

Until Wayne mentioned it, I hadn't realized there was a community room in the basement. I knew there was a laundry room down there, along with a utility-type area where the various heating and air units sat, blowing hot and cold air to the rest of the building. The other side of the basement had a line of small storage rooms: one for each condo, with enough room for a couple of bikes, a few boxes of Christmas decorations, maybe some old clothes, and a chair or two. As Derek had said, the small community room was beyond: 10 by 15 feet, maybe, with a couple of rows of metal folding chairs in it. When I passed through the door at seven o'clock, most of the seats were taken and Wayne stood at the front of the room, preparatory to making his announcement. I raised a hand in greeting, and he smiled. "Hi, Avery."

Heads turned, and Wayne added, "For those of you who don't know her, Avery Baker and her boyfriend have bought the Antoninis' condo and are renovating it. Where's Derek?"

"Portland," I said, avoiding all the eyes. "Bachelor party."

Wayne nodded. "Find yourself a seat. We're about to get started."

I slid onto the chair next to Josh, who gave me a distracted look and smile. Probably because Shannon was leaning up against his other side, whispering in his ear. Next to her was Gregg the resident and the young man with dark hair we'd seen a couple of days ago—the one Derek had said looked Hispanic and must be Mariano. In the row behind, Jamie sat next to Amelia Easton on one end, while on the other was William Maurits. There were several empty seats between them. Candy was nowhere to be seen, so maybe she was working tonight.

In the far back were Robin and Bruce with little Benjamin; the boy had a coloring book on his lap. This was the first time I'd seen Bruce, and he turned out to be a stocky man around my own age, with a shaved head, a little goatee, and a tattoo of a skull and crossbones on his neck.

Robin, once I saw her up close and personal, was pretty in a washed-out sort of way, like a faded watercolor. Little Benjamin had gotten all the color in the family, it seemed, with that shock of jet-black hair and—when he looked up for a second, gnawing on his crayon—big, dark eyes.

While I'd been looking around, Wayne had explained the situation. Hilda Shaw was dead, most likely from natural, or seminatural causes—the medical examiner had completed the autopsy and had confirmed anaphylactic shock as the cause of death—but there were just a few questions that Wayne hoped the neighbors could help out with.

"She obviously had food allergies," Wayne said, looking around the room. "Dr. Lawrence, the medical examiner, thinks the allergic reaction was due to ingestion of a trace matter of peanuts, probably in her breakfast cereal yesterday morning."

I had met Dr. Lawrence once, about six months ago, after Derek and I had found the body of a young girl floating in the water between Rowanberry Island and the mainland. She'd been a nice lady, who knew Dr. Ben, Derek's dad. As she'd said, "Doctors of the dead are doctors, too."

I raised my hand. "I spoke to John Nickerson earlier today. You know, from Nickerson's Antiques? He went to school with Miss Shaw, and said she had allergies back when she was a child, too. Severe ones. She had a bad reaction to pecan sandies once."

"Corroborating evidence is always nice," Wayne said, "although the contents of her cupboards speak for themselves. I've also spoken to her doctor and had the allergies confirmed that way. Thank you, Avery."

He addressed the rest of the room. "Someone with long-standing, severe allergies should have had an EpiPen. For those of you who aren't familiar with it, it's an emergency self-administered dose of epinephrine that someone with severe allergies can take in the event of an allergic reaction. The same way an asthmatic would carry an inhaler around."

A couple of people nodded, Gregg the resident among them. Robin put her hand on Benjamin's head and stroked his hair; maybe the boy had asthma. He shot his mom a quick grin.

"Her doctor confirmed that she had a standing prescription for one at the local pharmacy," Wayne continued.

He glanced around the room. "We've spent quite some time going through Miss Shaw's apartment and her things, and so far, there's no sign of an EpiPen. Which seems unlikely. In every other aspect of her life, Hilda Shaw seems to have managed her illness very carefully. It doesn't make sense that she wouldn't have made sure she had a dose of epinephrine in case of emergency. So I thought perhaps one of you might know what happened to it. Whether she ran out of medicine and hadn't gotten around to ordering a refill. Whether she'd misplaced it and told you she'd lost it. Whether she came to visit and accidentally left it behind."

Silence greeted this statement. Gregg leaned toward Mariano and whispered a few words in his ear. Mariano nodded. Nobody else spoke.

"Moving along," Wayne said. "We have to track down any extra keys Miss Shaw may have given out. Her next of kin is a sister in Oklahoma City, who will arrange for everything long distance. The condo will be cleaned out and, I'm sure, sold. There will be no funeral or memorial service, unless you'd like to arrange your own."

There was another long pause, during which I imagined I could hear the wind rustling through the grass on the lonesome prairie. Obviously nobody felt the need for a memorial service, and no one wanted to confess to being in possession of a set of Miss Shaw's keys. In the back of the room, the door to the hallway opened, and Candy slipped through. After a quick look around, she dropped onto the last seat in the last row of chairs. She didn't sit down with Jamie and Amelia Easton, and although Jamie glanced over her shoulder, she didn't acknowledge Candy in any way, nor did Candy acknowledge Jamie. Maybe they'd had a tiff. I'd never had a roommate other than my mother—I lived at home during the time I went to Parsons School of Design—but I could imagine it might sometimes be grating to be on top of one another, especially when there was a lot of added stress in the situation. Such as when one of the neighbors dies suddenly and the police are all over everything.

"I'm going to need all of your fingerprints," Wayne added, "as well as a statement from each of you regarding where you were last night between the hours of ten P.M. and eight A.M. today."

Another pause ensued, this one fairly humming with tension.

"Why?" Bruce asked eventually, with a glance at Robin.

Wayne turned to him. "To match with fingerprints found in Miss Shaw's apartment. Someone was there overnight, after we sealed the place and locked up. We'd like to know who, and what that person was looking for." He took in the rest of the room with a glance. "I don't suppose any of you would like to tell me?"

No one did.

After a few moments, William Maurits raised his hand. "Are you still investigating, or is the case closed?"

"The case is open," Wayne said. "But we're finished with the apartment. I'll make sure it's locked up and leave it for Mrs. Carroll to deal with. If you'll all go to your apartments, I'll be by to get your fingerprints in the next few minutes, as well as a record of your whereabouts last night. And any keys you may have. If there's anything else you'd like to confess, you can do it at the same time. Dismissed."

There was a scraping of chairs and quiet whispers as everyone got up and filed toward the door. Robin helped Benjamin close his coloring book and gather his crayons while Bruce watched, the look on his face somewhere between doting and fierce. When she straightened and gave him a smile, he smiled back, and put his hand on the small of her back as they walked out. Mariano and Gregg had their heads together, whispering. Candy and Jamie, on the other hand, each seemed to be taking great pains to pretend the other wasn't there. They departed separately, without looking at one another.

I turned to Wayne. "I don't suppose you need my prints, do you?" He'd taken them before, last summer, when everything was happening in and around Aunt Inga's house.

He shook his head. "I already have yours. And Josh's and Shannon's. You're free to go."

Not until I'd gotten a little more information. And shared some. "Is the medical examiner sure it was an accident? When I told John Nickerson that Miss Shaw was dead, he thought she'd been murdered. Said he'd wanted to kill her himself."

Wayne's eyes sharpened, and I added, "It was a long time ago. I think he said he was thirteen. Hilda Shaw found out that he liked this girl named Susie Lawrence, and she threatened to spill the beans to Susie unless John gave her his dessert every day."

"What happened?"

"His mom sent pecan sandies instead of chocolate chip cookies one day. Miss Shaw ate them and had a bad reaction. Her mother found out what was going on and made it stop."

Wayne tried unsuccessfully to hide a smile.

"He said," I added, "that she was the kind of person who liked to know things about people. And who liked holding them over people's heads."

"Blackmail?"

"Maybe. Or maybe she just felt unimportant, and knowing things about people made her feel better about herself. Both Kate and Shannon told me that she knows everything there is to know about everything in the building. Maybe she found out something that someone didn't want her to know."

"Huh," Wayne said. "I'll look into it. But I doubt anyone

will admit it if she was holding something over their heads, Avery."

Likely not.

"It's a reason why someone might have broken into her apartment last night, though. If Miss Shaw knew something, and had proof, maybe in writing, someone would have wanted to make sure the police didn't find it, wouldn't they?"

"I imagine they might," Wayne agreed. "But it's gone now. And they're not going to tell me what it was. Especially if they killed Miss Shaw over it."

"I guess we'll just have to find out what it was on our own," I said.

He gave me a beady stare. "You mean that I'll just have to find out on my own, don't you? Since this is a police matter, after all."

"Of course," I said. "That's exactly what I meant."

"Humph," Wayne said, and made no effort to make it sound like he believed me.

—8—

Wayne headed upstairs, and so did I—to our condo to have a look around without Derek's distracting presence.

I love him, but he can be loud, with his sawing and banging and swearing, and apart from that, I'm usually pretty aware of his presence anyway. It can be hard to concentrate on anything else when he's around. So I welcomed the opportunity to take a look at the space by myself, and to get some thinking done on what I might do to make it look fabulous.

The hallway was small and dark, since it opened on an interior staircase and had no windows. We'd paint the walls a light color to make it appear bigger. Not white, though. White is blah, and it gets dirty quickly. And not eggshell, either. Every unimaginative renovator in the universe paints the walls eggshell white, because it is supposed to appeal to the greatest number of people. I hate eggshell white. Much better to make a statement, and if that alienates a few potential buyers, then those were probably people you wouldn't want to do business with in the first place.

So light walls, pale blue or pale green maybe, or yellow.

Pale gray if Derek wanted bland—and sometimes he does. A big mirror on the wall to reflect what little light there was, and to make the space appear bigger. Maybe we could mount it right on the sliding door to the bathroom. It's nice to have a full-length mirror you can look in right before you walk out the door. Most of us like to make sure we look OK before we take on the world. And from that location, it would catch any light coming in both from the living room and the kitchen. Maybe I could do something fun with it, instead of just buying one at the store. Glue seashells or beads or glass tiles around the frame, maybe. Or etch it. Something unique. It'd look great.

I'd already designed the kitchen—on paper—and it would look fantastic, too. Painted cabinets that'd look lacquered after copious amounts of shellac. Maybe some white subway tile on the backsplash; it's classic, all-purpose, and goes with any style, from cottage to industrial. Concrete counter, or maybe a bright and colorful Formica?

The possibilities were endless . . . and for another day. I moved on.

The bedrooms would be simple: carpeted floors maybe, to cut down on noise, and painted walls, light and airy. And the living room/dining room combo . . .

I stopped in the middle of the floor, hands on my hips, to look around.

It wasn't a bad-sized room for a small apartment. Fairly generous for a living room. Not quite so big when you took into account that you'd need to fit in a dining room area as well. But sufficient for both.

Pivoting slowly, I did a visual 360-degree of the space. There should be wood floors; an unbroken expanse of the same flooring throughout the condo would make the space flow better and appear larger. Derek could hang a chair rail around the part of the room that would serve as the dining area, from the hallway door to the door to the back bedroom. The vertical line would visually extend the space. The wall on the right was unbroken, so we'd probably have to leave that wall bare, since we couldn't very well stop the chair rail in the middle.

Or could we?

Maybe we could do something funky. Like extend the chair rail through the dining area and then turn it in a different direction. Down. End the rail at the baseboard instead. And then perhaps fill in with something. Like a pattern of other rails. A fake paneling of sorts, something almost like a half-timbered look. Or—here was a thought!—aluminum. Corrugated. Industrial.

Head spinning with the possibilities, I made another half turn. If we painted the ceiling the same color as the top of the wall, that would serve to open the space up even more. Metallic paint, possibly. And outside on the balcony—I pushed the door open and walked out—maybe a bench. There really wasn't enough room out here for a table as well as chairs; someone would have to be really thin or else a contortionist to make it past any table I put out. But a bench would fit perfectly. One of my recently acquired DIY magazines had instructions for a slender bench with metal legs and an upholstered lid for seating with a shallow compartment underneath for storage.

Making a mental note to dig out the magazine and take a look when I got back to Aunt Inga's house, I sat down in one of the hard plastic chairs that populated the porch currently, and looked out onto the darkening lawn. A few stars were starting to appear overhead, along with a slim sliver of a moon. I put my feet up on the railing and inspected my toes. It was still warm enough to wear sandals to tomorrow's wedding, and I might have to touch up my polish after wearing sneakers to work all week.

My toes were watermelon red. And in spite of the rough treatment of the past few days, they didn't look bad at all. I might just want to give them a quick coat of extra polish when I got home, but other than that, I was good to go.

The dulcet tones of "Saturday Night Fever" cut through the air, and took my attention away from my toes. Moving my feet down and leaning forward, I peered over the railing. I'd thought I was alone out here, but maybe I was wrong.

Or not. There was still no sign of anyone below, so unless the unknown cell phone owner was downstairs on Hilda Shaw's porch, where he or she had no business being, I was still alone.

"What took you so long?" a female voice said, and I leaned back on my chair as I realized the truth. The person with the cell phone was above me, not below. Over my head, where Candy must be sitting on her own porch. It was her voice I was hearing. "I called you hours ago!"

"Yes," she added a second later, "I know I'm not supposed to call you at home, but this is important!"

That sounded like my cue to leave. I leaned down, soundlessly, and grabbed my shoes.

"Yeah, it's over," was the next thing I heard. "The chief of police said it was an accident. That's not the problem here."

I wiggled my toes into a shoe while I tried not to make any noise. It was a tricky situation to be in. I didn't want to eavesdrop on Candy's conversation. She probably had no idea I was here, or she'd have gone inside when her phone rang, to speak in private.

Or maybe she did know I was here, and it wasn't a confidential conversation. Maybe she had heard me come outside and she didn't care whether I overheard or not. After all, I hadn't heard the door upstairs open or close, so she must have been here before me.

Nonetheless, I started fussing with my second shoe. Other people's conversations, whether personal or not, are not something I feel I need to overhear.

That was until I heard Candy say, "Not on the phone. I want to meet in person."

There was a pause while the caller spoke, and then Candy's voice came back, petulant. "What do you mean, we decided? *We* didn't decide. *You* did."

If I concentrated hard, I thought I could hear a faint quacking noise that must be the other person in the conversation. Or maybe I was just imagining things.

"I know that's what you said," Candy continued. "But you'll get in more trouble than I will. And don't you forget it!"

Another pause ensued, longer this time. I waited, holding my breath.

"I'll be there in ten minutes," Candy said. "And if you know what's good for you, so will you!"

And that salvo must have been the end of the conversation, because the next thing I heard was the balcony door closing upstairs. Hurriedly, I finished slipping my foot into my other shoe and followed suit: ducked through the door into the living room and closed and locked the balcony door behind me. Then I scurried across the condo to the front door, snagging my bag from the floor of the hall along the way.

I opened the front door and listened for a second. There were no sounds of steps on the stairs, neither above nor below me. Candy must have either been super fast, and was already down and out, past my floor and outside in the parking lot, or she was still upstairs, preparing to leave.

I took a chance that it was the latter and headed down myself, after quickly locking the door behind me. Every second I spent standing there, and every step I took down the stairs, I expected to hear Candy coming, but she didn't, and by the time I reached the parking lot, I fully expected to see her car already gone.

But it wasn't. The small hybrid was still there, like a smear of white in the gathering dark, parked in front of the building. I hurried over to the Beetle, three spaces down, unlocked the door and slid behind the wheel, and snapped off the overhead light just a second before the front door opened again, and Candy came through.

She was dressed in her usual tight jeans and a Barnham College hooded sweatshirt, with the ubiquitous ponytail and pink bubble gum. I could see her jaw moving from where I was.

She stopped for a second just outside the door and looked around, as if she thought she might have heard something. I slid down in my seat until I could just barely see her above the dashboard, hoping that if I could hardly see her, maybe she wouldn't notice me.

After a moment she took a left and headed for her car. I watched her go past the Beetle without a sideways glance, and heard the sound as she beeped off the hybrid's car alarm. She slid behind the wheel and closed the door gently, and after a moment, the engine purred to life.

I expected her to turn on the headlights, but she must have forgotten about that little detail, because she just reversed out of the parking space and rolled slowly across the lot over to the road. There was no traffic to speak of this time of night, and a second later, she was on her way down the Augusta Road in the direction of town and Barnham College.

I left my own lights off as I followed, just in case she happened to look in the rearview mirror. When I got out onto the road itself, though, I thought I'd better adhere to the law, so I flipped them on. Candy had done the same; I could see her taillights a hundred yards or two up ahead.

With her lights on, she was fairly easy to follow in the dusk, and there wasn't enough traffic on the road to cause a distraction. And as it turned out, she didn't go far. Once we hit the Portland Highway and took a right—away from downtown Waterfield, toward Barnham College—only a minute or two passed before she signaled a right turn. I slowed down and followed. Right into the parking lot of Guido's Pizzeria.

Well, that was a disappointment. She must have been talking to a friend on the phone, someone who knew what had happened in Candy's building and who wanted to hear about the meeting with Wayne. There wasn't anything sinister about it at all, no matter how adamant she had sounded on the phone.

Nonetheless, I slotted the Beetle into a parking spot and turned off the lights.

There was no sign of the hybrid, so after a brief battle with myself, I exited the car.

Guido's is a low one-story cinder-block building that looks exactly like what it is: a roadside tavern. There are no windows save the one in the door, and no landscaping or other attempt to prettify the place. What you see is what you get: a squat, square building surrounded by parking spaces, and a neon sign flashing HOT-HOT-HOT, like a strip club.

That made me think of Derek, who was in Portland by now, probably into his third or fourth beer—or other alcoholic beverage—and who, for all I knew, was at a real strip club, toasting Ryan's impending nuptials, with big-bosomed women strutting their stuff in front of him.

Not that I was worried. Derek isn't the cheating type, and if he were, it wouldn't be with someone whose bra size is bigger than her IQ. No offense.

And besides, I had more immediate matters to occupy me than the possibility that Ryan was corrupting my fiancé with women, wine, and song. Peering around the corner of the building, I saw a ghostly shape in the dark corner of the parking lot, under an overhanging tree: Candy's hybrid.

The rest of the parking lot looked deserted, and she was parked nose forward into the corner. I knew she was meeting someone, so she'd probably be watching the lot in the rear-view mirror. If I tried to move closer, she might see me, especially as I was wearing a pale yellow shirt, almost as bright as the neon sign on the roof. If I'd known I'd need to sneak through the dark spying on someone, I'd have chosen something black or navy blue, the better to blend into the shadows, but hindsight's 20/20 and all that. It was what it was.

So I stayed close to the building, hiding between the cars and getting as close as I could to Candy without crossing the open expanse between the parking spaces around the restaurant itself and the parking spaces around the edges of the lot. I couldn't get very close, but I comforted myself with the knowledge that I wouldn't have been able to see anything even if I did. The corner under the tree was dark, and the interior light in the car was off. I couldn't see Candy at all, not even as a dark outline.

Out on the road a car slowed down to pull into the parking lot. For a moment, the headlights illuminated the narrow space between the two cars, and I threw myself on the ground, heart pounding. If Candy had looked out at that moment, she would probably have seen my head lit up like a halo.

I thought this might have been whoever she was waiting for, but the car parked in a space near the front, and two people got out. A young couple, laughing and holding hands as they walked toward the entrance to the restaurant. I went back to watching and waiting.

There were sounds off to the left, around the back of the building, and for a second or two, the ground lit up. A shadow appeared, the elongated outline of a man, then the whole thing disappeared again, and I heard footsteps—hard soles slapping against the blacktop of the parking lot. Someone had opened the back door to the restaurant and had stepped through before closing the door again. A moment later, I could see the outline of a man walking briskly across the lot toward the hybrid in the corner.

By now it had gotten too dark to recognize anyone. It was a man, and his hair looked dark, but that was all I was able to see. I had no idea who he was, whether he was young or old, employee, patron, or what. He was just a shadow moving through the night. Until he reached Candy's car and opened the passenger side door. Then the interior light came on for a moment. I saw the top of Candy's head move as she turned to him, and saw him slide in next to her. The light went off again as soon as he closed the door behind him, but I'd seen enough to recognize him. It was the same man Candy had spoken to last time Derek and I had been inside Guido's.

They spent five minutes together, nothing more, while I crouched between cars, eyes peeled to see what I could. It wasn't much. As soon as the light went out, the interior of the car was plunged into stygian blackness again, under the tree. I couldn't even see movement. Basically, they could have been doing anything at all in there. Although the car didn't move, so whatever they did involved minimal activity. Chances were they just sat there and talked.

After a few minutes, the passenger side door opened again, and the guy got out. He walked back across the parking lot to the restaurant, his movements quick and sort of angry. After he'd disappeared inside—the light and sound from the restaurant came back for a moment and then was cut off again when the back door closed—everything was still and quiet. Candy's car didn't move. The minutes ticked by, and I fidgeted.

Had something happened? Was she OK?

Had the guy killed her?

Should I go check?

I had just decided to stand up and make my way over there when the hybrid's engine cranked over. I ducked down between the cars again, hurriedly, as the taillights came on and Candy backed out from under the tree. The tires squealed, and I wondered if she were angry, too. She drove as if she was.

She took a right on the road, heading back toward the Augusta Road and—I assumed—home. I thought about following her, but I was pretty sure I'd just be tailing her back to the condo.

Instead, I thought maybe I should follow the boyfriend.

If that's what he was. He was much too old for her—late thirties, at a guess, while she was Brandon's age—but there was definitely something going on between them. They were sneaking around, meeting in dark corners. From what I had been able to make out from hearing Candy's side of their conversation, they'd been together last night, after the restaurant closed, and Candy had lied to Wayne about it. And besides, the fact that he was a man—good-looking, well-dressed, seemingly well-off—and she was a young, attractive blonde, made the assumption sort of automatic.

What was he doing here? He didn't look like the type to frequent Guido's. It caters to the college crowd, with student waitresses, cheap beer, and pizzas. Barnham College was just a couple of miles down the road. A slick professional-looking guy in a designer suit didn't fit the marketing demographic at all. He wasn't a teacher, not unless he was brand-new this semester. I'd taught a couple classes at Barnham myself last spring, and I knew pretty much everyone on staff there.

Maybe he was the owner? Guido himself?

I had no idea who owned Guido's Pizzeria. A lot of Italian places are family-run, with all the relatives pitching in. Stefano works the kitchen, Maria is the hostess, and Tony and Joey wait tables after school while Mamma Rosa folds napkins in a corner of the dining room. New York City's Italian neighborhood, Little Italy, is full of restaurants like that.

This wasn't one of them. The waitresses were all Barnham students, and so was the kitchen staff, at least from what I'd seen of it. But someone had to own Guido's, whether his—or her—name was Guido or something else.

I made my way back to the Beetle and pulled out my phone.

It took a few rings, but finally Derek answered. "Yeah?" I could barely hear his voice over the din in the background. Loud music and what sounded like yelling.

"Where are you?" I asked.

"You checking up on me, Avery?" But his voice was amused, so I didn't think he minded.

"I had a question."

"Shoot." It sounded like he took a drink of something while he waited.

"Where are you?"

"That's the question?"

Not the one I'd called to ask, but now I wanted to know. "Strip club?"

"Something like that. Don't worry, I'm just looking."

"I'm not worried," I said. "I'm sitting in the parking lot outside Guido's."

"Why? Afraid to go in?"

"Of course not. I just wanted to know if you knew who owns the place."

"Guido's?" He took another swig of whatever-it-was. "Why?"

"Just tell me if you do. It's hard to hear with the music going on in the background. I want to get off the phone and let you get back to it."

"I don't know who owns it. Nobody local. Flatlanders, I think."

"Thank you."

"Don't mention it," Derek said.

"Are you having fun?"

He chuckled. "Oh, sure. A half dozen bachelors, a bunch of almost naked women, booze, and loud music. What's not to enjoy?"

I laughed, too. "Stupid question, I guess."

"Not really. I'd just as soon be home with you, with a pizza and a movie and Mischa trying to lie between us."

"I miss you, too," I said, touched. "But I'll see you tomorrow."

"You know where to go?"

"I'll look up the directions on the Internet before I leave. I'll see you around eleven." The ceremony started at two, and it would take me a little time to get ready first.

"See you then," Derek said, just as the music in the background changed to something that sounded suspiciously like the intro to "Pour Some Sugar on Me." The yelling intensified. "What the . . ." Derek said, sounding suddenly very awake.

"What?"

"Nothing. Or nothing important. Just thought I saw someone I recognized."

"Melissa?"

"Hardly," Derek answered, but with a smile in his voice. "I'll see you tomorrow, Avery."

He hung up. I did the same, and leaned back in the seat, trying to get comfortable. It was just after nine thirty. I had nowhere to be and no one to get home to. I could stay awhile.

. . .

I was still sitting there an hour later, but I was seriously contemplating leaving. College students and other young people of both sexes had come and gone, but there had been no sign of Candy's boyfriend. And I had to pee. I suppose I could exit the car and use the bathroom in Guido's—or alternatively, hide under the tree where Candy had parked her car earlier—but Guido's restrooms are meant for patrons only, and although I doubted anyone would stop me if I pushed my way through the restaurant to use one, I didn't want the boyfriend to see me. And the second option was just plain undignified. I was thirty-two—too old to squat behind a Dumpster.

And it was a good thing I didn't, because just at the time I would have reached the bathroom at the back of the restaurant—or alternatively, just at the time I'd have been squatting, pants down to my ankles—the back door opened again, and Mr. Tall, Dark, and Handsome came out. If I'd been inside the restaurant, I'd have missed him. If I hadn't . . . well, let's just say that the idea of running through the parking lot zipping up my jeans so I could get to the Beetle and follow him before his car moved out of sight was just mortifying.

The car was a sleek BMW, late model. Convertible, although the top was up now in September. The color was difficult to ascertain in the dark, but it was either black or navy blue, possibly green. And when it left the parking lot, it took off in the same direction as Candy: toward Barnham College and the condo building. I waited a few seconds and fell in behind.

I expected to trail him to the condo, and be back where I started, but the Beemer's taillights kept going past the turnoff for the Augusta Road. The BMW's more powerful engine easily outstripped the Beetle's, and by the time we zipped past the incline where I'd turned Derek's truck nose-first into the ditch last autumn, beside the Stenhams' now defunct property development, Devon Highlands, the Beemer's taillights were yards and yards ahead.

Next we passed the turnoff for Primrose Acres, a 1950s suburban development where Becklea Drive is located. I figured we were headed for Barnham College, but before we got there, the BMW signaled a left turn and zoomed across the road into another recent real estate development. This one was called Wellhaven, and from what I could remember from driving by in the daylight, it had a tall fence around it, with impressive wrought-iron gates that stayed closed unless a car just happened to be passing through.

I slowed down as the BMW did just that. The heavy gates clanged shut behind it with a dull thump, and the headlights disappeared behind the wall, out of reach.

—9—

The Cathedral of the Immaculate Conception on Congress Street in Portland was stunning—almost enough to make me reconsider our decision to get married in the church in Waterfield, with Derek's friend the Reverend Bartholomew Norton officiating. It was a big red brick structure in the neo-Gothic style, with pointed arches, three steeples, and a huge, round stained glass window. The plaque outside said it was dedicated on September 8, 1869, and the plaque next to that named it a National Catholic Historic Site and a Portland landmark, and said that it was listed on the National Register of Historic Places.

"See that steeple?" Derek nudged me and pointed.

I nodded. It was the tallest of the three, so it wasn't like it was easy to overlook.

"That's the tallest structure in Portland. Two hundred and four feet."

I glanced at him. "How do you know?"

"Middle school field trip," Derek said. "We climbed to the top. You can see the New Hampshire mountains from there."

"Can we go up?"

"If it's open." He put a hand on my back and guided me forward, toward the entrance. "And if you can make it in those shoes."

I'd driven to Portland this morning and changed my clothes in the hotel room. The shoes were the same pair I'd worn to Kate and Wayne's wedding in December: black, strappy sandals with four-inch heels that I'd unearthed in Filene's Basement in Boston last winter.

The dress was new. For Kate and Wayne's shindig, I'd worn an icy blue 1950s gown I'd seen in John Nickerson's shop window and fallen in love with. I'd thought I'd looked pretty good in it, and Derek had certainly been very complimentary (even if Melissa had told me, rather condescendingly, that I looked "cute"). But you're not supposed to detract from the bride on her wedding day, and my 1950s prom gown did make a bit of a statement. I hadn't been worried about upstaging Kate—nobody could outshine Kate on her wedding day—but I didn't know Carla, and I didn't want to get off on the wrong foot. So I'd come up with a new dress: less eye-catching, but hopefully just as flattering.

It was my own design, and my own fabric. Raw silk, dyed in shades of deep yellow, with hand-painted black vines and flowers. I'd worn it as a sundress this summer, since it had a halter top and open back, but because I didn't think the excessive exposure of skin would be terribly appropriate for an afternoon wedding—in the Cathedral of the Immaculate Conception, no less—I'd thrown a black shawl with silver threads around my shoulders. I'd even made an attempt to straighten my hair before pulling it back in what was supposed to be an elegant chignon. I hadn't been too successful; strands were already escaping to frizz around my face.

Nonetheless, Derek had told me I looked great, and had reinforced the compliment with a kiss that had curled my toes in the strappy sandals.

"Wait till you see the stained glass windows," he said

now, leading me up the shallow stone steps to the church. "And the tile."

"That stained glass window?" I pointed up as we passed under it and into the coolness of the old brick cathedral.

"That's one of them," Derek said. "There are almost twenty. From the conception to the coronation of Mary in heaven. Munich glass. Thank you." The last was directed at a young man in a tux who had handed us a program for the ceremony.

"Excuse me?" I said.

Derek glanced down. "From the Royal Bavarian Glass Factory in Bavaria. Germany. Munich."

I knew where Munich was and said so. "The windows are German?"

"Designed by Franz Mayer. They're from 1909, most of them. The Immaculate Conception window—the round one, it's behind the main altar—is from 1902. Also by Franz Mayer. So is the Rose window behind the pipe organ. The Cathedral of the Immaculate Conception is one of very few cathedrals to have all Franz Mayer stained glass windows."

"And you remember all of this from middle school?"

"Oh no," Derek said, "I've been here since then. Remember I told you I restored the stained glass windows in the church in Waterfield a couple of years ago? The windows here"—he gestured to them—"the whole cathedral, for that matter, was restored in 2000. I tracked down the guy who was in charge of it and got some instruction."

"And a bit of a history lesson at the same time?"

He grinned. "He did like to talk. And I learned a lot."

Derek looked pretty good himself today, in a gray suit and tie with a blue shirt that matched his eyes. They were a little bloodshot, but not too bad, considering that he'd told me the bachelor party had kept going until almost four in the morning.

"Will you be wearing that suit to our wedding?" I wanted to know.

He glanced down. "I can. I thought you might want me to wear a tux."

My mind derailed for a moment, picturing Derek in a tux. He'd look fantastic. "Do you have a tux?"

"Somewhere. I think. Or we could rent one."

I shook my head. "Afternoon wedding. Suit's fine. And cheaper. Besides, you look great in it. Maybe I'll just wear that dress I bought for Kate's wedding so we'll match. It's such a pale blue it's almost white anyway. I can stick a veil on to jazz it up."

"You're not going to wear a white wedding gown?" He sounded almost disappointed.

"I don't exactly qualify to wear white," I reminded him.

He smiled. "News flash, Avery. These days neither does anyone else."

That was true. Melissa had worn white when she married Derek, and they'd already been going at it like rabbits. Kate had worn oyster white, and not only had she and Wayne been keeping company for years, but she had a daughter. I supposed I could find a white wedding gown somewhere if he wanted one.

But then we were inside the cathedral, and I forgot everything else in my openmouthed awe.

OK, so I grew up in New York City. I'm not Catholic, but I've been inside St. Patrick's Cathedral once or twice. I've seen religious splendor before. Nonetheless, the Cathedral of the Immaculate Conception was impressive. There were tall arches along both sides, held up by white pillars, and there were those stained glass windows Derek had talked about, gleaming with afternoon sun streaming through them. There was a white marble baptismal and a huge pipe organ that reminded me of the one in St. Patrick's. There were bas-reliefs and lots of paintings, and there were those tiled pictures Derek had also mentioned. The Stations of the Cross, in shimmering, translucent tile.

"Venetian glass mosaic," Derek whispered in my ear when I halted for a better look at one of them. "Six thousand tiles per picture. A quarter-inch each."

"Wow."

He nodded. "Let's sit. You can look at everything later.

Including the tower, if it's open. We have a couple of hours to kill between the ceremony and the reception."

I nodded, and slid into a row on the left, on the groom's side of the church, tucking my skirt nicely and properly around my legs. Derek sat down beside me and took my hand. "So what did you do last night?"

"Didn't I tell you? After the meeting with Wayne, I went up to the condo and spent some time looking at it." I told him some of the thoughts I'd had, and how I thought we'd be able to enhance the look and feel of the place. "I ended up on the balcony. And while I was sitting there, I overheard Candy talking on the phone."

"To?"

"That same guy we saw her with at Guido's last week. Remember?"

"I'm not old enough to be forgetful, Avery," Derek said. "How do you know it was him? Did you recognize his voice?"

I hesitated, and contemplated lying. Since I was sitting in a church, I thought better of it. "I followed her."

He straightened up. "Excuse me?"

"It sounded suspicious, OK? They were talking about the meeting, the one Wayne called, and Candy said that the police hadn't asked her any questions about him. The guy she was talking to. I wanted to find out who he was, so when she left to meet him, I followed."

Derek didn't say anything for several seconds. I braced myself, sure he'd chastise me for being careless and getting into trouble while he was gone. Not that I'd actually gotten into trouble, but you know what I mean.

He opened his mouth. "Was Jamie there?"

I blinked. "What?"

"Jamie. Candy's roommate. Was she at the meeting?"

I nodded. He didn't say anything else, and after a moment I added, "Why?"

"I saw a girl last night who looked like her."

A girl? "One of the strippers, you mean?"

"Yes, Avery," Derek said patiently. "But if Jamie was in Waterfield, I guess it must have been someone else."

I shook my head. "Not necessarily. It's only forty-five minutes to Portland. When did you see her?"

"Just after I hung up the phone with you," Derek said.

That would have made it 9 P.M. Plenty of time for someone to drive from Waterfield to Portland and take her clothes off. Still . . .

"That's hard to believe. I mean, she looked so sweet when we met her. Didn't she? No makeup or anything. I have a hard time imagining her taking her clothes off in front of a bunch of drooling deviants. Don't you?"

"I'm not a drooling deviant," Derek said mildly. "And no, I don't. Because I saw her. Or someone who looked a lot like her. With a lot more makeup and a lot less clothes on."

"Maybe she has a sister."

"Maybe. Although she's not exactly from around here, is she?" He looked around. "Pretty place, isn't it? They decorated it nicely."

I squinted at the interior of the church, and then at him. "Are you trying to change the subject?"

"It doesn't seem quite right to sit in church and discuss strippers," Derek said. "I've never been all that religious, but I've gotta draw the line somewhere, and I think that's it."

He rested his cheek on the top of my head, and we sat in silence while the church filled up with people.

One of the ladies passing by caught my eye, and I lifted my head from Derek's shoulder to follow her with my eyes. A woman in her late fifties, with short, blond hair going gray, dressed in a lavender dress with a matching cardigan.

"What?" Derek said.

"She looks familiar."

The woman ended up on the other side of the aisle, the bride's side, on the second row.

"Relative of the bride," Derek said.

"I've seen her somewhere before."

"She'll be at the reception later," Derek said. "You can get a better look at her then. Maybe you'll remember where you've seen her."

I nodded.

The processional started shortly thereafter, with traditional music from the pipe organ. Ryan and his best man came out to stand at the altar, while Carla's maid of honor walked up the aisle, taking minuscule steps in her tight column of a dress.

"Sister," Derek muttered out of the corner of his mouth. "Doreen."

Doreen was followed by a little flower girl throwing handfuls of rose petals to the left and right as if she were pitching at a softball game, and then a ring bearer who looked acutely uncomfortable in his Little Lord Fauntleroy suit. The color theme for the wedding seemed to be baby blue with pale pink roses, so the poor kid was decked out in shiny satin with a lacy collar and buckled shoes, with blond curls under a little cap. He was too precious for words, and a picture of him in this outfit would probably be prominently displayed at his own wedding, twenty-five years from now.

"Do we need a flower girl and a ring bearer for our wedding?" I asked Derek, sotto voce.

He gave me a sideways glance. "If you want them, we could ask Jill and Peter if we can borrow their kids. Or Alice's. Although they live two hours away."

Alice is Derek's stepsister, Dr. Ben's wife's elder daughter. She and her husband live in Boston.

"Jill and Peter's brood would be easier. They're here in Waterfield."

Derek nodded. "Or we could ask Josh and Shannon." He grinned.

I shot him an incredulous look, and then had to giggle at the mental image of six-foot-five-inch Josh in the Little Lord Fauntleroy getup. Shannon would look great dressed as Little Boo Peep, but Josh would look absolutely ridiculous. It might be worth asking, just for the laugh.

And then the wedding march started, and Carla came down the aisle.

I'd only met her once or twice, and had thought she was

an averagely pretty girl with soft, brown hair and a little too much junk in the trunk. The gown—with a nipped-in waist and big bell skirt—took care of that problem, while the bead-encrusted bodice and deep boat neckline made the most of her pale skin and slender neck. Her hair was curled and piled on top of her head, with a few strands pulled out to frame her face, and the whole thing was topped with a tiara and a frothy veil. She looked gorgeous, and when he saw her, Ryan forgot all about the solemnity of the moment and broke into a big, delighted grin. I fumbled for Derek's hand. He shot me a surprised look and then a grin of his own, before he pulled the handkerchief out of his breast pocket with a flourish and presented it to me.

I took it, but shook my head. "I'm not going to cry."

"You cried at Irina's wedding." His voice was low and tickled the hair at my ear.

"I didn't cry at Kate and Wayne's. Irina's wedding was special."

"This is special, too," Derek said. "Every wedding's special to the people involved."

True. But I wasn't involved in this one, and knew the people involved only peripherally. So although I might have gotten a mite glassy-eyed when they said their vows and the priest declared them husband and wife, nothing overflowed.

"You OK?" Derek turned to me when the bride and groom had passed by on their way out of the church.

I nodded and handed him the handkerchief back. "Fine. Nice ceremony."

"Too stuffy," Derek said.

"You and Melissa eloped, right?"

"If you want to call it that. We got married at City Hall. Spur of the moment. I guess we thought it was romantic." He shrugged.

It probably had been romantic. They'd been quite young and crazy about each other. It happened more than ten years ago. Eleven or maybe even twelve. They'd been in their early twenties, both of them.

"Let's go see if the steeple is open," Derek said, cutting into my reverie. I shook off the thoughts to give him a smile.

"Let's."

The steeple *was* open, and the view was just as nice as he'd promised, once I'd made the climb to the top. There was the harbor and Casco Bay on one side, with the Atlantic and the small islands dotting the blue expanse beyond, and on the other there was land as far as the eye could see—all the way to the New Hampshire mountains. The green trees were starting to give way to some yellow and orange, and the city, with its red brick buildings and mansard roofs, was spread out below us. Derek put his arm around my shoulders, and I snuggled into his side and pulled my shawl a little tighter around myself. It was colder up here, two hundred and four feet above the ground, and it wasn't really warm down below today, either. I should probably have worn a dress with sleeves, or at least a proper jacket.

"Cold?" Derek said.

"Just a little."

"Want to go up to the hotel room while we wait for the reception to start? I'll help you warm up." He wiggled his eyebrows.

I smiled. "Maybe later. This is pretty."

"Yes," Derek said, looking around, "it is."

"I like living in Maine."

He smiled. "No plans to change your mind and run back to Manhattan?"

I shook my head. "None at all."

"Glad to hear it," Derek said. "You didn't finish telling me what happened last night. You were on the balcony and you heard Candy talking on the phone . . ."

"About the meeting and how Wayne didn't know anything about this guy. I wanted to know who she was talking to, so when she said she'd meet him in ten minutes, I followed her."

"To Guido's?"

I nodded. "She sat there a couple of minutes, in a corner of the parking lot, and then that guy came out and got into her car. They talked, and then he went back into the restaurant and she drove away. Both of them looked angry."

"Let me guess," Derek said, sounding resigned, "you sat in the parking lot and waited for him to leave, and then you followed him."

"There didn't seem to be any sense in following Candy. I figured she was just going home."

"Of course. And what happened when you followed him? He led you on a cat-and-mouse high-speed car chase through Waterfield?"

Hardly. We hadn't proceeded above 45 mph the whole time. A real waste of a BMW convertible, if you ask me.

"He drove to Wellhaven and disappeared inside. It's a gated community, so I couldn't follow."

"And you didn't park the car and climb over the gate and slink through people's yards peering through their windows until you figured out where he lived? I'm surprised." He turned toward the door to the stairs, pulling me along.

"There's no need to be snarky," I said, going.

"Who's being snarky? If it hadn't been a gated community, isn't that exactly what you would have done?"

Since it was, I didn't answer, just pretended to be busy navigating the treacherous stone steps on my four-inch heels. It wasn't all pretend, to be honest. I'd been used to wearing heels in New York, but in the past year, I'd spent most of my time in sneakers, boots, Wellies, and flip-flops, and I had gotten out of practice. I appreciated having Derek's steadying arm under my elbow, and not just because his hand was warm and rough and hard and felt nice. There was a time or two I would have pitched forward if he hadn't held on.

"So tell me about this strip club you went to yesterday," I said when we were in the Beetle and on our way back to the hotel. (We had decided that the Beetle was more appropriate for the occasion—and my outfit—than the truck was.)

Derek was driving, even though it was my car, and he slanted a look my way. "Why?"

"I'm curious."

"Uh-huh." I could tell he didn't believe me. "No way. If I tell you the name of it, you'll sneak out of the reception and go there, to see if you can find Jamie."

"I won't. I promise." I crossed my fingers in the folds of my dress, where I thought he might not notice.

"Uh-huh." I could tell he didn't believe me. "No way."

"Come on!"

"Nope." He shook his head. "But if you're a good girl, I might tell you tomorrow morning, before we check out. You can drive by on your way out of town."

"It won't be open then."

"Exactly," Derek said.

—10—

The hotel where Derek had spent the night—and where the reception would also be held—was the Tremont, just a few short blocks from the Cathedral.

It was a lovely old place, a boutique hotel located in one of the old red brick buildings from the late 1800s. Five floors, thirty rooms, plus a restaurant and bar and a ballroom on the first floor. The reception was to be held there, where sparkling chandeliers cast prisms of light over white-draped tables with centerpieces of baby's breath and pale pink roses.

We were among the last guests to arrive, since we'd taken that break upstairs in our room that Derek had suggested. I was relaxed and warm and rested, even if my fancy hairdo was a thing of the past. I'd given up on the chignon and simply let my hair down the way I normally do. The formal part of the occasion was probably over with anyway, I figured, and now it was time to celebrate.

We ended up at a table with some of the other participants in last night's outing to the strip club, along with their wives, girlfriends, and significant others, and they turned out to be a nice group of people. A few of them I had met before, like the Reverend Bartholomew Norton from Waterfield, who would be officiating at Derek's and my wedding in October. He had been friends with both Derek and Ryan in school, and I was a little bit shocked to learn that he'd been among the celebrants the night before.

"I can't believe you guys dragged a priest to a strip club!" I whispered to Derek in a quiet moment.

He whispered back, "He wasn't born with a collar and cassock, Avery. The man's seen naked women before. Besides, he's married!"

He was, to a very nice woman named Judy, who was a couple of years older, as well as a couple of inches taller than him. Barry is barely taller than me, with a compact and muscular upper body and extremely short legs. I've seen him preach before, and he stands on a box behind the pulpit. At this moment I was willing to wager money that his feet were dangling above the floor.

I smiled, and Barry, sitting on the other side of the table, smiled back. "Having a good time, Avery?" He also has a beautiful, resonant voice, very fitting to his chosen profession. Listening to Barry reading from the Psalms is a thing of beauty. I could hardly wait for him to say, *I now pronounce you husband and wife*.

I nodded. "Lovely, thank you. You have a nice group of friends."

Barry and Derek both looked around the table. "We don't see each other much anymore," Derek said. "Ryan's in Portland, Alex is in Bar Harbor, and Zach drove in from New Hampshire."

Alex, a big burly guy with a beard, nodded. So did Zach, who was a tall and skinny redhead with a job in the technology industry. Unlike Alex, who was loud and boisterous, he hardly spoke at all.

Derek continued, "Some of the others live even farther away. Of the seven of us, it's only Barry and me left in Waterfield. And Jill."

Alex grinned. "How *is* Jill? I thought for sure the two of

you would end up together. Until you showed up with that other girl, the blonde . . ."

"Melissa," Derek said. "That didn't work out. But by then, Peter Cortino had moved to Waterfield and Jill married him instead. And then I met Avery." He winked at me.

"Sorry, Avery," Alex said.

"No problem. I know both of them. Jill and Melissa. We're . . ." I hesitated, because the word got stuck in my throat when it came to describing Melissa. "Friends."

"Good for you. But I meant sorry for hooking up with this guy." Alex gave Derek a punch in the shoulder, which the latter returned.

"Don't give her a reason to rethink, Alex. We've got a good thing going. I don't want you to screw it up."

"Sure, Derek," Alex said, "I won't say a word about the time we went on the senior trip to Boston and you met that girl, what was her name?"

I laughed, and so did everyone else, and the conversation evolved into the men reminiscing about their high school years and the hijinks they got up to. Judy Norton turned to me.

"How are the plans for the wedding coming, Avery?"

"Good," I said. "Things are coming together. The invitations have gone out."

Judy nodded. "We got ours, thank you for thinking of us."

I grinned. "Not like we could exclude the minister, is it? And besides, he and Derek have been friends since high school. Of course we want you both there."

"Do you have your dress yet?"

I shook my head. "I'm thinking of wearing the same dress I wore to Kate and Wayne Rasmussen's wedding. With a veil and without the black fishnet stockings and the fifteen necklaces." It had had a slight Gothic edge at the time. With color. A sort of throwback to Cyndi Lauper. Back when I was a little girl, I'd wanted to be Cyndi when I grew up.

"Yes," Judy said with grin, "it might be best to omit those."

"There's a lot to do, so I'm trying to make things easy. No tuxedos or long gowns. A simple afternoon wedding. Reception in the church hall. And I just can't imagine buying my wedding gown off the rack, you know?"

Judy nodded.

"I'm a designer. I always figured I'd make my own. But we just took on another renovation project, and I don't have the time. So I thought if Derek could wear what he's wearing now, with the same blue shirt, then the blue dress would match, and there were little blue flowers on the wedding invitations, too . . ." Or *in* the wedding invitations, more accurately.

"It'll be OK," Judy said, her voice warm and comforting. "Derek won't care what you wear."

I nodded. "He liked the blue dress. He said he did."

"It was a lovely dress," Judy said. "If you add a veil to it, and maybe an overskirt or trail of some kind . . ."

"That's a good idea. I'll have to look at it when I get home. Tomorrow."

I glanced over at Derek, who was laughing about something that had happened in high school, twenty years before I met him.

"Marrying you will be good for him," Judy said. "He needs to get up on the horse again. He was a pretty sorry sight for a while after the divorce from Melissa."

"I'm sure." By the time I entered the picture, it was five years later—plenty of time for him to have gotten over the experience. Except he hadn't, totally. "I think he's been a little gun-shy, you know? I mean, how do you guarantee that you won't fail again? You can't."

"You can decide that you'll do whatever it takes to hold it together," Judy said. "To do the work you need to do to keep things going. Too many people don't."

True.

"I didn't know him then," Judy continued, "but from

what Barry has told me, Derek and Melissa's marriage was rocky almost from the beginning, and there was nothing that could be done to save it. Lord knows Barry tried, but he said it was one of those marriages that shouldn't have happened, because they were too young to know what they were doing. In the end, he just had to admit that the best thing they could do was cut their losses and go their separate ways."

"I didn't know they'd gone to marriage counseling," I said. Derek had never mentioned it to me.

"I don't know how formal it was," Judy answered. "Barry does do marriage counseling for the parishioners, but I think this was more in the way of a favor to a friend."

She shrugged. "Things will be different now. You're both mature enough to know that it's going to take work, and that it won't always be easy."

I nodded. And then I leaned a little closer and lowered my voice. "So this strip club they went to last night . . ."

Judy rolled her eyes. "Boys will be boys."

"Would you happen to know the name of it?"

She looked surprised. So surprised, in fact, that her eyebrows disappeared beneath her bangs. "Why?"

I thought about lying and telling her that I wanted to hire a stripper for my fiancé's bachelor party. And then I reconsidered lying to the minister's wife and told her the truth instead. "Derek said he saw a girl there he thought he recognized. I wanted to see if he was right."

"You want to go to a strip club?"

Not really. I mean, that'd be kind of weird, me walking into a place where women were taking their clothes off to loud music. But I didn't know how else to find out whether it really was Jamie that Derek had seen. I mean, I could ask her . . . but how would I know that she told me the truth?

"I guess I thought I'd go and just ask someone if she works there. Or see if maybe they have pictures of the . . . um . . . attractions."

"I see," Judy said, her lips twitching. "I don't think Derek would be too happy about the idea, Avery. No offense."

"You could come with me."

"I think Barry would be even less happy."

Probably so.

"I just want to know if it was her," I said plaintively.

Judy tilted her head. "If she wanted you to know, don't you think she'd tell you? If she hasn't, don't you think that's reason enough not to snoop?"

Interesting reasoning. But no, the fact that it wasn't common knowledge was exactly the reason I wanted to find out. Something was going on at the condo building, and I wanted to know what. The more I found out about all the neighbors, the more likely it was that I'd stumble onto something.

But it probably wouldn't do any good to keep talking to Judy about it. She obviously wasn't going to tell me the name of the place, or agree to go there with me. She might not even know what it was called. If Derek hadn't told me, Barry might not have told Judy. So I put Jamie and Candy and Miss Shaw and the whole business out of my head and concentrated on taking part in the conversation and enjoying the rest of the reception. And it worked wonderfully—for about ten minutes, until the food service started.

The Tremont had lovely food service, very upscale and snazzy. All male waiters, all in pinstriped pants and starched white shirts, with pale pink cummerbunds and bow ties for the occasion, to match the wedding party. All were young, handsome, and clean-shaven, with hair that was either short-cropped or slicked back. It seemed the Tremont Hotel had the same policy on personal appearance as did the New York Yankees.

Our waiter even came with a sexy accent. *"Perdon, señorita,"* he murmured when he leaned over my shoulder to place the first course—soup—in front of me.

Derek turned, of course. So did I. And there was a moment of mutual—and uncomfortable—silence while all three of us looked at one another.

After a moment, my eyes dropped from the man's face—familiar—to the name tag on his chest. It was also familiar, but wasn't the name I had expected to see. The face belonged to Mariano, our upstairs neighbor at the condo. The name tag . . . well, it identified him as Gregory.

Neither of us spoke, but I didn't doubt that Derek had noticed the same thing I had. And Mariano knew we had noticed. He had big, brown eyes with long, curving lashes—Bambi eyes—and for a second, they scanned the room as if he were looking for the nearest exit. Then he pulled it together.

"Perdon," he muttered again, and picked up the next bowl of soup, which he put in front of Derek.

My boyfriend and I exchanged a look, but waited until Mariano—*perdon*: Gregory—had wheeled his cart to the next table before saying anything.

"Am I crazy?" Derek muttered.

"If you are, then I am, too," I answered, keeping my voice low so the others wouldn't hear.

"Mariano, right?"

"It looks like him." And Josh had said Mariano worked in the hotel business in Portland.

"Huh," Derek said.

I nodded. "My thought exactly. But now's probably not the time. Or the place."

Derek picked up his spoon. "You're right. Let's focus on the important things. I'm starving."

"You're always starving."

"I need to build up my strength for later," Derek said.

"Dancing?"

"That, too. But I was thinking of tonight."

"What happens tonight?"

He didn't answer. But he smiled.

"Oh," I said. And blushed.

. . .

We did dance, though. A lot. Derek's a good dancer, and I'm not too bad myself. And we danced with other people as well as each other. Which was how, at one point, Derek found himself dancing—and laughing—with the woman I'd noticed walking past us in the cathedral earlier.

I caught his eye from where I was dancing with Zach, another of Derek's friends from high school, the one who lived in New Hampshire. He winked at me. Derek, not Zach. And after the dance was over, he came and found me, as I knew he would.

"Well?" I said when the music had slowed down and we were rocking back and forth on the dance floor. Everyone was dancing by now, including the kids, and there wasn't really room to do much but rock.

"Well, what?"

"Who is she?"

"Dr. Lawrence," Derek said. And added, "The medical examiner."

Of course. I'd met her once, over a gurney with a dead body. But I hadn't expected to see her again in this setting.

"I can't believe I didn't remember her."

"I imagine she probably looked a lot different the last time you saw her," Derek said.

"She did. But still."

Back then she'd been dressed in slacks and a heavy wool sweater, because it was cold in the morgue. And I'd had my mind on other things, like the dead body on the gurney and my friend, who was there to identify it if she could. Now Dr. Lawrence's hair was fluffed and she was wearing makeup and a nice dress and jewelry and heels.

"What is she doing here?"

"She's the aunt of the bride," Derek said. "Carla's mother was Susan Lawrence before she married Carla's father."

"You're kidding."

"No, why?"

I grinned. "John Nickerson told me that when he was thirteen, he had a crush on a girl named Susie Lawrence. Do you think it's the same one?"

"Probably," Derek said. "They're from Waterfield. The girls grew up there."

"What's Dr. Lawrence's first name?"

"Sandra," Derek said.

"She never married?"

He shook his head. "I guess it might be tough for a pathologist to get a date. Especially a female one."

"Men being more squeamish than women?"

"When it comes to that," Derek said and swung me around. "She's a nice lady."

"She seemed nice when I talked to her. Although the dead body was a bit of a distraction."

"I can imagine. She remembered you. Asked how you were."

"That's nice of her." I snuggled into his arms, and we danced in silence for a while. "I wonder what's up with Mariano. Gregory."

"I have a pretty good idea," Derek said.

I did, too. "Illegal alien, you think?"

"That'd be my guess. He's probably using his boyfriend's Social Security number to work."

"That's illegal, isn't it?"

Derek nodded. "Highly. Social Security fraud of some sort, I'm sure. I don't know what the penalties for something like that would be, but I doubt they'd be good."

Probably not. Being in the country illegally is a crime, although tons of people do it. Back about six months ago, I'd done a little bit of research on immigration, and I had learned that most of the illegal immigrants to the United States—other than the ones crossing the border from Mexico—come through the airports on tourist visas, and when the visa runs out, they just don't go home. New York City is full of young English and Irish men and women who came over that way. I'd known lots of them during my twenties. Baristas, waiters and waitresses, bartenders and shopgirls. It's much easier to disappear in a city like New York, so there were fewer of them up here in the snowy wastes of Maine, although Irina had been an illegal alien, living and working under the radar, until she'd gotten married this summer.

If Mariano was an illegal alien, he'd be deported if he was caught. If he was using someone else's Social Security number—even with that person's knowledge and approval—he probably faced jail time. And Gregg—because it was probably his identity Mariano was using—would face some sort of criminal charges, too, most likely.

"Should we talk to him?"

Derek looked down at me. "Why?"

"To tell him his secret is safe with us. That we won't report him."

"We won't?"

"Of course not. It's none of our business, is it?"

"He's breaking the law," Derek said.

"Irina was breaking the law, too. You didn't report her."

"I didn't know she was illegal," Derek said. "And she wasn't using anyone else's Social Security number."

"Not that you know about. But that's water under the bridge anyway. She's married now. But it's not like Mariano and Gregg can get married, is it?"

"They could if they moved to Massachusetts," Derek said. "It's just an hour away."

That was a pretty good point. But . . . "Maybe they don't want to move to Massachusetts. Gregg's got a job here. Or maybe there's another reason they can't get married. Maybe they just don't want to. It's none of our business."

"Then let's not worry about it," Derek said. "At least not tonight." He swung me around again. I subsided as the room spun.

▪ ▪ ▪

Checkout was eleven the next morning, and we waited almost that long to get ourselves together to head back to Waterfield. It had been a long night, the bed was comfortable, and that's all I'm going to say about it.

"So about that strip club . . ." I told Derek when we were ready to go, with our suitcases packed and my dress and his suit in garment bags.

He folded his arms across his chest. "I hoped you'd forget about that."

Fat chance. "C'mon. It's a Sunday morning. They're not going to be open. Can't you just tell me the name of it so I can drive by on my way home?"

"Why do you need to? Like you said yesterday, it's none of our business how other people make their money. Not Mariano or Jamie."

Boy, it's annoying to have your own words thrown back in your face!

"I just want to see the place," I argued. "Just in case there's a picture of her out front. To know if it's her."

"But why?"

I told him what I'd told myself last night: that something was going on at the condo complex, and that the more information we had about all the residents, the better our chances were of figuring out what it was.

Derek sighed. "Fine. There won't be anyone there anyway. C'mon." He picked up his bag and my suitcase and headed for the door. I followed with the suit and the dress.

In the hotel garage, he got into the truck and I got into the Beetle, and then I followed him out of the lovely historical neighborhoods by the harbor into a more industrial part of town, full of used car lots and wire-topped chain-link fences, until he slowed down in front of a long, low, cinder-block building painted virulently purple. It had a sign on the roof saying GIRLS—GIRLS—GIRLS, sort of the same way Guido's Pizzeria said HOT—HOT—HOT. At night, this sign probably flashed in neon colors, too.

There are plenty of titty bars and X-rated theaters in New York City. I'd walked past them almost every day of my life, tucked into storefronts on Eight and Ninth Avenues in Hell's Kitchen, with their blacked-out windows and their photo lineups of the big-busted attractions to be found inside.

This was my first experience with a strip club in the wholesome heartland, and it looked different, yet eerily similar. A big warehouse-looking building—it might have been a warehouse at some point, given the industrial makeup of the rest of the neighborhood—with no windows and only one door. The door was solid, so it must be pitch-black inside with the lights off. The equivalent of New York's blacked-out windows. There was a tasteful and discreet sign above the door indicating that this was the Pompeii Gentleman's Club, which was ironic, considering that the people who frequent strip clubs—present company excepted, since my boyfriend had been here two nights ago—often bear no discernable resemblance to gentlemen.

Unlike the burlesque theaters of New York, there were no photographs of scantily clad women hanging next to the only door. When Derek got out of the truck, slamming his door behind him, and came to crouch at my window, I greeted him with a pout. "There's nothing here."

"I told you so," he said.

The big parking lot was empty. I guess the customers drew the line at watching women take their clothes off before noon on a Sunday. Or maybe the owners had a conscience and drew the line there.

Derek straightened. "Let's go home."

I nodded, and watched him jog to the truck and get in before I put the Beetle back in gear and pulled away from the curb.

. . .

I trailed him all the way out of Portland, only to lose him once we hit I-295 North. By the time I exited the interstate and got on the Portland Highway, which would take me through Brunswick and past Barnham College into Waterfield, the truck was nowhere to be seen.

Instead of scrambling to try to catch up, I took my time. It was a lovely fall day, with bright blue skies and blushing trees on both sides of the car. I turned the radio up and was singing along with Taylor Swift when I passed the old red brick buildings of Barnham College. A few minutes later, I saw the wall surrounding Wellhaven in the distance, and the roofs of the McMansions peeking above.

I slowed down as I neared the entrance. There was a car there, waiting to exit, and just in case the driver decided to make a break for it, I thought I'd better proceed with caution. Accidents happen, and I didn't want this one to happen to me.

As I got closer, I saw that the gate into the development gaped open. That's when I flicked on my turn signal, and earned myself a dirty look from the guy in the convertible as he roared past me and onto the highway in a cloud of exhaust. A grating sound split the air as the heavy iron gates began to close. I pushed the gas pedal to the floor, and the Beetle shot through the narrowing opening two seconds before the gate shut behind me with a shuddering clang. Drawing a deep breath, I settled my nerves, and maneuvered the Beetle onto the well-manicured streets of Wellhaven.

—11—

I don't know what I was hoping to find. I'm not sure I thought I'd find anything. But I'd been kept from going in here after Candy's boyfriend two nights ago, and when I'd seen my chance to snoop, I'd taken it. And besides, I'd never been inside Wellhaven before, so I was really just taking the opportunity to look around.

It was a pretty place, in that planned-development, everything-in-its-place, nonorganic Stepford sort of way. The houses were big and distinctive, on postage-stamp-sized lots; no cookie-cutter subdivision, this. Every McMansion looked a little different from the others: Some had the appearance of English manor houses, some were Tudor mansions, and some would have looked at home in Normandy or Tuscany, with their French château or Italian villa styles. And while I had sometimes thought that the houses my cousins, the Stenhams, built looked a little chintzy, like a good strong storm could knock them down, these looked solid.

In spite of all being different, they had the same look to them, though. A little pretentious and self-satisfied. And everything was manicured to within an inch of its life. There wasn't a blade of grass or a dry leaf out of place. The edges of the lawns must have been laid out with a ruler, and there was lovely landscaping with evergreen bushes in front of every home. The colorful big-wheel tricycle sitting in the middle of a lawn on the second street I drove down looked like an obscenity.

Upon consideration, my bright green Beetle probably looked out of place, too. Judging from the cars I could see parked in the wide concrete driveways, the residents of Wellhaven drove luxury cars in tasteful colors like black, white, and silver. Here and there, there was a stab at a little more individuality with a fire engine red convertible or bright yellow Hummer.

I'd driven a couple of blocks when I saw a navy blue BMW convertible parked in a driveway. It wasn't the first of its kind I'd seen, not by a long shot. There'd been plenty of navy blue BMWs in Wellhaven. This one had the standard Maine license plate, the one with the chickadee and pinecone, and the word "Vacationland" across the bottom in italics with the word "MAINE" in chunky capital letters across the top. Between the two was the letter-number combo BFL-496.

I'd spent ten minutes trailing that license plate the other night, from Guido's all the way here. I remembered it. BFL—big fat liar.

I slowed my own car and crawled past the house, peering intently out the window.

It was a pseudo-Italian villa: pinkish-tan stucco with terra-cotta roof tiles and curved, wrought-iron balconies on the second floor. The BMW wasn't alone in the driveway; next to it sat a sleek Lexus SUV, jet-black. A woman with long dark hair was herding two little girls and a small excited dog into it.

I slowed my car almost to a standstill as I looked intently at her.

She looked like she might be a few years older than me. Thirty-three, maybe thirty-four. A good ten years older than Candy, and a little heavier in the hips and thighs. She looked as Italian as her husband, assuming that's who he was. Dark hair, olive skin, strong nose. She was dressed in slacks and blouse, clearly designer originals and expensive. Something Melissa would wear. Classic, elegant, and costly.

The girls were both brunettes as well. Long-haired, long-legged little girls, one in a green dress and one in blue. The dog wore pink: some sort of little sweater that picked up flashes of sunlight. Sequins maybe. Or silver thread.

There was a movement on the periphery of my vision, and when I turned in that direction, I saw that Mr. Guido had come out of the house. He was standing on the front steps staring straight at me, and his expression wasn't what I'd call welcoming. I had no idea whether he could see me or not—the Beetle has tinted windows, so probably not—but the Beetle itself is distinctive. If he'd noticed me behind him the other day, he might put two and two together. I put my foot on the gas pedal and rolled off down the street. Not too fast—I didn't want to make it look like I was running away—but at a good clip nonetheless.

I kept an eye on him in the rearview mirror. If he made a move toward his car, I'd step on the gas and hopefully be out of Wellhaven by the time he got himself together to follow me.

He didn't. He just stood on the steps and watched me drive away. When I got to the end of the street and turned, he did, too. The last thing I saw was him walking toward his family.

. . .

"What happened to you?" Derek said fifteen minutes later when I pulled up in front of Aunt Inga's house. "You were right behind me when we left Portland."

"I lost you on the highway. You drive faster than me. And then I took a detour." I opened the backseat, preparatory to hauling my suitcase out. Derek leaned in instead.

"Where did you go?"

"I just drove around Wellhaven for a few minutes," I said innocently.

Derek straightened, suitcase in hand, and looked at me. "Wellhaven?"

"The gate was open when I drove by."

"And you thought you'd just have a look around." His voice was resigned.

I shrugged.

"Did you see him?"

"Who?"

He just looked at me until I grimaced. And nodded.

"Did something happen?"

"Of course not. What could happen?"

Derek didn't answer, and I added, "He has a wife and a couple of kids. Girls. Eight and ten maybe. And a small, fluffy dog. At least I assume they're his."

"So he probably isn't Candy's boyfriend at all, then," Derek said. "Not if he has a family at home."

Maybe not. Not that having a family stops scme people from cheating. Mr. Guido could just be one of those people. For all I knew, he and his wife might have an "open" relationship.

"Do you think I should tell Wayne about that conversation I overheard? And how it sounded like Candy and this guy knew something about something?"

"Yes," Derek said, opening the gate to Aunt Inga's yard and holding it for me, "I think you should. Later. Whenever you have a chance to talk to him without going out of your way." He closed the gate behind me. "Right now I think you should go inside and greet your guard cat, before he busts through the window to get to you."

I looked up, and saw Mischa's triangular face peering out at me from the parlor window.

Aunt Inga's house is a Second Empire Victorian from the 1870s. It has a square tower in the front, and a porch on one side. When I first saw it a year ago, the yard was overgrown, the mansard roof was missing tiles, and the wood was rotted. Now that Derek (and, to a lesser degree, I) have been over it, it's a gorgeous confectionary item in periwinkle, mustard yellow, and brick red. I love Aunt Inga's house. One of these days I might even get used to calling it mine.

Anyway, to the left of the hall inside, there's a small front parlor. I use it for an office. It has sliding pocket doors and a big window overlooking the porch, so when Derek's working on something out there and I'm working on the laptop inside, I can talk to him. Mischa was now draped along the windowsill watching us come up the stairs, eyes unblinking. The tip of his tail twitched.

"You go first," Derek said when I'd unlocked the massive, carved wood door. "He'll attack me if I'm in front of you."

"I thought he'd stopped doing that."

After Derek saved my life back in July, Mischa had become nicer to him. Before that, Mischa's worldview had been of me as the queen, himself as rightful consort, and Derek as an interloper who must be chased off every time he showed his face. But after I almost died and Derek saved me, Mischa seemed to realize that Derek wasn't so bad. It had helped that Derek took care of Mischa, too, while I was recuperating, with both my hands bandaged. These days, I thought the two of them got along pretty well.

"Mostly," Derek said. "But if I'm blocking his path to you, I wouldn't give much for my chances of survival."

"He's nine pounds!"

"It's what's inside that counts," Derek said, "and inside, he's a mighty warrior."

"One you could dispatch with a swift kick."

He looked insulted. "I'd never kick your cat."

"Of course not." Although I have been known to nudge him out of the way with my foot myself, if he becomes too much. I pushed the door open and stepped inside the dusky hallway. Immediately, Mischa launched himself at me and started twining around my ankles, purring like a rusty saw.

"I'll take everything inside," Derek said and pushed

past me, carrying my suitcase, garment bag, and purse. "You won't be able to move for a while."

Not while Mischa was twining around my legs, no. I was stuck here until he finished, unless I wanted to run the risk of stepping on him.

"You want me to make some lunch?" Derek said when he came back after disposing of the bags in the bedroom at the top of the stairs. Mischa was still twining, but less hysterically. I leaned down and scooped him up. He hung from my hand like a feather boa, still purring.

"I'll do it. Tuna OK?"

I swear Mischa's ears pricked up and he began purring louder.

"Fine," Derek said.

Mischa sat on the floor next to me the whole time I prepared the food, eyes fixed and unblinking.

He's a pretty cat, a silvery-blue gray with brown eyes. His mother was Pepper, a Russian Blue that belonged to Gert Heyerdahl, the thriller writer—now Irina Rozhdestvensky's husband. Mischa's father was some Rowanberry Island tomcat that Pepper got involved with. I have no idea who. All I know is he must have had brown eyes. Pepper's eyes are bright emerald green, as they should be, so Mischa must have gotten his from his father. The rest of him is pretty solidly Pepper, though. You'd most likely think him a purebred Russian Blue . . . until you saw those eyes.

The eyes that were now staring fixedly at my lunch.

Mischa loves tuna. All the cats do. They have their own diet, dry and crunchy bits mixed with canned cat food—and I don't doubt that Jemmy and Inky at least may supplement with the occasional small rodent they run across outside the house—but Mischa looked so cute sitting there that I shortchanged the sandwiches a little, just enough to scoop a spoonful or two of tuna into a bowl that I put on the floor for him. He attacked it as if he hadn't eaten for weeks, in spite of having been fed canned food twenty hours ago, before I left for Portland, and having had dry kibble to tide him over while I was gone.

While he licked the bowl clean, I carried the sandwiches over to Derek, who was sitting at Aunt Inga's enameled-top kitchen table watching me.

"Thanks." I got a flash of blue eyes and a grin before he fell on his food, almost as eagerly as Mischa had done. I picked up my own sandwich and bit into it.

Last summer, when Derek and I first met and started renovating Aunt Inga's house together, we'd spent a lot of lunches at this table sharing tuna fish sandwiches. I'd probably fallen in love with him over this table. Or at least in this kitchen. He'd kissed me here, for the first time. He'd taught me to tile the kitchen counter with pieces of Aunt Inga's broken china. And once he'd peeled his T-shirt off, preparatory to painting the hallway, and had pulled it over my head to protect the clothes I was wearing, leaving me speechless and blushing as he sauntered off, half-naked.

Derek half-naked is a very pretty sight.

"What?" he said now, eyeing me over the table.

I pulled myself together. "Nothing."

"It doesn't look like nothing. You're pink."

"I was thinking," I said.

"About what?"

"Last summer. When we were working on Aunt Inga's house."

Derek looked around. "Turned out good, didn't it?"

It did. I loved my house. And look at that: I even called it *my* house, and not Aunt Inga's. "We'll live here after we get married, right?"

"Course. There isn't enough room in the loft. Especially after we start adding kids."

"If you prefer, we could sell both of them and buy something that would be ours. Together."

He tilted his head to look at me, and that damnable lock of hair fell over his brow again. My hand twitched. His voice was quizzical when he said, "Is that what you want?"

"I thought maybe it was what you wanted. Something that hadn't belonged to either of us before. Somewhere we could start over. Together."

"Don't be silly," Derek said. "This is a great house. I should know, I renovated it."

"If you're sure."

"I'm sure. As long as it's what you want. I don't care where we live, as long as you're there, too."

Awww.

"So tell me about the ideas you had for the condo. You said you were there on Friday night thinking about things we could do."

"Right." It was hard to remember what I'd thought about before the conversation between Candy and her maybe-boyfriend had derailed my attention. "It was something about aluminum, and a chair rail in the dining room, and maybe an etched mirror in the hallway, on the sliding door . . . Can we go over there? Maybe I'll remember when I see it again."

"Sure," Derek said with a shrug. "I'm not doing anything else this afternoon."

"Just let me visit the bathroom first."

"I'll clear the table." He got up and suited action to words. I headed down the hallway and up the stairs to the bathroom with Mischa dogging—catting?—my heels.

. . .

It was business as usual when we got to the condo. The only difference was that there were more cars in the parking lot today. Most people seemed to be home. Robin's station wagon sat next to what must be Bruce's truck, while Candy's hybrid and Jamie's compact were rubbing elbows on the other side of the lot. William Maurits's sedan was in its usual space, but the space next to it was empty of Mariano's Jeep. Perhaps he was working the early shift at the Tremont today. Or maybe he and Gregg had gone out for a Sunday drive. Josh's Honda was also missing; he was probably hanging out with Shannon, or perhaps having Sunday dinner with his dad and stepmom. Or he might be in the computer lab at Barnham College, working.

It must be laundry day for someone, because as we entered the building, we could hear water running and the sound of the dryers tumbling behind the wall on our right.

Everything was quiet on the first floor, of course. Hilda Shaw's apartment was unoccupied, with yellow crime scene tape still strung from doorjamb to doorjamb, and William Maurits must not be into music or television, because not a sound emanated from behind his closed door.

"Should we knock?" I asked Derek when we got up to the second-floor landing and I was waiting for him to fit the key in the door to the condo.

"Where?" He followed the direction of my gaze across the landing to Gregg and Mariano's door. "Why?"

"Remember last night? Mariano was working at the Tremont with Gregg's name tag?"

"It's none of our business," Derek said, pushing the door open.

I walked in and turned to look at him. "But aren't you curious?"

"No," Derek said and shut the door behind me. "I'm sure he has his reasons. They don't concern us."

"But—"

"No," Derek said. "He saw us yesterday. He knows we saw him. If he wants to talk about it, he can come find us."

"But—"

"Tink." He put his hands on my shoulders and pulled me closer, until he could look down into my eyes. His own are a lovely, clear blue, the color of forget-me-nots, surrounded by long, curved lashes. That particular blue might look very nice on the hallway walls. "How Gregg and Mariano choose to structure their lives is up to them."

"But what if he's worried that we'll tell on him? Shouldn't we reassure him?"

"No," Derek said, "it's none of our business. Leave it alone."

"But what if it has something to do with Hilda Shaw?"

He sighed and let his hands drop from my shoulders. "Why would it have anything to do with Hilda Shaw?"

"Well," I shrugged apologetically, "everyone says she liked to know things about people. What if she'd figured out that Mariano is an illegal alien and is committing Social Security fraud—"

"*If* he's an illegal alien who's committing Social Security fraud," Derek said.

I waved the objection away. "What if she found out, and told him that she knew, and he killed her to shut her up?"

Derek's eyes widened for a fraction of a second, and I wasn't sure whether it was in amusement or shock. Then he said, "First of all, we don't know that he's doing anything illegal. Maybe he accidentally put on the wrong shirt in the dressing room yesterday, and it had someone else's name tag on it. Maybe he didn't even realize it."

"That's highly unlikely."

"But not impossible," Derek said. "Secondly, even if he *is* doing it deliberately, we don't know that Hilda Shaw knew. And even if she did, can you imagine Mariano killing anyone?"

"If the provocation was great enough, I could imagine almost anyone killing someone. Even you. Or me."

He arched his brows. "Who would you kill, if you were going to kill anyone?"

Right now, him. He was annoying beyond words. In reality, though . . . "Probably no one. I can't imagine anything important enough to kill for. But if Mariano is an illegal alien, and he's looking at being put in jail, or maybe even deported, and he doesn't want to be separated from Gregg, he might think that getting rid of Miss Shaw was worth it. We've talked about that before, remember? How what's a legitimate reason for murder to one person isn't necessarily legitimate to someone else."

"There's no legitimate reason for murder," Derek said. "But be that as it may, you're forgetting the most important point, Avery. Hilda Shaw wasn't murdered."

Oh. Yeah. I bit my lip. "Are you sure?"

"It's not up to me to be sure. Wayne seems sure, and it's his job."

"But what if he's wrong? What if Miss Shaw had found out something about someone, something they didn't want her to know, and they killed her?"

"How?"

He hadn't been at the meeting Friday night, when I'd explained all this to Wayne. "By planting something in her food they knew she was allergic to. Wayne said cause of death was a trace amount of peanuts in her cereal. It wouldn't be hard to manage something like that. Buy a bag of peanuts, put a few in a plastic bag, and smash them with a hammer or a mortar and pestle. And then eat the rest. Get rid of the evidence, like the wife in that short story, who bashed her husband over the head with a roast and then cooked it. And invited the police to dinner."

Derek blinked at me.

"You know the one I'm talking about. Anyway, that's not important. Someone could have bought the peanuts, crushed some of them, eaten the rest, and then gotten into Miss Shaw's apartment under some pretext and poured the crushed peanuts out of the Ziploc and into the cereal. And then whoever it was took away her EpiPen, so she wouldn't be able to give herself the emergency medicine she needed. It would look like an accident, and maybe whoever did it would get away with it."

Was getting away with it, the way things were going. Of course, we had no proof it had happened that way, and no real reason to think it had.

"Do you have any evidence at all?" Derek wanted to know.

I shook my head.

"I don't think that's going to be enough for Wayne, Avery."

"What about motive?"

He arched his brows. "What about it?"

"Doesn't it seem like a lot of people in this building are doing things they're trying to hide? Mariano, Candy, Jamie . . ."

"You don't know that," Derek said. "Just because Jamie didn't tell you that she's picking up extra money as a stripper doesn't mean she's trying to hide it. We don't really know her, and it isn't something someone would just come out and say. 'Hi, nice to meet you; I'm Jamie and I take my clothes off for money.' I'm not even sure it was her I saw. It looked like her, but I'd had a couple beers by then, and with the flashing lights and the music and the way she was dressed—or not . . ."

I arched my brows and he trailed off, blushing. "Sorry. Even if Candy is having an affair, it doesn't mean she'd bump off poor old Miss Shaw to keep it quiet. Why would she?"

No reason I could think of. I mean, he was right. Even if word got out that Candy was sleeping with the man from Guido's, it wasn't like she'd get in trouble over it. *He* was the one who'd want to keep things quiet, if the woman and children I'd seen were his family. Candy was, as far as I knew, unattached, and could sleep with anyone she wanted. Morally and ethically one might object to her sleeping with a married man, but it was the married man who had everything to lose if they were found out.

"Maybe he killed Miss Shaw," I said. "So she wouldn't rat him out to his wife." That might be a strong enough motive for murder. "How can I find out who he is?"

"Check the property records," Derek said. "They'll tell you who owns the house in Wellhaven. But you should probably leave it alone, Tink."

"Why?"

"Because if he killed Miss Shaw because she found out about the affair, he'd probably kill you, too, if you started asking questions."

He had a point. I ignored it. "If he killed her, it was probably because she was blackmailing him. The guy must have money; he drives a very nice car, and that house didn't look cheap. The wife had some killer clothes on, too."

"Properties in Wellhaven go for over half a million," Derek confirmed. "So yes, he's probably got money. But I doubt he killed anyone. Especially Miss Shaw. It was an accident, Avery. Just because we happen to have stumbled onto a couple of murders in the past doesn't mean every death that happens in Waterfield is a murder. Wayne is the chief of police, Avery. Not you. And if he says it was an accident, then it was an accident."

"He could have made a mistake. It's not like he's infallible."

"No," Derek said, "but in this case, I happen to agree with him. So does the medical examiner. Why do you have this need to make it into something it isn't?"

"I don't. I just don't want anyone to get away with murder." I changed tacks. "What about the fact that someone went through her condo the night after she died? Doesn't that seem sinister?"

"It seems strange," Derek admitted. "But the murderer wouldn't have done that, Avery. It'd be stupid. All it did was draw more attention to Miss Shaw's apartment."

"So who do you think did it, then?"

"Maybe it was just someone who was curious," Derek said. "Or maybe you're right and Miss Shaw knew things about people. Things they didn't want her to talk about. It could have been one of the neighbors who was doing something he or she shouldn't be, someone who wouldn't kill for it, but who saw the opportunity to go into Miss Shaw's apartment and maybe look for whatever proof the old lady may have had."

Someone like Candy. At the behest of her boyfriend perhaps. If Miss Shaw had known that the two of them were carrying on, and they were afraid that she'd had proof, Mr. Guido might have sent Candy in to look for it.

"I'm going to go talk to Candy."

"I'm not sure that's a good idea, either," Derek answered,

but he followed me out on the landing. And when I headed up the stairs, he followed then, too.

Upstairs, I rang the bell and waited. And waited some more. I was just about to ask Derek whether we should get the screwdriver to remove another lock when the door opened.

"Oh." Jamie looked from me to Derek and back. "It's you."

She looked awful. Deathly pale, her skin almost transparent, with black circles under heavy eyes. Her hair straggled down her back like a sheet of crumpled silk, and she was dressed in a shapeless sack of a sweater and pajama pants, with fuzzy socks on her feet.

"Gosh," I said, "are you all right?"

She passed a hand over her forehead. It was shaking. The hand, not the forehead. "Don't feel too good."

"Something you ate?"

"Drank," Jamie mumbled. "Wine last night. I think."

So she was hungover. Great. The sympathy I'd been feeling vanished. I mean, hangovers are awful—I've had a few of my own over the years—but they tend to be self-inflicted, and so not worthy of too much consideration.

"Is Candy around?"

"Basement," Jamie muttered. "Laundry day."

Derek wrinkled his brows. "She's just sitting down there while the clothes spin?"

"I used to do that," I said. "In New York. I'd go to the Laundromat on the next block and sit there with a book until the laundry was done. Watching clothes agitate is very calming. All those suds."

"If you say so. But this isn't a Laundromat on the next block; it's in the basement. It would take her twenty seconds to run back upstairs."

"She's not feeling good, either," Jamie whispered. "But she was out of clean clothes. She had to do wash."

"We'll go look for her." I tugged on Derek's sleeve.

"Take care of yourself," he told Jamie—always the doctor. "Drink lots of water. Or sports drinks and chamomile tea. Avoid coffee. No aspirin or ibuprofen, but acetaminophen is OK. And get some rest."

Jamie waved a limp hand and closed the door.

"So what do you think?" I asked Derek.

"I think we should go downstairs and look for Candy," Derek said.

"That's not what I meant. I know she didn't look like herself, and I'm sure she didn't look like the girl you saw on Friday night . . ."

"I still think it could be her. But the more time that passes, the less sure I am."

I nodded. That made sense. By now, he'd probably see the resemblance whether it was there or not. "She looked awful."

"She'll be OK. No one ever died from a hangover. You might feel like you will, but it just won't happen. She'll be back to normal tomorrow. Although I think the Pompeii will probably have to do without her tonight."

No doubt. Jamie had barely managed to lift her hand to close the door; bumping and grinding with a pole would be far, far beyond her.

We continued down to the basement, which looked just as it had when we arrived earlier. There was no sign of life, except for the sound of the dryers from the utility room.

I twisted the doorknob and pushed the door open. "Candy?"

We both stuck our heads in.

The utility room looked just as it had when I'd looked at it a week ago. Three washers, three dryers, a utility sink, and two uncomfortable metal chairs. Unlike then, when everything had been quiet, now two of the dryers were turning while the third had just finished, and one of the front-loading washers was going through the final spin cycle. A couple of wet shirts were drip-drying on a small rack in the corner, and a paperback novel was sitting on one of the chairs, spine up. The cover showed a scantily clad female swooning in the arms of a brawny, half-naked male.

Beyond that, the room was empty.

"Huh." I looked around.

"Maybe she went outside for some fresh air," Derek suggested. "It's a bit stuffy in here."

It was. Or maybe not stuffy so much as clammy. Steam from the hot water and heat from the dryers had combined into the sort of humidity that was almost solid. And if Candy was suffering from the same ailment as Jamie, she might have thought some fresh air would feel good.

I closed the utility room door behind me, muffling the sounds of washer and dryers and sealing in that awful humidity, and headed toward the front of the building, where the grass was, with Derek on my heels.

"What exactly is it you want to talk to her about?" he wanted to know as I pushed open the door to the outside and we passed into the cool temperature of autumn.

I opened my mouth to answer, but closed it again when a roar sounded from over to my left. We both whipped around, in time to see Robin and little Benjamin come hurtling across the grass with Bruce in hot pursuit. He was the one who was roaring. Benjamin's little legs pumped as fast as he could manage, and his mother was right next to him, pulling him along. They were both laughing. At least until Bruce made a mighty leap, and tackled both of them and they ended up in a heap on the ground. Benjamin rolled, shrieking with delight. Robin, on the other hand, curled up like a hedgehog, cowering on the ground. When Bruce prepared to fling himself at her, she squirmed backward, her voice too high-pitched for me to understand. The grin slid right off his face. After a moment, he reached out and hauled her into his arms, and folded her in a bear hug. When Benjamin trailed back to ask why Daddy had stopped playing, Bruce stroked the boy's head, but without loosening his hold on Robin. His voice was low, just barely high enough for us to hear.

"I'll be right there, Benjamin. Mommy needs a minute."

"I don't see Candy," I said softly.

Derek shook his head. "Nobody out here but the Mellons. And I don't think this is the time to ask them if they've seen her."

Definitely not. Bruce had let go of Robin, who was squatting to give Benjamin a hug. There were tears on her cheeks. Bruce, meanwhile, was looking around, his face fierce. Before he could turn in our direction, I ducked back into the building, and pulled Derek with me.

"What was that all about?" I said when we were on our way back toward the utility room.

He shot me a look. "How would I know?"

"She looked afraid, didn't she?"

He nodded. "I think she's probably got some abuse in her background."

"Surely not by Bruce?"

Derek shook his head. "Wayne was living a floor down from them for a while. If there was something going on, he'd have noticed. Police officers are trained to look for signs of domestic abuse, same as doctors. Besides, she didn't look afraid of Bruce."

She hadn't. She had turned to him for comfort, and he'd immediately stopped doing what was making her uncomfortable. Whatever her problem was, it didn't seem to be with him.

And it was none of our business. I pushed open the door to the utility room again, and stuck my head in, just in case Candy had appeared in the couple of minutes we'd been gone. "Still empty."

"Maybe she's across the hall," Derek said, and headed for the door to the community room and storage units. He pushed it open and let me go in first, and then he followed me.

The storage space was just as deserted as the laundry room across the way. There was no sign of Candy.

"Should we check the community room?"

"We're here. We may as well." He moved past the doors to the storage units and pulled open the heavy door to the community room. And froze in the doorway, as if he'd walked into an invisible wall. "Shit."

"What?" I moved to join him, looking past his shoulder. "God."

Candy was on the floor, curled in a fetal position, and she didn't react at all when we came through the door.

—12—

"She's still alive," Derek said.

Unlike me, who was still standing there petrified, staring, my heart beating so hard I thought it might knock a hole right through my chest, Derek had shaken off the shock and inertia and had fallen to his knees next to Candy. When I didn't answer, he raised his voice. "Avery!"

The word cut through the rushing in my ears, and I blinked. "What?"

"She's still alive. There's a pulse."

"There is? God. I mean, good. I mean . . . what do you want me to do?"

My voice was jittery and uneven. Derek's was level and perfectly calm. "We have to keep her alive until the paramedics get here. I need you to call them."

"Sure. Um . . . My phone's upstairs."

"Use mine." He dug into his pocket and pulled it out.

"What do I tell them?" I took the phone from his hand and watched the display, searching for a connection. There wasn't one, down here in the bowels of the building.

"Female," Derek recited, "early twenties, full systemic shutdown."

I looked up from the phone. "You don't know what's wrong with her?" How could that be? He was a doctor, wasn't he?

"I know she'll die," Derek said tightly, "if we don't get help."

Right. "There's no connection. I'll have to go outside, to make sure I can get a signal."

"Hurry," Derek said.

I scrambled through the door and out.

Two minutes later I was back, feeling a little calmer and a bit more like I could breathe again. "They're on their way. How is she?"

"Still breathing," Derek said. "Barely."

"Is there anything I can do?"

"Do you know CPR?" He had flipped Candy over on her back and was on his knees beside her, pushing on her chest.

"Um . . ." Theoretically, yes. In practice, not so much. I'd gone through the training at some point, trying to breathe life back into a rubber doll, but I'd never had occasion to use what I'd learned on anything living. And it was years ago, so I was afraid I'd probably forgotten everything but the basics.

"Never mind," Derek said. "I can keep going for a few minutes on my own. When will the paramedics be here?"

"They said about five minutes."

I hadn't taken my eyes off Candy. She was breathing, but so shallowly I could barely see her chest rise and fall. And she was deathly pale, even paler than Jamie.

"What's wrong with her?"

"Not sure. But it isn't a hangover. Alcohol poisoning maybe." He kept the heart massage going. When he straightened, he added, his voice still calm but tighter now, "You're not doing anyone any good standing there. Run upstairs and see if Gregg's home. I could use another pair of hands. A pair that knows what they're doing. It's been a while since I did this."

I nodded and took off. Two minutes later I was back. "No answer."

"Damn," Derek said. He had turned paler, too, in the time I'd been gone, probably from the exertion and the worry. "Any sign of the ambulance?"

"I'll go look." But I didn't. I couldn't look away from Candy. She was so still, and so pale that she looked dead already, and coupled with Derek's obvious worry, it froze my feet in place. I felt light-headed, and as I reached out a hand to brace myself against the wall, a couple of splinters embedded themselves in my palm. While I usually don't enjoy splinters, I welcomed these, since the pain gave me something to focus on rather than the dizziness that was making my head spin.

Derek looked up at me over his shoulder. "Go outside, Avery."

"What?" I managed.

He raised his voice, put some sharpness into it. "Go outside. Now! Make sure the paramedics don't waste time getting in here. And get some fresh air before you pass out. I can't deal with more than one body at a time, and right now, she's the priority."

I nodded and stumbled out, catching myself on the walls along the way. The banging of the dryers rolled in my ears until I was outside.

The fresh air did help a little, and so did the sight of the ambulance shrieking up the Augusta Road, lights flashing and sirens screaming. It took thc turn into the parking lot on two wheels, tires protesting loudly. I waved both arms above my head.

The next couple of minutes were frantic, disjointed. The paramedics grabbed their gurney and hustled inside while I held the door. They loaded Candy up with Derek still pushing on her chest, and wheeled her back out to the ambulance, where they started hooking her up to various IVs and monitors. Meanwhile, the sound of the siren and the appearance of the ambulance had summoned all the residents currently in the building, who had clattered down the stairs to gather in the downstairs hallway, gabbling and rubbernecking and trying to get a bead on what was going on. Poor Jamie was almost as pale as Candy, weaving back and forth, being supported by Amelia Easton and William Maurits, while Bruce still had an arm around Robin, who kept Benjamin's hand in a tight grip. In the middle of it all, another siren sliced the air, louder and louder until it cut off with an electronic wail as a police car came to a stop in the lot. Wayne popped out and raked the assembly with a comprehensive look.

"What the hell happened here?"

"Avery can tell you," Derek said from inside the ambulance. "I'm riding in with her."

One of the paramedics glanced at him. "Sir, you can't—"

The other shook his head. "Shut up and drive the bus, Coleman. Dr. Ellis and I've got this."

Paramedic number one snapped his mouth closed and hopped in the front seat, his cheeks pink.

"I'm not actually Dr. Ellis anymore," Derek said mildly as the doors shut, and that was the last thing I heard.

As the ambulance headed out of the lot, sirens and lights going, Wayne turned to me. "Explain what happened."

"I have no idea," I said. "We came out here this afternoon to talk about what we wanted to do to the condo. I wanted to ask Candy a question, so we knocked on her door. Jamie said she was downstairs doing laundry. When we didn't find her in the laundry room, we went into the community room and found her lying on the floor. I called nine-one-one while Derek did what he could for her. That's all I know."

"What happened to her?"

"I have no idea," I said. "Whatever it was, it happened before we got here."

"Did Derek say anything about it? Did he notice any injuries or anything?"

I shook my head. "If he did, he didn't mention it. He didn't say much at all. Too busy trying to keep her alive."

He had mentioned alcohol poisoning, but I found that explanation hard to believe, in the middle of the afternoon on a Sunday. Jamie had mentioned drinking wine the night before, yes, but from everything I knew about alcohol poisoning, it didn't work like that. People who die from alcohol poison have been drinking pretty steadily for a long time; they didn't share a bottle of wine at night and suddenly collapse twelve hours later.

"Jamie?" Wayne said.

Jamie looked up. She was wedged between Amelia Easton and William Maurits, who were more or less keeping her upright, and she'd been crying. There were tear tracks on her cheeks, but she made no attempt to reach up and wipe them away. With the tears, and in her extra pale face, her eyes looked a bright emerald green. "Yes?"

"Do you know anything about this?"

Jamie shook her head.

"Can you tell me what Candy did this morning?"

Jamie sniffed. "We slept late," she said, her voice rasping. "It must have been eleven by the time we got up. Neither of us felt great. We had some wine last night."

She looked guilty. I couldn't imagine why, since she and Candy were both into their twenties and legally allowed to get as drunk as they wanted in the privacy of their own apartment. It wasn't like she'd done anything wrong.

"Candy always does her laundry on Sundays. We have school the rest of the week, and on Saturdays she likes to do other things." Her eyes brimmed over again, and big, fat tears rolled down her pale cheeks. "She felt awful, and so did I, so I wanted to wait to do laundry until I felt better. But she was out of clean clothes, and she said she could be hungover in the basement as well as upstairs."

"When did she go down?" Wayne wanted to know.

It had been just after noon, when the laundry room opened. "We put our names on the schedule from week to week," Jamie explained.

"And then?"

"She stayed downstairs. She had a book. And it's nice

not to be right on top of each other every minute. I went back to bed until Avery knocked on the door." She glanced at me.

So that was why it had taken her so long to answer the summons when we knocked.

"You didn't see Candy again after she went downstairs?"

Jamie shook her head. She seemed a little disoriented, almost as if she wasn't just hungover, but still a little intoxicated. It must have been quite the celebration, if the alcohol stayed in her system this long.

Wayne must have noticed the same thing, because he asked, "How much did you have to drink last night? Between the two of you."

"Just a bottle of wine," Jamie said. "Red."

"Have you had anything to drink since last night? Hair of the dog to chase the hangover this morning maybe?"

Jamie shook her head, as her pale face took on a green tinge. "No."

Wayne looked around. "Did anyone else see Candy this morning?"

Nobody answered.

"I want to go to the hospital to see her," Jamie whispered.

"I'll take you." This was Amelia Easton's contribution. She had her arm around Jamie's waist, holding her up. "We can go right now."

"I need to change first." Jamie glanced down at her duckie pajama pants, and wobbled.

Amelia guided her toward the stairs. "We'll go upstairs first. Maybe get some food into you. It might help to settle your stomach."

"I don't think so . . ." Jamie muttered, but she allowed herself to be herded up the stairs nonetheless.

William Maurits gave me a polite little nod before he followed, his step springy and his posture ramrod straight, as if to make up for his lack of inches. Last were the Mellons: Bruce with his arm around Robin's shoulders, Benjamin clinging to his mother's hand. With Candy on her way to the hospital, Derek riding with her, and Miss Shaw in the morgue, the group of neighbors was severely diminished.

"Avery?" Wayne said. I turned to look at him. "Everything OK?"

I nodded. "I'm just a little shook up. But I'll be all right."

"Do me a favor. I want to go upstairs, to pick up that bottle of wine the girls shared last night. Brandon's on his way. Will you wait for him and let him in if he arrives while I'm upstairs?"

"Sure," I said. "You think there was something wrong with the wine?"

"It's hard to say. A young, healthy girl shouldn't have this kind of reaction to half a bottle of red wine. I want the bottle and glasses tested, along with anything else the girls ate or drank last night. If Brandon gets here while I'm upstairs, tell him to have a look around the laundry room and the community room for anything unusual."

I told him I would, and he headed up to the third floor. I sat down on the ground with my back against the building, wondering what the hell had just taken place and how it was that this peaceful, quiet condo complex had turned into such a bloody battlefield.

Brandon pulled into the lot a few minutes later. I was feeling better out in the crisp air and silence, and by the time he'd pulled his forensic kit out of the trunk of the police cruiser and was coming toward the door, I was on my feet and ready to do my duty.

"What happened?" Brandon wanted to know, blue eyes a little wild in his pale face.

"I'm not exactly sure," I admitted. "She was on the floor of the community room. Unconscious. Barely breathing."

"How?"

"I don't know."

"Well, was she shot? Beaten? Was there something wrong with her?"

"Nothing I could see. Nothing Derek mentioned. She

was hungover, or so her roommate said. They'd had some wine last night and woke up late, feeling sick. Jamie's in pretty bad shape, too, although nowhere near as bad as Candy."

Brandon furrowed his brows. "How much wine did they have?"

"Not enough to account for this. Unless there was something wrong with the wine. Wayne is upstairs picking it up, along with anything else they ate or drank. He said to take it to the lab and have it tested when you're done here."

Brandon nodded.

"He said to get started in the laundry room and community room, to look for anything unusual."

Brandon nodded and pushed open the door. No sooner had he stepped through into the hallway than Wayne was there, along with Jamie—looking pale and wan—and Amelia Easton, looking motherly and solicitous with a hand under Jamie's arm.

"We'll stop for a cup of coffee along the way," she told the girl, "and see if that won't make you feel better."

Jamie shook her head, her eyes teary. "I just want to get there."

"There'll be coffee at the hospital," Wayne assured Professor Easton at the same time as he passed the bag in his hand off to Brandon. It contained the bottle of wine along with the glasses from last night, I gathered, when I heard them clink together. "Put this in the car, please."

Brandon nodded and headed back out to the parking lot.

"I'll be there myself in just a few minutes," Wayne continued, addressing Jamie and Amelia Easton, "to see what, if anything, the medical team can tell me."

They both nodded, and Amelia Easton supported Jamie toward the door, held open for them by Brandon. They passed through into the parking lot, and Brandon came back inside the building.

"Anything else?"

Wayne shook his head. "She swore up and down they just drank the one bottle. I've got it, empty now, as well as the glasses and also a box of chocolates. Have a quick look around here, for anything out of the ordinary, and then drive it down to the lab in Portland. I know they won't get started on it until tomorrow, but at least it'll be there first thing in the morning."

Brandon nodded.

"Avery can show you where she and Derek found Candy. I'm going to the hospital." He headed for the door.

"If you see Derek," I called after him, "tell him to call me when he's ready to get picked up."

Wayne didn't turn, just waved a hand to signal that he'd heard me.

As soon as he was out of sight, I took Brandon into the laundry room, where he picked up Candy's paperback romance to add to the bag in the car, and then into the community room, where I pointed to the place on the floor where Candy had lain. Brandon looked around. "Nothing here that I can see."

I shook my head. "No blood. She wasn't shot or stabbed. Unless there's something wrong with the wine, it looks like natural causes."

"Girls her age don't die from natural causes," Brandon said grimly. "Thanks, Avery."

"Sure." But I couldn't quite bring myself to walk out.

Brandon looked at me. "Something on your mind?"

I hesitated. I knew something he didn't—or at least something I assumed he didn't. About Mr. Guido and what I thought was Candy's affair with a married man and what had looked like an argument between them on Friday night . . . as they got together to discuss something that had to do with Miss Shaw's death.

If what had happened to Candy wasn't natural, Mr. Guido was at the top of my suspect list. Or perhaps Mrs. Guido, if she knew her husband was diddling Candy on the side.

Always assuming he *was* diddling Candy on the side, of course. And assuming he and his wife didn't have one of those "open" relationships where he was allowed to.

It was information I felt like the police should probably know. Except it was all pretty much supposition on my part. I assumed they were having an affair, but they may not be. I assumed they'd had an argument Friday night, but they may not have. And I'd assumed the conversation I'd overheard had had something to do with Miss Shaw—it had sounded like it might—but I hadn't heard the other side of it, so I couldn't actually be sure of that, either.

And if I was wrong, and they weren't having an affair, and Mr. Guido hadn't done anything to Candy, did I want to be responsible for siccing the police on him? What if he was just a concerned boss wanting to make sure his employee was all right after the sudden death of her neighbor? The police would interrogate him, and maybe interrogate his wife, and upset those two pretty little girls I'd seen—and it would all be for nothing.

Brandon was still looking at me, waiting for my answer. I shook my head. "I'm just a little shook up, that's all. I think I'll spend a couple minutes folding the laundry and throw the rest of it in the dryers, and then I'll head down to the hospital."

"I'm gonna get the stuff to the lab," Brandon said.

I nodded and headed back to the laundry room.

. . .

I hadn't been kidding when I told Derek I enjoy doing laundry. There's something very peaceful, almost hypnotic, about watching clothes agitate through a front loader's window. And folding clothes is one of those mindless activities, like washing dishes, that keeps your hands busy but leaves your mind free to wander. Great for puzzling over solutions to mysteries. These days I have other activities that serve that same purpose—removing wallpaper and scraping paint come to mind—but as I folded Candy's tight jeans and cropped tops and silky little bits of underwear, I found myself going back to what had happened.

For a second, when we'd first walked into the community room and had seen her on the floor, I'd been sure she was dead. She'd been so still, so pale, her back hardly rising or falling at all. And in the ambulance, with all the tubes and machines hooked up to her . . . not to mention the look in Derek's eyes. He wasn't one to worry overmuch, my boyfriend—when Melissa had gotten shot, he'd acted like it was no big deal—so when he did, I tended to take it seriously. Candy was in a bad way.

And Brandon was right: Girls her age didn't just drop dead—or almost dead—from natural causes. Not unless they had some kind of hidden medical issue. Which she might well have, but if so, no one had mentioned it. People knew that Miss Shaw had had severe allergies, and several of them had said so. But no one—not even Jamie—had said anything about Candy having health problems. Chances were she didn't, that she was just as healthy as she looked. Or as healthy as she had looked, up until today.

That was something the doctors would figure out anyway, and while I could keep my fingers crossed, mentally, for a simple solution, I was pretty sure this would turn out to be something more sinister than a hidden case of, say, diabetes. Wayne must agree, since he'd determined that the wine and glasses and chocolate needed to go to the lab. To be tested for poison, I assumed.

Did she have any family? She grew up in Waterfield—I knew she'd gone to school with Brandon—so she probably did. Although if she'd chosen to live with Jamie instead of saving money by staying at home, they might have problems.

Either way, Wayne or Brandon—or the hospital—would notify them. And if they'd had anything to do with this, the police would find out.

Would anyone notify Mr. Guido?

Not likely, I thought. Jamie probably knew what was going on, but if Candy was trying to keep it secret—and judging from where she'd parked the other night, in the far corner of Guido's parking lot, almost out of sight under the branches of a tree, she wasn't eager to broadcast her relationship to the world—Jamie might not mention it. Or could be too rattled to think of it.

Maybe I should make a quick trip out to Wellhaven to tell the guy what was going on. It would be a kindness. If he and Candy were carrying on, he must feel something for her. Even if he didn't, if she were just a fun diversion, he should know that she was in the hospital, that she'd almost died. That sometime soon, the police might stop by to talk to him.

—13—

I ran up the two flights of stairs and into our condo, where I grabbed my bag and headed back out. I was on my way down the stairs again when the phone rang. I fished it out.

"Yes?"

"Where the hell have you been?" Derek asked, without so much as a by-your-leave.

"What do you mean, where have I been? Downstairs, with Brandon."

"You haven't been answering your phone."

"It was upstairs, remember? In my bag? That's why I used yours to call nine-one-one."

"Oh," Derek said, and it sounded like he took a deep breath. "Right."

"I didn't even think about it until just now. So are you ready for me to pick you up?" I crossed my fingers that he'd say no.

"No," Derek said. "Dad's here, visiting a patient. He'll give me a ride."

"Oh." Well, that was convenient. For both of us.

"They want us to come over for dinner. Cora's making lasagna."

Yum. Dr. Ben's second wife, Derek's stepmom, is a wonderful cook. "I'll be there," I said, mouth watering. "What time?"

He told me six o'clock. "Beatrice and Steve will be there, too." Cora's younger daughter was back in Waterfield with her husband after a few years of living in Boston. "Why can't you come right now?"

"I want to run an errand first," I explained. "It might take me a half hour or so."

"Oh. OK. Fine. I'll see you later."

He moved to hang up, and stopped when I yelped. I could hear him put the phone back to his ear. "What?"

"What about Candy? She made it to the hospital, right?"

"She's hanging on," Derek said grimly. "No news yet on what's wrong. She came in in a full systemic shutdown, but no one knows why. They've managed to stabilize her for now. She's getting oxygen to help her breathe, and an IV to keep her hydrated, and they've pumped her full of medications. All we can do is keep our fingers crossed. And pray."

"I will," I said.

"I'll see you over at Dad's." He hung up. I stuffed the phone back into my bag and continued down the stairs.

Two minutes later, I was in the car and on my way to Wellhaven. The gate was still hanging open, and now that I knew exactly where this guy lived, I drove straight to his house, and it wasn't long at all before I was parked at the curb outside the McMansion.

The wife's SUV was still missing from the driveway, and now so was the BMW. It had looked to me like the little girls were going to a birthday party, so maybe the wife had stayed there with them. The husband must have gone off on his own after they left. Maybe he was at Guido's, ready to open the restaurant for the night.

It looked like I wouldn't be able to talk to him after all. At least not there. Although I could stop by Guido's on my way back to town and see if he was there.

On the other hand, if the house was empty, maybe I should take the opportunity to do a little bit of snooping. Carefully, of course, since there were neighbors all around. But if nothing else, maybe I could at least come up with a name for this guy.

I turned the Beetle off and got out, pocketing the key. A quick look around assured me that none of the neighbors were out on their front lawns, watching me as I moseyed innocently toward the mailbox at the curb.

It was red and ornately engraved, with a slot at the top where the mailman could deliver the mail, and a drawer on the bottom, with a keyhole, where the owner could retrieve it. In between the two were the words *Cassetta per le Lettere* and *Regie Poste*. Italian. It's not a language I speak, but I know enough about it to recognize it when I see it written.

The mailbox was the perfect accompaniment to the house, with its Mediterranean look. However, because of that pesky keyhole, I couldn't open it to see whether there might be mail inside listing the names of the owners. It was Sunday anyway, with no mail delivery, so it had been a long shot, but I'd thought it was worth a try.

All righty, then. I turned to the house. Maybe there was a name on the doorbell. Or on the door itself.

Squaring my shoulders, I started up the shallow steps to the front door.

It seemed to take forever to get there, as I counted each step—thirteen, fourteen, fifteen; there were a lot of them—and felt the skin between my shoulder blades prickle. It felt like someone was watching me, but another look over my shoulder, more thorough this time, showed me no one. Just my Beetle, sitting forlorn at the curb, looking jazzily bohemian and out of place in these refined surroundings.

The front door—or doors, since they were double—were twice my height and made of heavy, carved wood, polished to a high gloss. There was no doorbell that I could see, but an ornate brass knocker hung in the middle of the door on the left. It was almost the size of my head, and consisted of two mermaids clutching at the feet of a guy I assumed was Neptune, their tails curving down to form the handle of the knocker. Before I realized what I was doing, I found myself casting one mermaid with Candy's features and blond ponytail, and the other with the strong exotic beauty of the woman I had seen herding the little girls into the SUV earlier today. When I realized what I was doing, I shook my head to dislodge the image, but it was stuck.

Each side of the door had etched glass sidelights, and I stepped over to one and pressed my nose against it. If I squinted just right, maybe I'd be able to see some of the interior through one of the designs.

"Can I help you?" a voice said behind me.

I jumped, and accidentally banged my forehead against the glass. "Ow!"

Swinging around on my heel, I slapped a hand to my brow. And lowered it again when I met a pair of cold, dark eyes.

Oops.

I'd thought it'd be one of the neighbors, someone who had noticed me sneaking around where I had no business being. I hadn't expected it to be the homeowner. I'd been confidently sure he'd left a couple of hours ago. Obviously I'd been wrong.

"Oh," I said lamely.

He smiled, but it wasn't a nice smile. "That your car?"

He gestured to the Beetle. I nodded.

"I've seen it before."

I swallowed. "Lots of green Beetles around."

He shook his head. "Not in Waterfield. You were here earlier. And I saw you a couple nights ago, too."

"I don't know what you're talking about," I said.

"Sure." He tilted his head and looked at me.

Up close, he must be a just a couple of years shy of forty. And I suppose he was good-looking in an overly macho, Neanderthal way, if one likes the type. Slicked-back black hair, hooded eyes, olive skin. Unfriendly expression.

"Why don't we go inside," he said, taking my elbow.

Note the lack of a question mark. That's because it wasn't a question.

"No . . ." I tried.

But resistance was futile. I'm five two; he was almost a foot taller, and outweighed me by at least sixty pounds. Before I knew it—certainly before I had time to weigh the pros and cons of screaming for help to try to attract attention—I was through the door and into the house, with the door closed and, for good measure, locked and bolted behind me.

"Now." He steered me into a small antechamber off the hall to the right, his hand tight on my arm. "Sit."

I sat, rubbing my arm, and in spite of the way my heart thudded and my palms were sweaty, I couldn't help looking around. The interiors of people's houses are interesting to me, both as a renovator and a designer, and besides, I didn't want to look at him.

I was in a little sitting room with reproduction furniture of the same quality—and monetary value—as the stuff my former boyfriend Philippe Aubert used to make. The same stuff I used to design textiles for. Expensive, in other words.

(And in case you wondered: No, Philippe had not received an invitation to the wedding. When I'd told Kate I still had friends in New York, friends I'd invited, I hadn't included Philippe in that description. We had parted on fairly amicable terms the second time, since I'd met Derek by then and had realized I didn't care quite so much that Philippe had cheated on me. But he had lost the right to partake in the happiest day of my life when I'd learned that he hadn't been able to keep Little Phil zipped in his pants for the forty-eight hours I spent in Waterfield, and he had gone to get his needs met by Tara, the receptionist, instead. She was twenty-two, vapid, and blond, and now that I thought about it, very similar to Candy in appearance. What is it with middle-aged men and young blondes?)

"Who are you?" this particular middle-aged man asked.

I pulled my attention from the room—a little too presumptuous, not quite lived in enough, like a photo spread in a home and garden magazine—to the man standing in front of me. "I'm Avery Baker. You?"

He didn't answer, but his eyes narrowed into dangerous slits. "D'you work for my wife?"

I shook my head. "What kind of business does your wife have?"

He muttered something, but I couldn't hear what it was. I'm pretty sure it was the Italian equivalent of "stupid idiot," so I didn't ask him to clarify. The more time I spent with him, the less I understood what Candy saw in this guy.

"What are you?" he asked next. "A private detective?"

"Of course not," I said. "I'm a designer."

He blinked. "Francesca wants to redesign the place? After all the money she spent decorating it in the first place?"

"I have no idea what your wife wants to do. I came to talk to you about Candy."

At the sound of that, his eyes narrowed again. "You *were* following me the other night."

"I was following her," I said. "From home to Guido's. And then I followed you from there."

"Why?"

I hesitated. It was probably best, and smartest, not to tell him that I'd overheard Candy's phone conversation and suspected that he—or they—might have had a hand in killing Hilda Shaw. My situation was precarious enough right now, without telling him that I suspected him of murder.

"Just curious, I guess. That's not the point."

He put both hands on his hips, a very girly gesture for such a masculine man. "What's the point?"

I glanced around the room. "Have you been here all day?"

"At home, you mean? Why?"

"Something happened," I said.

"What?"

I watched him carefully. "Candy almost died this afternoon."

I think he may have turned a shade paler, but it's hard to be sure, since he flushed a deep red almost immediately. A vein beat in his temple. "And you think I had something to do with that?"

"You argued with her on Friday night, didn't you?"

He didn't answer, just looked at me. It wasn't a nice look, and it went on much too long for comfort.

"Sorry," I said eventually, pressing my back into the chair in an effort to get farther away from him. He looked ready to pop. Either a blood vessel or me.

After a few seconds of heavy breathing through the nose, he pulled himself together. "Why would you think that?"

"I don't," I said. And added, "Not necessarily. For all I know, she just had an attack of some kind. Would you happen to know if she suffered from any kind of illness?"

He shook his head. "What happened?"

"I'm not sure. All I know is that when we found her, she was in a full systemic shutdown. My fiancé has a medical degree, and he kept her alive until she got to the hospital. Last I spoke to him, he said she's on a ventilator and drip, and nobody knows what happened, just that she almost died."

This time I definitely wasn't imagining it; he *had* turned paler. "What hospital?"

I told him. There's only one, after all. He must be fairly new in town if he didn't know where the hospital was. "If you call them, they might give you her status. If you don't want to go down there yourself." And he might not, just in case he didn't want his wife to know what was going on.

And then there was a tense little moment while we stared at each other. He looked like he was contemplating doing something to me, something I wouldn't necessarily like. Like bashing me over the head with one of the marble statues of old Etruscans decorating the mantel, or tying me up and stuffing me in the closet until he had time to deal with me.

"I'll . . . um . . ." I slipped out of the chair and sideways.

"I just wanted to tell you what happened. I thought you should know. So I'll go now. Let you deal with this."

"Not so fast." His hand shot out and grasped my arm again, fingers digging in. I winced. "Who else knows you're here?"

"A lot of people," I said, twisting. I'd probably have bruises. Derek wouldn't be happy when he saw them. "My fiancé. A couple of Candy's neighbors. You're hurting me." And while he was at it, making me seriously consider whether he might not be capable of hurting Candy, too. Not to mention Miss Shaw.

His hand tightened for a second, as if he knew what I was thinking, but then he shifted his grip and pushed me away. More or less flung me in the direction of the door. "Get the hell outta here."

His voice was rough.

He didn't have to tell me twice. I scurried to the front door. It took my shaking fingers a few seconds to unlock it, and every moment I stood there, I expected to get hit over the back of the head with a bust of Julius Caesar.

But nothing happened. I got the lock turned and the bolt slid back, and then I yanked the door open and headed out, not concerned with closing it behind me. Once in the car and behind the wheel, I made sure the car was securely locked before I peeled rubber out of Wellhaven. I don't think I drew a deep breath until I was outside the gated entrance and waiting to join the traffic in the direction of downtown.

. . .

I had every intention of going straight to Cora and Dr. Ben's house, to meet Derek and his family for dinner. I'd already kept him waiting, and I knew he wanted me there. But as I sat there waiting for a gap in traffic so I could swing my Beetle onto the road, a small blue Honda zoomed by in the opposite direction, a whole lot faster than it should have been going. Josh was lucky none of his dad's deputies were out looking for speeders this afternoon.

He drove like he had the hounds of hell on his tail, and I couldn't help wondering if something else had happened, something I didn't know about. So at the first opportunity, when there was a gap in traffic, I swung the Beetle out, and instead of going east, toward Waterfield, I headed west, into the sun and in the direction of Barnham College, trailing the Honda.

He was way up ahead, and gaining ground fast, but I was pretty sure I knew where he was headed. When I reached the entrance to Barnham, I turned the Beetle into the parking lot and wasn't surprised when I saw Josh's Honda parked in a corner of the lot. As I slotted the Beetle into a parking space, a couple of cars down, the Honda's door opened and Josh swung his long legs out. By the time I'd gotten out of my own car and slammed the door, he was on his way across the parking lot toward the computer building, a manila envelope in his hand.

"Hey!" I called.

He turned, and for a second I swear I saw a flash of fear cross his face. "Avery." He stopped to wait for me as I trotted toward him, his smile looking a little forced.

"Something wrong?" I wanted to know when I stopped in front of him. "You passed me up on the main road a minute or two ago, driving like a bat out of hell." I gestured with my thumb toward the road.

"I just heard about Candy," Josh said.

I could feel myself turn paler. "Is she . . ."

"In the hospital."

Oh. I started breathing again. "I already knew that. I thought maybe something more had happened." It had been a half hour or so since I'd spoken to Derek and gotten his assurance that Candy was still among the living. The situation could have changed.

"Nothing that I know of," Josh said, shifting from foot to foot. He looked guilty, and he'd put both hands—and the envelope—behind his back as if he hoped I might not notice it.

"Are you two close?" I wanted to know.

He shook his head. "Not really. Neighbors. And I see her at school sometimes. But she's a couple years older than I am. I know Jamie better than I know Candy."

For some inexplicable reason, he flushed.

"I see," I said. That was interesting, considering that Candy was a native Waterfielder and Jamie had only been here for a year or so. But if she'd lived across the hall from Josh for that year, maybe it wasn't so surprising after all. I could see where he might like the quiet Jamie more than the vapid Candy. "What's in the envelope?"

His shoulders slumped. "I can't tell you."

"Why not?"

"It isn't mine," Josh said.

"Whose is it? Jamie's?"

He shot me a surprised look, and that was all the answer I needed. "Does it have anything to do with the Pompeii Gentleman's Club in Portland?"

This time the look wasn't just surprised, it was somewhere between floored and respectful. "How do you know about that?"

"Derek was there on Friday," I said. "Bachelor party. He recognized her."

"Damn." Josh glanced past me out across the parking lot and the Barnham quad, brown eyes serious behind the glasses.

"I think she has more important things to worry about right now," I said.

Josh shook his head. "You don't understand. Her family will have all kinds of fits if they find out. They're religious. Fundamentalist. Some small sect where the women wear dresses and aprons and bonnets."

"Amish? Or Mennonite?"

"Something," Josh said with a vague wave of his hand. "Somewhere in Mississippi. The Bible Belt."

"She's a long way from home."

"As far as she could get," Josh said grimly. "Her folks didn't want her to go. Something about someone else leaving and never coming back. They wanted her to stay home and get married and start having babies instead."

I could feel my eyes widen. "Straight out of high school?" What kind of parents actually *want* their daughters pregnant at seventeen or eighteen these days?

Josh shrugged. "I guess it's one of those groups that think women aren't good for anything but cooking and having babies."

So it seemed. "Stripping seems a strange career choice for someone who grew up like that."

"She got a scholarship," Josh explained. "That was how she convinced her parents to let her come here. It pays for her tuition and her books, and for her dorm room. But once she actually got here, she decided she wanted to live off-campus instead, and the scholarship didn't cover off-campus housing, so she got a job. If her parents find out what she does, or even if they just realize she's not living in the dorm anymore, they'll drag her home. By the hair, most likely."

"They can't do that," I protested.

"Yes, they can," Josh answered. "Jamie's twenty. The age of majority in Mississippi is twenty-one."

"You're kidding." In New York it was eighteen. As far as I knew, it was eighteen in Maine as well. To be honest, I'd assumed the age of majority was eighteen pretty much across the board, and across the country.

"There are only a few states where it's higher," Josh explained when I voiced this thought. "Mississippi is one of them."

"Wow."

He nodded. "She's terrified that her parents will make her move back home. When Miss Shaw . . ."

He snapped his lips shut, but it was too late. "What?" I said.

Josh shook his head, his cheeks pink.

"Don't give me that. You can't mention Miss Shaw and then refuse to say anything else. When Miss Shaw what?

Died?" Or had she, per chance, threatened to call Jamie's parents?

Josh made a sound that was somewhere between an exasperated sigh and a raspberry. "When Miss Shaw died, Jamie was afraid Dad was gonna call her parents."

"Why would he do that? She didn't have anything to do with Miss Shaw dying, did she?"

"Of course not," Josh said, sounding offended. "I told her he wouldn't care. Stripping isn't illegal. And it wasn't like Miss Shaw was murdered. But she—" He stopped again, and once again pressed his lips together.

"What?"

He sighed, and this time it *was* a sigh. "She came knocking on my door that night, after Brandon had gone home. Late. Or early morning, really. Four o'clock or so."

No wonder he'd looked tired when I'd seen him around nine that morning. "What did she want?"

"She wanted me to let her into Miss Shaw's condo," Josh said.

"You're kidding."

He shrugged. Obviously not.

"Why didn't you tell her no?" Frankly, I was more than a little surprised, not to say shocked, to hear this. I mean, he was the son of the chief of police; how could he even consider letting a civilian into a crime scene?

"It was one of those offers I couldn't refuse," Josh said. When I looked at him, brows arched, I saw that he was squirming in a very guilty way. His cheeks were flushed and he avoided looking at me, quite determinedly.

"Oh my God," I said, putting two and two together, "you slept with her, didn't you?"

—14—

Josh's shoulders hunched, and he pulled his head down, like a turtle.

"I can't believe it," I said, full of righteous indignation. "I thought you and Shannon were getting serious. How could you sleep with someone else?"

I'd assumed he'd been pining for Shannon forever, and here it turned out he'd been getting it on with an exotic dancer instead.

His head snapped up. "I didn't! For God's sake, Avery!"

I blinked. "But if you didn't . . ."

"Not then!" He took a breath, and when he spoke again, his voice was a little calmer. "It was last year sometime. November, maybe December."

Almost a year ago. Long before Shannon had given his long-standing crush on her any encouragement. That made it a little better.

He added, "It was back when Shannon was spending all her free time with Gerard. I was frustrated. Jealous, even. I didn't know at first that Gerard was Shannon's dad. Jamie was nice. She'd just moved in across the hall, and the new job was making her feel"—he hesitated—"dirty, I guess. Like nobody decent would want her."

I nodded, and bit back the several snide comments I could have made.

"It only happened once. She's busy with school and work, and I"—he blushed again—"I'm in love with Shannon. I don't want a relationship with anyone else."

"Does Shannon know?"

He shook his head. "And I don't want her to."

Small wonder. I wouldn't like to hear that my boyfriend had had a fling with a stripper, either. Might make me feel just a little inferior, yeah? As far as I was concerned, Melissa was bad enough.

"So Jamie knocked on the door and wanted you to let her into Miss Shaw's condo. And made you an offer you couldn't refuse."

An offer which obviously didn't include another session between the sheets. I was pretty sure I could trust Josh on that.

"She said if I didn't do it, she'd tell Shannon about us," Josh said.

Ah. *That* kind of offer he couldn't refuse.

"That wasn't very nice of Jamie."

Josh shrugged.

"So you let her in. And left her there?"

"Of course not." He sounded offended again. "I stayed with her. And I didn't give her the stuff. I kept it."

"What stuff?"

He ran a hand through his curls. They were in disarray, so it obviously wasn't the first time. "Miss Shaw had information she'd dug up on people. Everyone in the building. People who used to live there but don't anymore. Even people who never did, but who just know someone in the building. Like Kate and Shannon."

"Miss Shaw had information about Kate and Shannon?" I don't know why that should strike me as worse than Miss Shaw having information about her own neighbors, but it did.

Josh nodded. "And you and Derek. And me. And Jamie. And Candy—" He broke off.

"Let me guess. Miss Shaw found out that Candy was sleeping with what's-his-name."

"David Rossini," Josh said, nodding. "Her boss. I guess I shouldn't be surprised that you know about that, too."

I wasn't quite sure how to take that, so I decided to let it pass without comment, even as I suppressed a quick shudder as I remembered the look in those cold, black eyes. David Rossini probably hadn't been thinking about killing me and fitting me for concrete shoes before tossing me off the cliffs into the Atlantic, but it had felt that way.

"Did Miss Shaw blackmail them? Candy and Jamie?"

"For money? I don't think so. Jamie was just worried about her parents finding out. And she told me that Rossini's married, so . . ."

Candy had been worried about his wife finding out. Naturally. "Did Jamie know about Candy and Mr. Rossini?"

"Before we found the pictures?" Josh said. "I don't think so. She seemed pretty surprised."

"Really?"

Josh nodded. "She kept saying she couldn't believe Candy would be so stupid. And that Francesca was going to hit the ceiling."

"What about the rest of the neighbors?"

"What about them?"

"Did Miss Shaw blackmail anyone else?"

"I don't think so," Josh said. "None of us have any money. Besides, what does it matter?"

I sighed, exasperated. "It matters because I'm trying to figure out why someone would go to the trouble of killing her."

"Someone killed her?" Josh said. "I thought Dad said it was an accident."

"He could be wrong. I'm sure it happens."

"Not often," Josh said.

"Well, what about David Rossini? If Miss Shaw had

been blackmailing him—he does have money, quite a lot of it, plus a wife who probably wouldn't be very happy to find out he's cheating—then maybe he would kill Miss Shaw to shut her up."

"She did have pictures," Josh said slowly. "Of Candy and Rossini. Fairly explicit pictures."

He blushed, the sweet thing.

"Those are in the envelope?" I glanced at it.

Josh nodded and took a tighter grip on his prize. "We looked everywhere we could think of for the stuff. It was Jamie who found it, behind the books in the living room."

"Why didn't you put the books back on the shelves? If you had, maybe Brandon wouldn't have noticed that someone had been there."

"No time," Josh said. "By then it was morning, and Brandon was already on his way. He called and told me to meet him with the key. We got out of there as fast as we could."

Understandable. Brandon would realize that someone had been there, but he wouldn't know who or why.

Something struck me. "You didn't take her EpiPen, did you?"

"Of course not," Josh said. "We took the envelope, that's all. Just the information she'd gathered on all the residents."

"Did you say that Miss Shaw had information about me and Derek?"

Josh nodded.

"Show me." I held out my hand.

Josh hesitated, clutching the envelope close to his chest. "Not here."

"Where, then?" Because if Miss Shaw had dug into my life, and Derek's, I wanted to know what she'd found. Not because I had anything to hide—my life is an open book—but because it's hard to resist something like that.

"Lab," Josh said with a quick glance around.

Fine with me. I followed him across the parking lot and the grass into the building that held the computer lab, and up the stairs to the second floor. When we were seated—him in front of his computer, me on another rolling chair I'd pulled up beside it—I held out my hand again. "Let me see."

Josh blew out a breath, but he dug into the envelope and brought out a couple of snapshots. Digital photos, computer-printed. I fanned them out in my hand and caught my breath harshly when I got a better look. "That nasty old witch!"

Miss Shaw must have shot the pictures through her kitchen window with a telephoto lens. And although they certainly weren't indecent or in any way criminal, they were personal. The first showed me and Derek outside the condo building, next to the Beetle, and we were wearing the clothes we'd worn the very first time we'd come there to see the Antoninis' condo. I remembered telling Derek she'd been watching us, and he'd grinned and asked if I'd be up for giving her a thrill. Apparently we had. In later photos, she'd caught Derek with his hand on my butt—a fact I'd forgotten until now—and also a close-up where I had my hands fisted in his hair. I blushed looking at it.

"They're not so bad," Josh said as he watched my expression. "You should see the ones of Candy and Mr. Rossini."

"I'll pass, thanks." I'd already seen all I cared to of David Rossini. I especially had no need to see him and Candy naked, which was what I assumed Josh was intimating. "What clsc is in thcrc?"

"About you and Derek?"

That wasn't exactly what I'd meant, but when he started dragging out pieces of paper, my jaw dropped and I reached for them. "What the . . . what is all this?"

"I'm gonna say everything she could dig up on the two of you on short notice," Derek said. "Obviously, there was a lot more information available on Derek than on you."

Obviously. She had a copy of the newspaper announcement that ran when he came back to Waterfield to join his dad's medical practice some eleven years ago now, plus a couple of clippings of him with Melissa on his arm during the time they were still married. Then there was Melissa on Ray Stenham's arm, and Melissa when she received her award as Maine Realtor of the Year a couple years ago. There was the announcement the paper had run when Derek opened Waterfield R&R, and so on and so forth. She also had copies of the property records for both Derek and Melissa, and although there were no notations on them, I wondered if she'd realized the fact that they were directly across the street from one another and that if Derek didn't keep his curtains closed, Melissa could look straight into his loft.

And vice versa, of course, but I knew Derek wouldn't be looking to sneak a peek at Melissa. She, I wasn't so sure about.

As Josh had pointed out, there was less dirt about me, probably because I'd only been in Waterfield for a year. There was a copy of the announcement that had run in the *Waterfield Clarion* just a few weeks ago, after Derek and I had gotten engaged, as well as a newspaper clipping from the spring, after we helped the police in Boothbay Harbor, up the coast a bit, break up a human trafficking ring. There was the newspaper coverage from last fall, when we were renovating the house on Becklea Drive, when we found the skeleton in the crawl space, and from even longer ago, there was a small news article about my aunt Inga, who had been Waterfield's oldest resident—almost ninety-nine—when she died. That article also included the information that her second cousin a few times removed, Avery Marie Baker, textile designer from New York, had inherited her house. Miss Shaw had scribbled the words "Murder?" and "Inheritance?" in the margin.

She'd been right about the first, but not about the second. Aunt Inga had indeed been murdered, but it certainly hadn't been me pushing her down the stairs. I'd been in New York when she fell, and at that time I'd had no idea she was planning to leave me her house. I hadn't seen her since I was five.

I sniffed, insulted, and lowered the clipping to my lap. "I can't believe it. Why would she do something like that?"

"Believe it," Josh said. "There's more like it in here." He tapped the envelope with a fingernail.

"Does the rest of it have as much basis in fact?"

Josh shrugged. "Some of it has more. Miss Shaw had computer pictures of Jamie at work; people take them sometimes, and upload them to their social networking profiles. I have a Google alert on her name, and I take 'em down whenever I come across them, but I don't catch everything. They say her name's Jamaica Lee, but anyone who knows her can tell it's Jamie. Good thing her family thinks the Internet is evil and they stay away from it."

Guess so. We were sitting in front of a computer, and my fingers itched to do a Google search on Jamaica Lee, but I contained myself.

"She also had Jamie's parents' address in Mississippi," Josh added, "so I don't think Jamie was exaggerating when she was afraid that Miss Shaw would contact her parents. It looked like Miss Shaw had thought about it. Or at least she was prepared."

So it seemed.

"A lot of what's here is stuff that's more or less commonly known," Josh added. "No huge secrets. Even Jamie's job is a secret only from her parents, really. Gregg and Mariano are gay, and Mariano is an illegal alien working without a permit. I'm sure everyone at the hotel knows it, and probably everyone in the building, too. Bruce has a police record from when he was a juvenile. Underage drinking and joy-riding. Half of Waterfield remembers that. Robin's been married before, and Benjamin isn't Bruce's kid. Big surprise there; he doesn't look anything like Bruce, and Robin had him when she moved in here last year. I can't imagine why Miss Shaw thought any of that was newsworthy."

I couldn't, either. "Who was Robin married to? Anyone interesting?"

Josh shook his head. "Someone named Guy Quinn. In

Alabama. I've never heard of him. And if he was somebody, I'm sure Miss Shaw would have had a newspaper article about him."

I nodded. "Hard to see how that's anyone's business but Robin's. Obviously she left him and married Bruce instead. And I'm sure he told Robin about his misspent youth. If *you* know about it, there's no reason why he wouldn't share it with her. As for Gregg and Mariano, it's not like they're trying to hide, is it?"

Josh shook his head. "She even had a picture of a picture—or I should say a copy of a painting—that William Maurits's insurance company paid out on a few years back. Here."

He dove into the envelope; obviously the picture of the picture—or copy of the painting—was something he felt he could share with me.

I took the computer printout he handed me and stared at it. An off-white oval with a slash of red across it, crowned by a half circle in orange and gold on a purplish-black background. There was something compelling about it, although I couldn't have told you why. I tilted my head. "What is it?"

"It's called *Madonna*," Josh said, "so I assume that's what it is. Or was. Although I'm not sure whether it's supposed to be the religious figure or the singer."

I could see his point. The painting didn't look like either of them. Nor did it look like anyone else, really. It certainly didn't look like something I'd want to hang on my wall. However, the accompanying article said it was valued at a cool half-million dollars, and that it had perished when the gallery where it hung had burned to the ground. This was only one of the pieces that had gone up in smoke, and not even the most valuable. The article noted that since the cause of the fire was undetermined, the insurance company had tried to claim arson, probably so they wouldn't have to pay out the six million dollars on the claim. However, there was no proof that the gallery owners had had anything to do with the fire, so eventually the insurance company had to bite the bullet.

"Maurits couldn't have been happy," I said.

Josh shook his head. "I have no idea why she'd focus on this painting. There were at least a dozen of them that were lost, some of them more valuable. But I guess she had a reason."

"Probably." I did a quick tally of neighbors in my head. Maurits and Miss Shaw herself on the first floor; Derek and I and Mariano and Gregg on the second; Josh and Candy and Jamie on the third; and Robin and Bruce along with Amelia Easton on the top floor. "What about Professor Easton? Did Miss Shaw dig up any dirt on her?"

"Not apart from that old story that everyone knows," Josh said.

Old story that everyone knew? "What old story?"

"Haven't you heard about that? It's not a secret, either. All of Barnham was talking about it last year."

"I was still trying to settle in last year," I said. "Tell me." So sue me, I'm as interested in good gossip as the next person. And if everyone at Barnham knew about it already, it wasn't like it was private, was it?

Josh shifted on the chair, getting more comfortable now that we were far off the subject of him and Jamie. "It happened about twenty years ago or so, when Professor Easton was in college herself. Apparently her roommate died mysteriously."

My ears pricked up. "How mysteriously?"

"Not as mysteriously as you're thinking," Josh said. "Suicide."

"Why?"

"You should probably just read the newspaper articles." He tapped the computer open and then keyed in a search for Amelia Easton and Southern Mennonite University. It took the computer only a few seconds to pull up thousands of matches.

"Knock yourself out," he said, getting up from the chair. "I'm gonna go get a cup of coffee."

I slipped into the chair he'd vacated, my eyes already scanning the available links.

"You want one?"

"No thanks." I picked a link and clicked on it. "I'm on my way to Cora and Dr. Ben's house for dinner after this." And I should probably hurry. Derek would be waiting. But what I was reading was too interesting to leave quite yet.

"Suit yourself," Josh said, and strolled out, taking the manila envelope with him. A part of me had hoped he might forget and leave it, since that part wanted to dig in and see what else was inside; but the other part was relieved, since I didn't really want to turn out like Miss Shaw, too interested in other people's business. All in all, just having Josh's word for what the envelope contained was enough.

I turned back to the screen, to what turned out to be an official interview on the Barnham College website, most likely in response to the unrestrained gossip when Professor Easton was hired last year.

The article wasn't long, and as Josh had said, the crime wasn't all that mysterious, either. Twenty years ago or so, while Amelia Easton had attended Southern Mennonite University, her roommate, Nanette Barbour, had been found dead, hanging from the ceiling fan in the bathroom. It was no wonder Amelia had been so pale while she and I were standing outside the door that day when Miss Shaw died. It must have brought back memories of Nanette.

The two girls had come to SMU together, from what was essentially a closed religious community. It was their first experience with the outside world: Up until then they had spent their time entirely within the commune. College was a whole new world to them. Nanette was the one who had wanted to go, and Amelia had agreed to accompany her. But Nanette had gotten into trouble almost immediately. Amelia had caught her talking to a boy, alone. She had phoned the elders, who had made immediate plans to fetch both girls and bring them home. Amelia had told Nanette what was coming down, and the next morning, Nanette was dead.

It seemed pretty open and closed to me, and obviously it

had seemed equally simple to the local police, who had determined that Nanette self-terminated rather than allow herself to be brought home in disgrace.

With the gossip settled, the article went on to detail Amelia Easton's accomplishments after Nanette's death. Instead of returning to the commune, the way one might expect that she would, she had changed her major from home economics to history—in honor of Nan, who had wanted to study history—and had settled in to become a scholar. From Southern Mennonite University, she'd gone on to postgraduate work elsewhere, had become a professor, and had eventually ended up at Barnham, taking over as history professor when Martin Wentworth died. If she'd ever gone back to the commune, even to visit, the article didn't say anything about it.

"I can't imagine why Miss Shaw would be interested in this," I told Josh when he came back into the lab, coffee in hand but without the manila envelope. "It seems pretty cut-and-dried."

He nodded. "I can't understand why Miss Shaw would be interested in any of it. It's none of her business that Robin's been married twice, or that Gregg and Mariano are gay, or that Jamie's a stripper. Or that Candy's sleeping with her boss."

His face sobered as he remembered Candy and what had happened. Mine did the same.

"What did you do with the envelope?" I asked after a minute.

"Put it in my locker," Josh answered. "Shannon won't find it there."

"Why don't you just get rid of it?"

He shot me a look as if he suspected I'd lost my mind. "I stole it. Took it out of someone else's condo. Someone who just died. I can't do that."

I guess I shouldn't have been surprised. More than a year ago, when I'd first moved to Waterfield, Josh, Shannon, and their friend Paige had been withholding evidence then, too. Specifically, they'd been hiding Professor Martin

Wentworth's daytimer, with all his appointments in it. They hadn't been able to bring themselves to destroy it then, either. Thankfully, since the information it had contained had helped the police—and me—figure out what had happened to Professor Wentworth.

"Couldn't you give it to your dad? And explain? Wayne would understand about Jamie not wanting her parents to find out, wouldn't he?"

"Maybe," Josh said. "I'm not sure he'd understand about Mariano, though. Or about me taking the stuff out of Miss Shaw's condo."

I opened my mouth to continue arguing, but he shook his head. "I'm gonna hold on to it for now. If I think there's anything in it that Dad might need to know, I'll give it to him."

I nodded. "I should go. Derek's expecting me. Thanks for sharing what you know."

"My pleasure," Josh said politely, although I hadn't given him much of a choice in the matter. He glanced at the computer screen. "I'm gonna stay here, get some work done."

I nodded. "I'll see you later."

—15—

By the time I made it to the small green Folk Victorian on Chandler Street, dinner was but a distant memory. The table was cleared and everyone had settled into the family room to play Chinese checkers.

Everyone except Derek, who seemed to be watching the door and the game alternately. When I walked into the room, apology on my lips, he jumped up. "Are you OK?"

"Of course I'm OK," I said. "Why wouldn't I be?"

"You know how he worries," Cora said with a smile. "There's a plate for you on the counter, Avery. It should still be warm, but if not, you can put it in the microwave for thirty seconds."

"I'm sure it'll be fine. Thank you." I headed in the direction of the kitchen with Derek on my heels, my stomach rumbling. I hadn't felt all that hungry while I'd been talking to Josh and driving back here, but now that I was inside the house, still redolent of tomato sauce and Italian spices, I found I was ravenous.

The plate was right where Cora said it would be, covered with aluminum foil. I removed the foil and stared greedily at a generous piece of lasagna, dripping with tomato sauce and cheese. My stomach signaled approval, and Derek grinned as he reached past me to the silverware drawer for a fork. "Here."

"Thank you." I plunged the fork into the lasagna, which was still plenty warm enough.

"Breadstick?"

"I wouldn't mind," I said around the first bite of lasagna. It tasted even better than it looked and smelled.

"Coming right up." He slipped on an oven mitt, yellow with orange stripes, and pulled a tray out of the cooling oven. "Careful. They're still hot."

I waved the warning away as I reached for a breadstick, and burned my fingers as a reward for being careless. "Ow!"

"Told you," Derek said, and put the tray back in the oven. He slipped the oven mitt off and continued, "You said you'd be here in thirty minutes. What took so long?"

"I swear I didn't do it on purpose. I was on my way back, just coming out of Wellhaven, when—"

I stopped, narrowly escaping choking to death on a piece of pasta when I realized what I'd said. Derek's eyes narrowed. "You went back there?"

I blinked as I looked for a rational explanation, something that wouldn't make me sound like I was a weird stalker. "Someone had to tell him his girlfriend was in the hospital. I didn't think Jamie would remember to call."

I did my best to sound virtuous, for all the good that it did me.

"One of these days, Avery . . ." Derek said, and stopped. He shook his head in exasperation, and that hank of hair that tends to fall into his eyes whenever he moves, fell into his eyes. My hands were full, so I resisted the temptation to reach out and brush it away. Didn't want to risk gouging his eye out with either fork or breadstick.

"I know. But I'm fine. And when I was leaving Wellhaven, I saw Josh driving in the opposite direction, like a bat out of hell. So I followed."

"Let me guess," Derek said. "Barnham College was burning."

"Of course not." I popped another bite of lasagna in my mouth and chewed. "He was going to Barnham, but not because anything was burning."

"So you spent the past hour with Josh?"

I nodded as I dug the fork back into the lasagna. "Remember the other morning, after Miss Shaw died, when Brandon swore up and down that someone had been in her condo during the night?"

Derek nodded. "Josh said he'd locked up."

"He did. What he neglected to mention was that he unlocked the place again, too, at four o'clock in the morning. And that he and Jamie Livingston tore it apart looking for pictures Miss Shaw had of Jamie."

Derek's eyebrows disappeared behind his hair. "Josh and Jamie?"

"Just so. Apparently they had a one-night stand sometime last fall. Jamie threatened to tell Shannon about it unless Josh let her into Miss Shaw's condo."

"That wasn't very nice of Jamie," Derek said judiciously.

I shook my head. "In justice to her, she was pretty freaked out. Miss Shaw had figured out about the Pompeii Gentleman's Club—it *was* Jamie you saw on Friday—and she was threatening to tell Jamie's parents. Jamie's under twenty-one, so by Mississippi law she's still a minor, and she's afraid her folks are going to come and drag her back home."

"If she has left home and is supporting herself, her age doesn't matter," Derek said. "She'd be considered an independent minor. And anyway, she's in Maine now. Legal age here is eighteen."

"I'm sure she'd be thrilled to hear that. But when Miss Shaw died, Jamie was afraid the police were going to find the information Miss Shaw had, and that they would call her parents. So she made Josh help her search for it."

"Did they find it?"

"Behind the books in the living room, Josh said. But by then it was morning, and they didn't have time to clean up. Anyway, the pictures of Jamie weren't all they found. Miss Shaw had dug up little tidbits of information about everyone in the building. Even you and me."

"You and me?" Derek echoed.

I nodded. I'd finished the lasagna now—inhaled it more than chewed and swallowed, or so it felt—and I was rinsing the plate in the sink preparatory to putting it in the dishwasher. As soon as I was done, I dug the stuff out of my bag. Josh hadn't asked for it back, and I hadn't offered it. As I spread it out across the counter, I detailed what it all was. "Newspaper articles about you, all the way back to when you came back to Waterfield after medical school and residency. Articles about Melissa. Pictures of you and me, kissing in the parking lot that day when we first went out to see the condo."

"She took pictures of that?"

"Sure did." I handed them to him.

Derek fanned them out in his hand like a deck of cards, and winced. "I feel violated."

I tilted my head. "You're not serious, are you?"

He glanced up at me, his eyes a stormy blue. "A little."

"I didn't think you were a prude."

"I'm not. It was in the middle of the day, in broad daylight, so it wasn't like I expected no one to see us. Hell, Josh and Shannon were hanging out the window cheering! But Miss Shaw had no right to take pictures of us. It was a private moment."

Since that same thought had crossed my own mind when I'd seen the pictures, I didn't argue.

"Apparently the pictures she had of Candy and her boss, David Rossini, were worse," I said instead. "I didn't see those. Josh only showed me the things that had to do with us. Did you see this article about Aunt Inga? Looks like Miss Shaw suspected me of having done away with my aunt to inherit the house."

"Shrew," Derek said, and I don't think he was referring to Aunt Inga. "So Josh didn't show you anything else that was in the envelope? Stuff she'd dug up on other people?"

I shook my head. "He told me what it was, though. Said it was information most people knew about anyway. Not the kinds of deep, dark secrets someone would kill for."

"I certainly wouldn't kill over these," Derek said, indicating the pictures.

I nodded. "Same thing with the rest of it. It was all pretty minor stuff, according to Josh. A lot of it from a long time in the past. Professor Easton's roommate in college committed suicide, twenty-plus years ago. Robin's been married once before, and Benjamin isn't Bruce's kid. Bruce was in trouble as a teenager; that must be at least ten or fifteen years ago now . . ."

"I could have told you that," Derek said. "He's a couple years younger than me. I remember he set the school trash cans on fire once. Most of Waterfield probably knows that."

That's what Josh had said, too.

"Jamie's up on stage in front of hundreds of people every week; it's not like she's hiding. She just doesn't want her parents to find out what she's doing. And Candy . . ." I hesitated.

"What?" Derek said.

"I don't suppose there's any chance that what happened to Candy was self-inflicted, was it? If she killed Miss Shaw and was afraid she'd get caught?"

"I don't think Candy's smart enough to get away with murder," Derek said. "And so far, we may have suspicions, but there's no proof that Miss Shaw's death wasn't an accident. Whoever did it, if someone did, would have to be a lot smarter than Candy. Besides, she almost died."

All right, then. I switched gears.

"She and her boyfriend had an argument on Friday night. If he threatened to stop seeing her, could she have done it herself? To try to get his attention?"

"Not sure," Derek admitted. "I still don't know what happened to her. Something did, but the doctors hadn't figured out what it was by the time I left the hospital, and I haven't had any revelations myself since I got here, either."

"Do you think your dad might have some idea?"

"We could ask," Derek said. "It's probably time to go out there anyway. They'll wonder what's keeping us."

"Just show them the pictures."

I should have known better than to joke about it, of course. Derek isn't someone who backs down from a challenge. Cora looked up at me and smiled, and opened her mouth—I'm sure to ask how the food had tasted—and Derek dropped his load right in the middle of the table.

There was a beat of silence, then—

"What on earth?" Dr. Ben said and reached out.

Derek's dad is a little shorter than his son, with cropped gray hair and a set of eyes almost as pretty as Derek's, but more gray. Derek inherited his from his mother, Eleanor, Dr. Ben's first wife. Cora is his second, a short, pleasantly plump brunette who likes to cook and to garden. Dr. Ben's hobby is watercolors. The family room was full of paintings of Cora's flowers that he'd done.

Derek pulled me down next to him on one of the sofas. "Josh Rasmussen found them in Hilda Shaw's condo a couple days ago."

Beatrice looked up. She has her mother's blue eyes and brown hair, but she's taller and very thin, and her hair is straight and long instead of short and curly, like Cora's. "Your neighbor had pictures of the two of you kissing? Why?"

I explained that it wasn't just us, it was all the neighbors. "She was confined to home, I guess. So she lived vicariously through other people."

"That's sick," Bea's husband Steve said. He's tall and lanky like his wife, with glasses and a beaky nose. "And probably illegal." He's also a lawyer.

"She's dead," Derek said. "It's too late to sue."

"Damn." Steve picked up a newspaper clipping. He did it with the tips of two fingers, as if afraid it might contaminate him. And I don't think it was the newsprint that worried him.

I glanced at my future father-in-law. "Did you know Hilda Shaw, Dr. Ben?"

"We were a few years apart in age, so we went to school together," Dr. Ben said. "Of course, that was a lifetime ago. She wasn't one of my patients, if that's what you're asking."

"I guess she probably went to an allergy specialist?"

Dr. Ben nodded. "Someone in Portland, or maybe Boston. I hadn't seen her for years. And I don't remember her well from when we were children."

"You didn't miss much," Derek grunted, still scowling at the pictures. The rest of the family were no better: Cora, Beatrice, and Steve were trading pictures and clippings back and forth, muttering darkly.

"She had this kind of information about everyone," I said. "Including Candy, the girl who's in the hospital."

I turned to Dr. Ben. "Any chance that what happened to her was self-inflicted?"

"You mean, she took something herself, to cause what happened? On purpose?"

I nodded.

"Anything's possible," Dr. Ben said. "When I left the hospital this afternoon, they still had no idea what had caused the shutdown, just that something had. The jury was still out on whether it was natural or induced. If she did it herself, it was a big, stupid chance to take, though. She came very close to dying."

"Do you think she was trying to?"

Dr. Ben tilted his head. "Depends on what Hilda Shaw had on her, I guess. Whether it was worth taking her own life over."

"She was sleeping with her boss," Derek said, not pulling any punches. "He's married."

"They had an argument Friday night," I added. "I saw them. He might have broken up with her, I suppose."

With the extra attention after Miss Shaw's death, that

might make sense. To cool things down for a bit, wait for the added interest to die down before they picked things up again.

Dr. Ben shrugged. "She's how old? Twenty-two? Twenty-three? Hurting herself sounds like something a teenager might do to get back at a boyfriend who jilted her. I'd expect someone that age to be more mature. But of course it depends."

Of course it did. And although I didn't know Candy well, I thought she just might be more immature than her real age, judging from the pink bubble gum and all. And the fact that she'd been sleeping with a man almost twice her age.

Maybe she had a daddy complex.

"Can we run up to the hospital tonight?" I asked Derek. "Maybe they'll have come up with some new information by now."

"We could call," Derek suggested.

We could. But—"I'd like to stop in and see how she's doing, since I didn't get a chance to go with you earlier. Maybe she's conscious."

"That's optimistic," Derek began, and then added, at a glance from his dad, "but sure. We can run up to the hospital after dinner. It's only—what?—eight miles?"

"No more than four. But I can drop you off at home first, if you want."

"No," Derek said. "If you're going, I'm going. You've gotten into enough trouble. From now on until we're married, I'm not letting you out of my sight."

"On that note," Cora said and got to her feet, "I think it's time for dessert. And then we'll talk about the wedding. Who wants cannoli?"

Everyone wanted cannoli, and five minutes later we were munching happily as the conversation drifted from blackmail and murder to wedding dresses and centerpieces. Cora informed me that she'd be doing my wedding flowers, and she'd also volunteered to help Kate with the food.

"What about the dress, Avery?" Beatrice wanted to know. "Have you decided?"

I swallowed. "I'm thinking of getting married in the blue dress I bought for Kate and Wayne's wedding. All I need is a veil and some sort of headdress. That way Derek can wear his gray suit and blue shirt, and we'll match."

"You don't want to wear white?"

"I don't have a white dress," I said, "and no time to make one. And I can't get married in an off-the-rack dress. I just can't."

Cora and her daughter shared an amused look. I added, "Besides, what am I going to do with a wedding dress after the wedding? It's not like I'll ever need it again."

"That's true," Cora admitted.

"And it isn't like it's the wedding that's important. It's what happens afterwards."

"The wedding night?" Derek said with a glint in his eyes.

I blushed even as I shook my head. "The marriage. It's getting married that matters. Not the wedding. Do you care if I get married in a blue dress?"

"You could show up in what you're wearing," Derek said, looking at my jeans and T-shirt, "and I'd marry you in a heartbeat."

Likewise.

"See?" I said. "The ceremony and the dresses and the flowers and the food, those are for everyone else. We just want to get married."

There was a beat of silence.

"In that case," Cora said, "I'm sure the blue dress will be just fine. It's practically white anyway."

"You can borrow my veil," Beatrice added. "And my gown, too, if you like. I still have it in storage. And you're right, I've never worn it again. Probably never will." She took Steve's hand. He smiled at her.

▪ ▪ ▪

"They're cute," I told Derek an hour later as we made our way out of the house on Chandler and toward the Beetle.

He glanced down at me. "Who? Beatrice and Steve? I suppose."

"It's good to see that they've worked everything out. Things were touch and go there for a while."

"Once she got kidnapped and almost died," Derek said, "Steve came around in a hurry. Nothing like mortal danger befalling the woman you love to bring a guy in line." He put an arm around my shoulders.

"You've had more than your fair share of that, haven't you?"

The arm tightened. "I have. And that's why, from here on out, I don't want you to be alone with anyone. Not even Amelia Easton or Robin. You wanna confront someone you think is dangerous, you call me first."

"Deal," I said, and unlocked the car.

. . .

Waterfield is a small town. Small enough that we don't have our own medical center. Instead, we share with the rest of the county. However, since we're the biggest town in that county, the hospital is located just outside the city limits. As Derek had said, in a roundabout way, it's roughly four miles there, and four miles back.

We were pulling into the parking lot, looking around for a space, when a pale blue minivan came screeching around the corner and darned near clipped the bumper of the Beetle before it straightened up and careened on, in the direction of the emergency room entrance.

"Stop the car!" Derek said, fumbling for the door latch.

"What? Why?"

"That's Jill's car." He had his door open and swung his legs out while we were still moving. "Just do your thing. I'll come find you."

He slammed the door and ran hell for leather across the parking lot, following the minivan. I sat there, in the middle of the lot, engine running, gaping after him.

After a moment, I pulled myself together and continued the hunt for a parking space, while my mind now worried over two different people and two widely different scenarios. Candy and her coma and recovery; Jill and her baby.

Candy hadn't looked good when they hauled her out of the basement earlier, and if Peter came barreling in here on two wheels, maybe something was wrong with Jill or the baby as well.

Or maybe not, I tried to reassure myself. Maybe she was just one of those quick birthers. Once she went into labor, it was all over in under an hour. Must be nice. If I ever had children, that's how I wanted my experience to be.

Once I got to the reception desk, I asked for Jill first, and was told she was in the process of being admitted. Yes, the desk nurse confirmed, she was in labor. No, I couldn't see her; it was family only.

"That's fine. I just saw her car in the parking lot and wanted to check. I'm really here to check on Candy . . . um . . ." What the heck was Candy's last name? I'd known her—or known about her—for more than a year; how could I not know her last name?

"Morrison?" the nurse suggested. "The girl who was brought in this afternoon?"

"That's her."

"Another neighbor?"

I nodded. "Has she had a lot of visitors?"

"She's still unconscious," the nurse said, "but yes, there's been a lot of people looking in on her. Friends, neighbors. Good thing she got here when she did. Her body was shutting down. I heard Dr. Brewer say that in another few minutes it might not have been possible to save her."

"Good thing." I swallowed at the thought of finding Candy just a few minutes after we did. If we hadn't thought to look in the community room, she would have died there, on the floor. "Can I go up and see her? Just for a minute?"

"Room 304." The nurse went back to work.

"Thank you," I told her bent head, and headed for the elevator.

Room 304 was on the third floor, and Candy must have been upgraded from critical to stable, because it wasn't part of the intensive care unit. Or maybe they'd just done everything they could for her for now, and the rest was up to Candy herself. Either way it was just a regular room, shadowed and still except for the low beeping and whirring of the machines that kept track of Candy's breaths and heartbeats. The room was empty now, but the nurse hadn't been kidding about the visitors: The windowsill was one after another of flower bouquets and potted plants, while the table next to the bed held a small stack of boxes. Chocolates and other candies, with a white teddy bear on top.

I stepped inside quietly and made my way over to the bed, peering down at her.

She was pale, her skin almost as white as the sheets. The staff had taken down her ponytail, and all that sunny yellow hair framing her face looked healthy, out of place, against the pallor of her skin and her sunken eyes and colorless lips. Her breathing was so shallow I could barely see her chest move, and the tubes and needles going into her arms and her nose and everywhere else were disturbing, but the steady *beep-beep-beep* of the machines was reassuring in a strange, sort of unreal way.

A sound from behind startled me, and when I looked up, I saw that Jamie had come into the room. She looked almost as bad as earlier, and to top it off, now her eyes were red and swollen from weeping.

"Oh," she said when she saw me, her voice tired and the words slurred. "It's you."

"Sorry. Didn't realize you were still here." The way she looked and acted, it seemed like she'd be better off in bed. Maybe I should just ask the staff nurse to wheel in another bed so Jamie could lie down there.

"I went to get another cup of coffee." She was clutching an oversized cup in a shaking hand, and her steps were unsteady.

"How is she?" I looked back at Candy.

"The same." Jamie settled into the chair beside the bed with a sound halfway between a relieved sigh and a painful groan.

"How are you feeling? Any better?"

"Weird," Jamie said. "Sort of hungover and drunk at the

same time. My head's a little fuzzy. My stomach's upset. Maybe I have the flu."

Maybe. Although the flu didn't explain what had happened to Candy. The flu doesn't throw someone into a full systemic shutdown. And besides, Jamie was stumbling over her sibilants, almost as if she were still drunk.

Maybe she had spiked her coffee with more alcohol. She sure was acting strange, and seemed to have lost a few of her inhibitions along the way, too. Then again, maybe this was the real Jamie. The one who was OK with taking her clothes off in front of strangers.

"Stupid David," she added. "This is all his fault."

"Candy's boyfriend? Has he been here?" I glanced around the room.

"The carnations are from him." Jamie gestured limply. "No card. Too chicken to put anything in writing. He didn't yesterday, either." Her voice was disgusted.

"What do you mean, yesterday?" I couldn't keep my own nose from wrinkling, although for a different reason. I don't like carnations. They're funeral flowers.

Or maybe that's just my own preconceptions. There had been carnations at my dad's funeral when I was thirteen. The smell of them still brings to mind death, almost twenty years later. That sickly sweet smell . . .

Meanwhile, Jamie must have realized I'd said something surprising. She blinked owlishly at me. "How d'you know about that?"

"David Rossini and Candy? I've seen them together a couple of times. At Guido's." And outside in the parking lot.

"He owns it," Jamie nodded. "Or so he'd like to think anyway."

"He doesn't?"

She shook her head. "Francesca's family does. That and the Pompeii. And a lot of other places. David just married into the family."

Ah. That explained a lot. Including why he'd been so upset at the thought of his wife finding out about his infidelity. If Francesca realized he'd been diddling Candy, not only would he lose his wife, his children, and his cushy lifestyle, but his father-in-law might have him outfitted with concrete shoes, too.

"Is that what you and Candy argued about on Friday?" I ventured.

Jamie blinked at me again. "How do you know about that?"

"I watched you," I said. "At the meeting in the community room Friday night. You didn't sit together. You didn't look at each other. And you didn't say good-bye when you left."

"It was my fault," Jamie said. "I found out about her and David that morning."

When she looked at the information in Miss Shaw's manila envelope, I guessed. Candy must have kept it real quiet, then, if that was the first time her own roommate realized that she was having an affair. Point to Miss Shaw for figuring it out earlier.

"I couldn't believe it," Jamie added. "It's stupid enough to get involved with a married man, you know, but her boss's husband? She could lose her job. If Francesca finds out what's going on, Candy will be lucky if that's all she loses."

I nodded encouragingly.

Jamie continued, "And she's put me in a really bad position. I work for the Rossinis, too. I like Francesca. I've babysat for her kids when she and David have gone out on dates. And now I have to choose between telling her that my roommate and her husband are getting it on, or lie about it so Candy won't call my parents and tell on me!"

She flung herself back in the chair.

"I'm sorry," I said. "Is that what happened? Candy threatened to call your folks?"

Jamie nodded.

"About the Pompeii?"

Jamie nodded again. And then—"How do you know about that?"

"You told me," I said. "Francesca Rossini's family owns Guido's Pizzeria and the Pompeii and a lot of other things. You work for them."

"Yes, but . . ." She stopped and shook her head. I guess the intricacies of the conversation were beyond her in her current condition.

"So what did you mean when you said it David's fault?"

She blinked at me again. "I said that?"

I nodded. "When I first came in. You said it was all David's fault."

"Oh." She thought for a moment and then her face cleared. "Candy talked to David on Friday night. After the meeting."

I nodded. I knew that already, but she didn't need to know that I did.

"They had an argument. And last night he sent wine and flowers and chocolates to apologize."

Pretty stupid, a small voice in my head said, *to send the stuff in his own name, if there was something wrong with it.*

"Was there a card with it?

Jamie nodded.

"With David's name on it?"

She shook her head. "The card just said *Sorry.* But who else could it be from? It wasn't me. And I don't think she'd argued with anyone else."

Right.

I glanced around the room. "Looks like a lot of other people have stopped by, too, not just David. Where did all this come from?"

Jamie looked around, too. "Candy grew up in Waterfield. She has a lot of friends. Most of the neighbors were here, and some people from school, and her mom."

"Candy's mother didn't stay?" When her daughter was in a coma and looked near death? What could be more important than that?

"They aren't close," Jamie said. "That's why Candy's living with me and not at home. And her mom had to go back to work anyway. Bruce and Robin were here, with Benjamin—they brought the bear—and William Maurits . . .”

“What about Gregg and Mariano?”

“Gregg’s here,” Jamie said. “Working. He worked on Candy. All the doctors did. I haven’t seen Mariano.”

I hadn’t seen Mariano, either. Hopefully he hadn’t made a run for the border. Seeing Derek and me at the Tremont yesterday had rattled him, I knew, but had it scared him enough to hightail it out of town?

Jamie covered a yawn with her hand, and I changed the subject.

“Amelia Easton brought you here, didn’t she? Is she coming back to take you home?”

“She’s been back,” Jamie said. “Brought me a Slushie. My favorite. Blue.” She smiled, but her eyes were at half-mast.

“Why didn’t you go home with her?”

“I didn’t want to leave Candy alone.” She glanced at the bed.

“She won’t be alone. There are nurses all over the place.” And she was in a coma, so it wasn’t like she’d know the difference. But that would sound callous, so I didn’t say it out loud. “You need to take care of yourself so you can come back tomorrow.” Especially as what had happened to Candy seemed to have affected Jamie, too, if to a much lesser degree.

She nodded. “I don’t feel so good. I think I need to sleep.”

“I can drive you home if you want. I just have to stop by the maternity ward first. A friend of Derek’s is in labor and I want to see how far along she is before I leave. You’re welcome to go with me, or do you want me to come back for you?”

Not surprisingly, Jamie elected to stay where she was until I was ready to head out.

“Can I get you anything before I go? Another cup of coffee? Something to eat?”

“I think I’ve had enough,” Jamie answered. “Stomach’s

still upset. I'm just gonna sit here and wait." She pulled one knee up to her middle and wrapped both arms around it. I guess pole dancing keeps you pretty limber.

"I'll be back in a few minutes," I said, and headed for the door.

Jamie nodded before fixing her tired eyes back on her friend.

—16—

Little Pepper Cortino was born at twelve minutes past seven, while Derek was pacing the waiting room as diligently as Peter was no doubt pacing the delivery room.

"Pepper?" I said when he told me. "That wasn't in the running, was it?"

"Late contender," Derek answered. "It seems Jill went into a sneezing fit at the dinner table, causing her water to break, and they decided to name the kid in its honor. I guess they were both ready for this one to make its appearance."

"Everyone's OK?"

"Everyone's fine." He put an arm around my shoulders and pulled me forward toward the window into the nursery. "There she is, look."

He pointed to a little bundle of joy with a pink hat on its head, tightly swaddled in a green-and-yellow blanket, blinking owlishly up from a bassinet just inside the window. The sign hanging off the end of the bed said "Cortino" and "girl." As I watched, Pepper opened her mouth and yawned, showing a small pink tongue. For a moment, she reminded me weirdly of Mischa the kitten.

"Cute," I said, although between you and me, she looked just like all the other babies I could see behind the glass: small, wrinkled, yellowish, and newborn.

"They all look the same when they're born," Derek said and turned me away from the window again toward the exit. "Anyway, Jill's fine. She's been through this enough that by now she can just squat and get the job done. The whole thing was less than an hour from start to finish."

"She's lucky." I've heard horror stories about women and labor. Twenty-four hours and counting before the baby makes its appearance. It's enough to make one seriously reconsider the whole concept of procreating.

"Women are made to give birth," Derek said. "Some have a harder time than others, but it's a natural process. Unless there's some sort of medical issue, most women don't have a problem getting through it."

"Have you ever delivered a baby?"

"By myself?" He shook his head. "But I did an ER rotation back in medical school, and we had a couple come through then. I've assisted in births. I've heard tell that afterwards, it's like the pain never happened."

Easy for him to say. He may have delivered a baby from the outside, but not the inside.

"I find that hard to believe," I said.

"It's kind of like you and the nosey parkering." He gave my shoulders a squeeze. "It's gotten you in plenty of trouble over the past year. You've almost been killed a few times. And yet every time something happens, you throw yourself headfirst into it, even if you know that this might be the time when things could go wrong."

He had me there.

He added, "So how's Candy?"

I switched mental gears. "Alive. Unconscious. Her room's full of boxes of chocolate and flowers. I told Jamie we'd give her a ride home. We have to go fetch her."

"Sure," Derek said. He pushed the button for the elevator and we stood and listened to it setting itself into motion a couple of floors above or below. "How is she?"

"She looked pretty bad. Almost as bad as Candy. Except Candy's flat on her back in bed and Jamie's walking around. Sucking down coffee. She needs to go home and rest."

"We'll get her there." Derek waited for the sliding elevator doors to part all the way before giving me a nudge. "Go ahead."

I went, and pushed the button for the third floor. We were halfway there when an alarm cut through the air.

"What the hell?" Derek said, looking around.

I did the same, my heart beating in my throat. For a second I was concerned that there was a problem with the elevator, that we'd be stuck in here for an hour or two while they worked to get us out. I'd been stuck in an elevator in a building in New York once, between the forty-seventh and forty-eighth floors, and the experience hadn't made me want to repeat it. But the elevator kept moving; the problem must be elsewhere.

After a moment, a disembodied voice came over the intercom system, faint and fuzzy from outside the doors.

"All available personnel to room 304. Repeat, all available personnel to room 304. Stat."

"That's Candy's room!" I exclaimed.

"Damn!" Derek shifted from foot to foot as he watched the elevator creep upward. It took a small eternity for the lighted number to go from 2 to 3, and then another eternity before the doors slid apart.

"Go!" He gave me a shove. I stumbled out of the elevator into the hallway and tried to get my bearings, while my stomach churned with dread. I've seen enough television to know that *"stat"* coupled with *"all available personnel"* probably meant that Candy had relapsed.

"What do you think happened?" I asked Derek breathlessly while we pounded down the hallway in the direction of Candy's room.

"Don't know. Save your breath for running." He sounded less winded than me. He was probably in better shape. And his legs are certainly longer. I concentrated on moving.

Already I could hear voices and lots of activity from Candy's room. When I got closer, I saw a half-dozen doctors, orderlies, and nurses buzzing about, the doctors in white lab coats over their scrubs, the nurses in pale blue and green. One of the lab coats contained Gregg Brewer, and I tugged his sleeve. "What happened?"

He shot me a distracted glance. "What? Oh, Avery. What are you doing here?"

"Visiting," I said, trying to peer around him to figure out what was going on.

"Get out of the way," Gregg said. "They're coming through."

He gave me a nudge. I moved, and pressed my back against the wall as a couple of nurses and orderlies pushed a bed on wheels through the door into the hallway. One of the doctors was on top of the bed, performing CPR as they went.

"One, two, three, four . . ." he counted, along with pushing down on Candy's chest.

"What happened?" I asked Gregg.

"Some sort of relapse. Or that's what it looks like. Excuse me."

He hustled after the gurney, in the wake of the other nurses and doctors. It was like a procession going down the hall, at warp speed, with the counting giving the whole thing the surreal appearance of a parade. I half expected the music to start at any moment. *A one, and a two, and a one, two, three, four . . .*

As they disappeared around the corner, still counting, I turned to Derek. "This is crazy."

He nodded, peering into the room. Jamie was still there, standing next to where the bed had been, her hands folded so hard her knuckles were showing white, with tears silently trickling down her cheeks.

"Let's get out of here," Derek said. I nodded. Since it

didn't look like Jamie would, I snagged her purse from the hook by the door on my way over to her. "C'mon. We'll go down to the ER and see what's happening, and then we'll go home."

Jamie nodded, her eyes still on the open doorway where the bed had disappeared, her stare vacant and filled with horror. I put an arm around her waist and guided her toward the hallway, asking Derek over my shoulder, "Should we call Wayne?"

"I'm pretty sure the hospital has already done that. He'll be here within the next few minutes."

I nodded and concentrated on getting Jamie out of there.

. . .

When we got downstairs, the ER was in an uproar, with doctors and nurses running frantically to and fro, doing their damndest to keep Candy alive. It looked like they weren't going to succeed. They had brought out the defibrillators, and while I watched, they tried to shock her back to life a couple of times.

"What's wrong with her?" I asked Derek, my voice shaking, and he put his arm around my shoulders and pulled me closer. His body felt warm and solid against mine, and his voice was strong and steady, bringing comfort, even if the words he said were chilling.

"I'm guessing some sort of poison. There are natural, medical reasons why someone might present with symptoms of intoxication and nausea—concussion, Bickerstaff syndrome, or even just a heavy migraine would do it—but they aren't usually followed by a full systemic shutdown. It's more likely it's some kind of drug or poison."

"She didn't do drugs," Jamie said from behind me, her voice shaking as she watched the doctors and nurses frantically trying to save Candy. "I swear. All she had was a bottle of wine last night. I had half a glass. I'm not as used to wine as she is. I had only a little, and she had the rest. Although I think there was alcohol in the chocolates, too."

Liqueur-filled, maybe.

"Wine and chocolates shouldn't be responsible for this," Derek said, I guess in an attempt to be comforting. "Not unless there was something wrong with them. Did everything taste all right?"

Jamie's bottom lip quivered, and she sank her teeth into it. "I don't know. I grew up religious. I'm not used to alcohol. It tasted strong, but alcohol always does. It wasn't bitter or anything."

"It wouldn't have to be," Derek said. "A lot of substances don't taste like anything at all. And some taste sweet. In fact . . ."

He didn't get any further, because now the double doors at the end of the hall opened and Wayne strode through, looking like a slightly older avenging angel in a uniform.

"What the hell happened?" he demanded when he was about twenty feet away. His voice was low, but vibrating with fury. Beside me, Jamie shrank back, quailing. I patted her arm and raised my voice.

"Gregg Brewer said it looked like a relapse."

Wayne shot a look through the window into the ER, where Gregg, along with everyone else, was bent over the table where Candy lay. When he turned back to Jamie, he had visibly simmered down and was making an effort to control his temper.

"Were you with her?"

Jamie nodded and swallowed. "I've been here since this afternoon. She seemed fine. She had a tube to help her breathe, you know . . ." She made a move toward her throat.

"Intubated," Derek shot in.

"But she was all right. Quiet. Sleeping."

Or unconscious, rather.

"The machines all sounded fine. Beeping. Steady. I was . . ." She flushed, looking guilty, "I think I might have dozed off. I don't feel great, either, and it's been a long day."

I patted her arm.

"I heard something, and I sat up, and the machines were going crazy and Candy was . . ." She swallowed. "She was arching off the bed. Shaking."

"Convulsing," Derek translated.

"I didn't even have time to call anyone. They came running; I guess they monitor the machines from somewhere else. They pushed me out of the way and started working on her, and then they took her out of the room and down here, and Derek and Avery came and got me . . ." She swallowed, tears trickling down her cheeks again. She was swaying, and I put my arm around her.

"Maybe we should get out of here. She needs to rest."

"Not until I know . . ." Jamie whispered and turned back to the window. In time to see everything come to a standstill. The doctor with the defibrillators lifted them from Candy's chest and took a step back. So did everyone else. For a moment, everything was frozen, like a still from a movie. Gregg Brewer looked at his watch. I could see his lips move, but I couldn't hear the words. I didn't have to, to know what he said. "Time of death, eight-oh-four P.M."

Jamie wailed, and fell on my neck, bawling into my shoulder.

"Damn," Derek said.

. . .

"This is crazy," Josh said forty minutes later. "I can't wrap my brain around it. Dad and I have lived here more than eight years, ever since my mom died. Nothing like this has ever happened before."

We'd loaded Jamie into the car, still crying, and Derek had driven us back to the condo. By the time we got there, Jamie had fallen asleep with her head on my shoulder. Rather than waking her, Derek had scooped her up and carried her the three flights of stairs up to her apartment while I ran ahead and held the doors.

Josh must have been waiting for her to come back, because as soon as he heard us outside, he swung his door open. "Jamie . . . oh."

He looked from me, to Jamie in Derek's arms, to Derek himself.

"She's out cold," Derek said. "I was just gonna put her in bed."

But somewhere along the way—perhaps when Josh had spoken—Jamie had woken up, and now she wiggled, her cheeks flushed. "I'm awake. You can put me down."

She squirmed so much that Derek almost dropped her before he managed to put her on her feet. "I'm OK," she added, taking her keys out of my hand.

"What happened?" Josh wanted to know, looking from one to the other of us again. "Jamie?"

Jamie's eyes filled with tears, and her lip started quivering.

"Candy . . ." I began, and Jamie's eyes overflowed.

"Oh, shit." Josh did the only thing he could, and hugged her. She sniffled into his chest as he gave me a helpless glance over her head. I shrugged. This was his own fault. If he hadn't slept with her in the first place, she probably wouldn't feel OK about crying on him now.

"We have to talk," I told him.

"About?"

"That envelope. The stuff Miss Shaw had."

I could see Jamie stiffen. After a second, she pushed away from Josh and glared at him, accusing. "You told her?"

"She knew already," Josh said. "Derek recognized you."

"Excuse me?" She turned to look at Derek, who shrugged.

"Bachelor party Friday night."

"Oh, great." Jamie blushed. She looked like she wasn't sure where to look—at him or me or Josh—or for that matter where to put her hands. She ended up folding her arms across her chest, in a classic defensive position.

"Don't worry," I said, "he's not imagining you naked. At least he'd better not be."

Derek grinned and put an arm around me. "No worries, Tink. I've been married before. I know the rules." He dropped a kiss on the top of my head.

I grinned back and turned to Josh. "You have to give the

stuff in the envelope to your dad. There's something going on here. Something more than just Miss Shaw being nosy. That envelope may have something to do with it." It probably did, if Miss Shaw had been murdered, too. As I assumed Candy had been. Two unexplained, suspicious deaths in the same building in just a few days were too much of a coincidence for me.

Josh looked stubborn. "It's personal stuff. None of my dad's business. Bad enough that Miss Shaw found out about it."

Jamie nodded. "What if he tells my parents where I work?"

"Why would he?" I said reasonably. "You're an adult. Maybe not in Mississippi, but here in Maine. You can make a living any way you want, as long as it's legal. And stripping was legal, last I looked."

Jamie didn't look convinced, but she didn't say anything else. I turned back to Josh.

"If it doesn't have anything to do with what's going on, he won't have to share it. But he has to know. I know you don't care who killed Miss Shaw, if someone did, but what about Candy? Don't you think someone should pay for that? And who knows if whoever it is will stop there? Who'll be next? Jamie?"

Josh glanced at her, and for a second, they wore identical expressions of horror and fear.

I pushed my advantage. "Wayne has to know. Anything that's gone on in this building, no matter how innocent it seems, might have something to do with Miss Shaw and Candy. If he doesn't have all the information, how can he figure it out?"

"But what if Shannon finds out?" His glance as Jamie was fearful, and quick enough that he missed seeing the corresponding flash of hurt that crossed her pale face. Maybe she liked him more than he liked her. To him, their encounter had been a one-night stand he didn't want the girl he loved to find out about, but maybe Jamie had hoped for more.

"Tell her," Derek said. "Keeping secrets never works. Better just to come clean and throw yourself on her mercy. Women love a man who knows how to grovel." He winked at me.

Josh looked uncertain.

"If you don't want to tell him," I said, back to Wayne again, "I will. I don't have any of the stuff Miss Shaw collected, but I do have the information. Enough of it that he can figure out the rest. But he'll have to dig for it, and it'll take time, and that's time he can use to figure out the deaths instead. It would be better just to give him what you've got. He's your dad. Don't you trust him?"

"Of course I do," Josh said. "They're not just my secrets, though."

"But you said it yourself. Most of it is innocent enough. Wayne isn't gonna care that Robin's been married before or that Jamie works as a stripper. That's not illegal. I'm sure he already knows that Bruce has a juvenile record and that Professor Easton's college roommate committed suicide. And unless Mariano moved in with Gregg in the past eight months . . ."

Jamie shook her head.

"He and Wayne lived in the same building for a while. Wayne must have suspected that Mariano is working without a permit. If he didn't say anything about it before, why would he say anything about it now? He isn't ICE. And Candy . . ."

Jamie sniffed, and Josh sent her a wary glance. Maybe he was afraid she was going to start bawling and latch on to him again.

I included Jamie in my next statement. "It's too late to protect Candy, or even try to keep things quiet for Francesca Rossini's sake. Wayne needs to know what was going on."

Jamie looked tearful, but she nodded. I turned to Josh, who sighed.

"Fine. But I'm not going to spring it on them without warning. The least we can do is let them know what Miss

Shaw knew, and that the police will probably want to talk to them about it."

After a second's hesitation, he added, "They should hear about Candy anyway. As soon as possible."

I glanced at my watch. Just after nine. Most of the neighbors were probably still up. Gregg wasn't even here. Mariano might not be, either. I hadn't seen him all day, and I hadn't noticed whether the Jeep was there in the parking lot when we arrived.

"I'll go door to door with you," Derek said.

"Me, too," Jamie added.

"Are you sure you don't want to go to bed? You look beat."

She shook her head. "She was my friend. I need to do this."

Very well, then. We turned toward the stairs and started climbing.

—17—

We started with Bruce and Robin Mellon. I could hear the TV going when we stood outside the door—something that sounded like Barney the Dinosaur or similar—but when I knocked, the sound was muted. Tiny feet pattered toward the door, followed by heavier ones. "Hold on, son," Bruce's voice said. "Let me get the chain for you first."

I heard the sound of the lock sliding back and the chain rattling, and then the door was opened. Slowly, as Benjamin exerted all his efforts. When the door opened, they both looked at us, Bruce over Benjamin's head.

The boy was dressed in little footie pajamas with pictures of tiny, green crocodiles wearing sunhats, and he looked too precious for words, with his big, dark eyes and shock of black hair. Bruce, meanwhile, looked a little less precious, with his shaved head, his pierced ears, and his black T-shirt with Gothic symbols on it.

"Hi," I said. "I'm Avery."

Bruce nodded. "I know who you are."

This was the first time I'd actually spoken to him, or even seen him up close, and he was bigger than I'd realized. At least as tall as Derek and beefier. One big hand was wrapped around a bottle, the nails grimy with what was probably motor oil or other engine fluids he wasn't able to get rid of anymore. Though I expected beer, the bottle turned out to be green tea.

He looked from me to Jamie, next to me, and then to Derek and Josh, behind us. Eventually his eyes, pale blue, came back to me, questioning.

"Can we come in? There's something we'd like to talk about." I smiled.

Bruce hesitated for a second, but eventually he stepped back. I stepped forward, across the threshold and into a condo that was the exact replica of my own, except for the decor. Behind me, Jamie moved across the threshold, followed by Josh and Derek.

Either Bruce or Robin must like color, because the hallway was a bright burnt orange. The kitchen was sunny yellow, and the bathroom was bright blue. I could see a shower curtain with colorful tropical fish through the half-open door, as well as a little red stepstool that must be there to help Benjamin reach the sink. I thought I'd heard somewhere that primary colors are good for the development of babies' brains, so maybe that was why Bruce and Robin had painted everything in such bright colors: to stimulate Benjamin's brain activity. Or perhaps it was just because the little boy enjoyed it.

"This way." Bruce walked to the door into the living room and gestured us through. I put some hustle in my step and headed that way.

Again, the room was an exact match to our own, but while ours was a mess of tools and materials right now, Bruce and Robin's was a mess of toys and other stuff. Parenting magazines were spread across the surface of the coffee table, Benjamin's toys littered the floor, and there were colorful balls of yarn everywhere, as well as what looked like a half-finished sweater on knitting needles in a corner of the sofa. The sofa itself had seen better days: It was a big, black leather couch that looked something like the front seat in an old truck, and it was cracked and faded in places. It looked like Bruce might have owned it since before Robin moved in and attempted to put her feminine touches on the place.

She was sitting at the dining room table, a cheap pressed wood and white laminate construction, doing some sort of craft. When we walked through the door, she looked up, and the smile turned to a puzzled sort of look when she recognized me. When the others came in behind me, and she recognized Josh and Jamie, the puzzlement changed to fear.

I opened my mouth, but before I got the first word out, she'd gotten to her feet.

"Why don't you go watch TV in Mommy and Daddy's room, Benjamin?"

Benjamin looked obstinate—he was already watching TV here, and besides, he probably didn't want to miss out on any of the adult fun—and Robin added temptingly, "I'll get you a special snack."

The special snack did the trick. Benjamin trotted off to the bedroom door, dragging a stuffed giraffe behind him by the neck. His own neck was twisted so he could keep his eyes glued to the television screen in the living room, where Barney the Purple Dinosaur and his friends were singing about popcorn. *Pop-pop-pop-popcorn is really neat; fun to make and fun to eat . . .*

Welcome, earworm.

"That stuff's like crack," Bruce muttered, as if he'd read my mind.

"Popcorn?"

He shook his head. "Barney. I swear, there's subliminal messages all over that show."

Robin hid a smile. She went to the kitchen and came back a minute later with one of those kiddie cups with a spout, filled with fluorescent green liquid, and a plate with a few chocolate chip cookies.

"Not too many," Bruce warned, "or he'll throw up."

Robin nodded. "I know." She ducked into the bedroom—

I caught a glimpse of dark blue walls and a striped duvet before she pulled the door shut behind her—and after a moment, the TV kicked on in there and Barney continued to drill a hole in my head.

A few seconds later Robin was back out, and shut the door gently. "Now we have a chance at a little bit of privacy for a few minutes. Have a seat." She gestured to the living room. Bruce and I perched awkwardly on the leather sofa with Jamie, while Derek leaned behind me. Until Bruce carried two chairs over from the dining room table and nodded to one. "Have a seat. So what's going on?"

Robin brought the last chair over and placed it next to Bruce's, as close as she could get to him without actually touching, before sitting down. She twined her skinny legs around the chair legs, pretzel-like.

Josh glanced at me. I looked back at him. They were his neighbors; he knew them better than I did. This news shouldn't come from me.

"Candy's dead," Jamie said.

Robin shot the bedroom door a wide-eyed look, probably afraid that Benjamin had overheard. "What?"

"It's true," I said. "She died about an hour ago. Still in the hospital. Complications from whatever was wrong this afternoon."

Bruce leaned back, and the cheap chair complained. "What was wrong this afternoon?"

When nobody answered, he looked at Derek. "You're a doctor, right?"

"I used to be. Retired my license six or seven years ago. Ben Ellis is my dad."

Bruce nodded. "What was wrong with her?"

"It looked like some kind of poisoning. Ethylene glycol maybe."

"Shit," Bruce said, and shot a guilty look at the bedroom door.

I turned to Derek. "What's ethylene glycol?"

He glanced at me. "Antifreeze. Highly poisonous, easy to come by, for sale in gas stations everywhere. Tastes sweet and mimics the effects of alcohol. It's often used in suicide attempts, less frequently in murders, but it's been known to happen."

"You've seen it before?"

"Once," Derek said. "I was still in medical school. The police had hauled this guy in for intoxication. When he went into cardiac arrest in the back of the police car, they drove him to the ER instead of the drunk tank."

"What happened to him?"

"It was too late by the time they got there," Derek said. "We couldn't get him back." His expression lightened. "They got the wife, though."

"She'd ingested antifreeze, too?"

He shook his head. "She'd given it to him. In his orange juice. She's serving twenty-five to life in some prison somewhere now."

"So she was trying to kill him?"

"Oh, yeah. Ethylene glycol is colorless, odorless, sweet-tasting, and extremely easy to come by. It's the perfect murder weapon, as long as you're able to administer a big enough dose. Mix it with something sweet, and people won't even notice they're drinking it. Most of us have a bottle of it sitting around at home or in the car, and if we don't, we can go to the auto parts store or a gas station and pick up a bottle."

"Yow." Who'd have thought something so toxic was so easy to acquire?

"I know," Derek said.

We sat in silence for a few seconds.

"We also wanted to talk to you about something else," Josh said eventually. "Although I wonder . . ."

He glanced at me. It didn't take special powers to read his mind. I'd wondered, too, and now I wished we'd planned this a little better. Bruce's wild youth wasn't a secret to the people of Waterfield, many of whom had watched him in action, but Robin wasn't from here, and it was possible he hadn't seen the need to tell her. And although I would certainly have made sure to tell my second husband about my first one, if I'd had one, we couldn't be sure that Bruce knew about Robin's previous marriage, either.

"Robin," I said, getting to my feet, "would you mind showing me your kitchen?"

"My kitchen?" Robin repeated with a glance at Bruce. He scowled at me.

"What's this about?"

Josh cleared his throat and drew their attention. "Before she died, Miss Shaw had gathered some information about her neighbors. All of us. Even Derek and Avery."

Bruce and Robin exchanged a glance. "OK," Bruce said.

"The night after she died, Jamie and I"—Josh shot a look at her—"went through her apartment. And found it."

"It?"

"An envelope. Full of dirt she'd dug up on everyone in the building."

Nobody said anything. In the silence, Bruce wrapped his thick fingers around Robin's slender ones and held on. It must have been a signal of some sort, or maybe Robin just decided to stop pretending. When she looked up and across the table at us, her eyes were steady. "If this is about Guy, Bruce knows all about him."

Ah. Well, that made things easier. I don't think I was the only one who breathed a sigh of relief. In fact, I'm pretty sure I could see Josh become visibly less tense.

"I have no idea why she'd care," he said apologetically. "It's nobody's business if you've been married once, or twice, or even three times . . ."

"Once."

"But with everything that's going on, we need to . . . what?"

Robin's eyes were still steady, even as a wave of hot color crept into her pale cheeks. "I've only been married once."

"But . . ." We all looked at Bruce. Unless he'd changed his name from Guy, something wasn't right.

"I'm still married to Guy," Robin added.

Bruce rolled his eyes. "Way to go, Roberta."

"But . . . I thought the two of you were married."

So much for our impression that the information in the envelope was harmless. Robin having a previous marriage to Guy, and a new one to Bruce, was way different from Robin being married to both of them at the same time. Divorce isn't a crime, no, but bigamy sure is.

Robin shook her head. "I can't divorce Guy. If I file for divorce, he'll figure out where I am. I might even have to go back to Mobile." The way she pronounced the name of the town, returning there sounded like a fate worse than death.

"Bad marriage?"

"You have no idea," Bruce said grimly. He was still holding Robin's hand, the gentle way he stroked the back of it in harsh contrast to his voice and the expression on his face.

"Did you know that Miss Shaw knew about it?"

They both nodded. "She liked to let people know that she knew things about them," Robin whispered, echoing John Nickerson.

"It wasn't any of her damn business—" Bruce began. But his voice broke, and his other hand, the one that wasn't holding Robin's, clenched into a fist on his thigh. "Somehow she got it in her head that Benjamin would be better off with his proper father. Like Guy gave a damn!"

Robin nodded. "I got pregnant out of wedlock," she explained. "His mother made Guy 'do the right thing—'" Her soft voice twisted as she said the words. "But his heart wasn't in it. He'd just wanted to have some fun, he hadn't expected me to get pregnant, and being tied down didn't suit him at all. It wasn't long before he started taking his frustrations out on me."

"You mean he hit you?"

She nodded, and Bruce's expression darkened further.

"It wasn't so bad while I was pregnant," Robin continued. "His mother would have killed him if he did anything to hurt the baby. But after Benjamin was born, and I was tired all the time, and Jamin had colic and cried all night, and Guy had to stay home instead of going out with his friends . . . that's when it got bad. I stood it as long as I could, and then I left."

"Why didn't you report him to the police and have him arrested?" That's what I would have done. Not taken my baby and fled.

"I was afraid," Robin said simply. Bruce patted her hand. "The Quinns are an important family, while I was some little upstart from the wrong side of the tracks who everyone thought had gotten myself in the family way so Guy would marry me." She made a face. "The mayor was Guy's uncle. The chief of police used to bounce him on his knee when he was little. I knew nothing would happen to Guy in Mobile."

"How did you end up in Maine?"

"I drove to New Orleans," Robin said, "and sold the car at a used car lot. I thought it would make Guy lose the trail. If he bothered to look for me at all, that is."

I nodded. Around me, Josh, Jamie, and Derek were also listening intently.

"From there, I took a train to Chicago, and another train to Boston. I didn't want to fly because there would be a record of my name if I did."

"Why Boston?"

"It was where the train stopped," Robin said. "And it was as far away from Mobile as I could get without going out West."

"And Maine?"

Robin blushed and shot a glance at Bruce. He picked up the story.

"Robin and I met in Boston. She was looking for a car, and a friend of mine has a used car lot. I happened to be there when she came in."

"I freaked out a little when I realized I had to fill out paperwork," Robin said softly. "I didn't want my name recorded anywhere, just in case Guy came looking for me. For Benjamin." She looked over at the closed bedroom door. Behind it, I could hear Winnie the Pooh singing about being short and fat and proud of that.

"We got to talking," Bruce said, "and Robin put up the money while I put my name on the registration. I gave her my phone number and told her to call if she needed anything. Two days later she did."

Robin was still blushing, and the look she slanted at Bruce was almost shy. "He was so nice. And he'd already been so helpful. I felt bad about imposing any more than I already had, but I didn't know what else to do. I needed a job, but I was afraid to apply anywhere, since I thought they'd want to check references, and—"

"You didn't want Guy to find out."

She nodded. "So I called Bruce and asked him if he knew of something I could do, maybe under the table. I ended up telling him the whole story. He told me to drive up to Waterfield and we'd figure something out."

"She spent a couple of months living in the spare bedroom with Benjamin," Bruce said. "I have a job, enough to pay the bills, and she doesn't eat much."

He grinned at Robin, who smiled back, a little tremulously.

"Eventually we decided to try to make something more of it. That's when we bought the rings and started telling people we were married. Robin needed a new name, just in case Guy was still looking for her."

Robin nodded. "Guy couldn't care less about me, or for that matter about Benjamin, but he's still Jamin's biological father, and he and his mother have a lot more money and power than we do. If they want Benjamin back, they can cause a lot of trouble for us."

"And Miss Shaw figured that out?"

Bruce nodded. "I don't know how, but she stopped me going upstairs one day, waving that damn paper in my face and asking if I knew that my 'wife' was already married to another man. Guess she thought Robin hadn't told me."

"What did you do?" I asked.

His face darkened. "Threatened to rip her tongue out if she caused any more trouble."

Derek smiled faintly. I swallowed. "That would have been good enough for me."

Bruce shrugged. "Musta been for her, too, I guess, 'cause I never heard about it again. And Guy never showed his face around here."

Probably a good thing for Guy, since I was pretty sure Bruce would have rearranged it for him if he had.

We sat in silence another few seconds. Again, it was Josh who broke it. "I'm really sorry, but I have to give the envelope with the stuff to my dad."

Both Robin and Bruce looked ready to interrupt, but he continued before they could. "If someone's going around killing the people in the building, I can't not share it with him. It might be relevant. And I want to stop this person, whoever it is, before someone else dies."

"Wayne isn't unreasonable," I added. "He's a nice guy. He'll understand your situation. And it's not like you've done anything illegal. You didn't really commit bigamy; you're just pretending to be married. Just tell him the truth. He might even have something to suggest for how you could divorce Guy for real."

Robin didn't look convinced, but she nodded.

"Sorry to be the bearer of bad news," Josh added and got to his feet. "We'll leave you guys alone. Sorry to spring it all on you. I just . . . *we* just"—he took in the rest of us with a glance—"we wanted you to have fair warning. So that when Dad shows up to talk to you, you'll know what happened."

Bruce nodded. "We appreciate it. Let me see you out."

He herded us toward the front door while Robin made a beeline for the bedroom and Benjamin. I guess she probably felt the need to see him and hug him and reassure herself that he was there, and whole, and hers. I know that's what I would have wanted to do.

"You gonna visit everyone in the building tonight?"

Bruce asked as we filed past him out of the apartment and into the stairwell.

Josh nodded. "Pretty much, yeah."

"She dig up dirt on other people, too?"

"Everyone in the building."

Bruce nodded. "Good luck."

"Thanks." Hopefully the rest of the visits wouldn't turn out to be as surprising as this one had been.

. . .

Across the landing, we knocked on Amelia Easton's door and stood back to wait. We could hear music from inside, 1980s techno-pop or something like it, and when Amelia came to open the door, she looked happy and relaxed, too, in jeans and a bright turquoise T-shirt, with her hair down, a big balloon glass of something pale green and slushy in her hand—frozen Margarita?—and her feet bare with matching turquoise polish. Hardly the statement I'd expect from a staid professor of history.

Of course, the happiness slipped right off her face when she saw us. Her eyes turned wary and the corners of her mouth drew down. "What's wrong?"

And then she noticed Jamie, and must have realized what had happened. "Oh, no. Candy?"

We nodded. Jamie's eyes filled with tears again.

"That's terrible," Amelia said. "Any idea what happened?"

Since Derek was the one who had tackled the answer to that question last time, we left it to him to bring her up to speed. I was a bit surprised when he simply said, "Heart failure."

But Amelia didn't question it, just nodded. She seemed to have realized she was holding a ginormous glass of alcohol, and I could see her eyes flicker as she looked for somewhere to put it down.

"Can we come in for a minute?" Jamie asked. "We need to talk about something."

Amelia hesitated, but it wasn't like she could say no, really. "Of course." She stood aside to let us in.

"Thank you." We filed into the hallway and looked around.

Here, everything was a mirror image of the apartment across the hall, and of ours downstairs. The kitchen was right instead of left, the living room left instead of right.

But unlike Amelia herself, who was bland to the point of boring—at least when she wasn't barefoot—the place was full of color and excitement. The walls in the hallway were light purple, with tasteful black-and-white landscapes in black frames flanking a beautiful sunburst mirror. The bathroom had been updated with marble tile and what looked like a big soaking tub, and the kitchen had white high-end cabinets with glass fronts, a bright blue counter, and stainless steel appliances. It was gorgeous, especially against the big bowl of oranges sitting on the counter.

"Wow." I looked around. "This is beautiful."

"Thank you." Her voice was sort of toneless. Usually people get excited when you compliment them on their homes, but Amelia was more stiff. But maybe she was just worried about the other shoe dropping. The shoe Jamie had intimated was coming when she'd said we had something else to discuss. "Why don't we sit down in the living room?"

She led the way without waiting for our answer.

Like the kitchen, hallway, and bath, the living room/dining room combo was gorgeous, and bespoke excellent taste, enough money to indulge it, and a love of luxury and fine things, albeit in a more personal—and less ostentatious—way than in the Rossinis' home. There, there'd clearly been a designer at work. Here, it looked like Amelia had lovingly put it all together herself. The floors were polished hardwood, and two Persian rugs defined and separated the living room and dining room areas. The dining room set was upscale modern: dark wood with simple Quakerish lines and tasteful seat cushions. A huge flower arrangement sat in the middle of the table: what looked like at least two dozen calla lilies in a hand-blown glass vase. Both flowers and vase must have cost a small fortune, separately or together. I'd priced calla lilies for my wedding bouquet, and they don't come cheap. Nor does art glass.

The living room sofa and chairs were leather, but that was the only thing they had in common with Bruce and Robin's cracked couch across the hall. This stuff was the color of eggplant, and looked brand-new. When we sat down, it was like sinking into a mound of pillows. The leather didn't even squeak.

"This is gorgeous," I said, stroking it. It was as soft as butter, or the proverbial baby's bottom.

"Thank you." Amelia didn't sound any more excited about that compliment than she'd been about the previous one. "What's going on?" She took the matching chair while the four of us made ourselves comfortable on the sectional. It was plenty big for all of us.

Jamie glanced at Josh and Josh glanced at Jamie. It was a tiny bit disconcerting to watch them, since I had the impression that if it hadn't been for Shannon, Josh and Jamie might have been very happy together.

"It's about Miss Shaw," Jamie said eventually, turning back to Amelia.

Amelia looked wary. "Yes?"

"Remember I told you about Miss Shaw finding out about my job and threatening to call my parents? And remember that envelope of information I told you we found in Miss Shaw's condo after she died?"

Jamie didn't wait for Amelia's nod. "It didn't have just information about Candy and me in it. There was stuff about everyone in the building. The two of us, Josh, Robin and Bruce, Mariano . . . even Avery and Derek."

Amelia glanced at me. "What kind of information?"

"Jamie's job," I said, sticking to the things I figured she already knew about. "Candy's affair. My aunt's death." She might not know about that last one, but I didn't care if she found out. Better I talk about that than any of the other neighbors.

"Now that Candy's dead," Jamie continued, "the police need that information. I don't want to believe that her boyfriend or his wife did something to her—but someone did." She sniffed. "She was always so healthy, at least until she drank that stupid wine he sent."

"Of course," Amelia said. "It's all right, Jamie. Candy can't be hurt by anything we do anymore. What we need to do now is help the police figure out who did this to her."

Jamie nodded. "That's why we're going to give the police the envelope tomorrow. With everything in it. We just wanted to let you know."

Amelia nodded, but I thought she looked a little confused, or perhaps "concerned" is a better word.

"We wanted to warn you," I tried to explain, "in case Wayne brings up that old story about your college roommate again. That information was in the envelope, too. I guess maybe Miss Shaw didn't realize it was common knowledge. Maybe she thought there was something more sinister to it than there was."

Amelia shook her head. "It was nothing more or less than it looked like. A terrible tragedy, and a great personal loss. I loved her, in spite of her failings. I'm just sorry her weaknesses caused her death." She sighed.

We sat in respectful silence for a few seconds until I got to my feet. "Is this her?"

It was a small strip of photographs, the kind you get out of a photo booth, tucked away in a corner of the shelving unit, sharing space with a few strategically placed books—chosen more for their looks than for Amelia's enjoyment of them, I thought—another glass vase, a few glass animals—birds—and other knickknacks. Other than the landscapes on the wall in the hallway, clearly professional quality, these were the only photographs I'd seen since entering Amelia Easton's apartment.

Amelia nodded. When I picked up the strip for a closer look, I think she twitched a little, but I might have been mistaken.

The pictures showed two young women around the age of twenty squeezed into a photo booth together, mugging for the camera. Or at least one of them was. I recognized Amelia's face, even with her eyes crossed and her tongue sticking out. Her hair was longer then, thick and wavy, down past her shoulders, not pulled back in that no-nonsense knot she wore these days, and a pair of chandelier earrings almost the size of the real thing decorated her earlobes.

The other girl must be the dead roommate. They looked a lot alike, actually. Same round, unfinished face, same big eyes. Both were brunettes, but Nan had curlier hair she kept pulled back so only a few wisps framed her face. I understood that compulsion; curls—like kinks—can be hard to tame. No earrings for her, but she was wearing a crucifix on a chain around her neck. The same crucifix, or one identical, was curled next to the strip of pictures. The links pressed into my fingertips when I picked it up.

The crucifix was engraved, I realized. With a date and a name. The date was from the mid-1980s—maybe a confirmation or the Christian equivalent of a Bat Mitzvah, when Amelia had been thirteen or fourteen?—and was engraved on the crossbeam, while the name ran vertically down the shaft.

"We each got one," Amelia said, looking over my shoulder. "All the girls did. Confirmation gift."

"I have one, too," Jamie said from behind us. As I put the photograph back down on the shelf, she added hesitantly, "I know it's not my place to tell you what to do, Professor Easton, but you should consider going back for a visit. It's a different place now. At least that's what my mom says."

How different could it be, I wondered, if parents still threatened to drag their grown children back home by the hair if they strayed too far from the straight and narrow?

And then I caught on, a few seconds belatedly. "I didn't realize you two came from the same place." Judging from Josh's expression, he hadn't realized it, either.

"The same congregation," Jamie said. "Although Professor Easton had left by the time I was born, I think."

She turned back to Amelia. "There's no commune anymore, you know. That happened soon after . . ."

She trailed off. "Anyway, we live all over now. In normal houses in normal neighborhoods. The kids get immunized, just like all the other kids. We have medical records and dental records and birth certificates. I went to a regular school. A private Christian school, so it was stricter than the state schools, but I had friends who weren't part of our congregation. My parents even let me go on group dates once I turned sixteen. It isn't like it used to be."

Amelia nodded, but it didn't look like she believed it. Or if she did, it certainly didn't look like she'd ever consider going back, even for a visit. If I'd narrowly escaped a place like that, I'm not sure I would have, either. It must be just as stifling and horrible as Robin's bad marriage.

And none of this was any of our business. It was obvious we were making Amelia uncomfortable. We'd done what we came for. I got to my feet. "We should get going. We still have to tell the rest of the neighbors the news. Thank you for inviting us in."

Since she couldn't say it was her pleasure, Amelia simply nodded. "Thank you for stopping by to let me know about Candy. I'm sorry it ended that way. I hoped, since she got to the hospital in time, she might have a chance."

"She hung on for a while," Derek said as we made our way toward the front door. "But her system was just too compromised, I guess. The damage was already done by the time we got to the hospital. It was just a matter of time. But at least we can take some comfort in the fact that she didn't suffer."

"She didn't?" Jamie's eyes were huge in her pale face, and begging for reassurance.

"No," Derek said gently, "she didn't. She was beyond feeling anything at all the whole time she was in the hospital. From when we found her in the basement until she died, she didn't feel a thing. At least that's one thing to be grateful for."

Jamie nodded and bit her lip. When her eyes overflowed again, we all pretended not to notice.

—18—

"Two down," Josh said when we were outside in the stairwell, with Amelia Easton's door closed and locked behind us, "and two to go." He sounded as exhausted as I felt.

I nodded. "This is a lot harder than I thought it would be." However, it was also a lot more enlightening. I turned to Jamie. "I had no idea you and Professor Easton knew each other from before."

"We didn't," Jamie said and wiped her eyes with the back of her hand. "I'd never seen her before I came here last year. She left Mississippi when she was eighteen, and she never came back."

"Is that why you applied to Barnham? Because you knew she'd be here?"

Jamie shook her head, carefully navigating the stairs. Josh kept a hand under her elbow to steady her. "Professor Easton only got this job because the history professor that was here died unexpectedly. I'd applied to Barnham long before that happened. It was one of a handful of schools my parents approved of. Small college, small town, conservative values, no more than a three-hour plane ride away."

"But you knew who she was, right? You'd heard of her."

"Of course," Jamie said. If she had added *you idiot* to the end of the sentence, she couldn't have made her feelings any plainer. "It was one of those horror stories parents tell their children, about what can happen if you aren't careful and don't do as you're told."

"You die?"

Jamie shrugged. "My mother knew Nan. And Amelia. Whenever I behaved badly as a child, my mom always said, 'Don't do that. You don't want to end up like Nan Barbour.'"

Fantastic. Nanette had become the local bogeyman. Probably not what she'd hoped for when she went off to college full of hopes and dreams.

By now we'd reached the third-floor landing, and Jamie glanced at her own door.

"Maybe you should go rest," I said. "It's been a long day."

Jamie hesitated. She was clearly exhausted, but I guess maybe she didn't want to leave the rest of us in the lurch.

"It's OK," Josh said, and put a hand on her shoulder. "You need to take care of yourself. We can do the rest of this on our own."

"You sure?" She glanced up at him.

"Positive." He nodded. "Go ahead. We've got this."

"If you're sure you don't mind." Jamie fumbled in her purse for her key. "I really am tired." When she got it out, Josh had to help her get the key into the lock.

"Would you like some help?" I asked when she pushed the door open. I was honestly concerned that she wouldn't make it to the bed, but would simply collapse on the living room floor.

She hesitated a moment, and glanced at Josh, then at Derek, then back at Josh again, before she shook her head. "I'm fine, thank you."

That was clearly a lie, but we had other things to do, so if she said she was fine, I was willing to take her word for it.

"We'll see you tomorrow, then. Sleep well."

Jamie nodded. The last thing I saw before she closed the door were her eyes fastened on Josh's face.

. . .

"When we finish here," Derek said, his voice low, as we made our way down to the next floor, "find somewhere else to spend the night."

"Huh?" Josh glanced at him.

"Go stay with Shannon. Or sleep in your car. Hell, you can come home with us if you want. But don't go back upstairs."

Josh blinked. "Why?"

"Because in an hour or so, your doorbell's gonna ring, and it's gonna be Jamie, and she's gonna tell you that she can't sleep, that she just can't stop thinking about Candy, that the apartment feels so empty, that she's afraid to be alone . . . and because you're a nice guy, you'll offer to stay with her—on the sofa, of course—and thirty minutes after that, you'll hear her crying, so you'll go check on her, and then one thing will lead to another, and before you know it—"

"OK," Josh said, his cheeks flushed. "I got it. You can stop now."

Derek nodded. "Do yourself a favor, and just spend the night somewhere else. Problem solved."

"Right." Josh's ears were a bright red. When he knocked on Mariano and Gregg's door, it was with the expression of a man who feels wolves snapping at his heels. Derek grinned but didn't comment.

For a minute I wasn't sure we'd get an answer from 2B. Gregg, presumably, was still at the hospital, maybe pulling a twenty-four-hour shift—Derek had told me how he'd done that, too, as a resident—and I didn't know where Mariano was. But after waiting, and knocking again, the door was opened a crack and Mariano peered out.

"Yes?" He looked from Josh to me to Derek and back.

"Can we come in for a minute?" Josh asked. "Something we want to talk about."

Mariano hesitated, but I guess he couldn't really in good conscience say no. He stepped aside and we filed past.

Like Amelia, he was in jeans and T-shirt, with his feet bare. His nails weren't painted, but he had a silver ring on his big toe, which matched the one he wore on his thumb. His hair was damp, curling at the neck and around the ears, and he smelled clean and musky. I deduced he'd just come out of the shower.

The apartment looked like Amelia's, but it was decorated in shades of sand, brown, and black, and everything looked a bit less expensive. I guess a medical resident and a waiter weren't quite at the point where they could afford arrangements of calla lilies and hand-blown glass yet.

The sofa was overstuffed and looked comfy, but there was only one, facing a big screen TV, so we ended up at the round dining room table.

"You missed all the excitement earlier," I said in an effort to start the conversation on a light note.

So much for that. Mariano's face darkened. "I heard."

"Gregg called you?" Josh asked.

Mariano nodded. "I was hiking. Thinking." He glanced at me and Derek, and then just as quickly away. "Fretting. I like to hike when Gregg's working double shifts. It's something to pass the time."

This was the first time I'd heard him say more than a few words, and he had a light tenor voice with a slight Hispanic accent. A bit like Antonio Banderas.

"What were you fretting about?" I accompanied the question with a sweet smile, hoping it might make it seem less like I was interrogating him, but no such luck. His eyes—pretty and brown with long lashes—narrowed.

"Things."

Right. "I thought maybe you were worried about us seeing you at the Tremont the other night. Because of the name tag and all."

Mariano threw his hands up. "Why do you ask, if you already know the answer? *Dios mio!* We thought, when that old *bruja* Miss Shaw died—"

"Witch," Derek told me out of the corner of his mouth. I nodded.

Mariano shot us both a jaundiced look. "—we wouldn't have any more problems. And then you came along!"

"We haven't caused any problems for you," I protested.

"Yet."

He had a point there. Especially as we were here for the express purpose of causing those problems.

I glanced at Josh, who took over the conversation. Mariano knew him better; maybe it would help. "You said Gregg called you from the hospital?"

Mariano nodded.

"Then you know about Candy."

Mariano nodded again, those big, dark eyes limpid with sadness.

Josh leaned forward, elbows on the table. "We—my dad—is pretty sure someone did it on purpose. Just like someone might have killed Miss Shaw on purpose."

Mariano blinked.

"We have to give Dad all the information Miss Shaw had dug up on all the neighbors. There might be something in there that can help him figure out what's going on."

Mariano opened his mouth, thought better of what he was going to say, and closed it again. "I'll get deported," he said.

He was actually more likely to go to jail, I thought—Social Security fraud is a crime, after all—but like Mariano, I thought better than to voice what I was thinking. That little wrinkle wasn't likely to make him feel any better at the moment.

"Sorry," Josh said. "But people are dead. If we don't figure out why, someone else might die. I don't want it to be me. And I'm sure you don't want it to be you. Or Gregg."

Mariano shook his head.

"I'll talk to Dad, try to convince him that it's not his job to police the borders. That's what the ICE does. And he did live here with you for a while. I imagine it might not come as a total surprise."

Mariano shook his head again, but he did look a little bit better.

"Just hang tight," Josh said. "And if things get really bad, you can always run away to Massachusetts and get married."

"We plan to. After Gregg finishes his residency." Mariano tapped his lips with a well-manicured finger. "But if we have to, I guess we could do it sooner. Set up residence in Massachusetts. Get married. Gregg could commute to Waterfield for five days and come home for two. It would be difficult, but we could probably make it work."

He looked across the table at Josh, happy again, and looking for reassurance that his plan was a good one. Josh nodded and got to his feet.

"We appreciate your time. We just wanted to tell you about Candy, if you hadn't heard already, and to let you know that I'll be passing the information from Miss Shaw on to my dad in the morning."

Mariano got to his feet, too. "I'll let Gregg know when he comes home. Tomorrow."

Derek and I followed suit. "Thank you for your time," I said as we headed for the door. Mariano didn't answer. I suppose it was possible that he didn't hear me, but I got the impression that he just didn't like me much and might have preferred to ignore my presence.

"He had reason to kill Miss Shaw," I said when we were outside in the stairwell and our footsteps were masking the sound of my voice. "She knew that he's an illegal alien. If she threatened to call ICE, he could have killed her."

Derek murmured something. It wasn't an objection, so I ignored it.

"He works in food service; putting something in her food probably seemed like the logical thing to do. And Gregg's a doctor. He would have realized the need to take her EpiPen so she couldn't give herself the antidote. He could have taken it to work with him and disposed of it there. I'm sure there's all sorts of medical waste sitting around the hospital. And he could have arranged for whatever killed Candy, too. It might not have been the ethyl . . . whatever."

"Ethylene glycol," Derek said.

"It could have been something else. I'm sure there are lots of substances that would cause those same symptoms. Right?"

Derek nodded. "Plenty of things could cause those symptoms. Some of them things that would only be available to a doctor."

"He even worked on her. If he did want her dead, he was in a perfect position to make sure she died."

"Yes, Avery," Derek said, "but why would he want her dead? Why would either of them want Candy dead? Miss Shaw maybe. But why Candy?"

I shrugged. "Maybe she knew they'd killed Miss Shaw. Maybe she threatened them."

"Wouldn't they just have threatened her back?" Josh said. "She was sleeping with Rossini and trying to keep it a secret."

"They may not have known that. She actually managed to keep it pretty quiet. Jamie didn't even know, and she and Candy were roommates."

"How do you know that?" Josh wanted to know.

I turned to him. "She told me. Earlier tonight, in Candy's hospital room."

"You didn't tell me this," Derek said.

"I guess I didn't think it was important. And we were busy looking at Pepper Cortino."

I turned back to Josh. "When the two of you found the envelope the other morning, that was the first time Jamie realized Candy was sleeping with David Rossini. She may have known that Candy was involved with somebody, but if she did, she didn't know who. And she was upset when she found out. She works for Francesca Rossini, and she told me she likes Francesca. She thought Candy put her in a bad position. And then, when she confronted Candy about it, Candy threatened to call Jamie's parents and tell them about the Pompeii if Jamie told Francesca about Candy and her husband carrying on."

There was a beat of silence.

"As far as I can tell," Derek said, "that gives Jamie a better motive than Gregg and Mariano. Miss Shaw threatens to call Jamie's parents, and Miss Shaw ends up dead. Then Candy threatens to call Jamie's parents, and Candy ends up dead."

Josh was shaking his head, but Derek kept going.

"None of the neighbors would have had too hard a time getting into Miss Shaw's apartment, and Jamie especially looks young and harmless. She could have poisoned Miss Shaw. Peanuts are easy to come by. They serve them at the Pompeii too, so if she didn't want to risk buying her own, she could have just pocketed a few. And she had every opportunity to doctor the wine and chocolates. For all we know, she uncorked the bottle and poured the glasses. Hell, she even made sure she only drank enough to make herself a little bit sick, while leaving enough for Candy to make sure Candy died. And didn't you say she was in the room with Candy when it happened? Alone?"

I nodded. She had been. Completely alone, with no supervision.

Josh shook his head. "No," he said. "Not Jamie."

Derek turned to him. "Why not? Because you slept with her?"

Josh blushed, but was adamant. "I know her."

"Maybe not as well as you think you do. People can do crazy things when their status quo is threatened. Just look at Professor Easton and her roommate. The girl committed suicide rather than go back home."

"Suicide is one thing," Josh said, "murder another."

Now it was Derek shaking his head. "Two sides of the same coin. Fight-or-flight response. Something happens, someone gets backed into a corner, and they either run away or hit back. Professor Easton's roommate—"

"Nan Barbour," I shot in.

"—chose to run away. That's what suicide is. Running away. But someone else, with a different personality, might have chosen to fight. To do whatever they had to to win. Including killing the threat. That's why blackmailers so often end up dead. Their victims turn on them."

Josh shook his head. But his voice lacked conviction when he said, "I don't . . ." And then he stopped before he even completed the sentence.

"It's just one possibility," I said, trying to be comforting. "We don't know that that's what happened. Mariano and Gregg could be guilty, or even Robin and Bruce. Mothers will do anything to protect their children, and it sounds like Robin was afraid she'd lose Benjamin. And Bruce was afraid he'd lose both of them."

Derek nodded. "Maybe Nan didn't kill herself all those years ago," he said. "Maybe Professor Easton killed her, and Miss Shaw figured it out, and so Professor Easton had to silence her, too. Nobody's off the hook yet. And we're not even done talking to everyone." He nodded to William Maurits's door, across the landing from Miss Shaw's empty apartment. "He's her closest neighbor. Maybe they were carrying on an illicit affair, and when Miss Shaw wanted more, wanted marriage, Maurits got rid of her the only way he knew how."

The picture of the small and spare, nattily clad William Maurits and the oversized, somewhat slovenly Hilda Shaw, was irresistibly funny. I giggled. Derek winked at me, and even Josh was fighting a smile when he lifted a hand and rapped on Maurits's door with his knuckles.

"Let's get this over with. The sooner we're done, the sooner I can run out to Barnham and pick up the stuff and take it to Dad. And then all of this will be off my shoulders."

I nodded. My thoughts exactly.

It was getting late, so I wouldn't have been surprised to find that William Maurits had turned in already, with tomorrow being a workday and all, but he opened the door after just a few seconds, dressed in the same knife-pleat pants and starched shirt as every other time I'd seen him.

The only difference between these clothes and his work suits was that the pants were khakis, the shirt was unbuttoned at the neck, and he was wearing slippers.

"Oh!" he said when he saw us. "What a surprise!"

And then, no more than a second later, "Oh no. What's happened?"

We glanced at each other, to determine who would take the lead this time. Since Maurits was looking straight at me—we were about the same height—I took it upon myself. "It's Candy. I'm sorry. May we come in?"

"Of course. Of course." He stepped back and gestured us in, into an apartment just like Amelia Easton's and Mariano and Gregg's. However, there were no flowers here, no vases, and no little glass animals. What there was, was expensive furniture: postmodern, influenced by the 1950s and '60s, sleek and elegant. That, and modern art. Strange little sculptures on the shelves, paintings on the walls. Everything was painted white, like in a gallery: the better to display the art, I guess.

"Sit, sit." He gestured us to the living room, where we sank—at least in my case—gingerly onto the ivory-colored suede sofa. "Can I get you something to drink? Coffee? Wine? Something stronger?"

We declined, leaving Maurits to nurse his glass of what looked like cognac. He sat back on the sofa, folding one leg over the other, and jerked his chin up in that little way he had. "Tell me what happened."

He was still looking at me, so I answered.

"I'm sorry to be the bearer of bad news, but Candy passed. In the hospital about an hour ago. We drove Jamie home afterwards, and then thought we might just let everyone know. I'm sure Josh's dad will be by tomorrow, to talk to everyone about anything they may have noticed, but we didn't feel right about not sharing the news when we knew everyone would want to know."

Maurits nodded, twirling his glass. "What do you mean, Chief Rasmussen will want to talk to everyone about anything they may have noticed?"

"Well"—I shrugged apologetically—"it probably wasn't natural causes. Someone did something to her. He'll have to figure out who. And why."

"I see," Maurits said, looking past me to the wall. "She was murdered?"

"So we assume. Probably has something to do with Miss Shaw's murder."

Maurits blinked and came back to himself. "Dear me. Miss Shaw was murdered as well?"

"It's leaning that way. What with the missing EpiPen and now Candy and, of course, the envelope of secrets."

I waited. It didn't take more than a few seconds for him to take the bait. "Envelope of secrets?"

"Miss Shaw kept tabs on everyone in the building," Josh said. "You know that."

"Remember," I chirped before Maurits could think of denying it, "you told us about it the first morning we were here? What was it you called her? A nosy old biddy?"

Maurits didn't answer, but his cheekbones got a little darker. "What envelope?"

"I found it in her apartment after she died," Josh said. "Information about everyone in the building. Little stuff, mostly. I didn't think anything of it at first, just that I didn't want anyone to get in trouble over it. But then Dad started talking about how Miss Shaw's EpiPen went missing, and now Candy's dead—and I'm thinking I'd better give the stuff to my dad. Just in case there's something in there that can help him."

It didn't take more than a few seconds this time, either. "What was in the envelope?"

"About you? Just a picture of one of the paintings your company settled on a long time ago. Something called *Madonna*. D'you remember it?"

"Of course," Maurits said, his eyes stuck on the living room wall for a moment. I looked in that direction, but there was nothing to see. Just the wall between this room and the bedroom, and a different painting, one of—I thought—a field of flowers or possibly a view of outer space. "It was a terrible loss. All the other paintings that were lost in the fire, too, of course, but I have to admit the *Madonna* was a personal favorite of mine. Perhaps that's why Miss Shaw singled it out. She knew how devastating that particular loss was for me, not just on a professional level, because the company lost a lot of money on the claim, but because of such senseless loss of beauty."

"It looked very nice," I said politely. "I was wondering . . ."

"Yes?"

"The *Madonna* . . . is that the religious figure, or the entertainer? It wasn't clear from the picture."

I'd sort of been able to visualize a face, with a slash of red lipstick, topped by a circle of gold that could either be a halo or blond hair—but beyond that, I couldn't be sure. It seemed a reasonable question. Maurits obviously didn't think so.

"The religious figure," he said, his voice short.

"That's what I thought." I ignored Derek's amusement and Josh's not quite successful attempt to hide a smile. "The halo, you know? It could have been hair, but it really looked more like a corona."

Maurits nodded, and looked like he thought I might be trying to make fun of him. I wasn't, I swear. I just prefer art I understand.

"I'm sorry it was lost," I said. "Anyway, there was a picture of it among Miss Shaw's stuff. In the envelope Josh will be passing on to his dad in the morning. In case Wayne asks you about it."

"If he asks," William Maurits said, "I will tell him that it perished in a gallery fire five years ago, and that the company paid out on the claim, along with all the others. It's a done deal, settled long ago. Everyone's happy and no one's suing anyone else. I have no idea why Hilda Shaw would take an interest."

"We don't, either," I said. "We just thought you should know what's happening. And now that that's done, I guess we should get going." I glanced at Derek and Josh, who both got to their feet. "Thank you for your time, Mr. Maurits."

"A pleasure," Maurits said, without sounding like he meant it. He jerked his chin up in that little nervous tic that he had. "Thank you for letting me know about poor Candy. That's terrible news." He shook his head sadly as he herded us toward the front door. "It's enough to make one seriously consider moving, isn't it? Or at least take a vacation until things settle down."

A vacation sounded lovely. Somewhere sunny and tropical where there were no dead bodies.

Ryan and Carla were probably on the beach in Saint Thomas by now. I wished I were there, too. Just Derek and me, in the honeymoon suite, with no dead bodies distracting us from the more important things.

"I'm glad that's done," Josh echoed my feelings when we were out on the landing with William Maurits's door locked behind us. I nodded.

"Telling people that one of their neighbors has died is never any fun. I'm glad to be done, too."

"So what now?" Josh wanted to know.

"You have your car keys on you?"

Josh shook his head.

"Run up and get them. Don't look left or right, don't get distracted. If you see Jamie, say 'Excuse me' and keep going."

"She's not going to—" Josh protested.

"Yes, she is. But if you're lucky, she'll wait a few minutes. You'll have time to grab your keys and make it back down."

Josh rolled his eyes, but all he said was, "I'll be back in a minute."

Derek nodded. "We'll be downstairs."

—19—

"Any reason we wanted to be downstairs?" I asked a minute later, when we had left the landing outside Maurits's door and were standing in the basement, outside the laundry room, waiting for Josh to return.

"We wanted to make sure nobody could hear us. I don't trust these people." Derek looped an arm around my shoulder and spoke into my ear.

I didn't, either. "Did you get any vibes from William Maurits?"

"Other than that he didn't appreciate your talking smack about his favorite painting?" He grinned. "He didn't seem overly heartbroken about Candy. Although he was certainly more heartbroken than he was about Miss Shaw."

I nodded. No doubt. "You really think Jamie's going to try to waylay Josh?"

Derek looked at me. "Don't you?"

I did. The scenario he'd outlined earlier was only too realistic, right down to Jamie's excuses and Josh's responses to them. "Sounds like you've had some experience with scheming women."

"Melissa used to play games like that," Derek said. "She still does. Remember how she tried to foist a murder weapon off on me back in July?"

Vividly. I still hadn't quite forgiven her for that, although the fact that she'd gotten arrested and had to spend a few days in jail had gone a long way toward making me feel vindicated.

"You don't think Jamie's trying to frame Josh for anything, do you?"

"No," Derek said, "I think she's looking for comfort and reassurance and companionship, and he's proven himself to be susceptible. She just doesn't want to be alone, and I can't blame her. But that doesn't mean I want Josh to fall for it. For one thing, it would really upset Shannon. I like Shannon. And for another, he'll kick himself later. But by then it'll be too late."

I nodded. "Hence your suggestion that he find somewhere else to spend the night."

"Hence. You don't disagree, do you?"

I shook my head. "I don't trust Jamie, either. You made a good case for why she might be guilty of two murders. I don't really think she is, but I don't want her anywhere near Josh."

He arched his brows. "You don't still think it's Mariano and Gregg, do you? I'll give you Miss Shaw, if she threatened to turn Mariano in to the ICE, but they had no reason to do away with Candy."

"Actually," I said, "I think my money's on David Rossini for all of it. And not just because he's an outsider and I hate to think it's one of the neighbors. I don't like him. He's a cheater, and cheaters are by nature dishonest. He had reason to get rid of Miss Shaw, if she threatened to tell his wife about him and Candy, and if he killed Miss Shaw, and Candy knew, she could have held it over his head to try to make him leave his wife and marry her instead."

Derek nodded pensively.

I continued, "He wouldn't want to do that. Candy might have been a fun pastime, but Jamie told me it's his wife who has the money. Her family owns Guido's and the strip club and a lot of other businesses. David married into the family—and into the money. He wouldn't want to lose it, not to marry a twenty-two-year-old waitress. One his wife employed."

Derek nodded again, more certain this time.

"Jamie said the wine and chocolates were from him. He'd know what Candy liked. And he stopped by the hospital today. When I saw him this afternoon, I told him what had happened and that she'd been taken to the hospital. He got angry. Maybe because she was still alive. Maybe he'd thought she'd be dead already. He could have gone to the hospital and done something to her, when Jamie wasn't looking."

"Anything's possible," Derek said as we heard footsteps on the stairs, echoing through the building. It was Josh coming back, car keys jingling in his hand.

"I called Dad and told him I was coming. He's waiting for the stuff."

"I'll go with you," Derek said.

I blinked, surprised. He hadn't said anything about that.

Josh blinked, too. "Why? Are you afraid I'm gonna take something out of the envelope before I pass it to Dad?"

"No," Derek said calmly, "I'm just making sure you get there."

There was a beat of silence. Then Josh tried to laugh. "You can't be serious."

It sounded hollow, and then he stopped laughing and swallowed, his face pale in the bright light from the fluorescent bulb overhead. "Are you?"

"Just being cautious," Derek said. "If there's something in that envelope someone's been willing to kill for, that same someone might just decide to try one more time. You know what that's like. It's just a month since your car went off the road and into the ocean."

Josh swallowed again. "Sure," he said. "After that, I'd just as soon not be alone."

Derek nodded. "Did you figure out a place to stay? Other than here?"

"There are rooms at the inn," Josh said, referring to Kate's bed and breakfast. "I'll give Dad the stuff and crash there for the night."

"If you don't mind some free advice," I said, "maybe you should find the time to take Shannon aside for a talk, too. You're gonna have to tell your dad how you got the stuff, and he'll guess that Jamie must have pressured you in some way to get you to steal it. It's better for Shannon to hear about Jamie from you and not your dad."

Josh nodded, and drove a hand through his hair. "Guess I don't have a choice, really."

"Honesty is always the best policy," Derek said. "Much better to tell the truth and deal with the fallout, than lie and have it blow up in your face later. Let's get it over with." He gave Josh a push toward the front door. "C'mon, Tink."

I came, until we were outside in the cool air, and then I realized something. "I left my laptop here on Friday. I want to go upstairs and get it. And bring it home."

"Can't it wait until tomorrow?"

"There's something I want to look up," I said.

Derek looked mutinous, and I added, "I'll be fine. No one's going to try to hurt me. It's not like I know anything more than anyone else does. Just go. Pick up the stuff and take it to Wayne. I'll grab the laptop and be out of here in two minutes. I promise."

He relented. "Fine. But if you get yourself killed, I'll never forgive you."

"I won't get myself killed." Sheesh, talk about paranoia. "I'll see you at home later. Right?"

He nodded. "Oh, yeah. From now on, you're stuck with me whether you want to be or not."

"I want to be." I tilted my face up and got a kiss while Josh busied himself by unlocking the doors of the Honda and getting in, giving us a moment of privacy. "I'll see you in a half hour or so. Have Josh drop you off at the house."

Derek said he would, and then he jogged across the parking lot to where the Honda was idling, waiting to go. I went back inside the building and up to the second floor, where I let myself into the Antoninis' condo and locked the door behind me before going to look for the laptop.

It was exactly where I'd left it, on the floor of the living room, not too far from the balcony door, and I grabbed it and headed back out. Above my head, I could hear Jamie moving around. I had expected her to go straight to bed—to be honest, she'd looked beat—but maybe she couldn't sleep. Any minute now, she'd probably walk across the hall to knock on Josh's door for some company.

Yes, indeed: No sooner had I opened the door into the stairwell, preparatory to leaving, than I heard the door upstairs open as well. I held my breath as soft footsteps padded across the landing. The knock on the door sounded hollow as it echoed between the walls in the hallway.

There was no answer, of course—Josh was gone—and after a few seconds, there was another knock. Then Jamie's voice. "Josh? Are you there? Josh?"

I thought about telling her that he'd left, but I thought better of it. Instead I just waited quietly while she knocked again, called his name again, and finally gave up. I heard her footsteps move across the landing over my head, and then the door close and lock upstairs. I waited a few more seconds before I started pulling on my own. I was just about to shut it when Jamie opened her door again.

Damn. Maybe she was on her way out. Maybe, in a minute, she'd come down the stairs and see me standing here.

But no, it wasn't Jamie after all. These sounds came from below. Must bc William Maurits, since Miss Shaw's apartment, obviously, was empty. Maurits and I hadn't parted on the most perfect of terms earlier, so it might be best if I waited until he'd done whatever he planned to do, before I went downstairs. We were all stressed out and nursing fraying nerves at the moment; to be honest, I wasn't up for another conversation, especially with someone I'd annoyed earlier.

He locked his door and then headed down the stairs. I ducked back inside my own apartment and pulled the door shut behind me. And moved through the dark hallway into the kitchen, where I went to the window and looked out. If he was headed to the basement, to do laundry or root around in his storage bin, I might be here awhile. Derek would get to Aunt Inga's house and find it empty, and then he'd worry. If I got stuck here, I should probably call him and let him know I'd been delayed. But if Maurits was going somewhere, all I had to do was wait until his car had driven away, before I could get out of here myself.

It was rather late in the day to go for a drive, but even later to do laundry. I kept my fingers crossed as I peered down into the parking lot.

Yep, there he was. Walking across the parking lot from the building toward his car with something under his arm. Something square and brown. A pizza box?

But what kind of idiot carried a pizza box vertically under his arm? Pizzas have to be kept horizontal, or the cheese slides off. Everyone knows that.

Although when he got to the sedan and beeped open the trunk, he set the box right side up and stowed it carefully, even a bit reverently, inside. And then, almost as if he couldn't help himself, he lifted the lid and peered lovingly at the contents.

No, not pizza.

The trunk light had gone on when the trunk opened, and although I was far away and didn't have a fantastic view into the trunk, I saw enough. A rectangle, just slightly smaller than the box, with a dark background, an ivory oval, a red smear, and a golden halo.

"Whoa!"

It was the *Madonna*. The painting that supposedly had been destroyed in a gallery fire five years ago. The painting that the insurance company Maurits worked for had paid a half-million dollars in settlement for.

It could have been a copy, I suppose. But if it were, why was he carrying it around in a pizza box at ten o'clock at night? Just thirty minutes after we'd warned him that the police would want to talk to him about it?

Obviously he was getting it out of his condo before the

police arrived. It must have been in one of the rooms we hadn't seen. Maybe he kept it above his bed, so he could gaze at it before going to sleep at night.

Downstairs, Maurits lowered the lid of the box gently over the Madonna's face. I saw the logo of Guido's Pizzeria for a second before he closed the lid of the trunk on top of it. And then he headed for the door of the car.

"Shit," I muttered. I'd thought he might just be planning to keep the box in the car overnight, and take it to work with him in the morning. Leave it somewhere along the way maybe. But it seemed he was taking care of it now instead. He must be desperate to get it out of the house, if he was willing to risk heading out now. Going for a car ride at this time of night looked so much more suspicious than just waiting until the morning.

If I had any hope of keeping up with him—and of course I wanted to; for all I knew he might be on his way to destroy the *Madonna*—I'd better hustle. But not too fast, or he'd see me. So I scurried across the kitchen and out of the apartment while Maurits started his car. While I locked the door, he backed out of the parking space, and while I hustled down the stairs and along the basement hallway, he drove to the entrance to the parking lot. I stood just inside the front doors and watched him take a left, toward downtown Waterfield, Barnham College, and the ocean, and then, as soon as he was out of sight, I hustled to the Beetle, threw myself behind the wheel, and followed.

It was déjà vu all over again: just two days since I'd followed Candy along this same road. But unlike on Friday, William Maurits didn't stop at Guido's. He didn't stop at Barnham College, or Wellhaven. In fact, he kept driving until he was far outside the Waterfield city limits, and for a while I thought I'd have to follow him all the way to Portland. However, twenty minutes later we'd made it to a small town called Brunswick, and here he turned off.

I haven't spent a lot of time in Brunswick, other than to pass through on my way to or from Portland. I'd never been in the area where I tailed Maurits now. If Brunswick had an underbelly, this must be it. Pawnshops, bail-bonding companies, and used car lots surrounded by barbed wire fencing and guarded by watchful dogs. It was dark, and I had to follow a little more closely than I liked so I wouldn't lose Maurits in the labyrinth of streets. If I got too close, I was afraid he'd recognize the Beetle.

Through all of this, I hadn't given Derek a thought. When my phone suddenly signaled, I jumped. And because I did, I fumbled the phone, dropped it on the seat next to me once, and had to retrieve it before I could push the speaker button. "Hi."

"Where are you?" Derek demanded.

Oops. It had been more than thirty minutes. He must have gotten to Aunt Inga's house and found it empty.

"Sorry. Somewhere in Brunswick."

There was a moment of silence, when I wondered whether we'd lost the connection. "Derek?"

"I'm here. What are you doing in Brunswick?"

"Following Maurits," I said. "When I came out of the apartment with the laptop, Jamie was knocking on Josh's door. I didn't want to deal with her again . . ." Especially after Derek had so accurately predicted the chain of events; I hadn't been sure I could talk to her with a straight face. "So I had to wait for her to go back to her own condo. But then Maurits headed out, and I didn't want to deal with him, either. So I waited for him to leave."

"This doesn't tell me how you ended up in Brunswick," Derek said.

Right. "He had the *Madonna* with him."

There was another pause. "The entertainer or the religious figure?" Derek asked.

I stuck my tongue out at him, not that he could see it. "The painting. Hidden in a pizza box. He put it in the trunk of the car and then opened it. I saw it clearly."

"He didn't see you, did he?"

Not as far as I knew.

"You better make sure he doesn't," Derek said, "because if Miss Shaw knew he had that painting, and he killed her because of it, he might kill you, too. Dammit, Avery, why do you do these things?"

Because I couldn't not, I guess.

"Don't worry. I'm not going to confront him. I just want to see where he's taking it. So I can tell Wayne where it is."

"What if he tries to destroy it?" Derek said.

I hadn't thought of that. "I guess I might have to try to save it. I mean, if he destroys it, there goes the evidence. Right?"

"No!" Derek said. "If he tries to destroy it, you let him. I'd rather the painting go up in smoke—for real this time—than you hurting yourself. You were lucky to survive the fire back in July. It's just a painting. Promise me you won't do anything stupid."

I promised. I didn't want anything to happen to me, either. "But I don't think he will. If he wanted to destroy it, he could have done that at home. Taken a sharp knife or a pair of scissors and cut it to ribbons. I think he's just giving it to someone else. Or leaving it somewhere."

And possibly sooner than I'd realized. While we'd been talking, Maurits had slowed down. As I watched, he took a right into a driveway.

"Stay on the line," Derek ordered.

No problem. After a quick look around to make sure there were no cop cars waiting to pounce on me, I cut my lights and rolled closer, in time to see the rear lights of the sedan disappear through a sliding chain-link gate. Inside the fence were row upon row of storage units.

"U-Stor," I read the sign. "He must have a unit here. He's disappearing into the back."

"What's the address?"

It was posted below the name on the sign beside the gate. I read it off to him.

"He's probably just putting the painting there for safe-keeping," Derek opined. "I'll call Wayne. When it's light, he can get a warrant and search the unit. Come home, Avery."

"Yessir," I said, and turned my lights on and did a U-turn

that would have gotten me pulled over for sure in Waterfield, before I made a beeline for home.

. . .

"So you saw the painting?" Derek asked when I was back in Waterfield, inside Aunt Inga's house, with my feet on the living room table and the laptop in my lap and Mischa curled up between Derek and me on the sofa.

I nodded. "With my own eyes. He had it in a pizza box. It isn't very big."

"The *Mona Lisa* is only about twenty by thirty inches," Derek said. "I saw it when I did that exchange year in France."

I glanced over at him, where he was sitting next to me on the couch. "Surely you're not comparing the *Mona Lisa* to the *Madonna*?"

"Only the size. I haven't seen it, or even seen a picture of it."

"Here you go." I'd only just finished pulling the information up on the computer screen, and now I handed him the laptop.

He was silent for a moment after receiving it. "Huh."

"Yes?"

"It's not as bad as I thought. The colors are nice."

I slanted a sideways look at the screen. They were, sort of.

"And it's obviously a portrait."

"Obviously?"

"Face," Derek said, circling the oval with two fingers, "lips, hair. Or halo."

"If you say so." I took the computer back from him to manipulate the keys. "Your average medium pizza is twelve inches across and has eight slices, right? So this couldn't be any bigger than twelve inches to a side. Probably less. That's small for a painting."

"Maybe it was a copy," Derek suggested.

It could have been. I hadn't been close enough to get a good look. However—"If it wasn't the real thing, why would he want to get rid of it? He could just say it was a copy."

I shook my head. "Here we go. Yes, this says the *Madonna* was only twelve by nine. Barely bigger than your average sheet of copy paper."

"I called Wayne," Derek said, "and told him about it. He said he'd get a warrant and go out to Brunswick in the morning."

"Will he let us go with him? I'd like to see if I'm right. If it's a copy, I'll feel really stupid."

"Like you said," Derek said, "if it was a copy, why'd he bother to move it? He must have taken it out of the gallery before it burned. Maybe he set the fire. Or maybe it's some kind of insurance fraud. Maybe all the paintings were removed and then the place was torched. And the *Madonna* was Maurits's payment for facilitating the fraud. He seemed very attached to it."

He had. Right down to risking a peek at it in the parking lot within view of the other condos. Maybe he'd done the same thing when he brought it home five years ago, and that was when Miss Shaw had seen it.

"If Miss Shaw went to the police, he would have gone to jail, wouldn't he? For insurance fraud, at the very least."

"At least," Derek nodded.

"That might be enough reason for him to murder her."

"It might. But what about Candy?"

"No idea," I admitted, since I couldn't come up with a good reason why William Maurits would have wanted to do away with Candy. If it had been Jamie, that might have been a different story. She'd seen the contents of the envelope, and knew that the painting had something to do with Maurits. If she'd told him about it, he might have decided to get rid of her, too. "Unless the wine and chocolates were really intended for Jamie. Then Candy would just be collateral damage and Jamie would be the intended victim."

"Puts a different spin on things," Derek agreed. "Another explanation is that the two aren't related."

I shot him a look. "How do you mean?"

"Maybe Maurits killed Miss Shaw because of the painting. Or Mariano killed her because of the ICE. Or Bruce killed her because of Robin. And then Rossini decided to take advantage of that death to rid himself of Candy. Maybe she'd become a nuisance. Maybe she was pressuring him to leave his wife and marry her instead. So he killed her, thinking that whoever killed Miss Shaw would get blamed for Candy, too."

Also possible.

"My head hurts," I said plaintively.

"Poor baby," Derek answered. "Wanna go to bed?"

"Soon. I just want to look something up first."

"You already looked something up."

"Something else." I moved my foot away from the big toe inching its way up my ankle. "You're distracting me."

"Yes," Derek said, "that's the point."

"Ten minutes. I promise. Just let me look up this one thing."

He sighed and moved his foot away from mine. "What is it you're looking for? More pictures of the *Madonna*?"

"Not the painting. Or the entertainer. But in a funny way, sort of. I'm hoping to find a picture of Nanette Barbour."

"Amelia Easton's roommate? The one who died?"

I nodded.

"Why?" Derek said.

"Not sure."

"Didn't you see a picture of her in Amelia's condo?"

I nodded. That was why I wanted to see another one.

"What are you thinking?"

I denied thinking anything. "I'm just wondering why Miss Shaw had it. If there was nothing to the story."

"The same reason she had the article about you," Derek said. "She thought you might have pushed your aunt Inga down the stairs. You didn't."

"Of course not."

"Just like Amelia didn't kill her roommate."

"How do you know she didn't?"

"I don't," Derek said, "but I'm sure the police in Mississippi looked into it. It's been twenty years; if they suspected her, someone would have done something about it by now. And besides, she had no reason to."

"Maybe she didn't want to go back to the commune, either." She hadn't gone back, after all; not in the twenty years since Nan's death. She'd stayed in college and gotten an education and worked, and had never returned to Mississippi.

"If she didn't," Derek said, "all she had to do was keep her mouth shut. The only reason the elders got involved was because Amelia called them and ratted out her roommate."

"I'm sure you're right." It made sense, after all. "And there are no pictures here. Plenty of photographs of Amelia, from after she started college, but none of Nan. Not even the one Amelia has."

"Some religious groups think taking photographs is wrong," Derek said. "They equate them with graven images. You know, 'Thou shalt not make onto thyself . . .' "

I nodded. "The photograph Amelia had must have been taken after they got to college. It might be the only picture that exists of Nan. Not much of a legacy to leave, is it?"

Derek shook his head. "It isn't. I'm sure she had bigger hopes for her life."

Probably. She'd been the one who had insisted on going away to college in the first place, and who had made Amelia go with her so she could. She was the one who had decided to study history, while Amelia had chosen the wimpy and no doubt commune-approved home economics—at least until Nan's death had made her change her major. Nan didn't seem like the type who'd allow herself to be forcibly taken somewhere she didn't want to go. If nothing else, I would have expected her to run away. Just pack her things and leave, and never look back. She would have built a life eventually. And she'd had the time to do it. It wouldn't have taken much longer than the time it took to tie a rope to the ceiling light and the other end around her neck and to strangle herself to death. But it would have hurt a lot less.

"Ready for bed?" I said, and closed the computer, feeling inexplicably sad about a young woman I'd never met, who'd died more than twenty years ago, when I was just a little girl myself.

"I thought you'd never ask," Derek answered, and reached out a hand. "Can you walk, or should I carry you?"

"I can walk. But if you want to practice, I won't stop you."

"In that case," Derek said, and lifted me. I made the trip up the stairs hanging over his shoulder.

—20—

"Here she is," Wayne said the next morning.

We—that is, Derek and I—were standing outside William Maurits's storage unit in Brunswick, while Wayne and a couple of officers from the Brunswick sheriff's office had opened the door to the unit and were rooting around in there. It didn't take long before Wayne emerged holding the pizza box I'd seen Maurits carry to his car last night. He flipped it open in front of me, as if to make sure I'd received what I'd ordered.

"That it?" Derek said, watching over my shoulder.

Wayne glanced at him. "That seems to be it. It's a real painting. It's possible the artist painted more than one, sometimes they do, but unless that's the case, and unless Maurits painted this one himself, this is the real deal." He turned to me. "Can you confirm that this was the box William Maurits carried to his car last night?"

"I can confirm that it's the same kind of box," I said, "and that the painting I saw inside that box looks like the painting that's in this one now. Will that do?"

"That's great." He handed box and painting off to one of

the Brunswick cops, who slid them into a big, thick plastic bag, probably to preserve any evidence like fingerprints from getting lost. Wayne stripped off his latex gloves and stuck them in his pocket.

"Are you done?" I asked.

He nodded. "The sheriff's office will catalog everything in the storage unit. They'll be checking anything they find against missing artwork and antiques, but between you and me, I doubt they'll find anything. The rest of it looks like it's just old furniture and things he didn't have room for in his place."

It did. And not just William, but perhaps his parents and grandparents, too. Some of the things I could see were old, but not nice old, or antique old; they were just plain old and really not worth keeping.

"I get the pleasure of driving to Portland," Wayne added, "and coordinating with the police there to pick up Maurits and bring him in to the police station to help with our inquiries. I won't be back for a few hours at least."

"I'm sure we'll manage to muddle through," Derek said.

"Josh gave me the envelope last night. Looks like most everyone in the building has some kind of motive, at least for offing Miss Shaw."

Pretty much.

"At the moment, we really have no idea who did it. There were fingerprints in her apartment from several of the neighbors, but that doesn't prove anything, as she spoke to everyone in the building at some point or another."

"We weren't invited inside," I said.

Wayne nodded. "Several of the others were. She seemed to have preferred women to men. We found prints from all the women inside her place. Jamie and Candy, Robin, Professor Easton, even Shannon. She said Miss Shaw asked her to bring up the mail a while ago."

"I don't really think Shannon's anywhere near the top of the suspect list," I said. "And after what happened, I'm pretty sure Candy's off the list completely."

Wayne nodded. "There, we had a break. There were

traces of ethylene glycol in both the empty bottle and glasses, and some of the chocolates were intact, and still stuffed with the substance. Good call." He nodded to Derek, who grimaced.

"Not sure how much that helps, Wayne. Antifreeze is too easy to come by. I'm sure we've all got a bottle or two of it sitting around. I know I do."

"True," Wayne said. "However, we traced the other stuff. The wine was bought at a liquor store in Portland, the chocolates at a confectioner's in Portland, and the flowers at a florist in Portland, all within an hour of each other on Saturday afternoon. All within the same one-mile radius. All for cash, so there's no way to trace a credit or debit card. People are too savvy to make that kind of mistake these days. But the person who bought them was female. Brunette, long hair, big hat, and sunglasses."

"That takes Maurits out of the running," Derek said. "He's short, but he doesn't look like a woman. Not even in a hat and a wig."

"Have you ever seen him in a hat or wig?" I didn't wait for his answer. "It takes Gregg and Mariano out, too. They're both too tall. So is Bruce."

"Candy, Jamie, and Robin are all blondes," Derek said. "Not that Candy would have bought the stuff. Not unless she was trying to kill Jamie. But then she wouldn't have drunk so much of the wine herself."

"Hair color is easy to change, though. Wigs aren't hard to come by. I don't know about Robin, but Jamie probably has them at work."

Wayne nodded. "She does. One of the pictures Miss Shaw had has her wearing a long, brown wig. She could have taken it home on Friday night, and brought it back on Saturday. The place is closed during the day, so no one would have noticed that it was gone for a few hours."

Likely not. And Derek had already posited a good motive last night, when he suggested that Jamie had killed both Miss Shaw and Candy because they both, at different times, threatened to call her parents and tell them she was working as a stripper. He must have shared the idea with Wayne while he and Josh were dropping off Miss Shaw's envelope of shame. It was looking more and more like Jamie was the guilty party, much as I was loath to admit it.

"What about Francesca Rossini?" I said. "She's a brunette. And if she figured out that her husband was cheating, she could have come up with a way to take out Candy while framing David for it. Two birds with one stone. And since Jamie hadn't told her about it, she might have considered Jamie an acceptable sacrifice, too."

"I'll be talking to Mrs. Rossini this afternoon," Wayne answered with a snap of teeth. "And her lawyers. I'm sure she'll have more than one."

Probably. You don't get far as an Italian crime family—or even an Italian business family—without good legal counsel.

"Anything else in the envelope strike you?" Such as the fact that Mariano was working illegally or that Bruce and Robin weren't really married or that Amelia Easton's roommate died?

"No other reasons for murder, if that's what you mean. And unless I suspect someone of a crime, I don't see the need to dig around in their personal dirty laundry. Do you?"

I didn't. I was also relieved, since it sounded like Robin's secret was safe, at least for now, and like Wayne didn't know—or care—that Mariano was illegal.

"So what will you be doing the rest of the day?" he asked now, looking from Derek to me and back.

Derek glanced at me before answering. "Since it seems like things have settled back down, I guess we'll just go back to work. Lots to do on the condo still. And a bit of wedding planning to do, too. And we might stop by the hospital to see Jill and little Pepper during visiting hours."

Wayne nodded. "I'm going to Portland to deal with Maurits. While I'm there, I'll check in with the ME about the autopsy on Candy. Not that there's much doubt what killed her. I'll be back in Waterfield at one to talk to Francesca Rossini. Maybe I'll just schedule a chat with Jamie after that. See if she can get me an alibi for noon on Saturday."

"I was in Portland with Derek," I said. "Having lunch at the Tremont, before Ryan and Carla's wedding at two."

"I didn't really think I needed to ask you for an alibi," Wayne answered, "but thank you."

I shrugged. "Fair's fair. If you're checking everyone else's alibi, you should have mine, too."

Wayne nodded. "I'm off. If I need anything, I'll give you a call. If anything else happens, you have my number."

We did. He went off in his police car toward Portland, pizza box in tow, and Derek and I headed back to Waterfield and the Antoninis' condo.

Going back to work felt sort of anticlimactic. I mean, two people were dead, probably murdered, and here we were, just going about our business as usual, stripping wallpaper and scraping paint and ripping out plumbing.

Derek disagreed, of course.

"Yesterday was plenty climactic," he said, "and besides, I think it's nice that for once, at the end of a case, I don't have to worry about anyone holding you at gunpoint. You're just upset because Wayne gets to solve this one without you being there."

He might have a point. So far I had managed to insert myself, usually quite unintentionally, into a lot of Wayne's cases. I should be happy that I'd avoided having my life threatened this time around.

"It just feels like there should be somcthing more. A car chase or a burning building or a mad dash across a foggy island with a killer on our trail . . ."

"No," Derek said firmly. "This is the way it's supposed to be. You and me safe and sound going about our business of renovating this condo, and Wayne taking care of the police work. That's his job. This is yours."

I knew that. And I love my job. I do. I just felt like something was missing. But Derek was probably right. I was just subconsciously a little miffed at missing the big confession, when Francesca—or maybe Jamie—broke down and said, *Yes, it was me. I did it. Lock me up and throw away the key.* I'd always been there before. The murderer had always done something desperate—or something stupid—to give himself—or herself—away. But Derek was right. This was the way it was supposed to be. This was the way it usually was, when I wasn't involved. The police gathered the evidence, the police weighed the evidence, and then the police decided who the guilty party was based on the evidence and arrested him or her. Entirely without my help.

"You're right. I just feel . . . unsettled, I guess." I tore at a strip of wallpaper and let it drift to the floor.

"Tell you what." Derek put his wrench down on the floor. "It's almost lunchtime anyway. Maybe you need a break and something else to think about. We'll go grab something to eat, and then we'll stop by the hospital and see Jill and the baby. Maybe that'll make you feel better."

Maybe. At least it was worth a try.

So we went to Guido's, where everyone wore pink T-shirts in honor of Candy's passing—and where David Rossini was nowhere to be seen. I hoped that meant something, but even if it didn't, I was happy not to look at him. And then we went to the hospital, where I was vividly reminded of watching Candy's pale face as the doctors worked on her . . . but where a beaming Jill and tiny Pepper Cortino reminded me of the power of life over death, or some such thing. Jill looked tired but thrilled that it was over, and she assured us, even as she looked dotingly down at Pepper, that she was done; this was the last baby. We didn't see Gregg Brewer, but that wasn't surprising; if he'd pulled a double shift yesterday, he was probably at home in bed. With or without Mariano.

We were on our way back to the condo, full of food and feeling a bit more relaxed than earlier, when Wayne called. "I just wanted to update you," he said.

"Yes?"

"Maurits confessed to the insurance fraud, but he swore he wasn't in on it from the beginning. I'm not sure whether that makes it better or worse."

"How do you mean?"

"The paintings were on loan from a collector in Providence, Rhode Island. He had gotten into a little bit of financial difficulty. He could have just sold a painting, but I guess he just couldn't bear to part with any of them. So between him and the gallery owners, they cooked up the story of the fire. They removed the paintings first, of course, and put other, much less valuable paintings up in their place, so the investigators would see that there had actually been paintings in the gallery when it went up in smoke. The collector got his paintings back, he and the gallery owner shared the insurance settlement, and everyone was happy."

"And Maurits?" Derek wanted to know. I had put Wayne on speaker, so we could both talk to him, even as Derek was driving.

"He was the claims adjuster assigned to the case. And he figured out what they'd done. But he let them get away with it in exchange for the *Madonna*. He seems to have some kind of emotional attachment to it. The fact that he can't take it to jail with him seems to upset him quite a bit."

"So he's going to jail?"

"He'll be serving a few years, at least, for insurance fraud. But not for murder. He swears up and down he didn't kill Miss Shaw, that he was paying her to keep her quiet. His bank accounts bear him out. A thousand dollars passed from his account into hers every month. Automatic draft."

"He could have killed her to stop her from bleeding him dry," I said.

"A thousand dollars a month didn't even come close to doing that. He admitted he would have paid a lot more. And he had no reason to want to kill Candy. I put him on a lie detector just to make sure, and he passed. On both murders."

Fine. So it wasn't William Maurits. I hadn't really thought so, to be honest. At least not after I heard about the brunette.

"What about Francesca Rossini?"

"I haven't spoken to her yet," Wayne said. "I just finished interviewing her husband. He confessed to sleeping with Candy. Not much else he could do when we had the photographs to prove it. But he seemed sincerely distraught about her death, and very, very afraid we were going to try to pin it on him. He also said he'd never been inside Miss Shaw's apartment, and hadn't considered killing her."

"Maybe Candy killed her and then he killed Candy."

"He's not smart enough," Wayne said bluntly. "He married into a powerful family, with a wife who stood up to her father and insisted on marrying him, and then he put it all in jeopardy by getting involved with a college student, and one of his employees."

"But doesn't that make it more likely that he'd be worried about Francesca finding out?"

Wayne admitted that it did. "But it also makes him stupid. Too stupid to get away with murder. And whoever killed Miss Shaw has gotten away with it. If it hadn't been for Josh and Jamie digging around for that envelope, and drawing attention to the fact that something more was going on, we'd never have realized it wasn't an accidental death. David Rossini just isn't that smart."

"So his wife is next?"

She was. And after that, Wayne would be having a chat with Jamie. "She asked if she could bring a friend. I'm halfway worried she'll show up with Josh."

"I think she got the point last night," Derek said, "when she knocked on his door and he didn't answer. If she brings someone, I don't think it'll be Josh."

Probably not. And it wouldn't be Candy. Another friend from school maybe. A college advisor. Or maybe Amelia Easton?

"Let us know if you find out anything interesting," I said.

Wayne promised he would, and hung up. We continued driving.

We spent the rest of the afternoon working on the condo. After Derek finished with the plumbing, he started tiling the shower walls. We had decided on a basic white subway tile, high gloss, with a decorative band of glass tiles about halfway up the wall, along with floating glass doors and a very streamlined, square sink simply set into a shiny chrome base with a lower shelf. It was modern, just a touch masculine, and a bit utilitarian in look if not design or function.

I was in the kitchen, preparing the backsplash so we could start tiling that tomorrow, too, when I happened to glance out the window into the parking lot and saw a strange car pull into a space and park. It was a plain white Toyota, so in and of itself nothing strange at all, but I hadn't seen it before. It was parked with its back to me, so I could see that it had Portland plates, and it also had an Enterprise sticker on the back bumper. A rental car. I stopped what I was doing to watch.

After a moment, the driver's side door opened and a woman came out. From two floors up, it wasn't easy to get a good look—not when what I was looking at was the crown of her head—but I could tell she was a few years older than me, maybe around forty, and that she had soft, light brown hair, cut in a classic, if a little dowdy, Dutch pageboy. Other than that, she looked to be on the short side, and slightly plump, with ample breasts and a matching posterior. She was dressed in a classic—also a bit dowdy—A-line skirt that hit her just below the knees, a matching jacket, prim blouse, and a pair of sensible pumps. She stopped in the middle of the parking lot and looked around.

"There's someone outside," I told Derek.

He turned away from the tiling to look at me. "Who?"

"Don't know. Some woman. I've never seen her before. Maybe it's Candy's mother. The age looks right. Maybe I should go give her my condolences and see if she needs help."

"Sure," Derek said and turned back to his tiling. "You know where to find me."

"I do, indeed." I pulled open the door to the stairway and stepped through. "I'll be back in a few minutes."

If Derek answered, I didn't hear him; I was already pulling the door to behind me and on my way down the stairs.

By the time I got to the first floor, the woman had drifted over to the door, but hadn't made a move to let herself into the building. Maybe she didn't have a key. "Can I help you?" I asked when I'd pulled the door open.

"Please." She had a soft voice and soft blue eyes to go with it. "I'm looking for someone."

She also had an accent. Southern. I've never spent much time in the South, so I couldn't place it more specifically, but it sounded the way both Jamie and Robin spoke, and to a lesser degree, Amelia Easton. Of course, she'd had more time to get rid of hers. This woman was about her age, and she still had the accent, so she must still be living in the South, I figured. Jamie's mother? Or perhaps Guy's mother, looking for Robin and Benjamin?

"Who's that?" I held my breath. If she said she was looking for Robin, would I be able to lie and tell her Robin didn't live here? I didn't want to be responsible for Robin and Bruce losing Benjamin. And I certainly didn't want to be responsible for Bruce strangling this woman to keep his little family intact.

"My daughter," the woman said. "Jamie Livingston?"

Oh. I started breathing again. It was still bad, but not as bad. "I haven't seen her today. She's probably at school."

The woman—Mrs. Livingston—shook her head. "I've been there. They said she wasn't in class. When I tried to find her dorm room, they said she'd moved into an apartment almost a year ago. I had no idea."

"I'm sorry," I said, since she seemed genuinely distraught and not all that judgmental. Not so far. "I'm Avery Baker. My boyfriend and I are renovating 2A. A floor below Jamie and . . ."

I stopped, no longer able to say "and Candy."

"The staff at the college told me her roommate passed away," Mrs. Livingston said.

I nodded. "Last night. We're all a little distraught at the

moment. I'm sure your daughter just needed some time away. Maybe she went to see a movie or something."

Mrs. Livingston didn't answer, and I remembered, a second too late, that movies are surely the Devil's work. However, the other option was that Jamie was at work, or at the police station talking to Wayne, and I didn't think either of those suggestions would make Mrs. Livingston any happier. Entirely apart from the fact that I didn't want to be the one to tell her—this very religious woman—that her daughter was a stripper. I wanted to tell her even less that her daughter was the prime suspect in two murders.

"I'm sorry," I said. "I don't have a key to Jamie's place. And I don't have her cell phone number, either. You can come up and wait in our apartment, if you want, but there's nothing to do there. No TV or . . ." But maybe she didn't watch TV, either. That could also be the Devil's work. Considering some of the programs on television these days, I could sort of relate to that opinion. "We're renovating," I added. "You'd be able to sit down, but I suppose you might as well do that in your car . . ."

Mrs. Livingston glanced at it and nodded.

"I can try to track her down for you, if you want." If nothing else, I could call Wayne. He was supposed to talk to Jamie this afternoon. She might still be there. She might be sitting in a cell.

"If you wouldn't mind," Mrs. Livingston said.

"Of course. I'll just run upstairs and get my phone. Do you want to come upstairs, or—"

"I'll wait down here," Mrs. Livingston said, "in case she comes home."

Fine with me. I'd be able to speak a little more freely to Wayne if she wasn't listening to me. "I'll be right back. One minute. Maybe two."

"Take your time," Mrs. Livingston said politely and backed out of the doorway. I let the door close behind her—she made no move to keep it open—and dashed up the stairs.

"Uh-oh," Derek said when I'd let myself into the condo

and had told him who was downstairs. Not Candy's mother, but Jamie's. The one—if we were right—Jamie had killed two people to avoid seeing.

"I know. She didn't seem bad at all, actually. Maybe it's the father Jamie's afraid of." I hauled the phone out of my bag.

"You calling Wayne?" Derek said.

I nodded, dialing. "With any luck, Jamie's still there and he can tell me what to do. What to tell this poor woman. I don't want to say the wrong thing."

Derek opened his mouth to answer, but Wayne picked up the phone first, and I held up a finger to stall Derek. "Wayne? It's Avery. Is Jamie still there?"

"No," Wayne said. "Why?"

No? "You'll never guess who showed up. Her mother."

"Jamie's mother?"

"Looking for Jamie. She's down in the parking lot right now. I didn't want to send her to you before I knew what was going on. Where's Jamie?"

"I had to let her go," Wayne said. "She had an alibi for Saturday at noon. She and Candy had argued Friday morning, about David Rossini, and Jamie didn't want to go home to more of the same. So she spent the night with another of the dancers and went right back to work on Saturday morning. She said several of the other girls can vouch for her being there."

"Did you check with them?"

"Not yet," Wayne said, "but if she says she was there, on stage, with people watching, I'm sure she was. She'd have to be stupid to lie about it, and I don't think she is."

"So where is she now?"

"No idea," Wayne said. "Probably on her way home. Or maybe back to school. She brought Amelia Easton with her to the interview, by the way. I thought maybe she'd arranged with Francesca Rossini to borrow a lawyer, but no. She seemed pretty rattled. Very young and scared. Maybe Professor Easton is the closest thing to family she could come up with on short notice."

Maybe. "Well, her mother is here now. What do I tell her?"

"You're asking me? It's out of my hands, Avery. I'm the chief of police. My job is to arrest whoever killed Miss Shaw and Candy. I'm not a psychologist or a family counselor. Tell her anything you want. And let Jamie deal with it. It's her problem." He hung up. I stuck my tongue out at the phone.

"Bad news?" Derek asked.

"Yes and no. Jamie has an alibi for Saturday at noon. She didn't buy the wine and chocolates. The bad news is that Wayne had to let her go. She isn't at the police station anymore."

"So where is she?"

"That's just it," I said. "She could be on her way here. Or—if she did kill Miss Shaw and Candy, and she fudged that alibi somehow—she could be anywhere." Once she dropped off Amelia Easton anyway. "I'd better go tell her mom that I can't find her."

Derek nodded. "Want me to come with you?"

"Of course not. I'll be back in a minute."

"I'll be here," Derek said, and went back to tiling.

. . .

So down the stairs I went again, this time with my phone in my hand. Through the door and into the parking lot, and over to the rental car, where Mrs. Livingston was waiting. "I'm sorry. I called around, but I couldn't find her. I found where she was just a few minutes ago, but she's left now. I guess she's probably on her way back, either here or back to Barnham."

Mrs. Livingston nodded.

"I guess you can either go back there and see if she's there, or wait here."

"I'll wait here," Mrs. Livingston said. "Sooner or later she'll show up. If she lives here."

I nodded. "I'm in 2A. If you need anything, just . . ." Ring the bell, I was about to say. But just then, a pale blue nondescript compact came up the road and swung into the lot. "Here she is now."

Mrs. Livingston looked up as the compact pulled in next to us. Jamie leaned across the passenger seat, across Amelia Easton, to stare. "Mom?"

"Hello, Jamie Lee," her mother said, her lips stiff. She looked as if she'd seen a ghost. Either Jamie had changed a whole lot in the year and couple of weeks she'd been away at college, or something else was wrong.

And then Mrs. Livingston added, in a voice that barely carried the couple of feet to where I stood, "Hello, Nan."

—21—

Nan?

I waited for Amelia to explain that Mrs. Livingston was mistaken; she was Amelia, not Nan. It had been twenty years and the girls had looked alike; it was a surprising, if not precisely earth-shattering mistake. Except Amelia didn't. She just stared back at Mrs. Livingston, mesmerized.

"Nan?" I said.

Amelia—Nan?—snapped out of it. She glanced up at me, at Mrs. Livingston, and then over at Jamie. "Drive!"

"Wh . . . what?" Jamie stuttered.

Amelia didn't repeat it, but the gun she pulled out of her purse had the same effect.

"Mom!" Jamie shrieked.

"No!" I threw myself at Mrs. Livingston and knocked her to the ground before Amelia—it was too difficult to think of her as anything else—could fire. At least in our direction. The compact bounced backward and then squealed forward, headed for the entrance to the parking lot.

"Jamie!" Mrs. Livingston screamed, and pushed me off her. I picked myself up and glanced around.

The compact was almost to the road. Derek's truck was parked on the other side of the lot. We were standing beside the rental car.

"Give me the keys," I said. "I'll drive. I know the roads."

Mrs. Livingston didn't waste time arguing, just dug in her purse for the car key. I slid behind the wheel and shoved the key in the ignition while she got into the passenger seat. Up on the road, the compact didn't even slow down before it squealed onto the road toward Augusta. I wondered whether that was Amelia's instruction or Jamie's choice.

"Keep an eye on the car," I told Mrs. Livingston. "I'll watch the road. And use this"—I dug in my pocket and pulled out the phone I'd, luckily, brought with me downstairs—"to call my boyfriend and tell him what happened."

Mrs. Livingston stared at the phone as if she'd never seen one before. Maybe she hadn't. "Shouldn't we call the police?"

"Derek will do that. He's upstairs. We need him to follow us." I plucked the phone out of her hand, punched in the number, and hit Speaker before I handed it back. "Hold on to it. I need both hands on the wheel." The compact was booking it at twenty miles per hour above the speed limit, and if I had any hope of keeping up, I'd have to concentrate.

The phone rang a couple of times, then—

"What happened?" Derek's voice said from the phone, sounding resigned. "Avery?"

"You have to call Wayne. Amelia took Jamie's car and Jamie."

"What?" It wasn't a request for information, it was an exclamation of shock. His voice wasn't resigned at all anymore, it was quick and sharp.

"Follow us in the truck," I said. "We're on our way up the Augusta Road. They're ahead of us and I don't want to lose them. Get Wayne and tell him to come, too. She's got a gun."

"Why?" Derek said.

I wasn't entirely sure. Not until I'd had a chance to talk to Mrs. Livingston. But I knew enough to hazard a guess. "I don't think she's Amelia Easton. She's really Nan. And Jamie's mom recognized her."

"Shit," Derek said. "I'm on my way. I'm gonna hang up and call Wayne now. Stay in touch, Avery, OK?"

I promised I would.

"And don't do anything stupid!" was the last thing I heard before he was gone. Mrs. Livingston watched as the display changed and showed that Derek had ended the call.

"Just hang on to it," I said. "If he calls back, hit the button that says Speaker."

Mrs. Livingston nodded and stared at the phone as if she expected it to ring right away.

"So that was Nan?" I said.

She glanced over at me. "Nanette Barbour. We grew up together."

"Jamie told me. I thought her name was Amelia Easton." I wondered if Jamie knew the truth, or if she'd been as surprised as I was. "Are you sure?"

Duh. Of course she was sure. If she hadn't been right, Amelia—Nan—wouldn't have made a run for it.

Mrs. Livingston nodded. "I grew up with the both of them. Amelia and Nan. I was a couple years younger, so when they left for college, I was still in high school. Or the commune equivalent. I was fifteen or sixteen."

"And then word came back that Nan died."

"Amelia called first. To say that Nan wasn't behaving. The elders discussed it and decided to bring them both home."

"What did you think of that?" Up ahead, the compact kept going, straight up the road. I concentrated on keeping it in sight, and did my best to focus on what Mrs. Livingston had to say. Hopefully Derek was raising Wayne while at the same time hotfooting it down to the truck.

"I was excited," Mrs. Livingston said softly. "I missed Amelia. Nan was always more brash, more likely to get into trouble, but Amelia was a good girl."

"But instead of coming home, Nan died," I said. "Or so you thought."

"The police called. To say that Nan had committed suicide. We couldn't bring her body back, she had broken the commandments. I thought Amelia would be coming home, but she didn't. She never did. I never understood why. Until now."

"Because that isn't Amelia up ahead."

Mrs. Livingston shook her head. "That's Nan. They looked alike, but not to someone who knew them. Amelia's hair was curly, Nan's was wavy. Amelia's eyes were dark blue, Nan's were a little more gray. And Nan was the one who pierced her ears with a sewing needle when she was seventeen. Amelia wouldn't have done that."

"She could have changed her mind later," I said, the same way that she'd changed her major from home ec to history. Except of course she really hadn't. Nan had changed Amelia's major to history, because history was what Nan wanted to study.

Mrs. Livingston shook her head, adamant, back on the pierced ears. "The sight of blood made her sick. Physically sick. And she said once that because Christ's body was pierced on the cross, she would never willingly pierce her own."

It made sense, in a strange sort of way. Not that I really needed Mrs. Livingston to prove anything to me. If she said it was Nan up ahead, I was willing to take her word for it. Nan herself—Amelia—had proven that pretty much without a doubt when she'd taken off and taken Jamie with her.

"So I guess Nan started acting out once they got to college, and Amelia called home. And then Nan killed Amelia and somehow managed to make everyone believe it was Nan who was dead . . ."

"They looked alike," Mrs. Livingston said. "Cousins. We were all related. That's one of the reasons the Mississippi government refused to allow the commune to continue operating. That and the fact that the children didn't get immunized or properly educated or even registered with the state. Up until ten or fifteen years ago, there were no real records of any of us."

So Nan could have gotten away with killing Amelia, and no one would have known the difference. No DNA, no fingerprints, no dental records. No visual identification other than Nan's. The girls had only been at college for a week or so—not much time to make connections with other people. And if they looked alike anyway, that would have helped. Slap some lipstick on Amelia while making herself look sweeter and dowdier . . .

So for twenty years, Nan had pretended to be Amelia Easton. That explained why she'd never gone back to the commune after "Amelia" died. If she was Nan, not only wouldn't she want to, but she'd also have known she'd be recognized if she did. In fact . . .

"Shit," I said as the metaphoric lightbulb flickered on above my head. Mrs. Livingston winced, and I added, "Sorry. But I just realized something."

"What might that be?"

"Two people have died in the building in the past week. Both of them were threatening to call you. We thought maybe Jamie—"

"My daughter would never kill anyone!" Mrs. Livingston said, and drew herself up indignantly.

"Of course not. I realize that now. But Amelia . . . Nan. She knew that if you came to Maine, you'd recognize her." And what a motive *that* was. It blew everyone else's motive for murder right out of the water. If Mr. and Mrs. Livingston identified her as Nan, not only would she lose her entire life, she'd also go to jail for arranging Amelia's "suicide." There's no statute of limitations on murder. And if she'd already killed once, it probably came easier the second time. And the third. It was "Amelia"—Nan—who had bought the wine and chocolates and given them to Candy.

The phone rang and Mrs. Livingston hit the speaker button. "Yes?"

"Avery?" Derek's voice said.

I raised my own. "I'm here. What's up?"

"I'm a couple minutes behind you. Wayne's a couple minutes behind me. Where are you?"

I looked around. "Not too far from Clovercroft."

"That development the Stenhams were working on when they went to jail? I'll let Wayne know. He's contacted the police in Dresden, and they're on their way down to meet us. They'll set up a roadblock halfway between them and Waterfield."

"She may turn off the road before then," I warned.

"Yes," Derek said, "but where? There's only this one main road in this area, and it goes to Dresden. There are a few developments along the way, but mostly it's just woods. Where are they gonna go?"

I didn't know, and said so.

"Can you see them?"

"They're up ahead. It's been no problem keeping up with them so far. Thank God there's not much traffic."

I shot a guilty glance at Mrs. Livingston. She probably wouldn't like it that I took the Lord's name in vain. But her eyes were closed, and I guess she was praying, one hand holding the phone and the other tightly knotted in her lap.

"The Augusta police are sending a chopper," Derek added. "Keep an eye out for it."

I promised I would. "Actually, I think I hear it already." A faint *fwapping* noise was coming from outside, and when I bent and peered out of the windshield, I saw what looked like a tiny insect buzzing above the pine trees on the left, getting bigger with every second. "Yep, there it is."

"They're gonna keep an eye on them from the air," Derek began, and then stopped when I cursed. "What?"

"Sorry." Mrs. Livingston must think I was the worst heathen. "They must have noticed the helicopter, too. They're turning off the road. Into Clovercroft."

"That might work in our favor," Derek said. "We know the place. There isn't anywhere there that they can hide. And the road won't do that little compact any good."

Very true. It might not do the rental much good, either. But Derek's truck would be fine. It had big, beefy tires.

"I'm less than five minutes behind you," Derek said. "Don't do anything stupid, Avery."

He hung up before I could tell him that I wouldn't. It was probably better that way, since it wasn't a promise I was sure I could keep.

I had to slow down as I took the turn into Clovercroft. I couldn't see the compact right now, but that was OK; there was only one way to go from here: down through the copse of trees and into the development. I slowed down a little more as the rental bumped and skittered across the dirt road.

"I don't see them," Mrs. Livingston said nervously.

"They're up ahead. There's only one road in and out. It's a housing development my cousins were working on until they went to jail last year."

She shot me a look but didn't ask any more questions. By now she surely thought I was not only a heathen but a criminal, too.

"We'll get her back," I said, although I wasn't sure I could believe it myself. Depending on how desperate Amelia—Nan—was, she might end up shooting Jamie. I had no idea why she would, but when guns come into the picture, someone often gets shot, and it's not always the person you hope it will be.

We bounced out of the band of trees and saw the only completed buildings in Clovercroft up ahead: a row of commercial storefronts with apartments above. The banner that said Model Home was still hanging outside one of them, a lot more faded now than the last time I'd been here.

Then it had been Derek's sister Beatrice's small white car we'd been looking for—and had found, outside the model home. This time it was the pale blue compact. And like Beatrice's car last year, the compact was empty.

I looked around. There were only a few places someone could hide, and inside one of the buildings was the obvious choice. "Stay here," I told Mrs. Livingston. "Keep hold of the phone."

She nodded. "Where are you—"

"I'm just gonna look around." I opened the car door and put a foot on the ground. And just as quickly pulled it back inside the car when a bullet pinged against the open door. "Whoa."

"She's in there," Mrs. Livingston said, pointing to the office. At some point between now and the last time I'd been here, in November or December last year, someone had busted in the door and probably ripped anything of value out of both office and model home upstairs.

I nodded. "Call Derek back. Tell him what . . . never mind. Here he is now."

The black Ford F-150 burst out of the trees before I'd stopped talking, and roared toward us. He must have flown to get here so soon. He'd been five minutes behind us when we left the condo parking lot; now it was just about a minute or so since we'd pulled in here.

He stopped on the far side of the rental and rolled down his window. I hit the button to retract ours, and peered across Mrs. Livingston at my fiancé's irate face.

"I should have known it was too good to be true. You just wouldn't be you, would you, if you'd let the police take care of things for once?"

"I can't help it that she kidnapped Jamie right in front of me," I protested. "What was I going to do? Let her?"

"Of course not." He nodded to Mrs. Livingston. "Hello. I'm Derek Ellis. The chief of police is on his way. And there's the chopper the state police sent." He glanced up, where the helicopter was hovering above us. "We'll get your daughter back."

"They're in the office," I said. "And Amelia has a gun. She's already taken a potshot at me. That's why I'm still in the car."

"Of course it is," Derek said. "As long as she has a gun and bullets, I don't think we want to try to rush her. Just stay in the car and wait for Wayne. He should be here in a few minutes. I'll drive to the other side of the building and see if I can get a bead on anything."

"Be careful."

"Of course. I'm getting married in a month. I'm not about to do anything stupid."

He grinned and put the truck in gear. I watched him drive to the end of the row of buildings and turn the corner. Then I turned my attention back to the office again.

Wayne arrived after a few minutes. By then Derek had gotten in touch by phone to tell us he couldn't see much through the back, but that there was a door there that someone could use to get in.

"If I had a SWAT team on standby," Wayne said irritably, "or just more than one flak vest in the car, I'd be all for that. But it would take at least forty minutes to get a full team here from Augusta, and I'm not sure we have forty minutes."

I wasn't sure, either. I had no idea what Amelia—Nan—thought she'd accomplish with this crazy move. Or maybe she hadn't been thinking. Maybe she'd just reacted, her only thought to get away. Forcing her into Clovercroft had probably been a bad move on our part. It made her feel cornered, and as Derek had said yesterday, when someone feels cornered, sometimes they resort to desperate measures to survive.

"Tell me again what we're dealing with here," Wayne ordered. I explained exactly what had happened, and Mrs. Livingston added her assurances that, yes, the woman inside the building was Nan Barbour, not Amelia Easton.

"So basically she's got nothing to lose," I said. "If she comes out of this alive, she'll go to jail, probably for the rest of her life."

Wayne nodded. "At this point, I'm less concerned with arresting Amelia Easton—Nanette Barbour—than I am with getting Jamie out safe and sound. At the moment, she has no reason to kill Jamie. Let's make sure we don't give her one."

Mrs. Livingston agreed fervently.

"Is there some way we can make it beneficial to her to let Jamie go? She's already proven she knows how to look out for number one. If we can make her think Jamie's a hindrance . . ."

"If we do that, she might kill her," Wayne said tightly. "I won't play that card until I have to."

Fine. "Derek—or Derek and I—could cause a distraction in the back. Banging on the door or something. That might give you enough time to shoot her from out here."

"If she doesn't shoot you first," Wayne said. "Bullets have been known to punch through walls, and this is the Stenhams' handiwork; it won't be that solid."

Yet another reason to deplore my distant cousins.

"We could try calling. Negotiating. See if we can work out a deal. There must be something she wants."

"She wants to get away," Wayne said. "She's killed three people, and she wants to get away. I want Jamie out in one piece. At this point, I'm willing to let her think anything she wants. Do you have the number?"

I didn't. "Josh might."

"Why would Josh have Professor Easton's number? He's taking computer technology, not history."

"I was thinking of Jamie," I said. "He might have Jamie's number."

I added, for Mrs. Livingston's benefit, "Josh is Chief Rasmussen's son. He lives across the hall from Jamie. With his girlfriend."

Wayne arched his brows at the suggestion that Josh was living with Shannon, but he seemed to recognize that I was saying it to reassure Mrs. Livingston that nothing was going on with Josh and Jamie, because he didn't quibble. Although by now, surely Josh had told him that something *had* gone on with him and Jamie at least once.

Josh did have Jamie's number. He did not, however, inquire why his dad wanted it. I thought that boded well for Shannon, since yesterday, I thought I'd detected a little softness on Josh's part for Jamie—at least until Derek had warned him to spend the night elsewhere because she'd come knocking.

"Here," Wayne said, "you call. Don't say anything overt, but try to feel her out."

I nodded. And took a deep breath and dialed.

The phone rang and rang. At first it went to voice mail, and Wayne told me to try again, while I stepped out from behind cover so they could see through the window that I was the one trying to call.

I didn't think they were going to answer this time, either, but finally the phone was picked up. Jamie's voice was even softer than usual, the Southern accent more pronounced, and she sounded scared to death. "Yes?"

"It's Avery," I said. "Are you all right?"

"I'm fine." She sounded the opposite, and probably felt that way, too.

"Are you hurt?"

She said she wasn't. I resisted the temptation to complain. But darn, we couldn't use that as an excuse to try to talk Amelia—Nan—into letting her go!

"Your mom wants to talk to you," I said. "I'm gonna put you on speaker, OK?"

Hopefully she'd take the hint and do the same on her end, so Amelia—Nan—could hear, too.

I handed the phone off to Mrs. Livingston, who cleared her throat. "Hello? Jamie Lee?"

"Hi, Mama," Jamie said. "What . . . You didn't tell me you were coming. What are you doing here?"

"I wanted to surprise you," her mother said, with that slight hint of accusation that mothers excel at. "And I knew if I suggested it, you'd come up with some reason why it wasn't convenient."

That must have happened before, because Jamie couldn't come up with an answer. Then—

"I'm sorry. I knew you'd get upset if I told you I wanted to move out of the dorm and into an apartment with a friend."

"It doesn't matter," Mrs. Livingston said. "I don't care. I just wanted to see you. To know you were safe." Her voice was still shaking.

"I missed you, too, Mama," Jamie said, and sniffed. The whole thing was so sweet it made my teeth ache, and what made it worse was that if something went wrong, this might be the last conversation the two of them would have. And we were no closer to figuring out how to get Jamie out.

And then I straightened with a gulp when I heard the next thing Mrs. Livingston said. "May I speak to Nan?"

"I'm Amelia," Amelia's voice said from a distance. "Not Nan. Nanette's dead."

"She says Nanette's dead," Jamie reported. "She's Amelia."

Mrs. Livingston glanced at Wayne, who nodded.

"Of course. I'm sorry. May I speak to Amelia, please, Jamie Lee?"

Jamie must have conferred, probably silently, with Amelia/Nan, because the next thing that happened was that the older woman came on the phone. "Hello, Denise."

Mrs. Livingston smiled, but I wasn't sure whether it was in acid appreciation or just polite habit. In either case, the smile didn't reach her eyes. "Amelia. It's been a long time."

I'm sure "Amelia" was thinking that it hadn't been long enough, but she didn't say so. "You have a lovely daughter," she said instead. Wayne's eyes narrowed, as I'm sure he tried to discern from the tone whether the statement was intended as friendly conversation or a threat.

Denise Livingston must have wondered the same thing, but she managed to keep her voice steady. "Thank you. I'm sure she has appreciated getting to know you. I told her about you, you know. It made me sad that you never came home."

"I'm sorry, too," "Amelia" said, "but after what happened . . . it just felt disloyal to Nan's memory to go back."

She seemed determined to keep behaving as if she were, in fact, Amelia. As if there were a chance that we'd actually believe it.

Or was it possible that she actually thought she was Amelia? Had she taken the lie so far that she'd started believing it herself?

I glanced at Wayne, who shook his head, finger to his lips.

"I wish you'd come out, Amelia," Mrs. Livingston was saying plaintively. "I haven't seen my daughter for a year. And I haven't seen you for more than twenty. Not since you and . . . and Nan left for college. Won't you come out so we can all sit down and talk? And get to know each other again?"

"I already know Jamie," fake Amelia said, her voice suddenly sharper, "and Jamie and I want to stay here."

Jamie and I? Stockholm syndrome, or was she simply speaking for Jamie because *she* wanted Jamie to stay?

Probably the latter. Jamie was a smart girl; she wouldn't want to spend her time with the woman who had killed Candy and Miss Shaw and the real Amelia Easton. The woman who was keeping her from her mother. At gunpoint.

But again, maybe Nan—Amelia—really had gone around the bend and honestly believed she was Amelia.

Or maybe she just wanted us to think she did. Setting up that "innocent by reason of insanity" defense for later.

"Do you think she'll try to kill herself?" I asked Wayne out of the corner of my mouth. "If we push her too hard? Will she do that rather than let herself be arrested?"

He answered back the same way, not taking his eyes off the building. "It's possible. She's looking at going on trial for three murders. All the evidence is circumstantial, but it all hangs together, and taking Jamie hostage is an admission of guilt if I ever saw one."

"Will she shoot Jamie first, if she does?" I held my breath while I waited for his answer, my eyes on Mrs. Livingston, a few feet away, still arguing back and forth with "Amelia" about letting Jamie go. Hopefully she was too busy to listen to us.

"She might," Wayne said. "To punish Jamie's mother for recognizing her. It isn't impossible."

I had my mouth open and was about to respond when—

"Well, then," Mrs. Livingston said firmly, "I'm coming in."

She headed for the door to the office, still clutching the phone. It was squawking, but by now she was too far away for me to hear what "Amelia" was saying. Wayne made an abortive movement forward, perhaps thinking to stop her, but he checked himself.

"Are you just going to let her go inside?" I said.

He glanced at me, and then back to Mrs. Livingston. She was on her way up the steps to the door. "It's her daughter. If it was Shannon in there, Kate would do the same thing."

"Would you let her?"

He didn't answer, but it might have been because Mrs. Livingston reached for the door. I held my breath as I waited for "Amelia" to blow her away.

But the shot, when it came, came from inside the office. There was something like a thud, and then another bang I recognized as a gunshot, and then a really loud bang from right beside me that sounded like a clap of thunder. I blinked and shook my head as the front window of the office collapsed in what looked like slow motion, a cascade of glass. Wayne lowered his gun and said something, but I couldn't hear it. All I could hear was the reverberations from the shot.

He had probably told me to stay put, because the next thing he did was run up the steps to the office and kick the door in. In was quite impressive to watch, actually, and I'd have appreciated it more had my ears not been ringing.

And then I forgot my ears and everything else when I saw Derek through the now missing window, standing in the middle of the room inside, with his hand pressed against his side with blood trickling through his fingers.

I was up the stairs and through the door in seconds. "Derek!"

"Flesh wound," my boyfriend said. "I didn't get out of the way fast enough."

I looked around. Mrs. Livingston had wrapped Jamie in a hug, and it looked like both of them were crying, while Wayne was kneeling on the floor next to "Amelia Easton." The back door was standing open, the lock splintered. Derek must have kicked it in while Mrs. Livingston was distracting "Amelia." When he came through, she had shot at him, and then Wayne had shot at her. And dropped her.

"Is she dead?" My voice was perfectly steady. I wouldn't be sorry if she were.

Wayne shook his head. "I aimed for the stomach. The ambulance is on its way. It was waiting just beyond the trees."

"You called them earlier?"

"Guns," Wayne said. "Someone usually gets shot."

And in this case it had been my fiancé. I turned to him nervously. He didn't seem overly bothered by the fact that he was bleeding, to be truthful. He gave fake Amelia a visual scan—albeit without getting down on the floor next to her—and pronounced that she would survive. "No arterial bleeding. Although you may have nicked something in there. Intestines or kidneys or something. Nothing that can't be fixed."

"You?" Wayne asked.

"I'm fine. There's nothing in this part of the body that can be damaged. Just a flesh wound."

"Are you sure?" I said nervously.

He smiled and reached out to me. "I've seen a lot of gunshots, Tink. I used to work on them all the time in the ER. This one's no big deal. You're not getting rid of me that easily."

"Good," I said, and snuggled into his good side.

—Epilogue—

"Do you, Avery," Barry said, "take Derek to be your lawful wedded husband?"

He said a lot of other things, too, but I was too worried about missing my cue to listen. When he paused, I nodded. "I do."

Barry smiled approvingly before turning to my right. "And do you, Derek . . ."

"I do," Derek said, hitting his cue right on.

Barry nodded. "In that case, with the power vested in me by the state of Maine, I pronounce you husband and wife. You may kiss the bride."

He grinned at Derek, who grinned back before turning to me. "What do you say, Tink?"

"Do your worst." I braced myself.

"Ladies and gentlemen," Barry said above my head, "I'm happy to present Mr. and Mrs. Derek and Avery Ellis."

There was a round of applause that I didn't really hear because of the rushing in my ears, but when Derek let me go and I turned toward the pews, I saw my mom and Cora wiping away tears while Kate grinned from ear to ear, and a lot of other people looked quite happy for us both.

The ceremony had gone off without a hitch, something that couldn't be said for yesterday's rehearsal dinner. It had been raining cats and dogs outside, so we all arrived at the church soaking wet, leaving puddles in the vestry, after almost slipping off the road a few times due to the slick pavement.

"I hope it stops by tomorrow," I told my mother as I shook out the umbrella and leaned it in the corner.

She shook her head. "Rain in the wedding veil is supposed to bring good luck."

Great. So now I had to hope for rain on the most important day of my life.

The rehearsal itself started late, because the organist *had* run off the road in the rain—luckily with no injury to herself or the car—and then it limped along as everyone struggled with nerves and concentration. We'd gotten to the point where the minister said, "Speak now or forever hold your peace," when the doors to the church opened. When I turned around, I saw my friend from New York, Laura Lee, slip through and onto a pew in the back, her pink rain slicker shining wetly. She had been followed by what must have been her date for the occasion: a tall man in a leather trench coat, shaking raindrops from his shoulder-length brown hair.

"What the hell . . ." had slipped out of my mouth.

Barry had looked startled and my mother had looked shocked. Derek had looked at me and then over his shoulder. After a second he'd turned back to me, lips twitching. "Did you invite him?"

"No! Are you *crazy*?"

Why would I invite my ex-boyfriend to my wedding? I'd made a point *not* to invite him.

"You invited Melissa," Derek had pointed out.

"That's different." Melissa lived here. She'd been—unfortunately—part of both of our lives for as long as I'd lived in Waterfield. Excluding her would have looked petty.

Of course, I had hoped she'd be sensitive enough to decline the invitation, but no such luck. Sensitivity is not one of Melissa's conspicuous qualities.

"Think he'll object?"

I'd turned back to Derek, who still looked amused rather than upset or worried. "What?"

"Tomorrow. Think he'll object?"

"Lord, no." I shook my head. "And it wouldn't do any good if he did. I'm marrying you whether you like it or not."

"Good thing," Derek said, and turned back to Barry. "Carry on."

Barry nodded and got back to it.

I did exchange a few words with Laura Lee and Philippe after the rehearsal was done, but I had to get to the rehearsal dinner and they had to get to the B&B where they were staying after the long and treacherous drive. "We'll talk more tomorrow," Laura promised me, with a sort of significant look.

I nodded. No doubt.

And now here we were. Tomorrow. Going through the ceremony again, for real this time. The weather had cleared up. It wasn't precisely sunny, but it wasn't raining hard, either. Everyone had gotten to the church on time—"See?" my mother said. "A bad dress rehearsal means a good performance."—and we'd all remembered our moves and our lines. When Barry asked if anyone knew a reason why Derek and I should not be joined in holy matrimony, I held my breath. Not because I thought anyone would really object—least of all Philippe, who didn't want me back any more than I wanted him—but no one did. And then we said our vows, and Derek put a ring on my finger, and I put one on his, and I was Mrs. Derek Ellis.

"That was beautiful!" Mother sniffed afterward at the buffet-style reception next door to the church. She was dabbing at her eyes with a lace handkerchief and smiling through the tears.

I smiled back. "It felt beautiful, too."

"And you look lovely. Beautiful gown."

"Beatrice's," I said. "I had to chop off about a foot of fabric on the bottom, but that's OK. She'll never wear it again." Nor—if fate was kind—would I. "And this way I got to wear white to my wedding."

Mother sniffed again as more tears came to her eyes, and gave me a hug. Behind her, my stepfather Noel beamed.

Everyone who was anyone in Waterfield was there. Barry had changed out of his vestments and into a suit, and was walking Judy through the buffet line. She was almost a head taller than him due to the heels she'd put on with her purple dress, but neither of them seemed to care. Next to them in line was John Nickerson, who was talking to—I squinted. She had short hair and was dressed in lavender, and there was something familiar about both the lady and the dress.

Then it hit me. "That's Sandra Lawrence!"

"Who?" Mom said.

"The woman John's talking to. It's Sandra Lawrence. The medical examiner. From Portland."

"Who's John?" Mom wanted to know. I pointed him out, and Mom squinted at Dr. Lawrence. "What about it?"

"He used to be in love with her little sister fifty years ago. Susie. They went to school together."

"Yes," Mom said patiently, "but why are you so excited?"

"Oh, I don't know. Susie's married. We went to her daughter's wedding to one of Derek's friends a month or two ago. But Dr. Lawrence is single. And so is John. And they look awfully chummy, don't they?"

They did. Mother agreed with me.

Then Mother went off with Noel, who was beaming as proudly as my father would have done on this day—he'd walked me down the aisle in lieu of my real dad, of course—and Laura Lee came up and flung herself at me.

Back when I was living in New York, we both worked for Philippe. I was his textile designer and girlfriend, while Laura was his business attorney. There'd never been anything more between them that I knew of, although now I felt compelled to ask. Although I waited until after she'd finished hugging me and telling me how lovely the ceremony had been and how gorgeous Derek was. This was her first time seeing him, since I hadn't brought him to New York with me last August, and Laura hadn't come to visit me in Maine.

"Speaking of gorgeous," I said, "what's with you and Philippe? Are you dating now?"

"Lord, no!" Laura said, dismissing Philippe with a flick of a pink-taloned hand. She'd always had beautiful nails. "He dumped Tara after a few months—or maybe she dumped him. She couldn't have been more than twenty-two, and he's pushing forty, so it wouldn't be surprising if she got tired of him."

Not surprising at all.

"He hasn't been seeing anyone regularly. And I'm not stupid enough to take him on." She brushed a strand of her straight black hair behind her ear.

"Whose idea was it to bring him here?"

She grinned. "Oh, it was his. He liked it here when he was up last summer. Says he wants to buy a summer house."

Really? Maybe we could talk Melissa into selling him the house on Rowanberry Island. And soak him for every penny we could while we were at it. It seemed fair.

"Or," Laura added, winking, "maybe he just can't resist keeping his hand in."

"His hand isn't in," I said. "His hand is nowhere near any of this."

Laura smiled. "I can tell. You couldn't ask for a better guy than Derek. And you seem happy. When you left New York, I honestly didn't think it would last. I thought you'd be back after a few months."

It was my turn to smile. "Once I met Derek, there was no going back. And I love it here now. I wouldn't want to be anywhere else."

"It's a nice place." Laura nodded. "I don't think it's for me, but I can tell you're happy. So I'm happy for you!" She leaned in to touch her cheek to mine. I leaned, too.

She wandered off, and I looked around, at my friends and family, at my wedding reception. Mom and Noel had joined the buffet line now, while Kate caught my eye from a table over in the corner and smiled. She was sitting with Wayne, Shannon and Josh, and Paige Thompson and Ricky Swanson, who were back in town now. Ricky had his degree—in computer technology, the same thing Josh was going for—but Paige was Shannon and Josh's age, and had two years to go. Ricky had found a job with an IT company in Portland, and they had already put an offer on the apartment Derek and I had renovated. It had turned out very nice, actually, once we got down to business: Blond wood floors throughout the rooms made the space seem larger, along with pale shades of green on all the walls. We did put corrugated metal below the chair rail in the dining room; it made quite an impression, and looked great with the chandelier I'd made from empty canisters of spray paint. And Derek had shown me how to etch glass, so the mirror on the sliding door in the hallway had a border of Celtic knots, which suited Patrick Murphy Swanson just fine.

Some of the neighbors were here, too. Mariano and Gregg were on their way through the buffet line, dapper in suits and ties, while Bruce and Robin were sharing a table with Peter and Jill Cortino and their brood. Benjamin and little Pamela were about the same age, and were hopping on the dance floor, while Robin was holding Baby Pepper and making eyes at Bruce. Maybe she wanted another baby.

Pepper wasn't the only infant present. Ian Burns and his Ukrainian wife, Angie, had driven down from Boothbay Harbor, and had brought their son, Liam, who'd been born at the beginning of the summer. Irina was holding him; she and Gert had flown up from Florida to be with us. She looked awfully comfortable holding little Liam, and I wondered if we might not be on the receiving end of some good news from them soon, too.

Looking around, I located Derek on the opposite side of

the room, talking to his family. Cora and Dr. Ben were there, Beatrice and Steve, and Alice and her husband, Lon, up from Boston. Even Paw-Paw Willy, Derek's grandfather, had flown up from retirement in Florida for the occasion. Derek caught my eye, smiled, and beckoned. *C'mere.*

On the way there, I happened past Melissa, who was making eyes at Philippe aka Phil. She'd done that the last time he was in town, too, a year ago, and I thought, a little uncharitably—as I had done back then—that they deserved one another.

I was going to brush past with a polite smile, since I had no real need or desire to talk to either of them. But Philippe insisted on kissing both my cheeks and telling me how lovely I looked and how small-town life obviously agreed with me—all in his fake French accent—and once he was done, Melissa asked for a moment of my time.

"I'm on my way to meet Derek . . ." I demurred.

Unfortunately, a glance in his direction showed me that he was still talking to his family, laughing at something someone had said. His head was thrown back, his dimples were showing, and the sight of him in a tuxedo was one I was sure I'd remember forever. He was gorgeous, and for a second I got caught up in watching him. When I turned back to Melissa, she was doing the same thing, and the expression on her face was one I'd never seen before. Soft and wistful and a little sad.

After a moment she seemed to realize what she was doing, and when she turned to me, she was smiling that bright smile with the unnatural amount of teeth. "You're a lucky girl, Avery."

"No argument here," I said.

"I hope you'll be very happy together."

"Thank you," I said, "I'm sure we will be."

It was all very proper and—I realized—very fake. And because it was the happiest day of my life, and because I had Derek and she didn't, I could afford to be magnanimous. "Is everything OK, Melissa?"

"I'm moving away," Melissa said.

I blinked. "Where?" Surely not to New York with Phil?

"Portland," Melissa said. And added, "Tony left me his condo there. And there's nothing for me here anymore. With Tony gone and Ray . . . well, I wouldn't want Ray back anyway. Not after what happened."

"Of course not." I wanted to tell her that she didn't have to leave, that she could stay in Waterfield as long as she wanted, but I didn't think I had the right. I also didn't think Tony and Ray were the only reasons she was going. But I wasn't about to call her on it. If she still had feelings for Derek, and she didn't want to stick around now that he was married to someone else, I could hardly blame her for that. If he'd been my husband and I'd lost him, I wouldn't want to watch him be happy with someone else, either. For as long as we were only dating and there was the chance I'd get tired of Waterfield and want to go back to New York, that was one thing. But now, when we were married and presumably settled . . . well, I didn't blame her at all for wanting to make herself scarce.

So I smiled and said it sounded like a good idea for her to start over somewhere else, and she already had such a great reputation for real estate—she'd already done a few deals in Portland; after all, it's less than an hour away—and maybe we'd see her again if she came up here to work sometime. Oh, and by the way, if she wasn't too busy, maybe she could sell Philippe our big, white elephant on Rowanberry Island before she left?

I think we were both equally relieved when the conversation was over and she could go back to Philippe and I could go meet Derek, who had finally extricated himself from his family and was on his way across the floor toward me, a frown on his face.

"What was that about?"

"She wished us well," I said serenely. "It seems she's decided to move to Portland, to Tony's condo."

"Oh," Derek said, his face clearing. After thinking

about it for a moment, he added, "Well, it'll be good for her. A bigger pond. Waterfield always was too small for her."

"You're not going to miss her?"

"Why would I miss her?" Derek said and put his arms around my waist. "I've got you."

Awww. I went up on my tippy toes to brush my lips over his. "I love you."

He smiled down at me. "I love you, too, Mrs. Ellis."

And then his lips came back and settled in, and I forgot all about Melissa and everything else in the enjoyment of being well and truly married to the man of my dreams.

—Home-Renovation— and Design Tips

Tips to Maximize Space

1. In a small space, everything counts
A lot of people live in small spaces. Some because it's what they can afford, and some because it's what they choose. Some people enjoy the tight quarters. You may be one of them. If you thrive in a cozy, intimate space, you're in luck. By using soft, snuggly upholstered pieces, dark, warm tones, and dramatic lighting, your tiny corner can become a wonderful private space.

But if you feel the need to stretch out in your small space and make it seem lighter and airier, you can make some decorating changes to make the area look and feel larger without moving any walls. With color, furniture, and lighting, your space will feel less cramped.

2. Light colors make your room look bigger and brighter
Light-colored walls are more reflective of light, making a space feel open and airy, which will help maximize the

effect created by natural light. Dark colors, on the other hand, absorb light, making the room look smaller.

For optimum effect, select soft, calming tones of blues and greens, and always remember that brighter rooms look bigger and more inviting. Paint your wall trim and moldings a lighter color than your walls. When you paint your moldings light, the wall appears farther back, making your space appear bigger.

3. If you have access to natural light, make full use of it

Windows make a room seem bigger because a barrier between visitor and outside view has been removed. Instead of seeing a dimension-defining wall, visitors see an expansive view of the outdoors. Make sure window coverings are sheer, or are pulled back—or nonexistent—to bring more light in. If the view is bad, use hanging plants and potted flowers near windows.

Similarly, mirrors can make your room look larger by giving the illusion of depth. The mirrors also reflect both natural and artificial light to make a room brighter both day and night. They bounce light deep into the room, making it appear larger. Mirrors are especially effective near a window so the outdoors can be reflected.

4. Keep your room tidy and organized

Nothing makes a small space feel more cramped than having too much stuff in it. With things neatly arranged and out of sight, the space that is in view will feel orderly and open. A cluttered room equals a smaller room.

Use multifunction furniture with built-in storage: coffee table chests, sofa beds, benches with seat storage. An extendable dining table, folding tables, and nests of tables can be tucked away when you don't need them.

Place the large pieces of furniture against the walls so the open space in the middle isn't broken up. Consider having at least some of the furniture pieces the same color as the walls to make them recede.

Keep lines simple and scale the furniture to fit the size of the room. Don't block walking pathways. With furniture and accessories blocking the view into a room and out to open spaces, a room will look cramped. By moving furniture out and away from walkways, you'll open up the space and make it feel larger.

Setting your furniture at an angle works because the longest straight line in any given room is its diagonal. When you place your furniture at an angle, it leads the eye along the longer distance, rather than the shorter wall. As an added bonus, you often get some additional storage space behind the piece in the corner, too!

Choose furniture that has open arms and exposed legs. This allows light to filter under and through the furniture, making the room appear airier. Even better, choose a glass-topped table! Anything seen through glass appears farther away, and you'll allow light through the table, as well.

If you can see the floor, the room will look larger, so keep the floor as clear as possible. Carrying floor covering (and wall color) through two connecting rooms is a good way to help dissolve the lines between the two rooms and open them up to each other. This technique is only effective, however, when used for adjoining rooms that fall in the same line of sight.

Space-Saver Wine Rack

Make your own wine rack from mailing tubes. The process is ridiculously easy, and the results surprisingly cute, so you can have a bevy of bottle storage in no time.

MATERIALS

- Cardboard mailing tubes (big enough to accommodate a bottle of wine)
- Plenty of wine
- Measuring tape

- Pencil
- Handsaw
- Sandpaper (200 grit)
- Paintbrush (optional)
- Paint (optional)
- Round color-coded stickers (optional)

DIRECTIONS

1. Measure the space where you want to install the wine rack. If it's a shelf, make sure it's strong enough to support all of your bottles. (Avery installed her shelf vertically and stuck it between two cabinets in the kitchen for a built-in look.)
2. Measure and mark your tubes in increments of 9 inches (just enough to cover most of a wine bottle).
3. Cut the tubes along your marks with the handsaw, taking care to keep the cuts even. Sand off any cardboard fragments.
4. If you want to paint the tubes, do it now. Make sure they dry completely before continuing.
5. Stack your tubes inside the space meant for them.
6. Gather your wine. Obsessive-compulsive types may want to come up with their own systems of categorizing bottle caps with color-coded stickers (to parse out which vintages are for everyday drinking and which are for special occasions).
7. Raise a toast to your not-so-hard work.

How to Make Paper at Home

Here's how to make Avery's wedding invitations:
To make a sheet of paper, you must first get a suspension of cellulose fibers in water. Getting these fibers from a tree trunk is possible, but the process would take a lot of time and effort. A much simpler alternative is to reuse newspa-

pers, from which fibers are easier to extract. As a bonus, you'll be helping the environment by recycling.

MATERIALS

- Wooden boards
- Sieve with holes of about 1 millimeter (available in a hardware store)
- Nails
- Newspaper
- Water
- Mortar with pestle
- Rectangular bowl/container large enough to fit the frame
- Green and dried grass (optional)
- Flowers (optional)

DIRECTIONS

1. With wooden boards, make a frame to match the intended size of your piece of paper.
2. Mount the sieve underneath the frame with additional strips of wood and nails.
3. Soak some of the newspapers in water—soaking these overnight or longer works best.
4. Squeeze out the excess water.
5. With the mortar and pestle, crush a little bit of pulp at a time until you get a homogeneous paste consisting of fibers isolated from each other.
6. Repeat this until you have enough paste.
7. Fill the bowl halfway with water.
8. Put the paper paste in the bowl and stir it with your hand to separate the fibers. Remove any resulting clumps.
9. Immerse the frame in the watery suspension of the bowl with the sieve facing the bottom of the bowl and collect part of the fiber suspension.
10. Slowly remove the frame from the bowl keeping it steadily horizontal.
11. Move the frame to even out the layer of fibers and wait for the water to drain.

12. Let the piece of paper dry in the frame before taking it out. Using a hair dryer on a low setting can help with this, or just leaving the paper in a sunny or warm place will help it to dry faster.
13. Repeat with additional frames and additional paste until you have enough pieces of paper for your needs.

As Avery says, making your own paper is a lot of work, but for a special occasion, or a special gift or project, it can be worth it. The addition of flowers, leaves, and grass—like Avery's forget-me-nots—make a for a unique and beautiful finished product. Homemade paper can also be used as mats for pictures, as pages in scrapbooks, and other crafts and decorating needs.

Etch Your Own Mirror

Developed in the mid-1800s, acid-etched glass became popular for its ability to shield patrons of drinking establishments from view while letting in natural light. Victorian and Edwardian homes quickly adopted the look, and today, etched designs appear on windows, mirrors, and even glassware.

MATERIALS

- Glass or mirror
- Glass cleaner
- Microfiber cloths
- Glass etching kits (with stencils)
- Contact paper
- X-ACTO knife
- Smoothing tool
- Etching cream
- Paper towels
- Soft-bristle artist's brush
- Latex gloves

- Water
- Pencil
- Carbon papers

DIRECTIONS

1. Before etching, wash your surface with glass cleaner to remove dust and fingerprints. If you mop up the cleaner with a microfiber cloth, it will help eliminate residue.
2. For a big project, opt for a peel-and-stick vinyl pattern stencil, which is easy to reposition. Or draw your own on contact paper, then use an X-ACTO knife to cut the contact paper away from the areas that you want to etch. To avoid seepage and air bubbles, use a smoothing tool, such as a plastic square or an old gift card, to affix the stencil/contact paper and seal the edges.
3. Apply the etching cream over the open areas of the stencil in a thick coat using a paper towel or a soft-bristle artist's brush. Because etching cream is made with ammonium bifluoride, which can irritate the skin, you should wear gloves while working with the cream.
4. Wait the amount of time required for the brand of etching cream you are using—usually five to ten minutes.
5. Use a sponge to rinse the cream off of the glass. For best results, work from top to bottom. If the object is small enough, forego the sponge and rinse with cool water in the sink, or run water from a hose over the object outside.
6. Peel off the contact paper and rinse the glass under cool water again.

—Acknowledgments—

As always, thanks go out to a lot of people who had a hand in making this story what it is:

My editor, Jessica Wade, and the rest of the team at Penguin and Berkley Prime Crime, as well as agent Stephany Evans and everyone at Fine Print Literary Management.

Cover artist Jennifer Taylor, cover designer Rita Frangie, and book designer Laura Corless, for making the book beautiful.

Publicist Kayleigh Clark, without whom this book would be nowhere.

My critique partner and tireless cheerleader Jamie Livingston Dierks, who not only did her usual helpful job with the manuscript, but who also graciously allowed me to use her name for one of the characters. I hope you're happy with Jamaica Lee!

The wonderful Faye Pond for once again supporting a good cause and ending up with character names in one of my books. This time it's Benjamin Quinn and William Maurits, and I hope you're satisfied with the way they turned out.

Brad Sorensen, for the title.

All my friends within and without the publishing industry. By now there are way too many of you to mention by name, but know that I'm grateful for each and every one of you. I wouldn't be here if it weren't for your love and support.

Last, but certainly not least, thanks to my family, who knows the real me and loves me anyway. I couldn't do what I do without you, and I'll always be grateful that you let me be who I am.

xoxo